FORTUNATE

ALSO BY ANDREW JH SHARP

The Ghosts of Eden
Winner of the 2010 Waverton Good Read Award

FORTUNATE

Andrew JH Sharp

Matador
9 Priory Business Park
Kibworth Beauchamp
Leicestershire LE8 0RX, UK
Tel: (+44) 116 279 2299
Fax: (+44) 116 279 2277
Email: books@troubador.co.uk
Web: www.troubador.co.uk/matador

ISBN 978 1783060 016

British Library Cataloguing in Publication Data.
A catalogue record for this book is available from the British Library.

Typeset by Troubador Publishing Ltd, Leicester, UK
Printed and bound in the UK by TJ International, Padstow, Cornwall

Matador is an imprint of Troubador Publishing Ltd

For Marietta, who introduced me to Zimbabwe.

CHAPTER 1

Beth Jenkins, locum general practitioner, is about to log off her computer after a late afternoon surgery when her desk phone rings. It's been a long day but she hopes – she prays – that it's a request for a house call. Today, the 8th of November 2007, is the first anniversary of her marriage but she does not want to return home. She'd like to work all evening, all night.

Perhaps she'll be lucky and it'll be a call to a time-consuming visit, such as a new diabetic or someone having a prolonged panic attack. Ah, yes, that's what she'd choose: a case of sweat-soaked, palpitating, adrenaline-swamped panic. A tight tangle of knotted fears to unpick. She'd have no difficulty in empathising. There are, she has strong cause to know, aliens incubating under the skin of even the most ordinary of days and they are always ready – without so much as a warning twitch – to erupt, rending flesh, spilling blood. Her panic attack sufferers are the perceptive ones, the sane ones, although she'd certainly not let on that she knows about the beasts. No, she'd be a good GP and do her best to reassure and soothe.

She lifts the receiver. 'Hello. Dr Jenkins.'

'Twicare Nursing Home are on the line,' says Brenda, the receptionist. 'I'll put them through.'

The line clicks.

'Dr Jenkins here.'

'Doctor Beth! Ecstatic it's you. It's Sean. I'm duty manager tonight. Titanic apologies for ringing late but could you come and take a look at our Mr De Villier?'

Well timed, Sean. 'Hold on, I'll bring him up on the computer.' Beth displays Mr De Villier's medical record. He must be a new patient as she's not seen him before which will give her an excuse to take an encyclopaedic past medical history. 'OK, ready now. How can I help?'

'He's had a tickly cough for a while but it's suddenly got legs. I'd say he's coughing like… hmm… a goose with croup.'

'Sounds distressing for him.'

'Distressing? You'd think so, darling, but he's not complained himself.' Sean sighs theatrically. 'Not about his cough, anyway. I'm sure he can wait until tomorrow but Matron's worried the other residents will catch it. Don't quote me on this, but it's like a kennels in here, someone barking sets off all the rest.'

'I guess I'd better visit then or we'll both be in the doghouse.'

It's easy to slip into a clubby banter with Sean. He was a Ryanair cabin attendant before coming to Twicare and has brought with him a sunny attitude salted with wry asides. *This is just like my last job, Beth. I'm flying all my passengers to paradise.* She can jolly along airily with Sean, as if crash landings never happen.

Sean calls off and Beth prints out Mr De Villier's case history although there's little to it. He's new on the practice list and 'a refugee' but she can find no mention of his home country. His name doesn't sound remotely Iraqi or Somali. He's been seen once by Hector Moncrieff, the practice's senior partner. Hector's entry starts: *In Twicare at expense of the council tax payer.* Typical Hector. *Double amputee due to smoking related Buerger's disease. Still smoking. Started on simvastatin 20mg, aspirin 75mg. Reluctant historian. Seems to be bearing a grudge.* Does Hector not know that patients can request to see their medical notes?

But… a grudge? Beth's heart swells with a pleasurable rush of anticipation. That's more like it. There are only so many minutes that a consultation on a cough can be stretched to. For Hector to have noticed, Mr De Villier's grudge must be as plainly on show as the absence of his legs. He'll be loudly disgruntled, visibly embittered. Just the sort of consultation she loves even when she's not looking for an excuse to stay working late. She sees herself sitting down beside the old man, leaning sympathetically towards him, giving him plenty of time to talk and lay bare the roots of his resentment. She'll—

The door springs open and Hector bursts in as if she's set off her panic alarm. She jumps, her fingers striking the keyboard so that she makes an accidental entry in Mr De Villier's record.

'Good evening, Bethan,' Hector says with loud, precise articulation, as if addressing a platoon. He stands – short but stout chested – in front of her desk in his sand-coloured suit and a tartan bow. He's a man who Beth has never heard say thank-you, but she's respectful of the fact that he inspires loyalty from the practice staff for his tireless reliability (despite his age of something over seventy) and for the rumour of a tragic lost love four decades ago.

'Come in,' she says. 'Can I help?' She tries as always not to let her gaze slide to where a chunk of his forehead is missing – the cause of which she's never had the courage to ask.

'I have something to say to you.' His determined stance suggests someone has provoked him.

'Of course,' she offers.

'I see you were very late – a habit, it seems – in finishing your surgery this morning.'

'Oh!' He remains motionless and stiff-faced, looking towards her but through her. She feels herself shrinking in her chair. Soon her feet will swing free like a child's. 'I seem to have so many depressed and anxious patients. They do need a little more time...' Hector's working eyebrow twitches. 'I've not had complaints from patients about being a bit slow.'

'It's been on my mind to say something for months and there's no other way to put it: you shouldn't waste time on... the morose. There'll be no appointments left for anyone else.' He raises his voice. 'Truth is, it's not what I'm paying you for. Prescribe Prozac. We can't afford these talking therapies.'

'Sometimes it's... I'll try my best to speed up.' Dammit! Is he going to dismiss her? Previous locums had not survived more than a few weeks – come to think of it, she's lasted the longest.

The engorged veins in Hector's neck collapse and his expression softens with an almost imperceptible relaxation of his jaw as if he's making allowances for a wayward child. 'The trouble with you freshers is that you have to drag out the whole saga of your patient's life story before you can treat the simplest of ailments.'

She offers him a cautious grin and then, risking it, leans forward. 'If that's the case, I suppose there's a chance of helping them rewrite their story... alter their plot, make a better ending.'

'You're a doctor, not a bloody author.'

She holds herself from drawing back and says, 'It's more like being a co-author. David says—'

'Dr Green is an ivory-tower highbrow. He's a theorist, a metaphysician. What does he know?'

She continues, against a warning to herself to shut up. 'He says listening to patients is like reading a book. You have to inhabit alien points of view, uncover clues and motives, be open to empathy.' How lucky that her instinctive consulting style happens to be endorsed by academic theory.

'I see you're not going to take any advice from a geriatric like me.' Hector jerks his hand across his chest as if making a move in a martial art and inspects his watch. 'I'd better get down to the TA.' With a curt nod, he swivels on the back of his heels and leaves, his stolid shoulders never anything but rod-straight and level. He must have caused the natives to choke on their qat when he did his National Service in Aden and must now be the Territorial Army's oldest member.

Beth deletes the accidental entry she'd made in Mr De Villier's record when Hector burst in. She hears Hector stamp off down the corridor. If only she'd been a little less assertive with him, not tried to make excuses. She can't risk losing her job. No practice will employ a sacked locum. If she has no work, she'll be stuck in the house. That lonely, becalmed, house. The quiet, barely-furnished rooms. Matt.

She logs off the computer, snakes her stethoscope into her bag and collects her coat from behind the door. The fizzy anticipation of an absorbing consultation returns but she tells herself to take a little of Hector's advice and not get too engrossed in the talking treatment and so end up neglecting Mr De Villier's cough. After all, perhaps the old man doesn't want to lose his grudge, clings to it as his last friend.

She slips on her coat but as she lifts her hair away from her collar, the phone rings again. She hopes it's not Sean, saying that Mr De Villier can wait for tomorrow after all.

'Beth, it's your husband,' Brenda says in a tone that might be either sympathetic or pitying. 'He's rung through again on the private line.'

The air bleeds from Beth's chest. She hears herself saying,

'Tell him I've left.'

'You sure? OK.'

'On second thoughts, no, don't.' She straightens her back. 'Put him through please, Brenda.'

'Here he is.'

Beth hears fumbling noises over the receiver. 'Matt?' She waits. She hears him breathing. 'Matt?'

'When are you coming home?'

She pinches the telephone cord. 'Everything's alright, Matt. Remember I'm at the surgery. I've just got one visit and then I'll be back.' She knows she sounds tired and indifferent and a lump of guilt grows in her belly. It's up to her to make an effort, she must rouse a celebratory spirit, froth up good cheer, be strong and loyal. 'You know what? It's our anniversary! I'll make us your favourite supper and I've got you three Magnum ice creams for dessert!' It's their private joke, their tag for the moment when they first met: Tesco self-checkout, Matt – hair softly untidy, fit and appealing in his cycling gear – buying mixed nuts, wholemeal rice, apples, oats, and a three for two pack of Magnums.

'When are you coming home?' he says again flatly.

She readjusts. 'I can't be at home all the time. Please don't worry, Matt, it won't be long. I've got to finish seeing my patients first.' The line goes quiet and she feels herself suffocating in the long silence. 'Matt?'

'Am I a patient?'

She watches the computer screen announce *Shutting Down*. She picks up the ophthalmoscope on her desk and squeezes the light switch. The beam lances her eye. 'Sort of,' she says quietly. She tidies the ophthalmoscope away. 'Why don't you watch television until I get back? I expect *Friends* is on somewhere.'

'Come home.'

'I've got to go now.'

'There's a man here.'

Beth drops herself into her chair. 'What do you mean? Who is he?' She presses her fingers up her forehead to smooth the frown that threatens.

'There's a man at the door.' His words come out a little faster than usual, a pressure behind them, even if his voice is as toneless as ever.

'Who does the man say he is? What does he want?' She has to repeat herself before he replies, 'I'll ask the man.'

She hears the knock of the receiver being put down and then she waits for over a minute, beginning to think that he's forgotten that he's rung her. When she hears his breath on the phone again, she says, 'What did the man say?'

Matt's panting comes and goes, comes and goes. 'When are you coming home?'

The computer's fan dies with a moan as it finally turns itself off. 'Who is it, Matt? Who's at the door?'

There's a long pause, then, 'The door?'

Beth can hear Brenda turning off lights in the passage. 'The man at the door, what does he look like?'

'Like… a man.'

'Go back and tell the man he can't come in.'

'Tell the man he can't come in,' repeats Matt.

'Good, that's right. Say that if it's important he can come back at eight. Then come back to the phone so that you can tell me that the man's gone. Make sure you've closed the door.'

'Close the door,' Matt says slowly.

'Yes, close the door and then come back and tell me.'

She strains her ear and hears Matt's voice and then she hears the door bang shut. She lets out a breath. He picks up the phone again. 'When are you coming home?'

'I'm putting the phone down now, Matt, but I'll see you later. I'll be as quick as I can and then we'll have supper together.' She's attempted to be high-spirited again but Matt remains mute. 'It's our first... first... oh, never mind.' She's aware of the sound of her own brittle breathing on the mouthpiece.

She replaces the receiver but stays there, weighted to her chair. If Matt is her... she can hardly bear to think it... patient... then Matt's story, and so their story, is impossible to rewrite. It's a read-only document. She rises slowly from her desk, thinking she's become horribly pessimistic, a fatalist. Not the sort of doctor she'd want her patients to see. She fastens a button on her coat but finds she's put it through the wrong hole. No, she's simply asserting the truth. Being unsentimental. She can't go back in time to alter the text on what's happened or cross out the bizarre diary of the life that she and Matt lead now. She blinks determinedly, sorts her button, checks in the mirror that she's not smudged her mascara, picks up her bag and sets off on her house call.

The rain starts as Beth reaches the door of Twicare Nursing Home – the kind of bone-chilling, fine-droplet winter spray that must make refugees long for their home country. She has half a mind on Matt as she enters. Should she have gone home first to make sure that he'd not opened the door again? Perhaps he'd let the visitor into the house who'd then beaten him up before helping himself to credit cards and cash. It doesn't take people long to work out that Matt is a *vulnerable adult*. She should pay to extend the carer's hours.

Sean's not in the office and Beth doesn't know Mr De Villier's room number so she stands under one of Twicare's Victorian landscape paintings until a Filipino nurse comes towards her trying to keep up with three bedpans stacked, teetering, in her arms.

'Who have you come to see, Doctor?' she asks.

'Mr De Villier.'

'Ah,' she says as she swishes past, 'Mr Bledy, that's what we call him. He's from Zimbabwe. Best of luck, Doctor.' She gives Beth an edgy smile. 'Go straight down – he's last on the right.' She sweeps on into the sluice room with a busy gait.

Zimbabwe? She'll mention to Mr De Villier that her husband once worked there. It would be a point of connection – an ice breaker – with her new patient although she wouldn't like to be asked to point out Zimbabwe on a map of Africa.

She walks on down the corridor, a flowering pergola of flocked wallpaper, chintzy borders, polished oak handrails and pastoral paintings with gold-lacquered frames. The door to Mr De Villier's room is a little ajar and so she knocks but goes straight in. Mr De Villier is on a commode leaning forward and a male nurse is wiping his backside. Neither he nor Mr De Villier looks up. Hastily stepping back, Beth excuses herself and waits outside.

'For sure, my first name is Fortunate,' she hears the nurse say to Mr De Villier.

Mr De Villier clears his phlegmy throat and shouts, 'Fortunate, is it? How appropriate! You people have taken my farm. Now you're taking my dignity. Bledy bliks!'

Beth moves to march in and slap the cold side of her stethoscope on Mr De Villier's chest but hears Fortunate say quietly, 'I'm so sorry, sir; I'm a long way from home myself.'

She drops the hand she's lifted to the door and leans closer. Mr De Villier has started to sob. She moves her head a little so that she can see through the crack. The old man is shaking as if he's only just faced a cavernous grief, groaning in the full realisation of a terrible loss. Beth sees Fortunate lay a hand on his shoulder and bow his head.

Mr De Villier stops shuddering and takes deep breaths. 'Don't think I pity myself. I weep because… the bloody beauty of the land.'

Fortunate gives Mr De Villier time and then murmurs, 'The land, for sure, it's too beautiful. Too, too beautiful.'

Then they are silent. Beth waits in the hush, trying to understand how it can be possible to feel so strongly about a mere place, 'the land', in Mr De Villier's words. But then she concedes that she does like to imagine she's from the moistly romantic land of Wales, writes 'Welsh' in the ethnicity box on forms, although it's something of a fantasy. Born in Swansea but – admit it – never actually lived in Wales. All that moving from one foster parent to the next, from one unremarkable suburb to another in four different English cities. She never knew when she'd be given over to new carers in an unfamiliar location so she never allowed herself to feel attached. But she remembers the dizzy moment when she first met Matt, remembers that conviction that wherever she and Matt ended up would be the place she'd call home, the place she'd feel a fuzzy nostalgic affection for when she was away. What word had that homesick Welsh patient she'd seen last week used to describe a longing for home? *Hiraeth*. Mr De Villier and Fortunate are suffering a terminal case of *hiraeth*.

Fortunate's voice comes to her. 'Ready now, Doctor.'

Beth scans the room as she enters to pick up clues to Mr De Villier's family circumstances. It'll help in finding the background setting to his story, although she thinks Fortunate has already made a good start on that. She can't miss the huge cream-coloured safe in the corner. It squats, round-edged, smooth and fat, and sports an impressive black combination dial lock, the type that features in bank robbery films of the sixties. Other than the safe, she can see no personal effects: no family photos, no books, no cards, and no flowers. Surprising, that. Twicare places flowers, seasonal when possible – nice touch – in every resident's room so that those who are never visited can feel loved. Then Beth sees them on the bed table: headless stalks sticking out of a heavy Twicare-issue glass vase. Their ends are twisted and torn as if the flowers have been wrenched off – as if their necks have been wrung.

Mr De Villier is off the commode now and Fortunate has swung him across into his chair with a hoist as if he's a rickety crate on a dock. He sits slumped forward, a blanket covering the stumps of his legs, but raises his brambly eyebrows to appraise Beth with eyes of a weak blue that give nothing away. If she hadn't just heard it, she'd never have guessed he's just been weeping. Perhaps his eyes can't wet – the xerophthalmia of old age.

'Who the bloody hell are you?' he says.

'I'm Dr Jenkins from the surgery. I'm very pleased to meet you, Mr De Villier.' She steps forward and flashes him her best reassuring smile. He takes his time to take her proffered hand in his wide bony grip. Tired hands now, but Beth can sense that he had once been a powerful man. She can't understand why her eyes threaten to fill. She swallows and says, 'I'm here to see if I can help you.'

Mr De Villier takes back his hand and drops it to his lap as if it's too heavy to support. 'If that's the case, finish me off.'

Out of the corner of her eye, Beth sees Fortunate fidget awkwardly. She says, 'I'm sorry you feel like that. I don't think I'd be allowed to finish you off, and anyway, I'm sure there are people who'd miss you,' although immediately she thinks that she's seen no evidence for it. She turns, perches herself on the edge of Mr De Villier's bed and leans towards him. She'll start with his grudge.

'Can I ask what makes you say that?'

Mr De Villier watches her coldly for a few seconds and then snorts. He sets his jaw. Fortunate squats down to look earnestly into Mr De Villier's face. 'The Doctor's right, I would miss you, for sure.'

Fortunate has soft, broad cheeks and full, generous lips that even in his sincerity seem on the cusp of melting into a kind smile. Beth can't guess his age. Despite a youthful appearance, something in his manner and in his eyes and the rumple in his forehead as he looks steadily up at Mr De Villier, suggest maturity, tells her he's lived long enough to have become knowing of life's tendency to take unwelcome turns.

Mr De Villier hunches further into his chair.

Beth leans back to give him space. Then she tries again. 'The staff tell me you've got a cough. Can you tell me when it started?'

'I've had a cough since '84.' He speaks slowly into his lap with an exasperated tone as if reminding a fool of something they've been told many times.

'But I understand it's got worse.'

'Ever been a boiler man on steam, young woman?' He lifts his eyes to look at her again. 'No, thought not. Ever shovelled two tons of coal in a day? My lungs are tattooed black. As black as this boy here.' He flicks his eyes in Fortunate's direction. 'And then there were my tobacco farming years – all those golden leaves. Kept half for myself. So, a cough? What do you expect?' He spits into a ragged carnation of tissue paper.

'Will you let me have a listen to your chest anyway?'

'If it'll make you happy. Bloody hell, why can't people just leave me alone?'

Beth asks more questions and gets grunting, reluctant, replies. Fortunate helps her lift Mr De Villier's shirt. His back is a forest floor in autumn – all dry flakes in browns and siennas. *Keratotic*. Fortunate's arm is smooth-skinned and strong.

Her attention tightens. 'Deep breath.' She adjusts the position of the bell of her stethoscope. 'Deep breath, please.' She pushes the ear pieces further into her ears. 'Deep breath again.'

No, she's not mistaken: that harsh rasping sound. *Bronchial breathing*. She percusses down his left chest with her fingers. The timbre alters as she taps lower, starting resonant and airy, then woody, before becoming as dull as a barrel of tar. She slides her fingers into the notch above his collar bone. A sentinel lymph gland sits there as hard as a nut in a bowl. It's frightening: when she least expects to find trouble, is on automatic, already preparing a reassurance speech, she can stumble across the menace within.

She meets Fortunate's eye and sees his wordless recoil as he reads her thoughts. Her stethoscope is a noose in her hand.

'Have a chair, Doctor,' Fortunate says. He pulls one over from behind the door. Beth sits down beside Mr De Villier.

He raises his head and looks straight ahead and beyond her, like a military man awaiting orders. 'How long have I got?'

'I am a bit concerned about your chest.'

Mr De Villier crumples and laughs sarcastically. 'Concerned? Tell you what, boy,' he looks at Fortunate, 'if a doctor says she's an incy bit bothered about you then you'd better ring the local newspaper to buy two lines in tomorrow's Death Announcements column.'

Fortunate stands with his hands clasped in front of him, slowly twisting his fingers.

'Until we do some tests we can't be sure what's happening,' Beth says. 'I'd like to send you for a chest X-ray.'

'You would, would you? Let's just wait for the autopsy report.'

Fortunate takes a sudden step forward. 'Please Mr De Villier, why don't you let Dr Jenkins help you?'

'Depends what she wants to help me with. If it's sitting on plastic chairs in a hospital clinic to pass the time of day until I die I'm not interested. In fact,' his voice rises, 'she can bloody well piss off.' He grips the arms of his chair as if about to jump up and run away. The stumps of his legs spasm up beneath the blanket in his lap. 'Bugger.'

'Mr De Villier! That's no way to speak to the Doctor,' says Fortunate, pressing his hands to his cheeks.

Beth waits, concentrating on projecting an unperturbed expression, until Mr De Villier drops his weight into his cushions again. 'I can understand you being upset, Mr De Villier. You may be right; if you've got something serious, then we may not be able to cure you but we should at least find out what's going on. I don't know yet how to help you. It might be something treatable.'

'Something treatable? Huh! Like a little sniffle, you mean?' Mr De Villier's sneer is aborted by his dentures coming loose. He impatiently straightens them.

Beth reaches forward to place her hand lightly on his shoulder but Mr De Villier snaps, 'Are you deaf? Like I said already, piss off! Both of you!'

Beth stands up. 'OK, I… how about I come back tomorrow so we can talk about it some more?'

'Please yourself.'

Fortunate follows Beth out of Mr De Villier's room, saying, 'I'm so sorry, Doctor.'

'It could have gone better, couldn't it?' she says. 'But thanks for your help. I'll see if he's more receptive tomorrow.'

She starts off down the corridor hesitantly, as if she might have left something in Mr De Villier's room. Then, remembering Matt, she quickens her pace. Fortunate keeps close, as if attached to her bag. 'No need to show me out thanks, I'll be fine.' An image comes to her of Matt lying unconscious in the hall.

'I've seen that you're very kind,' Fortunate says.

What if he'd been seriously assaulted?

'What? Oh, er, thanks.' She feels herself blush.

She reaches the exit. Fortunate is still with her, hovering close, an uncertain expression on his face.

'Everything OK?' she asks as she presses the door release button.

'Yes, very fine,' he says, still lingering.

She sets out to the car park. The drizzle has stopped but an east wind ices her cheeks. The out-of-hours service has taken over the calls now so she'll not receive any more visit requests tonight. She must make Matt's supper. She must sit and eat it with him and try to make a conversation. She'll not distress him by becoming upset.

She's not far from the car when she hears Fortunate's hurrying steps behind her. 'Can I please speak with you, Doctor?' He sounds anxious.

'Sure,' she says, slowing a little.

'It's a personal matter.'

'Uh-uh.'

'I have a problem. It's about my girlfriend.'

She stops and turns to him. 'Your girlfriend?'

'You see, she has a problem.' He looks relieved to have said it, to have the nerve.

'Nurse… um… Fortunate, I'm very sorry but I'm in a bit of a rush this evening. Do you think it's the sort of thing I can help you with? Am I her GP?' Nine times out of ten a 'problem with the girlfriend' is the patient's way of broaching his fear that he has an STD.

'She's in Zimbabwe, Doctor. She's requesting something of me.'

Beth lifts her keys from her coat pocket. 'And so how would I be able to help? Perhaps we can talk tomorrow when I come back to see Mr De Villier.' She presses the key fob. The indicators flash urgently.

'You're very kind. Please lend me your forgiveness,' Fortunate says, 'but let me tell you straight. She wishes to know if I have a car. You see, she has to be sure I have sufficient remunerations. If I've been able to afford a vehicle, then she'll marry me.'

Beth has her hand on the car door handle but now releases it.

'Doctor, this is a small favour: will you take a picture of me in front of your car? Yes?'

Beth turns to face Fortunate. 'Maybe I've misunderstood you. You want to pretend this is your car?'

Fortunate's face twists. 'Dr Jenkins, I know that this that I'm requesting is out of order but I wish to spare you a long story when you have more important matters to attend.'

A long story. Beth hesitates.

Fortunate reaches for her, takes her hand and presses a small silver camera into her palm. She tries to give it back to him but he's already standing by the front of her VW Polo straightening his uniform. He stands to attention, except for his right hand which strokes the bonnet. A tender hand.

'Oh, OK,' she says. 'I'll take a picture of you in front of the car – but as far as I'm concerned, it's just a picture of you to send to your girlfriend. Anything else, you've made up yourself.'

'May God bless you!'

It's not easy to see the composition but she fires the shutter anyway. The quiet snick of the shutter sounds like a padlock engaging or the fall of a latch.

The image on the display is perfect: Fortunate smiling unreservedly, no red eye, his hand resting proudly on 'his' car. He's still beaming as she hands back his camera. 'So kind – you've saved me. I'll always remember this. Now Shungu will give me her hand in marriage.' He has a dreamy expression and Beth turns away. So tragic, knowing what can happen, everything that can go wrong.

'Good, well, best of luck.' She slides herself behind the wheel, thunks the car door closed and sets off home, home to Matt. Her headlights slosh a cold light on the road.

CHAPTER 2

Her five bedroom house is alienating, Beth thinks, even when it isn't dripping in the rain. Not that it belongs to her. It's owned by her mother-in-law and is a recent build on an exclusive estate (The Tees) behind a golf course. Acres of bowling-green-flat lawns separate the properties so that the mock Elizabethan homes with their half-timbered frames loom like galleons. Foreign plants with vicious, spiky leaves bristle in kidney-shaped flower beds. Fat stone pineapples (perched incongruously on thin Doric columns) front the dyed-brick driveways. Statuettes of Ancient Grecian women holding pitchers and nonchalantly exposing one breast stand about on the lawns, cold, lonely and disconnected. They remind her of floating objects in a Dali painting. She doesn't know her neighbours because they are either in their houses watching satellite TV on six foot screens or are in their muscle-bound Range Rovers, the rear-seat DVD screens flickering behind the darkened glass as their children are whisked to and from schools in southern counties. Unblinking electric eyes watch the approaches to the iron-studded front doors, triggering arc-lights as she passes. Their blaze burns a sketch of her retinal vessels on her vision.

Her mother-in-law, Penelope, and her husband had made their money buying and selling property. Matt is in line for a fortune. Their wedding present to Beth and Matt was two years' rent-free use of the house, for which they were grateful, although

Beth's friend, Alena, had said that was stingy considering his parents' immense wealth. If it had been up to Matt's father they might have been gifted the house but Penelope preferred to wait and see how the housing market turned out 'in the short term'. She said she might have to put it on the market at a moment's notice. But now it's too late for any alteration to the terms of their gift: Matt's father fell – or jumped – from his yacht not long after their wedding. His body was never found.

Although Beth felt like a four-year-old with a new (oversized) doll's house when she first moved in, since Matt's brain haemorrhage everything in the house reminds her of what will never happen. Whenever she steps through the door into that voiceless and cavernous hall she recalls how she and Matt discovered that they held a mutual, counter-culture ambition to have a large family. Max a dozen, said Matt. Maybe just seven, cautioned Beth. Their children would run around the house like some eccentric Edwardian brood; a family life in the retro style. They wouldn't have a television so that the children would have to play: hiding in wardrobes, skidding on the skittle-alley-smooth oak floors, sawing at violins, wheezing into trumpets, tobogganing down the stairs on trays. Their height measurements would be colouring the back of the bathroom door in felt pen, their school art BluTacked to the walls, and every room strewn with half-finished projects. The house needed that measure of exuberant family incarnation to give it a soul, to make it a home. Having no family history of her own Beth was intent on building one for her children and their children. Some have a passionate ambition to sail around the world or to write a novel or to create a ravishing garden. Her yearning was no less single-minded and, she thought, needed no more justification. But now she knows that her family tree is never going to so much as germinate.

In spite of their previous intentions, Beth has bought a TV and can hear its punchy noise when she lets herself in. Everything appears in order. There are no gaping, rifled drawers in the hall sideboard and Matt's not on the floor nursing bruises. She puts her head around the door of the lounge.

'Matt, I'm home. Are you all right?'

He's kneeling on the IKEA Persisk rug near the bookcase constructing a precarious tower of books, his back to the loud colours of the television. The jumble from previous attempts radiate out from where he sits: *The Rock Art of Southern Africa*, *Messages from Prehistory*, *Decoding Rock Art*. Just so much clutter on the rug. It looks to Beth like he's trying to recall their purpose, reassemble meaning, faintly aware that these objects once represented his joy and passion.

Matt looks up at her with a vacant expression and she's winded afresh by what he's lost. What they both have lost. The man on his haunches, wearing the short-sleeved, brushed-cotton shirt that she'd bought him for his thirty-third birthday, looks like Matt, but he isn't Matt. Her lover, her husband, her friend, is no longer in there, is not at home. He's gone missing. She can see no recognition of her in his eyes and no reflection of the accumulated memories of more than two years together or their interlocked hopes for the future, their plaited experiences, their evenings of teasing chit-chat. She misses the evenings the most. His humour was open and generous, whilst hers is dry. The day's tension and stress would be folded away in the pleats of their laughter. Now he's stranded, trapped on the rug, an abandoned, strained expression on his once lively, engaging face.

It happened nine months previously, three months after they were married. He strode, unsuspecting, into a lecture theatre to deliver a talk on the rock art of the Lascaux caves to his second year class. When he turned to greet his students he kept turning, toppling with a low-pitched sigh like a falling cedar. He landed with a resonating thud on the podium.

Beth read that on a student's blog. She wishes she hadn't. She still feels the thump. Sometimes it synchs with a sickening beat of her heart. A tiny blood vessel deep in his brain carrying a congenital aneurysm the size of an apple pip had ruptured.

Beth turns off the television and says, with all the cheeriness she can muster, 'What have you done, Matt?'

He stares at his books as if newly astonished to see them there. 'Broken.'

'Yes, broken, but never mind. What happened to the man?'

'Man?'

'There was a man at the door. You've forgotten, haven't you?'

'All broken.'

'OK Matt, I'm going to make supper. You tidy up.'

She gives him a quick smile and makes her way to the kitchen through the two reception rooms. They are barely furnished but their walls are crowded. She sees all the faces looking back at her. All those portraits she's collected, the prints she's framed and hung up since Matt's stroke. Her hobby. More like a compulsion. The faces make her feel less lonely. Vermeers, Hockneys, Schierenbergs and many unknown artists. Miniatures and oils and drawings, from any era, although she prefers portraits where the sitter is unidentified. She can then look at the face and make them who she wants them to be. Give them a story. The more faces, the more stories. Every now and then one of them gets a new chapter or a plot twist. Some become the lover of one of the others. A few have family problems which she has to solve for them. Some get to start new lives.

Jenny, the cat, warming herself on the worktop adjacent to the immense fire-engine-red stove, jumps guiltily to the floor as Beth enters the room. Beth opens the silo-sized fridge and takes out a packet of mince. Matt has lost his appetite and his appreciation of food since his stroke. She suspects he can't taste anything because he only shows interest if she adds spades of salt which she's reluctant to do because of his high blood pressure.

She's opening a can of adzuki beans to pad out the mince (whilst Jenny wraps herself around her ankles) when she hears Matt enter the kitchen. He comes up behind her, puts his hands around her chest and squeezes her breasts. 'Kiss.'

'Ow, Matt, you're hurting me. I've asked you not to do that.'

She peels his hands off and moves down the worktop. He looks wounded and at a loss. 'That's inappropriate behaviour,' she says. And then, with resignation, 'You just don't know, do you?' It's not only that Matt's memory has drained down a plug hole. He's been occupied by a lecherous stranger who has nothing in common with the kind-hearted, courteous man that she married.

In the bedroom she makes an effort to pretend that the BC (Before Catastrophe) Matt remains but as soon as he lies down at night he's snoring – a recent, alien trait. It's around the house that he's lascivious, and sometimes in public: a sudden hand on her backside when they are in the aisle at the supermarket just at the moment an elderly couple, who are her patients, start to smile in recognition; a smacking kiss in her ear when she's at the bank trying to hear what the cashier is saying behind the sound-proof glass; fingers slipped into the front of her shirt top as she passes him a drink when she takes him to the pub. There are a lot of places she can't return to.

She gives Matt a carrot to chop, showing him what to do again and then leaves him to it. Thankfully his disappointments don't last long: he can never remember that she's just told him off. She looks up from the worktop to the shelf where there is a photo of BC Matt. He's looking directly at her and she stops and looks back, reminding herself of why she keeps going with AD (After Disaster) Matt. But Matt in the picture is trying to say something to her, something like: *Damn it, Beth, I'm gone but I've carelessly left my shadow behind for you to dress and feed.*

She's peeling the potatoes to make the mash for the cottage pie (his homely favourite) when the doorbell rings in a refined four-tone chiming.

'What's that?' Matt says, startled, as if he's never heard it before.

'Let's go to the door and see.'

Beth thinks it might be the man who visited earlier but it's Penelope. She looms tall and thin in the frame of the door, her highlighted blonde hair cut short, her make-up pencil-sharp. She looks over Beth's shoulder at Matt. Beth turns to see him back away.

'How's my handsome boy?' Penelope says in booming voice as if she's speaking into a public address system at a political rally.

'It's your mother,' Beth says.

'Looking a bit thin, isn't he?'

Matt shoots Beth a bewildered look. 'My mother?'

Penelope steps forward, keeps her elbows in but opens her arms with her fingers rigidly extended to take Matt and peck him a kiss, but Matt puts out his hands to shoo her away and then escapes into the lounge, looking suspiciously behind him.

Penelope turns and looks down on Beth. 'Have you booked him into the aspirational therapist yet? You should. He needs goals. He needs self-actualisation.' Penelope runs her property business but also writes motivational books for business people with titles such as *Self-empowerment in Property Management*.

Self-actualisation? Beth can't hide her doubtful expression.

'If you can't inspire him to make progress,' Penelope says, 'you need to find someone who can. A professional.' She sets off ahead of Beth to the kitchen. 'Are you cooking? I'll join you.'

Jenny escapes urgently through the cat flap as Penelope enters the room. Penelope bends down to look through the glass of the oven door. 'Let's see, what are you doing for Matthew? Something special? It's his wedding anniversary, you know. Lots of protein I hope. He has lost weight, poor boy; but it must be difficult for you, working, although I keep saying, you don't have to.'

'Have to?'

'Have to work, of course. It can't be good for Matthew being on his own here all day.'

'He's not on his own all day,' Beth says a little sharply to compensate for a rush of guilt. She picks up a knife to chop the cabbage. 'He goes to the day-centre on Tuesdays and the carers are here for much of the day when I'm working. I only work three days a week. I'd go—'

'I guess it's understandable, it takes time to adjust,' says Penelope to herself. She goes to open the drinks cabinet and clinks around for some gin.

Beth says, 'Perhaps it would be best if Matt were in sheltered accommodation where he can have around the clock care.'

'He's already in sheltered accommodation.'

Beth massacres the remaining crisp quarter of cabbage. She can't remember hearing BC Matt say a wrong word against his mother, although he'd warned her before they were introduced that she always spoke her mind. With Matt by her side, she used to find her direct manner refreshing and it was sometimes a

source of conspiratorial amusement for Matt and her, but now…
now it's hurting. She has to remind herself, on days like this, that
her mother-in-law is in a state of denial and she understands why
– Penelope has lost both of her closest male relatives within a
year. But she wishes that Penelope would face up to what's
happened and cry, and then she'd be able to cry with her. After
all, she's her only kin.

Penelope looks at Beth sharply from pouring half a glass of
gin. 'Matthew can't help being ill and I'm sure he never thought
of you as the sort of woman that wouldn't drop everything for
him if he got sick. Do you want more money? You know that
Tobias left more than enough. What's the point of going out to
look after other people if you're not looking after your own
husband?' She finds a tonic in the fridge and then, as she pops
the tag, says in a conciliatory tone, 'You should start a family
while you're waiting for him to get better. A baby will speed his
recovery; having the responsibility. As I said in my book, *Going
Further for Property Success*, Bethan, think in six dimensions.
Think three ninety degrees.'

Matt has wandered in. For a second Beth tries to catch his
eye, to share the absurdity of his mother's suggestion, but there's
nothing there.

Beth returns to Twicare the following afternoon but just as she
reaches Mr De Villier's door she's overcome with a loss of self-
confidence. This has happened several times since Matt's stroke
but she can't remember it ever stopping her forward motion as it
does now. She touches her hand on the wall to steady herself. A
chasm has opened unexpectedly at her feet, swallowing her hopes
– and those all seem so presumptuous now, so immature. A dozen
children! – so it's hard not to expect another to gape wide at any

time. Putting one foot in front of another (as her friend Alena has gently reminded her to carry on doing) seems to be inviting another fall.

She pretends to study one of Twicare's pastoral paintings in the corridor outside Mr De Villier's room but all she sees is her insubstantial reflection staring weakly back. Here she is: late twenties and most of her life lived unremarkably in the suburbs; a bordering-on-dull, safe, childhood despite being fostered; never seen the world (there was the school French exchange trip to Lille which she missed due to chickenpox). But she is on her way to give advice to an old man, full of years and adventures, holding in his heart a faraway land that she can barely imagine. Trapped in his cell-like room, he wrestles fitfully against the creeping disintegration of his life, seeing with the cold blue clarity of his eyes that she is just another marker along the crumbling way. She isn't sure that she can go any further.

She becomes aware of Fortunate approaching with a bouncy step, his wide smile chubbing his cheeks. He says, 'Dr Jenkins, it's too wonderful, she's so happy.'

Beth gives him a puzzled look.

'You remember – the photo, for Shungu.'

'That was a quick response.'

'I email her every night. She's too happy.'

'Good, I'm delighted for you.' Fortunate's uncomplicated joy squeezes a smile out of her.

Fortunate suddenly switches his demeanour to serious. 'Do you wish me to accompany you to Mr De Villier?'

The chasm at her feet closes. 'Yes please. I'd much appreciate it.' Fortunate has breathed the same air as Mr De Villier, has an understanding of where the old man has come from, knows something of the terrain of her patient's life.

Mr De Villier is in bed. The angry vitality that he'd brimmed with the previous day has drained away into his pillow. He half-opens his eyes as they enter.

'Feeling poorly today?' Beth asks.

He drawls croakily, 'You do when you're bloody dying.'

Fortunate fills his glass from a jug. 'You're not drinking enough, sir,' he says. 'Let me sit you up so the Doctor can speak with you.'

Beth pulls up a chair, noticing again the enormous locked safe in the corner of the room. What could it contain? A wife's ashes? His life savings in gold bars? A precious manuscript? Fortunate is wetting Mr De Villier's lips with the glass. Water dribbles down his furrowed chin. Fortunate whips a tissue from the bedside box and wipes it away with precise attention as if he's putting the final touches to a painting. It's the absorption, the love, that Fortunate brings to his role as a carer that moves Beth. He's working in a higher, alternative dimension to Matron's *Dignity* policy with its schedules of behaviour that feel like pretence. Between them, she believes, they'll bear the old man along.

'I've been thinking about what you said yesterday,' Beth says as softly as she can, 'and I appreciate you don't want to have pointless investigations but I think you should have the chest X-ray. It'll help me to know how best to help you. It's just a round trip in the ambulance.'

'Like a coach tour, you mean? Do we get a toilet stop? Can I smoke?'

Beth smiles thinly. 'Would you like more time to think about it?'

'How much time do you think I've got? Can I let you know next year?'

Fortunate steps forward and looks with grave devotion at Mr

De Villier. 'Remember, sir, there are almost no doctors left in Zimbabwe, so let's be grateful that here, in this country, we have the medical care. Please take the help.'

'What about it?' Beth asks, wondering if this two-against-one is fair. This siege by institution.

Mr De Villier breathes out in a low groan, then with effort takes another breath and says, 'It's nothing personal but... no.'

Beth looks at Fortunate. He's shrugging his shoulders, his helpful hands turned palms-up in a gesture of exasperation.

Mr De Villier stirs himself again. 'There's one thing you can do for me, Doctor.'

'Yes?' She sits forward.

'Fly me back to Zim. You can package me up as cargo. Wheel me out past my farm into the bush. Lay what's left of me on Sable Kopje overlooking the vlei. I could die happy as a kaffir there.'

Beth flinches but Fortunate nods sympathetically. 'But you're comfortable here, aren't you?' she says. 'You're being well looked after?'

'Comfortable?' He gathers his breath, grips his duvet and shouts, 'As comfy as a corpse!' Outside in the car park, a pigeon, startled, flaps away. Fortunate goes to the door and clicks it shut. 'You see, Doctor,' Mr De Villier says, quiet again, 'I've been wrenched from the earth like a bloody weed. They've uprooted us from the land as if we're an alien species. They see us like the jacaranda trees and the bougainvillea in Bulawayo: non-indigenous. My family's decimated, my land is raped, my workers are mutilated. They cut off their lips, you know. It shuts them up.'

Beth says nothing for a while. That feeling of loss of self-confidence – the trap door, the chasm – has returned. *Uprooted, decimated, mutilated.* Mr De Villier and his country have suffered a far deeper trauma than she has but his words resonate. She looks out of the window where a plastic bag is being wafted over the cars. She finds herself saying, 'We get blown about, don't we? And we can't do anything to prevent it.'

Mr De Villier's eyes are almost closed but as Beth turns to him again she sees a flicker of blue as he shifts his gaze to her. She immediately feels guilty. It's not fair on the patient for the doctor to collapse into self-absorption, for roles to be reversed.

Something strengthens in Mr De Villier, a tightening of sinews, and he says, 'For all my bloody ranting, Doctor, I'll tell you this: I had it all once. For a few years I was where a man should be. Had a family, worked the earth, owned a piece of land in the most beautiful country in the world. What more can we hope for? For that, I'm bloody grateful.' He keeps his gaze on her now. 'Let me give you some advice, Doctor. Look for a place in this world, some land that you love, then live there with someone you find to your liking. You can't separate people from land. People are no people without land.' He turns his attention to Fortunate. 'We Zimbabweans know that, don't we? We whites, you blacks, we all understand it too well.'

Fortunate nods his head sagely.

Beth has little idea of what Mr De Villier is talking about. He's offering a few wise words – they sound biblical in their gravitas – but she thinks they apply to an era long gone. She lives in a house, not on the 'land'. She lives on carpets and laminates bounded by walls and skirting boards. Her place is little more than a postcode. She rallies herself. 'Thanks for your advice. Perhaps you'll now take mine and have that X-ray.'

'Boy, give me another drink.' Fortunate obediently brings the glass of water again to Mr De Villier's lips. He takes a sip and then closes his eyes, puts one hand over another on his belly and settles his head into his pillow. Beth looks at Fortunate who gives an exaggerated shrug. There is nothing more to be said. Not today. She resolves to be available, allow Mr De Villier the opportunity to change his mind, let him know that she isn't going to give up on him and walk away. She tells him that she'll be back again early the next week, thanks Fortunate for his help, and returns to the car park.

Beth sees a silver BMW convertible with its hood up near her Polo. It's idling with a hi-tech Teutonic hum and has smoked-glass windows. Through the darkened glass she can just make out the shape of a bulky man in the driver's seat although she can't see the features of his face as he wears a baseball cap low over his forehead and wrap-around sunglasses. They must be a fashion statement, given the dimness of the day.

As she seats herself in her Polo, she has the uncomfortable feeling that the driver of the BMW is watching her and that his attention is more than casual, but when she glances in his direction he has turned away. She drives off but then notices that the BMW is following her out. It keeps reappearing in her mirror as she heads home. When she turns into her cul-de-sac, it's a relief that it does not follow her in.

CHAPTER 3

I t's Friday evening and Beth is a little early at her table in the tapas-bar restaurant, Tres Hermanas. She's settled Matt in front of the TV watching the only DVD he'll happily sit through twice in a row: *South Pacific*. (The songs make her sad – all that romance and its promise of sunny futures – but he never tires of it, which is the sole advantage of having no memory). These times in Tres Hermanas are one of the few occasions in the week when she isn't looking after Matt or her patients and she is revived by its cheerful atmosphere. There are sea-blue mosaics on the white walls, tin-glazed pottery in reds and yellows in the alcoves, and sardana music playing unobtrusively in the background. A curvy wooden counter at the bar merges in an organic fashion with a wooden arch that doubles back over the counter. Gaudiesque, Beth supposes.

As she waits for her friends to join her, a memory surfaces. She's about fourteen, and has been taken on a Sunday morning to a Zion chapel by the aunt of her foster mother who lives in a tiny, cold-as-stone house in a Welsh valley. Three of the eight-strong congregation sing the hymns and she's daydreaming about the football captain at school when the preacher starts up. She forgets the football captain, mesmerised by the wiry little man who hardly fills his cheap suit, but who grips the pulpit as if he's riding a big-dipper, shaking the wet slates of the roof with his pounding rhetoric. She can see how the eighteenth century preacher, Wesley, had men beating their chests in shame and running out to free slaves and return scrumped apples. The preacher speaks of a smug, rich, man called Job who lost it all, regretted he'd been born, dressed himself in sacking, got some unhelpful advice from his friends and then, refusing to curse his bad fortune (the preacher says: his God), gets it all back again.

Beth wonders why the occasion has come to mind. She can't claim that her troubles are as bad as Job's or there is some sort of parallel to their lives. For a start Job had his camels stolen and she's still got Jenny the cat; Job lost all his children to a whirlwind and she has none to lose; Job had a fulminating attack of pustular psoriasis, while she just suffers mildly dry skin; and she keeps herself in Monsoon skirts rather than in sack cloth.

Another point of difference is that Job had three friends called Bildad, Eliphaz, and Zophar while hers are called Alena, Christina and Preeti. She can see them arriving now and coming to the table. She's thankful that, unlike Job's friends, none of hers believe that what has happened to her is a punishment for her wicked life. However, like Job's friends, they are happy to give advice, in their own ways.

'Leave him,' Christina says, in her world-weary voice, when they've sat down and Beth has told them about Matt's latest physical molestation. She slips off her faux-fur jaguar-print jacket, lays it on her lap, pats it as if it's a pet and then languidly stirs her Manhattan with a glass stick. 'Your udders will become like mushy windfalls. You've got to unload him to a nursing home or somewhere. Face it Beth, he won't notice. He doesn't recognise you, for God's sake. You're just his carer now. You can't do that for the rest of your life.'

'Whoa,' Alena says, leaning away from Christina. 'He's not an item of clothing that Beth can just cast off.'

Christina laughs and throws back her blonde hair. Two men at the bar look over at her. 'Give me a break. I'm loyal to Roma.'

'Dogs don't count, especially loveable red setters,' Beth says.

'You two GPs are too bloody cautious,' Christina says. 'What do you think, Preeti?'

Preeti, a pharmacist, has been a friend of Beth's since they met at their university's Comedy Society. 'Ah, I really, really don't know,' she says. 'It's so, so, impossible.' Beth thinks Preeti too dreamy to work with the public. 'But… he does sort of know you, doesn't he? He rings you at work all the time asking you to come home.'

'He rings me asking me to come home when I'm in the room next door,' Beth says. 'He can't remember back more than a minute, if that. And he's not making any new memories. It's like he's locked in the present.' Aren't we all? she thinks immediately, and then decides, no, we see the river behind and have at least a sketch map of the river ahead, we have a sense of orientation, of history and of destiny. Matt is inside the high hull of a boat, is blind to where he's come from and where he's going. He doesn't know who he is. He's lost his sense of self.

Alena – neat as always with her hair in a sharp, jet, bob and wearing skinny jeans and black roll-neck top – stacks the drinks menus and lines them up parallel to the table edge. She always tidies before she says anything considered. 'But you must be familiar to him in some way. Perhaps he's got emotional memory. I read somewhere that there are different sorts of memory – for music, for language, visual and so on and they're spread out in different parts of the brain. So maybe he's not lost everything.'

'At least he doesn't take fright at me, like he does his mother,' Beth says. She must make an effort to think like Alena, to have considered and hopeful insights, to hear birdsong above the trenches.

'Such a crying shame,' Christina says in a tone that suggests she's making a final pronouncement on the matter. The bird drops dead. 'He was OK, your Matt. I'm never going to find someone like that. I was jealous of you.' She reaches reflexively into her bag, takes out her cigarettes and then, reminded by Alena's finger that points to the recently posted No Smoking sign, says, 'Bugger!' and puts them away again. 'Choose freedom, Beth. You're still young. You should move away, start a new life by the sea. Why don't you go to Australia?'

Alena puts her arm around Beth's shoulders and gives her a light, precise, squeeze. 'I don't like the sound of that. What would we do without you?'

'Look after Matt?' Beth suggests and gets uncertain smiles in return.

'We'll be too busy visiting you,' Christina says airily. 'We'll hire a four by four and do the Outback. I might meet a Crocodile Dundee type. You could line up a few for me.'

'Might have taken my pick first and gone walkabout,' Beth says, and then shudders, thinking of the venomous insects and grotesque reptiles.

'Um… ' Preeti pulls the cherry off her cocktail stick and kisses it into her mouth. 'Manesh says you should meet his younger brother.' She shifts the cherry to her other cheek. 'He's not nearly as clever as Manesh but, according to Manesh, he's much more sensitive. I think he's very sweet; and he's not a womaniser or anything like that; he's still living with his mother but he's got a job. Door to door leaflet distribution or something. Although you'd probably think he should lose some weight.'

'Sounds pitiable,' Christina says, whilst Beth exchanges a smile with Preeti. 'But how *are* you going to meet anyone new to shack up with if your one social occasion of the week is a low key hen party with your friends?'

Alena is centring the nut bowl. 'I'm not sure what the situation is regarding divorce law in your circumstance. Perhaps you should go to a solicitor to find out – just so you know. A precaution.'

Beth picks out a pistachio nut from the bowl and concentrates on prising open its shell.

Alena sits herself up straight. 'We're all being totally presumptuous. I don't think Beth's going to run away anywhere. You're very loyal to Matt aren't you, Beth?'

They all freeze, looking at Beth as if they hope she'll tell them The Right Thing To Do.

She takes a long slow breath. 'I guess I am.' Christina's shoulders slump. 'But... I don't think I've got a choice. To split from him – to get divorced – I'd have to separate in my mind the two Matts.' She takes a quick sip of her piña colada. 'I can't do it. My husband's dead but his doppelganger is still sharing my bed, the teabag, the toothpaste. I catch myself forgetting my Matt's not there. I start to ask him to do something, or make a comment expecting back one of those looks he used to give me.' She wraps her fingers around her glass. 'And sometimes I want a kiss that doesn't leave a bruise.'

Alena and Preeti nod sympathetically and Christina says, 'Bloody hell, Beth. It sucks.'

'Penelope makes me feel guilty all the time. Perhaps I deserve it.'

Christina tuts and says, 'You've got a bloody tender heart, Beth – that's why your patients tell you their life stories – but you can't be loyal when the relationship's not there. Let's face it; you and Matt are a mega example of a relationship breakdown.

Ask me, I know all about that. I've dropped guys on far less.' She flings her hair back again. 'George: too tight with money. Stefano: detested his nosey sister. Seamus: found his accent bloody annoying. Jake: discovered his family history was riddled with genetic defects. I could go on.'

'Thanks for not,' Alena says.

They smile and sip their drinks, except Christina. For a moment Beth thinks she sees a swirl of distress – more than that: despair – in Christina's blue eyes.

'Look... don't give up, Beth,' Preeti says.

Beth feels uncomfortable: all this attention on her own circumstances. What if Christina wants to talk about hers, has got something to tell them? And she'd like to escape being the perpetual hub of her friends' concerns. They've become reluctant to bring up their own traumas, or will say: 'But of course, it's nothing compared to what's happened to you, Beth.' She's become a benchmark for catastrophe – even though she hasn't lost any camels. She's also impatient to get away from insoluble problems.

Preeti says, 'Perhaps Matt will be cured one day. Manesh says there are scientists working on making memories out of molecules or... something.'

'Perhaps,' Beth says, thinking how the neurologist wasn't so optimistic, telling her that Matt has other small aneurysms and one day another is likely to burst despite the pills he's on to keep his blood pressure down.

Christina raises her glass in an exaggerated motion. 'You're a saint, Bethan Jenkins. I nominate you as the offset to my sinful footprint.'

'I'll sully my beatification then by downing a Georgia peach and two buttered rums,' Beth says, picking up the tall drinks menu. 'How are the twins?' she asks Alena.

'Tiring. It would help if I could find a cleaner who can do a decent deep-clean around the house after them.'

'You should let things go a bit,' Preeti says. She hooks out a thin curl of orange peel from her glass with her little finger and nibbles on it. 'What does it matter if there's a wet nappy under the sofa? No one will see it.'

Alena stiffens. She'd once told Beth that she'd found her twins' birth 'messy' rather than wondrous and Alena's mother said that her daughter's first words were, 'Tidy, tidy.'

'The trouble is,' Alena says, 'Martin can't help me because he still has to get up at five to get the train to London and doesn't get back until eight. I don't even understand what he does. *Futures trading*. Sounds like they're swapping destinies. You have mine and I'll have yours.'

They are quiet for a moment and then Preeti frowns and says, 'Do you think we should stock shampoo for greasy hair anymore? Customers seem so embarrassed to buy it. They only want normal or dry brands even if you can see that they'd break an oil embargo if they travelled.'

'I never use anything except Elysian Organic on Roma,' Christina says.

They leave Tres Hermanas close to midnight in a cocktail-corrupted state. Christina props herself up against Beth in the taxi. Beth holds her hand and wonders why she so likes this loud, opinionated friend. Perhaps because she's known her so long. Her surrogate sister. They'd been schoolgirls together, by chance moving to the same new schools on three occasions; Christina following her mother and her mother's boyfriends from town to town. In the purple glow from the frontage of a night club, Beth sees that Christina's hair is yang-white against her own yin-black.

'Are you OK?' Beth asks, remembering the momentary look

of pain in Christina's eyes earlier in the evening. Sparky Christina, always the life and soul – but Beth can't remember a time, even at school, when she's not caught glimpses of something else, a dark river under the bubbles. It's ironic, thinks Beth. Her patients open up to her, but her close friend, Christina, holds something back.

'Course I'm fine,' Christina mumbles, putting her head on Beth's shoulder. 'I'll come with you to Oshtralia, Beff, don't worry.'

Beth arrives at work half an hour before her morning surgery – she likes to see off some of her paperwork before the first patient arrives. Her inbox is on the third shelf down in the reception office, beneath Hector's and David's. Their names – *H Moncrieff* and *D Green* – are engraved on brushed-metal signs and fixed with screws to their shelves. Beth's is marked with a taped-on paper label, saying *LOCUM*, despite her working at the practice for two years. It's a daily reminder that her role is transitory, interchangeable with any number of other free-floating doctors. Being a locum implies to the most dutiful of her colleagues that you might not be that serious about your vocation or, to the cynical, that no practice wants you as a partner due to something that you've failed to mention on your CV, like third degree halitosis or steadfast belligerence. The most positive interpretation for being a locum is that you are biding your time while waiting for an Australian work permit – about to make a new life for yourself in the great outdoors, a flighty hedonist. If only.

Her first patient is Sindhi Kaur, a thirty-five-year-old owner of three restaurants. She comes in busily and sits down on the edge of the chair. 'Doctor, if you'll just sign this.' She pulls a form from a large brown envelope and sets it in front of Beth, saying breathily, 'We're emigrating to India.'

'Emigrating?'

'Frankly we're fed up with this country. So many immigrants and the new ones are the worst sort. The place is going downhill fast. India's where it's all happening now. I want a better life for my children, for them to have opportunities I never had.'

'What about your parents?' Beth recalls that they attend the diabetes and heart disease clinics.

'They're coming with us. It'll be fantastic for them in India. For a start, there's better health care. The doctors there always give antibiotics and sleeping tablets when we ask – they don't care about the cost. My father doesn't even need his tablets in India. His blood pressure's one hundred per cent and his sugar diabetes goes away. Sign here, Doctor.' She jabs her index finger at a box at the bottom of the immigration form.

'But what about your mother? She's in a wheelchair, isn't she?'

'The funny thing is, Doctor, when she gets off the plane in Mumbai she no longer needs it. Straightaway she can walk. It's the sunshine. It makes you want to get off your backside.'

Beth certifies Sindhi Kaur as in rude health. 'Aren't you a little worried – starting a completely new life?'

'Pfff, not at all. It would be much more worrisome to stay here. You see, here we'll always have the life we have now. Everything will stay the same for us. Nothing will ever change.'

Beth finds herself staring in silence at her patient.

Sindhi Kaur's finger darts onto the form again. 'The date goes here and your stamp there, Doctor.'

'You're very brave,' Beth says as she breaks back to the form.

'Come and visit us. We'll have a boutique hotel in Kerala by the beach. I'll send you the details.'

'Thanks, and all the best. I hope you enjoy your new life.'

Beth tries to imagine herself doing the same, making a fresh start far away as Christina had suggested, somewhere very foreign. She sees snakes whipping and coiling on dusty floors and battalions of ants waving their amber pincers as they march up her legs. But even without a disgust of crawling animals, she knows she could never escape like that – she's too far down a trench of responsibility. She beats away the thought that she's simply too cautious and lacks courage.

Next is Dillin Malachy. He comes often. Today he has found the little bone at the lower end of the breastbone called the xiphisternum. Then there are a couple of mums manoeuvring four-wheel drive buggies with the expertise of yellow digger operators. Somewhere inside the deeply padded interior of the perambulator (beneath Gore-Tex rain covers, rollover bars, twelve tog blankets, four-point harnesses) is a baby – inside an all-in-one bear suit baby grow, with tight little poppers in its damp crotch. But she loves the babies – although they give her a wistful feeling. Wistful? It shreds her.

She keeps a box of tissues handy on her desk. She seems to have a lachrymogenic effect on her patients although they come back for more the following week. Lately though, she wonders if she exudes tragedy and that's why she attracts the morose. She hopes not as she keeps on smiling, keeps keenly listening, keeps conjuring up for them happier, more optimistic narratives.

Beth has to wait while an elderly couple try to agree on whether something is wrong or not.

'He's short of breath at night, Doctor.'

'No I'm not. Don't exaggerate, Marjory.'

'You don't know how you sound, George. You sound like a predator.'

'Thanks, Marj. There's nothing wrong with me, Doctor.'

'Don't listen to him; he'll be shouting there's nothing wrong up the chimney of the crematorium.'

'For goodness sake, Marj.'

'And what about your dickiitis?'

Beth butts in. 'Er, diverticulitis?'

'See Marj, you're making things up. I haven't had dickiitis since I was in the merchant navy.'

It's going to take a while to figure out the story of their relationship. But she must keep to time and make more effort not to upset Hector.

Much of the rest of the morning is spent listening to the old fighting the physical indignities of their age or the young fighting the mental indignities of their emotions. She's also the practice's gynaecologist, Hector admitting to being inclined to too-readily diagnose hysteria, and absent-minded David having occasionally forgotten that he already has a patient laid out – ready to be examined – on the couch behind his curtain, before calling for the next.

Beth is running forty-five minutes late when she calls in her seventeenth patient. It's Fortunate. His second name is Mukumbi, she now learns. He enters with his hand extended and a rapturous expression as if he's just found a long lost friend. 'Ah, wonderful, wonderful! So nice to see you again, Dr Jenkins!'

'It's nice to see you as well. Sorry to keep you waiting. Do sit down. How can I help you?'

'It's a pleasure.' He settles himself in his seat and has a leisurely look around her room.

'Likewise, so what brings you to see me?' she encourages.

'Is that your husband?' She has a picture of Matt on her desk, taken BC.

'It is.'

'He's very handsome.'

'Yes, er, thank-you.'

'It's a pleasure. I also want to say that you've been too helpful to Mr De Villier.'

'I'm not so sure, but thanks for saying so.'

'That's OK, it's nothing.'

They sit there, silent, Fortunate content to wait with a faint smile on his face, almost beatific. Beth has the feeling he is expecting something of her and is waiting for her to guess it.

'How's your girlfriend?' she says at last. 'Shungu.'

'She's too wonderful.' He smiles back contentedly.

'Good… is there something you want to talk about?'

Fortunate suddenly slaps his hand on her desk as if dealing his cards. 'For sure, I have another problem with regard to Shungu. You see, I'm wishing you to take another picture.'

'Oh.'

'Yes, Shungu is requiring to be sure about my financial situation here.'

'Ah, I thought you'd established your credentials on that. So what's it this time?'

'She wishes to know that I have some land.'

'Land!' Beth moves her chair forward.

'A farm. Only a small farm, Doctor.'

'A farm!'

'You know – with maize and tractors.' Beth feels her mouth go slack. 'Or oxen. Oxen will be fine.'

She tries to prevent a smile and hopes he doesn't think her rude. 'Mr Mukumbi, this seems a little bizarre. Very few people here actually own a farm and she can hardly expect you – working in a nursing home a long way from home – to be one of them.'

'You're correct but she's not too conversant with the situation here in the UK. I shall inform her at a later time but for the present it's best not to complicate matters.'

Beth starts to shake her head.

'Dr Jenkins, I'm relying on you alone. Maybe we can go out to the communal lands.'

'Communal?'

'The farms where the… farmers live.'

'You mean go and take a picture of you on a farm?'

'Exactly. It's very simple.'

She's had outlandish consultations before – such as the man who wanted her to go and choose an engagement ring for his fiancée – so she doesn't feel entirely floored.

'Mr Mukumbi, I'm very sorry. I can't help you with this one. Is there anything else I can help you with?'

'Dr Jenkins, I don't ask you as my doctor, but as my friend.' He smiles winsomely.

'Er, thanks, but I'm consulting at the moment. I'm very happy to try to help with any medical problems but it's not good form (she nearly adds, *in this country*, but stops herself as it sounds so priggish) for me to do those sort of favours for my patients.' She straightens herself and folds her hands to signal that the consultation has to close.

Anxiety brushes Fortunate's eyes. 'Shungu is all I have, Doctor. She's a very wonderful woman and if I fail this last test of my sincerity then I fear she'll have to find a better man.'

'Don't you think that Shungu should love you for who you are, rather than for your financial situation?'

Beth hopes her agony aunt insight will be enough but he's unimpressed. 'Of course she loves me, but these are hard times in my home country and she must think of our children.'

'You have children?'

'Our future children. She has to think of their well-being. In my country we don't have the luxury of the benefits.'

Beth shakes her head again resolutely.

A crestfallen expression spreads over Fortunate's face as if he's been struck by a bilateral Bell's palsy. He stands up slowly with a downward look as if she's just broken very bad news which, it seems, she has.

'I will leave now,' he says.

'I'm very sorry.'

'I'm going now.' He hesitates before moving towards the door, giving Beth one last chance to redeem herself.

Beth starts to feel as if she is being wholly unreasonable and that she's wounded him grievously. She says, 'I'm sure you can find someone else to take the picture.'

He shakes his head dolefully. 'You're the only one I can trust, Doctor.' Beth purses her lips. He opens the door slowly, but then says, 'There's one other matter for you. Mr De Villier has agreed to have an X-ray.'

'Really?'

'I persuaded him.'

'Well done. How did you do it?'

'I told him that I'm an orphan here in Britain without my family and he is a *madala* – that's an old man, an elder – from my country. Therefore he's my father. I respectfully asked him, as his son, not to leave me here on my own. Not to leave me alone in this place that's not our home, where we have no land.'

'But he's incredibly rude to you. He treats you like a slave. Like he's still in... ' her colonial history is poor but she remembers: 'Rhodesia.'

'Doctor, he's an old man.'

Her foreign patients! She's always out of her depth with them. 'I'll make the arrangements for the X-ray,' she says.

Fortunate closes the door softly behind him. Beth isn't sure what to write on the consultation note. She can't leave it blank. She writes, *Updated me on Mr De Villier's care*, and then sits biting her lower lip for a few seconds, worrying that she's an inflexible bureaucrat. It isn't that the request is reasonable (she can't imagine Hector or Alena acquiescing) but Fortunate has a beguiling faith in her and she's let him down. It's not his fault that he doesn't know the ground-rules, doesn't understand where her role ends. He sees her primarily as a friend or perhaps as a suburban shaman with the powers to help him navigate his courtship.

She calls the next patient, hoping for something easier to deal with like scalp eczema. Whatever it is, she's going to fix an unempathetic expression, fire out a prescription, and try to make up time.

Beth drives home that evening still wondering if she should so firmly have refused Fortunate's request. Maybe she should have used her imagination and come up with a creative solution to his dilemma. As she nears her road, she nearly collides with a BMW convertible that has wandered across the central white line. It's just like the one she'd noticed at Twicare. She puts more effort into concentrating on the road.

When she lets herself in, Matt rushes up to her. She braces herself, in case he gropes her, but he just holds onto her, breathing fast. He's frightened. Whatever has caused his fright must have only just happened unless his powers of memory have been miraculously restored.

'What's the matter, Matt? What's bugging you?'

He shakes his head from side to side as if unable to put a name to his fear.

'Let's go through to the kitchen.' Perhaps he's fiddled with an appliance and given himself an electric shock. The carer would have left about an hour ago. But everything is in its place. Still holding his hand she looks in the lounge and dining room but finds no clue as to the cause of his alarm. She remembers Matt's telephone call about the man at the door.

Then she remembers the BMW, how it might have just emerged from their cul-de-sac, and feels uneasy.

She takes Matt's arm with her free hand and turns him around to face her. 'Did someone come to the door?'

He grips her hand more tightly. She notices that he's wet his trousers.

'Oops, you did get a fright. We're going to have to get you changed. Did the man come to the door again?' He's frowning. 'Who came to the door, Matt? Did you let him in?'

He stares blankly at her and she can see that he's suddenly calmed and has no clue as to what she's talking about. Matt is sometimes like a frightened horse: is it rearing up in terror because it has seen a tiger on the loose or because it has seen a hedge?

That night she props herself up in bed beside Matt. He is on his back, laid out like Lenin, but his eyelids are only half closed, as if he's become snagged on the border between being alive and being dead.

'Shall I read to you, Matt? Like we used to.'

He doesn't respond. His lips fall open.

'You liked biographies.'

From her bedside drawer she picks out a biography of Shackleton. They'd been half way through it before Matt had his stroke. She opens it at the bookmark and reads it aloud and finds herself carried away. Men tramping into icy wastes, leaning against the biting wind. Huskies hauling. Glaciated seal meat. Clothes frozen rigid. Endurance. As she turns the pages, her voice becomes drowsy as if infused by the exhaustion of Shackleton's men. Then, for a moment, she expects Matt to nudge her like he used to and say, 'Hey, Bee. You're talking in your sleep again.' And then she'll yawn, let the book slide off the bed, lay her head on his warm chest while he strokes her hair and sleep will come.

But he says nothing and his arms – seized up beside him – do not reach for her. He starts to snore, drowning out her voice.

She lays the book on her stomach and drops her head on her pillow to look over at him. She sees the portrait of the man she'd adored. That dent on the bridge of his nose: 'Rugby injury,' he used to say to anyone whose eye was drawn to the depression. 'Tripped on a paving slab on my way to watch a game.' The truth was almost as banal: a direct hit by the gybing boom of a dinghy whilst in the university sailing team and never found time afterwards to have the bones reset. She'd loved his lack of vanity in a self-conscious culture.

And there in the hollow of his cheek is the trace of the crease that formed when he used to smile. It would deepen as if to embrace others in the arc of his quiet good humour. There is his strong brow that furrowed faintly, mysteriously, when he was in thought.

She reaches her hand across towards him and almost touches his face. Wake up Matt. Let's go to the rugby this weekend. She rests her hand on his pillow. Remember? We'd shout and groan and cheer and then after the game we'd collect a Thai take-away as we walked home in the crowd. Then we'd make a short cut across the unlit park, you talkative about the game, me content, enjoying being unafraid of the dark with you beside me. Remember that evening when we lay down in the middle of the park – the city looked like a distant shore strung with lights – and floated there under the moon? You suddenly said, 'Look out! Dolphin!' and sprang up to fend off an exuberant dog that had bounded over. I yelped with fright and then we laughed and laughed. Let's do that sort of stuff again, Matt.

Matt's eyelids flicker and his cheek trembles as if his face is about to disintegrate. He takes a shuddering breath. His jaw sags.

She will extend the carers' hours and try to bring Penelope around on that. Or she will have to give up work. The years, the decades, stretch ahead. She thinks of Sindhi Kaur. She thinks of Christina's suggestion that she run away and start a new life.

CHAPTER 4

When Beth returns to Twicare the next day she sees a singer in the residents' lounge. He has a slick of black hair that curls roguishly at his collar and has a matching shiny-black waistcoat and black trousers with silver piping. He stands beside enormous speakers, crooning passionately into his microphone as if he's at the O2 arena. Perhaps he imagines a vast, mesmerised audience filling an auditorium. But none of the residents is taking the slightest notice. An old man lies a few feet away in an armchair as if he's fallen there from a great height: limbs splayed, jaw slack, eyes rolled up under half-closed lids. The singer imagines he's on a world stage; the old man's world is inside his eyelids, memories like misty mountains and the burbling of hidden streams.

Beth walks on down the corridor, passing the hairdressing room where a woman resident sits, doll-eyed, under a hood hair dryer. Its cone sports enough lights and switches to launch a spaceship but not enough to spark up the old lady. Beth feels a new admiration for Twicare's matron: her masterly running and maintenance of the machinery of her ship whilst on the decks there is such attrition. But not all the hands are down. The man she's on her way to visit has shown himself able to fizz into life – but only when it suits him.

She comes across Fortunate in the corridor. He's accompanying a female resident who is taking tiny, slipper-shuffling steps, making barely perceptible progress and muttering, 'Got to tell Doris. Got to tell Doris.' She supports herself on Fortunate's left arm. Fortunate is singing softly and a little sadly, 'We are moving in the love of God. It's true, we are moving, moving, moving in the love of God… ' The tune has an African lilt and he dances his shoulders as he sings.

As Beth passes, he stops singing and says in an even tone, 'He's waiting for you, Doctor.'

'Thanks.' She avoids meeting his eye in case she receives a shaming look.

'Do you want some help?' he asks. He gives a sideways glance at the old lady and says quietly, 'But we're footing slowly so it may take me until Wednesday to get to you.'

Beth feels worse at his forgiving joke. She declines with a quick smile, even as she wonders if she should do him just one more favour.

Mr De Villier is sitting with his head lolling against the wing of his high back chair, his eyes closed as if catching the sun. Beth imagines him on some tropical veranda, pleasantly sozzled, limp in a teak rocker as the late afternoon sun casts a golden light across the far hills and birds in fancy dress squawk amongst the giant mahoganies down by the river. But the low-energy light bulb in his Twicare room casts a wintry light so that it seems she can see the white of his skull through the parchment-thin tissues of his forehead.

When she says hello he keeps his eyes closed and says, 'What the bloody hell is it this time?'

'Fortunate tells me you've decided you would like to have the X-ray.'

From his sour expression Beth thinks he might have changed his mind but he says, 'I've only agreed so I can get you and the black boy off my back.'

Beth explains to him what she's arranged and then he lets her take a blood sample. As she waits for the syringe to fill, she says, 'You had a farm in Zimbabwe?'

He doesn't reply immediately but then says in a grunting voice, 'Yes – a few cattle.'

'Was the farm… in the family?'

'No, bought it one year after Independence. Used my hard-earned loot: fireman on steam, cross-border sanctions-busting in the Rhodesia days, trucking, mining, foreman on a tobacco farm.'

Beth releases the cuff, withdraws the needle and presses on the puncture wound with a tissue.

'Sounds very adventurous.'

'Shangri-La.'

'Do you mind telling me what happened? Why did you have to leave Zimbabwe?' She's made an effort to take more interest in the news on Zimbabwe since meeting Mr De Villier. She's learnt of the violence by the ruling Party against supporters of the opposition Party and of the invasion of white-owned farms by the government's militias.

He doesn't reply. Beth tries again. 'Your farm was taken away from you?'

Without warning Mr De Villier spasms forward, grips Beth's arm with his free hand and yanks her close. For a moment she fears he's going to assault her. His breath smells of uncooked meat. Then, like the fleet and deadly strike of a venomous snake, he says, 'Murder!'

Beth freezes. She waits for him to go on but he releases her arm, collapses back again and says, 'You finished skewering me yet?'

'Do you want to tell me more about it?' she says, finding she's pulled the tissue away from his arm too early, allowing a small bruise to swell under his skin like a bloated tick.

'No.'

'You gave me a fright.'

He harrumphs dismissively. 'It gave me a bloody fright as well, the murder. Now let's get on with my autopsy.'

Beth has to write Mr De Villier's name twice on the sample bottle as her first attempt is illegible. She drops the needle into the sharps container and then turns to Mr De Villier. 'I hope you'll feel free to talk to me about it if you want to.'

He pretends not to have heard her.

'OK, I'll let you know as soon as I have the results, then perhaps we can have another chat.'

'Please yourself.'

Beth excuses herself and leaves, but stops just before Matron's office door to stare at one of the landscape paintings on the wall. A ploughing scene under a hot summer sky. She needs a moment to steady herself after Mr De Villier's eruption. It's taken her aback more than she'd have expected. It isn't so much what he's said to her – the single-worded outburst: *murder* – but that she has a sense that he's made a decision to open himself up to her in a calculated manner, teasingly, reeling her in under his own terms to reveal things that she doesn't have the emotional reserves for right now. Her mouth has gone dry and she frets that Mr De Villier is somehow going to stoke her mild self-diagnosed anxiety state (and how could any woman not admit to that?) into house-on-fire panic attacks. But as her eye is drawn to a man with a scythe in the corner of a field in the painting she's certain there's more. She sees herself as a reinterpreter of her patients' stories, aiding alternative narratives, but she has an intuition that Mr De Villier has no interest in her help on those terms. He sees some other role for her. And now, in the dislocated state she's in, she has no confidence that she'll be able to resist.

The sound of Matron using a stapler in the office comes through the door and Beth tears her eye away from the scythe and goes in to see her. Matron's office is lined with wall to wall protocols and policies. There are generic official ones such as *Respect and Dignity, Gender Discrimination, Equality*, but many more besides: *Meals, Access Rules for Relatives, Toileting, Policy for Policy Writing, Singing*. She gets stuck on *Singing* until Matron says loudly, 'Yes, Dr Jenkins? Can I help?'

Matron is as lightly built as her, but she has a strong jaw. Sean told Beth that once she bit down on something, only death would unlock her. She wears a sharply-cut black suit and has dyed, severely cropped, copper-red hair. There are rumours that she was a naval officer until she'd slapped her commander.

'I just wanted to ask you about one of my patients,' Beth says. 'It's Mr De Villier. He seems unsettled. Do you know if he has any family?'

Matron tuts and says, 'He damned well shouldn't be here. He should be in a detention centre where he can be forced to obey the rules and be made to be grateful.' She pulls his file from a cabinet. 'He tells us – if you can believe him – that he's not got a living soul left to him in the world. We've got next to nothing on him, can't write a single line in his *my life story* page.' Beth thinks that she and Fortunate have had more success there; they've made a small start on the curriculum vitae elements of his story: tobacco farmer, smuggler, fireman on steam engines – and also know that there was a murder on his farm. Matron breaks open his file. 'Look at all these blanks. See, we haven't even got a photo of him for the front page. He refused to consent to it. Said he'd urinate on the lens.' Beth suppresses a smile but Matron frowns at the page. 'Look, I can't fill in *Previous GP, Previous Address, Next of Kin*, not even *Aftercare Instructions* – he said he doesn't want to be buried or cremated in this country. But we can't dispatch his body back on the plane he came on, can we? He arrived with a wodge of South African rand and, I should point out, gangrenous legs. He got allocated to us after the amputations. Did I forget to mention the suitcase full of Zimbabwean dollar notes?'

'Really?'

'Yes, millions and millions of Zimbabwe dollars. Said it was his pension although they were worthless apparently. He wanted our nurses to use them as toilet paper.' She points up at the *Toileting Policy* folder. 'Not permitted.' She claps his folder shut. 'There's a social worker who's looking after his affairs although of course she's off with stress at present and they've not yet allocated a replacement. Another thing, he insisted we call a locksmith. Said he wanted a lock on the inside of his door that only he could open. I said that was unacceptable so, after demanding we change all his rand into pounds, he made Nurse Fortunate go out and buy the safe you've no doubt seen in the corner of his room.'

'It's huge. What's he got in it?'

'No idea. I hope it's nothing illegal. I'm now going to have to write a Residents' *Safe Policy*.'

Beth tells Matron that she thinks it likely that Mr De Villier is terminally ill. Matron receives the news calmly, reaches up to the shelf and pulls down the *Twicare Twilight Pathway*. She opens it, looks at her watch, and enters the time in a box and Beth's name in another.

'I'm waiting for confirmation of course from his tests.' Beth is suddenly worried that she's initiated some process that can't be reversed or altered – or that might even hasten Mr De Villier's demise.

Matron grunts and pulls the sheet from the folder, tears it in half theatrically and says, 'Let me know when you're sure, Dr Jenkins. Uncertainty and ambiguity are not conducive to the efficient running of my ship.'

As Beth leaves, now somewhat fortified by Matron's no-blather attitude, she makes a mental note to go through a formal questionnaire with Mr De Villier when she returns to assess whether he's clinically depressed. Perhaps he just needs Prozac.

Fortunate is coming out of a side room, still supporting the shuffling resident. He wears a patient, saintly expression. Another nurse is walking down the corridor: a slight, shy-looking young woman, her large eyes downturned to show her upper eyelids, delicate and smooth as eggshells in her small face. A discreet silver cross hangs from a necklace on her slender neck. Despite the lightness of her form she wears sturdy, brown, lace-up work shoes that suggest determination and reliability. She doesn't look at Beth but says quietly, 'Good afternoon, Doctor. Good afternoon, Nurse Fortunate,' as she passes.

'Is she Zimbabwean as well?' Beth asks Fortunate.

'Yes, her name's Hope.'

'Ah, why don't you get her to take that photo you wanted?'

Fortunate lowers his voice. 'It's not possible.'

'What's the problem?' she says.

Fortunate leans towards her and says in a low voice, 'I think she wants to be my friend.'

'What's wrong with that? Oh, I see, she doesn't know about Shungu then?'

'Not exactly.'

Beth is about to move on but stops to ask, 'Does Mr De Villier talk about what happened before he came here – what happened on his farm?'

'Speak up Doris! Speak up Doris!' says the resident on Fortunate's arm, suddenly clinging onto him with both hands.

Fortunate pats her hands and says, 'We're nearly there Mrs Francesca.' He turns to Beth and says, 'No, he only says what he wishes. He doesn't answer my questions. I've tried to find out if he has any family but that makes him angry and he shouts and then Matron calls me to her office and says that I'm upsetting the residents.'

The jumped-up BMW is near Beth's Polo again in the Twicare car park and she can see the shape of the driver behind the darkened glass. He holds a black mobile phone to his ear. She can hear a muffled conversation in a foreign tongue and he keeps hitting the wheel with his other hand as if driving home a point. He does not seem to be paying her any attention this time. She is reversing out when she sees the nurse, Hope, coming out of Twicare. Hope has changed out of her mustard-coloured Twicare uniform and brown work shoes and is now in a short dark coat, tight jeans and heels. She goes to the passenger door of the BMW. The driver pushes the door open from inside but before Hope gets in she catches Beth's eye. Her expression has changed from a cool nonchalance as she approached the car, to fear. Worse than that: terror. She disappears into the vehicle. Beth stops reversing and waits.

A dull booming starts up as some sort of woofer system comes on in the BMW and then the car reverses out, swinging around and coming rapidly along the other side of Beth's Polo. Beth squeezes her eyes shut waiting for the noise of metal scoring metal but instead hears a shriek of rubber and when she opens her eyes the BMW is accelerating past her. The driver has lowered his window and she has a sight of his forearm resting on the ledge. The BMW's rear end bottoms out over the speed hump inside the gates to the Twicare car park. Beth sits there. A sense of foreboding grows. She would swear to a coroner that the deep scar on the man's arm had been inflicted by a human bite.

CHAPTER 5

A s Beth sits down at her desk in the surgery and sorts through her post, she still has half a mind on the fearful expression she'd seen on Hope's face in the car park. She'll have to speak to Hope although these scenarios in ethnic minorities can be difficult to unlock. She thinks about the man in the car. She remembers her suspicion that he was watching her and had followed her. Could he have visited Matt? Matt had been as fearful as Hope about something. Was he the man at the door? Could he be from Zimbabwe? Had Matt met him when he lived there? She absent-mindedly opens a sealed white envelope and finds a letter from Hector.

Dear Dr Jenkins,

Dr Green and I have to look to the long-term wellbeing of the practice given the constraints we are under. We would like to meet you next Monday at one o'clock sharp in the education room.

Sincerely,

Hector Moncrieff

She folds the letter and pinches it tightly along the crease. This is it, she's going to be flung out. She should've seen it coming. That warning he'd given her on her late-running surgeries. Her locum contract allows for only a week's notice. She looks at the bright toy – a plastic turtle with a loveable face – that lies on her desk, the one she uses to distract children before wriggling her otoscope into their ears. She'll miss the children, whose guarded expressions she likes nudging into expressions of relief, even happiness; she'll miss her elderly patients who become friends within one consultation. Then there is Mr De Villier – she's not yet been of any help to him with his grudge, let alone his cough.

She'll have to look for another locum which will be just the opportunity Penelope is waiting for to insist that this is the moment to become a full time carer for Matt. Which friend to ring? Depends how she feels. She feels cross. She rings Christina.

'The bastards!' she says. 'And after all you've done for them. Using you, abusing you, and then dropping you. Total pillocks!'

So cathartic, surfing on Christina's outrage. The turtle grins at her.

She arrives home later to see Penelope's Mercedes estate stretched out along the driveway. Beth braces herself. Penelope normally turns up in her cream-skinned Mini with a Union Jack painted on its roof, except when she's going somewhere with Bruno. Bruno is a dog with an uncomplicated prejudice: he has a deep hatred of Beth. She accidentally trod on his head when he was a puppy. Now she wishes she'd trodden harder.

She opens the door with caution, calling, 'Hello, I'm home.' There seems no immediate danger so she moves into the hall but is stopped in her tracks by the sight of three large, padded, blue suitcases next to the stairs. 'Um, someone going somewhere?' she asks to the empty hall.

She hears the toilet flush and then Penelope strides through. 'There you are at last. Matthew will carry the suitcases upstairs later on.'

'What's happening?' Beth asks.

'An answer to your prayers. I've decided to move in. It makes perfect sense, doesn't it? I can look after Matthew during the day when you're not here. I've sent the carers packing and told them not to come back.'

'You've sent the... so... how long are you expecting... ?'

'Until he's better of course, or... ' Penelope looks at Beth pointedly, 'until you're ready to give up work and shoulder your responsibilities.'

Beth breathes deeply and imagines herself stacking up sandbags to hold back storm water. 'Where's Matt?' she asks.

'He's in the garden playing with Bruno. They're having fun.'

'Bruno's here?'

'Of course, part of the family, isn't he? You must try and make friends with him. He can sense your hostility, Bethan. Anyway, there'll be plenty of time to make up.'

The sandbags are giving way. Every one of the faces in the prints on the wall looks at Beth anxiously. She takes a wheezy breath and then, with steely effort, zips her lips and goes through to the kitchen. Something is different; no, a lot is different. A thick nauseating fug from no less than three Ginger Lily aroma bottles on the breakfast bar fog the air. The spice containers (which she normally keeps tidied away in a rack on the wall) have been placed along the back of the worktop. Penelope has loaded her supplements and vitamins – Glucosamine, Zinc, Horny Goat Weed, Hoodia Gordinii and many more – into the spice rack, ready to be knocked back with her gin or sprinkled onto her muesli. The radio is on, the channel changed from Beth's usual Radio 4 to something playing annoying adverts. She turns to stomp back to Penelope but then turns again and goes instead to the kitchen window. What can she do? The house is not hers. It's Penelope's.

Through the window she sees Matt and Bruno – a black Scottish terrier – playing on the lawn. Matt is waving a stick above his head preparing to throw it and Bruno is trying to mate with Matt's leg. Bruno sees Beth, dismounts and growls at her, presenting his vicious teeth. She can't see his eyes through his facial hair but can imagine their demonic fixity on her. If Bruno stays, he'll eat poor Jenny with the toasted bacon sandwiches that Penelope makes for him each morning.

'Aren't they getting on famously?' says Penelope behind her. 'Matthew plays so well with Bruno. Just think what a good father he'll be.'

'Penelope, I've got to go out again.'

'So soon? Thank God I'm here then.'

Beth leaves and sits in her car and then rings Christina on her mobile, hoping for another session of mutual spitting, but Christina is at the hairdresser. 'Can't talk now Beth, they're just about to break the eggs on my head.' Alena is on her way out to take her children to Discover Dinosaurs at the museum and when she rings Preeti she gets her mother who says that Preeti's gone to Walsall for a pre-wedding party. Preeti attends weddings and their attendant functions as often as Christina shops. Beth sits there for a moment and then she jumps out of the car, lets herself into the house again, runs upstairs, changes into a loose, short-sleeved shirt, jeans and trainers and collects an old black jersey and her pristine frog-green Wellington boots from a box in the cloakroom. She's going to do something that she's put off since Matt's stroke, waiting for an occasion like this when there's nowhere else to go.

Matt's allotment is a mile out of town on the edge of a farmer's field down a lane that bends along a pretty curve of the county. But as Beth drives cautiously along the lane, she's reminded that she is not remotely an outdoors person or gardener (manure under the fingernails, laden with tetanus spore and E. coli – she shudders). Matt, however, had been enthusiastic about the allotment in a quiet way. That's the most dangerous sort of fanatic, she used to tell him.

Matt had bought the allotment and so they own it full and square with no strings attached to his mother. He used to say that it was his outdoor sanctum, his hideaway, his arrière-boutique, somewhere he could escape to when he wanted to unwind. On a Sunday afternoon or a summer evening he would sometimes disappear there and do whatever was necessary to come back triumphantly – as the seasons moved on – with kale and rhubarb, calabrese and kohlrabi, fennel and celeriac, ending up with oyster flavoured salsify. Matt was something of a vegetable specialist. She'd asked him why he couldn't save himself the trouble of going out to the allotment by growing them in their garden at home but he said he liked being out of the city in a place where 'our ancestors learned to nurture and love'. His comment seemed overblown at the time but now she wishes she'd asked him what he meant.

The lane passes through a dense tunnel of trees. Beth senses the leafless branches meshing together in a sinister fashion, and psychopaths lurking, and organic stinks, and predatory owls and insects picking on creatures smaller than themselves. She tries to put away from her vision the source of her disgust and apprehension, her near phobia: the occasion when she was six and got lost in a wood for several hours. She was, as it happened, wearing a red, hooded anorak. She didn't come across the big bad wolf but even thinking about it now, after so many years, makes her short of breath.

On the other hand, from behind the window of her car, she does like the idea – the general concept – of there being a natural world, that it exists out there, and she does her bit to save endangered animals by supporting charities like Gorilla Rescue; but she would hate to actually meet a wild animal face to face. Apart from Jenny, she is quite happy to stay clear of supposedly tame ones as well, such as Bruno.

She tries to remember the last time she'd been out to the allotment. Sometime before Matt's stroke. Now she has to make a decision on what to do with it. She has a mind to sell it.

Just beyond Matt's allotment – which is the expected bad-hair-day of enmeshed and dead vegetable matter in the sodden winter soil – Beth sees a sinewy man, in his late sixties she guesses, picking up a vicious-looking long-handled fork. He wears black flannel trousers streaked with mud, held up to just below his nipples by braces. The sleeves of his plaid shirt are rolled up, revealing grey fissured skin like a mudflat in a drought. He straightens himself unhurriedly, placing one hand on his lumbar region in a my-damn-back sort of way, supports himself on the fork and turns with an almost theatrical slowness to look at her from under the shadow of his cor-blimey cap. She is still in her lily-white trainers and holds her wellies at arm's length, hoping not to have to use them. She gives him a wary nod.

'You're Matt Hallam's wife aren't you? How is he?' the man says, speaking each word slowly as if she's the country bumpkin.

'Thanks for asking,' Beth says, 'but much the same, really.'

He digests that, working his lips. 'Crying shame. We got on like brothers. Bit of a rivalry we had, although I admit he was better at growing celeriac than I am. My name's Jack.'

She recalls Matt mentioning him. 'I'm Beth, pleased to meet you. Not sure what I'm going to do about this.' She points at Matt's allotment.

'If you want a hand tending it, then I'm your man.'

'That's kind but I'm not green fingered, so I'm not planning on—'

'Very valuable, your allotment. They're hard to find. You should keep it. There's going to be less of it. Land, I mean. Rising sea levels, population growth, new towns. Don't they say to buy land, they're not making it anymore? All the fields will be bought up for solar farming. That'll be much more profitable than dairy.'

'It's not really my thing. I haven't got the right gear.' She points to her trainers but he looks unimpressed.

'It's a bit of this planet you can call your own and if you look after her, she'll give you back much more than you put in.'

Beth stares, unconvinced, at Matt's patch. It seems so time consuming and inefficient: a barrowful of vegetables that went rotten before they had eaten through them, in exchange for weeks of back-breaking labour.

'Don't do anything hasty,' Jack says. 'That's all I'll say.' He turns to collect his implements and doffs his cap at her as he leaves, but not before saying, 'And the Lord God planted a garden. And the Lord God took the man and put him in the garden to till it and keep it.' Then he adds gravely, 'That's Holy Scripture.'

Another prophet speaks, thinks Beth, remembering Mr De Villier's advice. She turns to leave as a smell of slurry gasses over her from an adjoining field. She can't stay here on her own; it's too close to the woods. Then she finds herself dithering. She shouldn't stay, but who to go to, where else to go? The airport? Dover? She turns back to stare at Matt's allotment. The place is saying something to her. But she can't understand its language, can't read its earthy signs. She turns away, and then she turns back again, and then, eureka, of course.

She takes out her mobile phone and rings Twicare. Matron answers.

'Hello Matron, it's Dr Jenkins here.'

'Wednesday afternoon, Dr Jenkins? You're normally off duty on a Wednesday afternoon, aren't you?'

'Yes, but I was wondering if I could speak to Nurse Fortunate.'

'Nurse Fortunate Mukumbi? Perhaps I can help. Which patient is it?'

'It's really only something that Fortunate can help me with.'

'Which patient, Dr Jenkins?'

'Ah… never mind, I'll ring tomorrow. Fortunate's the only one who knows the… er… details.'

'I can assure you that's unlikely,' Matron says brusquely, 'we have a strict policy on sharing of information. All staff must disclose all client matters at handover. There's nothing he could possibly help you with that my other staff couldn't do equally as well. We don't want any particular nurse to become indispensable, especially these migrants. You never know when they're going to up-camp and migrate off somewhere else.' She gives a huffing chuckle as if pleased at her own wit.

'It's a personal matter.'

The line goes quiet. When Matron speaks again her voice is detached and official. 'As it happens, Dr Jenkins, although he's not on duty, he's helping out a bit. I'll go and see if I can find him.'

Matron returns soon and says, 'Here he is, Dr Jenkins, I'll pass him over.' Beth can see her sitting herself down behind her desk with a sweep of her hand to smooth her already smooth skirt over her thigh and then pretending to get on with her paperwork while she listens in.

'Hello, this is Nurse Fortunate here.' His voice is friendly and open.

'Fortunate, do you have your camera with you? I'm going to take you to my farm. Are you free to be picked up in half an hour?'

He hardly hesitates. 'Yes, I'm free.'

'I'll see you soon then.'

'Ah! It'll be a pleasure. I'll wait for you in the car park. But Dr Jenkins,' he sounds mischievous, 'there's to be no mating.'

Beth thinks she hears a sudden movement in Matron's office and then hears a door banging shut.

'Sorry?' she says, as aghast as Matron.

'Oh, apology!' he says, laughing. 'I mean the animals – you know, on the farm. They don't do as they're told. We must be sure that there are no mating cattle or pigs in the field behind me when we take the picture. They won't know the importance of this photo.'

'Quite! Ha, ha. See you soon.'

Beth meets Fortunate in the Twicare car park although he must have been back to his room as is wearing pressed black trousers and a crisp white shirt. His patterned leather shoes shine, newly polished.

'You look far too smart for a farmer,' she says.

'I must look my best for the photo,' he replies, exuding an infectious enthusiasm. 'It'll be shown to our grandchildren and their grandchildren. They'll laugh plenty to think of these days but for now we mustn't give Shungu any reason to doubt my credentials.'

Beth catches a glimpse of Matron through the window of her office. Her head is bent over her paperwork but her eyes shoot up to glance at them. Beth's limbs feel light, her step effortless, her head airy, as she opens the car door for Fortunate.

The sun comes out as they drive along the lane towards the allotment. The fresh light rinses clean the murky winter scene. Fortunate looks around as if he's never been out of town in the

UK before. They pass sheep, scattered like newly puffed popcorn in the fields, and then a field of downy stubble, a pale lavender in the soft sunlight. Beth hopes Fortunate might want to be photographed in front of the allotment; not Matt's untended patch of course, but perhaps Jack's fecund plot bursting with kale, parsnips and leeks.

'Do they run wild?' Fortunate asks.

'What?'

'Those sheep. I see no herd boys.'

'Yes, they roam sort of free-range but it's like a huge zoo. There are fences and hedges to keep them in.'

'Ah, I see. Hmm, they're very fat,' he says approvingly.

A little later he frowns. 'It's too quiet in these fields. There's nobody working here. In my country, in the rural areas, the fields are where the women meet. The sound of the fields is the sound of women talking. They talk all day.'

'Um, no, I guess it's too cold and muddy out here to stay chatting.'

'That must be so difficult for you women – at home the lands are where the women make their plans and decide important matters.'

When they arrive at the allotments, Fortunate as good as prostrates himself on the ground in his excitement. 'This is like my family land. It's very fine.' He strokes the long pale-green leaves on Jack's rows of leeks. 'Too beautiful.'

Beth leads him to Matt's plot, feeling she should make every effort to feel proud of it. 'This is my husband's... er... farm. It needs some attention.'

Fortunate is taking in more than the shambles at his feet; he's looking with an expression of rapture down the incline towards the trees that line the small valley below the allotments.

Beth remembers Mr De Villier's crush on 'the land' and attempts to look at the allotment through different eyes; after all, this is the sole plot of land that she owns – jointly with Matt. But it remains a scrap of dirt covered in weeds and she's determined not to get dewy eyed over it. But, when she looks down the valley to a glassy pond ringed by white-barked beech trees, she has to admit that the scene is pretty in the slanting sunlight. Nature is aesthetically pleasing as long as it's observed from a distance, as in the landscape paintings hanging in Twicare.

Fortunate squats down and scoops up a handful of earth, holding it in the cup of his hands, happy to get his hands dirty. 'This is good soil for growing. You're a lucky farmer as well as a beautiful doctor.' He laughs his easy, comradely laugh.

His warmth and unforced compliment cause Beth to feel a swell of gratitude. She wants to do something more for him. She looks at the plot and then at Fortunate. He's content and caught in the moment like the small bird chattering in a tree nearby. 'You can have it, Fortunate. You can have our allotment.' It feels right, even after she's said it. 'You don't have to pull the wool over Shungu's eyes. It can be your own farm. I'll be so pleased to give it to someone who appreciates it.'

Fortunate lets the earth fall out of his hand.

'You must look after it, though,' she adds, reassuring him of her sincerity.

He looks at her square and grave and then slowly shakes his head.

'My husband would approve of it, if he could,' she says and then is aware she's now sounding desperate.

'No, no, Dr Jenkins. This is too difficult. You see, sometime I have to go back to Zimbabwe. I must return to my place. This is your husband's place. This is where his heart lies. This is where he'll know himself.'

The bird throws itself with abandon from its branch and passes like a feathery sprite across the allotment. Everything closes in on Beth in a rush. She blurts, 'Please call me Beth.' And then, through a pressure in her throat, says, 'My husband… Matt… will never be able to look after this ground again. He was like you, he loved the land, but he'll never be… never be able to come out here and… ' Fortunate gives a deep sympathetic grunt. 'Oh God! He's had a stroke. He's badly disabled, a shadow of himself, not even that, and he'll be like that until he dies.'

She ducks her head and tries in vain to find a tissue in her jeans' pockets. 'I'm sorry… I'm sorry to get upset… ' She breaks off. She's never before been swamped by such a wild wave of grief. It has come up the valley in a tsunami and has gushed from the earth beneath her feet.

Fortunate comes near and, after wiping his hands on the back of his trousers, gives her a clean, folded handkerchief. She nearly leans into his shirt but knows that if she does so, she will sob uncontrollably. She's disgraced herself enough already. She dabs at her eyes and then passes his handkerchief back to him, mumbling her thanks.

'It's OK. These are hard times for you,' he says quietly. Beth takes deep breaths of the cold, sharp air. Fortunate bends down again and takes a clod of soil. He stands in front of her and solemnly parts the clod with his hands to hold the earth like an offering. He looks her in the eye, unaffectedly sympathetic, and says, 'Dr Jenkins, take this land, broken for you by your husband. It's yours.'

Beth can't understand what he is trying to say to her. It sounds vaguely religious. She turns away from him to give herself space to recover her equilibrium. If being out here in 'the land' doesn't make her fearful it certainly makes her tearful. Then she turns back to him, holds out her hand and makes herself say in a strong voice, 'Give me your camera and I'll take that picture, Farmer Mukumbi.'

Fortunate immediately becomes animated, sparing her further awkwardness. He hands her his camera and, with a jaunty skip, positions himself so that she can frame the valley behind the allotment. Then, as quickly, he becomes dignified and formal. Behind Fortunate, Jack's plot looks verdant and productive. Even Matt's plot in the foreground looks full of promise.

They are silent in the car, Fortunate looking straight ahead all the way back. As Beth drives him into Twicare car park he says, 'I'd like to bring your husband out to his farm. We can work there together.'

'You'll be lucky,' Beth says. 'He goes to a day centre for brain injured people once a week. They're fantastic with him but even they find it's a struggle to get him to do anything. They can just about persuade him to play pool.'

But when Fortunate opens the door to leave, she says, 'You can try. I'd not thought of that. Thanks for suggesting it.' She scribbles her home telephone number on a page of paper from a notebook in the glove compartment.

Beth is so distracted when she arrives home that she enters the house as if it's her own. A stench of cigarette smoke escapes as she opens the door. Penelope will be having a last drag before going on a detox day-retreat and a fish pedicure. When she steps into the hall Beth hears the scrabbling of claws on wood and Bruno launches himself at her with a teeth-baring snarl. She screams and then saves herself by taking a swing at him with her Wellingtons. He backs away, growling.

Penelope shouts from the kitchen, 'He's just following his instincts. He only wants to defend his territory.'

Beth tells Bruno to get his own wretched patch, and then she thinks of Mr De Villier and his land. His bitterness at whatever had happened. Despite what Fortunate said on the allotment, it seems better for everyone to remain unrooted.

CHAPTER 6

On the morning of her meeting with Hector and David, Beth nearly lets on to one of her patients that she will not be seeing them again, but she holds back. She'd better wait for the official announcement. She finds them both sitting at one end of the long table in the education room. Hector nods an acknowledgement as she enters. There is a chair at the far end of the table which, she guesses, is where she's expected to sit to receive her dismissal. She picks it up and positions it next to David, saying breezily, 'Looks like a disciplinary if I sit down there!' She is not going to let them make this impersonal.

David, fuzzily bearded, his feral eyebrows breaking over the top of his heavy black-rimmed specs grunts in an unfathomable way. He's wearing a thick Aran jumper in diamond patterns of orange and black, and his enormous head of black hair looks so stiff that Beth doubts it ever needs combing. She's not faced him in such circumstances before and he seems ill at ease. She once tried to read one of his academic papers but had not got past the title: *The application of Cuzick's non-parametric test for trends across ordered groups as a tool in Health Literacy empowerment studies.* When she seeks his opinion on some medical matter he has the disarming habit of talking to her navel in a quiet, grave voice, and pulling the Educator's trick of asking her to 'reflect' on her question. 'Do you think you're grappling with a conceptual dilemma or a technical issue?' She is never the wiser.

As David is lost behind bottle-end-thick glass and fuzz, Beth ignores him and looks Hector in the eye, ready to take her sacking like a soldier. Hector says, 'Comfortable? Good! Let me say straight away that you're very fortunate – there are few partnerships on offer nowadays. It's mainly salaried posts out there but we need a female partner to provide some choice for our female patients and – I'm going to be frank – to keep up with political correctness.'

Beth stares back.

'You must be delighted.' He holds out his hand. She pretends not to notice.

'You're offering me a partnership?'

Hector drops his hand on the table and drums a tune with his fingers. 'I agree you're far too young and it will be subject to bringing in capital, of course.'

'Oh, of course, how much?' she blurts.

Hector winces as if it's an impolite question. 'Finsbury Wakefield, our accountants, will let you know in due course.'

'Thank-you, but… this is unexpected. I'll need to consider it carefully and get back to you later.'

Hector's functioning eyebrow shoots up. David opens his eyes and moves his jaw from side to side.

'Do you know what you're turning down?' Hector says.

'Don't misunderstand me. I'm not turning down your kind offer. It's just come as a surprise and so I'd like a few days to decide.'

'I suppose we can wait that long,' Hector says. He turns to David who nods his head rather too protractedly as if he's thinking about something else. 'Although you've had nearly a week to consider it already.'

She almost laughs out loud. 'I thought I was going to be sacked so this has come as a complete shock.'

'Hmm, well, now you know.'

Beth doesn't know where to look. She's had a proposal of marriage when she thought she was to be dumped. She should ask a shopping list of questions but her mind has gone blank. She forces out, 'How many sessions are you offering? What'll be my partnership share?'

'Sessions? Four days a week, although as a junior partner we'd like you to take on the responsibility for hitting all those tiresome targets the government keeps setting us. And you seem to have a way with the elderly so it makes sense for you to look after the nursing homes as well. Share? You'll work your way up to a pro rata share in due course.'

'And—' but she isn't given further opportunity for questions as Hector springs up, looks at his watch and offers his hand to her like he's pointing a gun, closing the interview. She gets to her feet, gives him a limp handshake, and says, 'Thanks for the offer.' David acknowledges her at last with a faint, inscrutable smile.

As she leaves, Hector says, 'Almost forgot. I take it you're not thinking of taking maternity leave any time? I – ah – assume it's not likely.'

Beth stares again at Hector. David coughs loudly and, after a prolonged clearing of his throat, says, 'Umm, Hector, you're not supposed to... er... ask that sort of question unless we ask all the... er... candidates the same question.'

Hector looks perplexed. 'There aren't any other candidates so we have asked all the candidates the same question.'

David says, 'This is definitely one of those situations in modern life, Hector, where... er... *non nostrum inter vos tantas componere lites* applies.'

'Ours is not to question why!' exclaims Hector, affronted.

Beth lets them continue their debate on their own and rings Alena on her mobile as soon as she steps outside. 'You won't believe it; I've been offered a partnership. They as much as said they want a token female.'

'Congratulations Beth! But what's the catch?'

'I mustn't become pregnant – as if. At least they've offered. I'll have to go back with a list of questions.'

'You must be chuffed although I don't think they deserve you. Are you going to take it?'

'It's nailing a foot to the floor, isn't it? And I'd have to throw away my bucket and spade – won't end up running away to the seaside or to Australia like Christina suggested.'

'And your mother-in-law?'

'Yes, quite. I'll be spending even less time at home. I guess she might boot me out as she'll see it as a deliberate snub.'

'Perhaps you should take it, Beth, so that you can put down roots here. You could start to make some changes to the practice. It can't be long, surely, before Hector retires, then you can get in someone like-minded.'

Beth drives home past familiar shopping centres and along streets of semi-detached houses in muted shades of brindled grey and maroon under a low, clay sky. If she accepts the partnership, these ordinary suburbs will be the landscape of her life for the years ahead. It's not so bad, so ordinary – it has associations with friends and with BC Matt. There is the mini-supermarket where they first met (she had picked up and handed him a twenty pound note that he had dropped and he'd insisted on buying her a coffee which – chemistry already stirring – she had accepted after only half-hearted resistance), and there is the Age Concern bookshop which Matt could never pass without entering to buy a biography. There is the gold and white facade of the Hindu temple, the dental surgery with its brushed-metal (queasily filling-coloured) signage, Tres Hermanas – its window frames painted a bold midnight-blue – and the florist whose gaudy displays spill onto the pavement and where Matt bought flowers for her within twenty-four hours of meeting her. If she stays she'll be drilling down a tap root here. Into the land, as Mr De Villier would melodramatically put it. But surely he'd got the objects of *love* and *like* the wrong way around when he'd said 'look for a place that you love, then live there with someone you like'?

Mr De Villier's chest X-ray report comes back two days later. It reads *Shadowing in right apical lobe consistent with lung cancer. Refer urgently to respiratory unit.* Beth notes the instructions. Instructions that she knows are to be frustrated by that implacable foil to politically-driven target or committee-written procedure: the wishes of the patient.

She drives straight to Twicare after morning surgery. When she makes the walk down the corridor past each closed door, it seems to her now like a death row, as if she's a lawyer coming to tell Mr De Villier that the last appeal against his sentence has been turned down. She hopes that Fortunate will be in so that she can break the news to Mr De Villier in his presence but is told by a nurse in the corridor that he isn't on duty until later.

Mr De Villier is asleep in his chair, head slumped forward. She quietly draws up a chair beside him and waits. Perhaps the kindest thing is to flannel: 'Your X-ray was as expected in a man who still breathes out clouds of coal dust.' Telling the truth sometimes clashes with benevolence.

He wakes with a noisy snore and, before she has time to say hello, he says, 'Is it bad news or bad news?'

She replies, 'I do have the X-ray result back now.'

'What's it show? My heart's missing? If that's what it reads, it'd restore my faith in the point of all the bloody tests you quacks order.'

She chooses her words and speaks them softly. 'It shows what you suspected.'

He grunts and then he beckons her closer. She's wary of being grabbed again but she leans forward to listen. 'I want to ask you something.' His voice has weakened as if it's the first casualty of his illness. 'You see that safe in the corner?' How could she not? 'Bought it with my last piece of silver. Inside is the only thing that matters.' His voice cracks and he looks away from her for a moment. 'In there is the original title deed to my land – my farm out in Zimbabwe. There's also a letter to my son.'

'Your son! Your son?'

'My only begotten son.'

She thinks he's being sarcastic but then, looking at his filmy eyes, she isn't so sure. 'I didn't know you had a son. Matron told me you had no family at all.'

'Depends what you mean by family. I wouldn't call what I've got now, family. Not anymore.'

'Oh, I'm sorry.' He seems to have shrunk and looks all alone in the world. 'Your son – does he know where you are? Has he contacted you? Where's he been all this time while you've been here on your own?'

Mr De Villier lets out a short exasperated breath. 'Dr Jenkins, will you do me a favour?'

'If I can, of course I will.' She'd overdone the indignation.

He speaks in a whisper, as if someone is trying to listen in at the door. 'Would you take the title deed and the letter to my son? They've got to be delivered by hand.'

Has she misheard him? No, she hasn't. She should wear a placard: *Make a wish come true! Want a car? Want a farm? Want worldwide personal postal delivery? Just ask Beth Jenkins.* 'I'm sure Matron could arrange for them to be posted by registered post. I'll speak to her.'

'No! Don't mention this to Matron.' His eyes bore into her. She's pinned down, fixed by his burning will. 'The title deed is priceless; it's what I worked for all those years. I sacrificed more than you can imagine for that deed. It's my son's future. The title deed, Dr Jenkins, is the land itself.'

She squirms herself back a little. 'I don't think you need worry at all. You know Matron: she does everything by the book.'

His whole body shakes and his jaw trembles. 'That's not going to be anywhere near good enough. You're the only one I trust to deliver the papers to my son.' His hand springs out to grip her tightly on her wrist. It seems his last ebb of strength is in his fingers. 'What I've said to you is between you and me alone. Swear to me that. No one else should be given access to the safe. Only you and I know what's in it. Let me put it this way, Doctor, I'd rather you got the title deed to my son than fixed me up with a lung transplant.'

He's stopped whispering but now he tries to shift himself closer on his stumps. Beth holds herself rigid. He hisses, 'That title deed was bought with blood.'

CHAPTER 7

Beth takes shallow breaths of the dense air. The safe in the corner has grown, is about to yawn open and swallow her. Mr De Villier's hand remains clawed on her wrist. She says, 'What do you mean? Bought with blood?'

'My son's name is Selous.'

She waits but he says no more. She says, 'Selous. OK. Where does he live? Have you got an address?'

'There's no address now. I guess he's in the bush.'

'In the bush?'

'Yes, I don't know where he's gone – somewhere in Zimbabwe – he'll not leave Zim except through a hole in the ground. It's his country.'

'If he's not got an address, how's anyone going to find him?' Mr De Villier again pretends not to have heard her, so she asks, 'Have you got a solicitor?'

He shrugs. He relaxes his grip on her wrist but leaves his hand resting on her as if ready to catch her if she tries to escape. It seems heavy with hope and horror. 'You see, Dr Jenkins, I've thought of every goddamn alternative, and you're the one to do it.'

There's surely a simple solution to getting some pieces of paper to his son. 'Can you give me a better idea on how to contact him?'

'The only way is to go out there and ask around. Maybe someone in Bulawayo knows where he's hiding out.'

'Oh, he's got no address *and* he's hiding!'

'That's why it's not going to be easy and so that's why I'm asking you, Dr Jenkins.'

His eyes hold hers. His dying eyes. Willing her. She's tongue tied. 'The combination is 20 12 60 10. Don't ever give the number to anyone else. Not Matron. Not Welfare. Not Fortunate. No one. Remember, that title deed is two thousand hectares of land and it was exchanged for a life.'

'Whose life?'

'20 12 60 10.'

She finds herself reaching for her pen with her free hand. 'Um, 20 12 60 10.'

'No, don't write it, remember it.'

There's a perfunctory knock on the door. Mr De Villier releases Beth as if her skin has become red hot. In comes Fortunate. 'Good afternoon, Mr De Villier, and good afternoon, Dr Jenkins. I'm a little early for duty today but I can't leave my friend all on his own for too long.'

His voice trails off as he sees Beth's sober expression. She gives him a small nod. It seems, for a moment, that she shares with Mr De Villier an anxiety that Fortunate is going to burst into tears.

Beth turns to Mr De Villier. 'Are you sure you don't want me to refer you to the lung specialist?'

His blue eyes fix steadily on her. She sees something new in his expression. Something she hasn't expected to find in such an embittered man. He has an air of nobility, as if he's fought demons and (although he's not prevailed, has been beaten down, has had everything taken from him, has out-Jobed Job) has, at the final moment, snatched a splendid victory from the jaws of defeat. It humbles her, this sudden flaring in the strength of his spirit but, at the same time, a noose has been drawn around her. He sees the vehicle of his triumph as her. He believes her to hold the breath that will blow on the barely glowing embers of whatever meaning his life once held, to resurrect it, Phoenix-like, after his death.

'You've made a dying man very happy, Doctor,' he says.

Beth leaves Fortunate with her patient to go and tell Matron the news on Mr De Villier's prognosis. As soon as she's out of his room she finds herself in the everyday again, the orderly routine of Twicare (tablet and laundry rounds, door handle and carpet cleaning). Outside there's humming traffic, people calmly shopping and on their mobiles or taking cadenced walks in parks, all on the steady chassis of Midlands England. She's in a safe zone again and just has to decide what to do about the contents of her patient's safe. Whilst he lives, she will, of course, not breach what he's begged her not to divulge. But after? Does she still have an obligation to keep his secret? There'll be advice available from her peers. All she has to do is follow the routine.

But as she stands in Matron's office while Matron works through the multiple requisites of her protocol, Beth finds herself imagining that she's trekking through the bush in a fetching hat, safari-suit and walking boots, documents in hand, looking for Selous. She comes across him (he has a certain safari man good looks to him and is single and enticingly mysterious) at a lookout that has an endless view over the savannah. He's speechlessly thankful at her efforts to reach him and—Matron snaps her file closed. Beth feels herself blushing. What's come over her? How can she entertain such shallow thoughts? She has responsibilities to her husband, she must conduct herself as a professional, she mustn't run any more errands for her patients, Zimbabwe is particularly dangerous.

That evening Beth goes upstairs to Matt's office. She's put off clearing Matt's work long enough. As she enters, she stops and stands. Her gaze travels along his shelves of archaeological and art books, horticultural encyclopaedias, guides to growing your own food and coffee table heavyweights on famous gardens. His expansive oak desk is piled high with papers and yet more books, leaving little space for his computer screen and keyboard. Everything is as it had been the day he'd had his stroke. She takes a determined breath and picks up a handful of the scattered academic papers and correspondence on his desk. She'll offer most of his books to Jeremy, his friend and colleague. Then she places the papers down again. Matt sometimes wanders into his office to look aimlessly around his shelves and wouldn't notice a difference but what if a miracle occurs and Matt recovers and returns to his research. How appalling it would then be to have thrown it all away. Even to have tidied.

She sees the large frameless picture mount on the wall opposite his bookcases. Each shot is charged with bittersweet memory: Matt standing next to rock engravings in Egypt, receiving his doctrate, a view in Wales, a sailing boat, he and his colleagues looking rugged by their Land Rovers in the Libyan Desert, their wedding day.

She sees under the computer screen a photo of her taken when they first met. How she'd been when BC Matt knew her. What had she been laughing at? Perhaps Matt had just said something funny when he took the picture. It shows off her look-twice shoe-shine-black hair. She looks away; she's lost her gloss since then.

When she picks up his papers again she comes across a To Do list written in his quick hand.

Student appraisals – Thursday
Order allotment manure – enough for Jack
B's bday – City gallery portrait print? Table for two, Casey's.
Friday?

Friday never happened. She puts the list aside. Her eye is drawn to the large photograph of a rock art painting which hangs from the wall behind his desk. Matt used to sit staring at it when he was thinking, as if it gave him inspiration. But she's never more than glanced at it before. As she looks, she places her hand on the back of Matt's chair and has a sense that he's there, that she can lift her fingers to massage his shoulders whilst he looks into the painting. She follows his gaze. The sable antelope is exquisitely rendered in bold charcoal strokes and a shade of ochre that borders on gold, giving an impression of grace and movement. It's hard to believe that the artist had lived many millennia ago. She recalls a lecture given by Matt that she'd attended as a guest about a year before his stroke. He'd been invited to deliver the prestigious Henri Breuil Lecture at the University and was the youngest archaeologist to have been given the honour. Her pride in his achievement was fit to burst as he stood on the lecture stage saying he was about to transport the audience back thousands of years to a time before writing had been invented. Matt suggested they might mistakenly think of the skin-and-bark-clad people living in those times as brutish, their imagination limited to how to chip out tools of flint for the sole purpose of survival; living an existence of killing and being killed; a grunting, short, uncreative life.

Matt gave a signal to a technician. The hall's lights were extinguished leaving them all in the dark. Only thirteen years ago, said Matt, three spelunkers found the long-hidden entrance to an underground cavern near the Ardèche River in France.

Lights then flickered on the screen behind Matt as if it were the cavers' torches playing in the dark. Then the rays picked out a wall of rock and travelled dimly up the face to settle on poorly-illuminated shapes. The audience gasped as the scene brightened to reveal a painting of four horses erupting from the rock as if the cave was giving birth to life. Here was art of a high order, given creative virtuosity by subtle shading and sharp delineation against the white of the limestone wall. And yet, Matt said, the artist who had had such an imaginative vision, such a gift to distil the essence of things, had walked out of the cave at least thirty thousand years before the modern cavers had walked in.

Rock paintings were amongst the world's greatest treasures, arguably the greatest, said Matt, because they were the first occasion in the history of our planet when a creature could project the world back onto itself; could paint back onto the rock the life that had emerged from it. 'You can think of it this way,' said Matt. 'After sixteen billion years of tiny but inexorable steps in complexity and mystery, the universe had reached the point where it could imagine itself.'

The picture in Matt's office, Beth guesses, shows an example of rock art from Africa although she'd never, to her shame, asked him, and it was to Africa that Matt turned for the latter part of his lecture. He called Africa 'the motherland', which sounded a little affected and pretentious to Beth at the time but there was no doubt that he found the art of that continent the most intriguing. He projected onto the screen glowing landscapes of beaten gold in the Sahara where ancient peoples engraved symbols on the blackened and bronzed faces of stones. Some symbols were common to sites separated widely in location, the same etchings repeatedly drawn over many thousands of years. Did these communicate a religion and culture shared across the ancient world over thousands of years? For hundreds of generations the conventions of their art, in subject matter and technique, remained little altered as if the culture it represented was fulfilling enough to its peoples to be in no need of revolution.

He projected images of feathery precision from southern Africa: giraffes and dancers, antelope and hunters, in passage across a landscape that wasn't depicted, perhaps because the figures had been rendered back onto the landscape itself, as if to draw the land was as pointless as a modern painter first depicting the canvas on which he paints.

He ran through the controversies that brought apoplectic rows to academic life in his discipline. Some researchers took polarised positions on the art, for example that it was all the doodling of bored prehistoric teenagers (the first youth culture), or universally represented the trance-induced visions of shamans, or was a pictorial language like hieroglyphs (a secret scripture) and just needed the discovery of something akin to the Rosetta stone for a great breakthrough that would allow it to be read like a book.

Matt thought that across the thousands of known rock art sites, the paintings and engravings encompassed at least the first two (he dismissed the last outright) but also much more. He suggested that future research might explore whether the paintings were a window into how the human brain developed, its early psychic history, giving clues on the cognitive patterns that became embedded early in the human story, that perhaps they were a pointer to why humans think in the way they do. He thought that there were interpretations of the art that hadn't yet been imagined. He was certain that there were extraordinary discoveries to come.

Beth lifts her hands from Matt's chair but lets her eye linger on the sable. Oh Matt, you used to be able to remember back thirty thousand years.

CHAPTER 8

Beth pulls out the drawer beneath Matt's desk, lifts out each neatly-labelled suspension folder and works methodically through the contents, sorting them into correspondence, timetables, student assessments, references, grant applications. All the scaffolding of an academic working life.

There's an unlabelled folder at the back and had it not gaped open when she took out the other folders it might have been years before she found the three photos in an unmarked envelope. She picks one out. It has the harsh lighting of a picture taken with a flash. She can see out-of-focus rock art in the background on a rock face divided by an almost horizontal crack. It's the foreground scene that makes her start. She takes the image to the desk lamp. On the ground in front of the rock are bodies. They must have been lying there for a long time because bones tent up the clothing and poke through sleeves and holes in the fabric. The dome of a skull is picked out, shockingly white in the light of the flash.

She turns it over. *Zim 99 Matobo Hills,* in Matt's hand. Above the writing he'd drawn a cross – a Rest in Peace symbol. She sits herself down at his desk. Matt had never spoken about this. There are two other photos taken at different angles as if for submission as evidence. She counts perhaps seven bodies. She half stands up to call out, *Hey, Matt, what are these?* but sits down again. The theme tune of *Friends* floats up the stairs.

How baffling and disturbing. There must be an explanation for why Matt had kept these from her. It feels as if she's come across a bank account that he hadn't told her about.

She tries to recall every conversation they'd had about his time in Zimbabwe. There were very few. Matt, she now realises, had been tight-lipped about his time there. As she remembers it now, he'd even been dismissive. When anyone found out that he'd been there (usually because she'd mentioned it) she'd heard him say more than once, 'Zimbabwe? It was a long time ago. I was too young to be asking the right questions of the rock art.' As if the whole experience could be dismissed in one pre-prepared statement. He would have their friends shaking with laughter when he recounted yarns about his field trips but she can't recall a single anecdote on his time in Zimbabwe. He'd referenced Zimbabwe only briefly in his Henri Breuil lecture.

Then she does remember one occasion when he'd mentioned Zimbabwe in passing. They'd taken a bed-and-breakfast weekend in mid-Wales. Leaning against a dry stone wall, they watched the sun extrude every luscious shade of green from the valley below. He said, 'This reminds me a little of Zimbabwe – not the view, of course, but the way the sun works on the colours of the landscape, brings out their intensity.' She'd asked him to tell her more but perhaps they'd been distracted, or else he'd changed the subject.

Now she peers closely at the photos in the picture mount. There isn't a single image from the year he'd spent in Zimbabwe. The images will be printouts from his computer. She turns it on. Perhaps all his photos of Zimbabwe are there. She tries to log on as Matt but it's password protected. She tries *beth, bethan, bee, password, rock art, rockart, jenny,* even *bruno*, but is locked out.

She thinks of ringing Jeremy to ask him if Matt had said anything to him about the photos. Then she isn't so sure that she should. She can't think of what to say to Jeremy that will not suggest that she's discovered some treacherous secret.

She looks up at the sable and finds she can't meet its eye. She hurries out with the photos and goes to find Matt, more in hope than expectation.

Turning off the television she sits down beside him. 'What are these, Matt?'

'Pictures,' he replies, pleased to find the right word.

'What do they show?'

He stares at them without expression and then looks at her for an answer.

'These are bones,' she says. 'Look, you can see a skull.' Matt carries on looking at her.

'Did you take these pictures, Matt?' She can't hide her frustration.

'What are these?' he asks anxiously, always sensitive to her mood even if he can't judge what will alter it.

'I don't know. I found them in your office. That's why I'm asking you. What do they show?'

'Are they pictures?'

Beth drops Fortunate and Matt off at the allotment the following Saturday morning. She waits by her car a few moments, watching Fortunate introducing himself to Jack, and then Jack is pumping Matt's hand and slapping him on the back. Is that a smile forming on Matt's face? They fetch spades and forks from Jack's shed.

Matt gives Beth a worried look when she turns to go but she knows it isn't about her leaving him there on the allotment. She's been angry with him since discovering the photos and found herself being less than forthcoming with the reassurances she usually dispenses when he becomes anxious. She's angry with BC Matt but has taken it out on AD Matt as if it's AD Matt's fault. She certainly wants to pin her misgivings about what she's found onto AD Matt and so keep BC Matt innocent. What a relief it was to hand him over to someone else that morning.

She expects to receive a phone call before long – Fortunate admitting defeat – but when she comes to collect them, three hours later, they have difficulty persuading Matt to leave. Beth is amazed at the transformation of the plot: all the dead stuff cleared, the bindweed and creeping thistle on the waste heap, the soil not far off being ready for planting in the spring. Matt and Fortunate are both grinning as if they've had a rollickingly good time. Fortunate talks non-stop on the way back, telling Beth how Matt had dug as if he might find buried gold and of his ability to distinguish between weeds and vegetables.

She notices a change in Matt that evening. He is calmer, less given to pacing the house; he's even lost a little of his puzzled expression. She's grateful to Fortunate, helping Matt like that and breaking her pessimism with an earthy wisdom as to what Matt needs. Fortunate is a man who can bring sunshine wherever he goes. What had she been thinking, punishing AD Matt for the mysterious photos? It isn't AD Matt who'd taken them. But that presents its own difficulty.

She finishes Monday morning surgery even later than usual and is anxious to get away as has to take Matt to a dental appointment. Just as she starts to clear her desk, Brenda rings through to say that there is a patient who wants to speak to her urgently. A patient named Fortunate Mukumbi.

She feels the pull of an obligation to see him and imagines Alena saying: *See, best not to get over involved.*

'Ask him if he can see the duty doctor,' she suggests. She wonders how he and Hector will get on.

There is a change in the timbre of Brenda's voice as if she's cupped the mouthpiece with her hand, 'He says only you'll be able to help. He says he's begging you.'

'All right, send him down but tell him I was just on my way out and I've only got a couple of minutes.'

When Fortunate comes through the door, she sees he's lost his ready smile. His shoulders droop and his eyelids are heavy. 'It's too terrible,' he says, sitting himself down uncertainly as if concussed.

Her heart races. Perhaps he's come to tell her that he'd taken Matt out to the allotment again and Matt has had a nasty accident with a fork. 'What's happened?'

'Too terrible.'

'Yes?'

'Shungu's brother has died. She's very upset.'

'I'm very sorry to hear that.'

Fortunate nods sombrely. The minute hand on the clock on Beth's desk flicks forwards. 'Mr Mukumbi, I appreciate this news is upsetting for you and that it's devastating for Shungu but I've got to be somewhere else soon. So, unless there's something I can do for you immediately, I think we'd better have a chat about this later. Let's see if I can fix another appointment for you.' She selects the appointments screen on the computer.

'Of course, but Shungu says that he was murdered.'

'Murdered?' Beth's heart accelerates again and she faces Fortunate and stares at him with new eyes as if there's something infamous about him. She now knows two people who know people who've been murdered: Mr De Villier and Fortunate. And there's also Matt with his photos of the bodies. What's happening to her? Another world – frightening and alien – is lapping at her ankles.

Fortunate says, 'Yes, assassinated. Shungu says he was shot by the CIO because of his political views.'

'The CIO?'

'Central Intelligence Organisation. The Zimbabwean security service. Shungu's brother was a member of the MDC, the opposition Party. That's why he was murdered.'

'And is Shungu involved in politics?' Beth says, trying to understand the implications for Fortunate.

'I don't know. She hasn't mentioned it.'

'But maybe it was an accident. Maybe the information that Shungu's been given is wrong.' Some nationalities seem prone to jumping, by default, to conspiracy theories.

'It was no accident. In Zimbabwe not a sparrow falls without our President knowing about it.'

'How spooky.'

'And now Shungu is asking me to do this one last thing. If I succeed, then she'll marry me.'

'One last thing?'

'But, this… this… what she asks me, I cannot.'

'You can't? So what is it?' She almost adds *this time* but it would be unkind to express scepticism.

'Just pray for me.' He bows his head and closes his eyes as if expecting her to lay hands on him and call down courage or protection.

'I don't know that I'm allowed to do that,' she says, thinking how inhumane such a rule would be. 'And, even if I am, I've not had the training.'

The minute hand advances again. Fortunate opens his eyes and stares at the carpet. Beth resigns herself to missing the dental appointment. 'Would you like to tell me what Shungu has asked you to do?'

Fortunate stands up abruptly and waits there for a moment with his fists clenched at his side. 'I'm sorry to have come to you like this.' He turns and leaves without a backward glance.

Beth stares at the back of the door. Then, slowly, she finds the keys on the keyboard and types in the notes: *Came to discuss personal problems. Stressful circumstances.*

When Beth visits Twicare that evening to see one of her other patients, Matron calls her into her office. Her tone is accusatory. 'Nurse Fortunate Mukumbi has left me a note,' she says.

'Yes?'

Matron lifts the note and reads it out in a perfunctorily tone as if it wearies her to have to play along with Beth's feigned ignorance.

'Dear Matron, I am sorry to inform you that I have to leave your employment with immediate effect. This is due to circumstances of a pressing nature. I've paid my respects to those residents who retain their faculties. I am most sorry not to be able to attend Mr De Villier anymore. Please accept the enclosed monies representing a week of my wages as I have not given you the requisite notice of five working days. Kindest thanks and regards, yours respectfully, Fortunate.'

Matron nails the paper to her desk with her thumb and glares at Beth.

'Oh!'

'As I said, these migrants.' She's made her point, sits down and pulls a file out of a cabinet marked *Staff.* 'Oh well, a good worker while he lasted.' She hole-punches his letter and files it.

Beth has the impression that she's now in Matron's way so she backs out of her office and goes to see her patient. Twicare seems an emptier place, its corridors and rooms have become more clinical and institutional, or perhaps the emptiness is within. She feels lonely. She fears that she will never see Fortunate again. People she might have got to know well and like, even love, can disappear from her life before she knows it. She thinks that Matt might miss Fortunate as well, even though he will not be able to remember that he's met him. It almost seems that, before he left, Fortunate had found BC Matt somewhere inside AD Matt.

Beth hopes to put her head around the door to see Mr De Villier but once she's attended to the other patient, she receives a message from the surgery to ask if she can take herself immediately to a woman with chest pain at a different nursing home.

At half past seven the next morning – whilst she clears the breakfast table and Penelope reads a glossy magazine – Beth receives a call from Matron.

'Sorry to ring you early but Mr De Villier has died. Can you come and confirm the death so that I can call a funeral director to remove his body?'

Beth sits herself down.

'You still there?' Matron says.

'I didn't expect it to be so soon.'

'Fits his contrarian nature, don't you think?'

Like an estimated date of delivery for the birth of a baby, an estimated date of departure in death is always uncertain, but...

'When did it happen?'

'Nurse Hope reported him as asleep at 3am as per protocol but when she went in to check him again at 4am, she found him dead. Anyway, we'll be ready for you when you come.'

'What's the matter?' Penelope asks.

Beth finds herself staring into space, still holding up the receiver. 'Oh, it's… I've just been told that one of my patients has died.'

'How very uncanny, I've just read your horoscope and it says here, *An unexpected difficulty will occur early in the day. You may experience a sense of loss which could last most of the morning.*'

Beth puts down the phone. 'He was on his own. No one comes into the world like some bug egg, all alone. And no one should leave all alone.'

'It goes on,' Penelope says, '*but a stranger will ask for your help and will point the way to learning from your loss.*'

'We're held when we're born and should be held when we leave,' Beth says to the wall. And our first sight is a smile, she thinks, and our last sight should also be a smile. She hopes the old man died in his sleep.

She will need to speak to the coroner before signing the death certificate. With no histological proof of his cancer, the cause of death is a supposition rather than a certainty. The coroner will have to decide if she wants a post-mortem or will accept an informed guess. Beth doubts the coroner will think a post-mortem necessary in Mr De Villier's case. It's an 'expected death'.

She visits Twicare on her way to work and mentally prepares herself to enter Mr De Villier's room. She thinks that a room in which a body lies is the most noiseless place on earth. The deep silence seems like a disquieting hole in existence, a vacuum before the fabric of life, of matter, rushes in again. She wonders if the sensation it gives her is due to an intense awareness of the absence of the body's workings: the stone-still chest, the cemented muscles, the deserted eyes. How can a person's anima just vanish like that? It's the nearest she comes to a sense of something sacred. The life departed is one of billions of lives lost over thousands of years in a world that is a tiny blue fleck in the universe and yet it feels as if the universe is insufficient to the enormity of that one loss.

Mr De Villier has been laid out as if he lies in State, his head on a thin pillow, his eyelids basted shut, his arms long against his side. Beth draws down the sheet a little to go through the motions of listening for a heartbeat. After, she lays a hand ever so lightly on his head and wonders where the drip of water that falls onto his cheek has come from, until she becomes aware that it's her own tear. She steps back, surprised at herself, and then is terrified that this is a sign of emotional instability following Matt's stroke that will render her unfit to do her job. She hardly knows Mr De Villier and he is an old man. Old men do pass on. He'd also been rude and ungrateful. On the face of it, there's no reason for personal grief. The only explanation she can come to for that single tear is the poignancy of his complete trust in her to do something important for him, and then knowing that she's powerless to oblige him.

Her eyes come to rest on the safe. She has the eerie feeling that Mr De Villier's anima has found its way inside, is waiting for her to let him out. She banishes the thought but goes and studies the lock. She'll have to open it and deliver its contents to Matron for passing on to social services. They'll have to work out a way of contacting Mr De Villier's son, Selous. Perhaps the British Embassy in Zimbabwe could help – although perhaps he wasn't British, perhaps he was Zimbabwean, or Belgian, or Mauritian. She realises now that she knows next to nothing about Mr De Villier, had never uncovered his story. He might as well have been Ruritanian.

20 12 60 10. The door swings open. The space inside is small; the safe's walls would survive a meteorite impact. She'd imagined the title deed would be scrolled up in a red ribbon or sealed with wax but it just comprises a stapled A4 document in an open brown envelope. There is also a smaller, white envelope. She almost misses the photograph on the floor of the safe – a black and white in an old square format. The family group of three had been photographed a little too far back for a portrait, as if the photographer was more interested in the landscape behind them: a great cube of rock dwarfing the human figures, and balancing on the rock is another immense block, and then another and another. They look as precarious as one of Matt's book towers. At the foot of the rock she recognises the much younger Mr De Villier from his large hands, one of which envelops the shoulder of a boy of about eight. Mr De Villier sports a black beard like some wild preacher and wears a black Boss of the Plains style hat. Standing with her hand resting on the boy's other shoulder is a youthful woman in a loose skirt. The upper part of her face is in the deep shadow of her wide-brimmed straw hat but Beth can see her full, widely smiling lips. The boy between them is in shorts and looks to have knocked-about knees from scrambling around in that landscape. He has an expectant half-smile, as if in his element, living a boy's adventure story. That would be Selous.

She turns over the photo to read the caption. It's written in a woman's hand in blue ink with a nibbed pen: *Matopos, Zimbabwe, 1982.* She now has a picture of Mr De Villier's son but it's unlikely to be of any use in locating him, even if that were her intention. He'd be grown up and in his early thirties now. She examines the white envelope. The seal is firmly stuck down and Mr De Villier has further sealed it with a strip of medical tape, perhaps given to him by Fortunate. On the front of the envelope, Mr De Villier had written unevenly: *For Selous, by kind hand of Dr Jenkins.* She looks over at Mr De Villier's body again and smiles, but then she feels guilty as if she's mocked him. She places the envelopes and photograph in her medical bag and closes the door of the safe. It locks itself. What she does next she can only put down to finding her heart and head in equally balanced opposition. Having confirmed Mr De Villier's death to Matron, she leaves Twicare with the deed, letter and photo still in her bag.

As she goes through the door of Twicare, she notices a lightly-built man pacing restlessly back and forth near her car. He's in a pallid brown leather jacket and clutches a briefcase in front of the crotch of his rumpled trousers as if he's hiding a wet patch or is making sure that no one can snatch the briefcase. His round wire-frame glasses are at an angle on his narrow face as if he's just collided with something. For a moment she wonders if he is the person she'd seen in the silver BMW but this man has none of the weight or suggestion of swagger. As soon as she starts out for her car he scurries over to her with a hunted look.

'Good morning. My sincere apologies for troubling you,' he says breathlessly. 'Are you Dr Jenkins?'

'I am.'

'Ah, thank the Lord I've met you! I understand that you were Mr De Villier's doctor. My name's Mr Robson Chiripo. Please call me Robson. You see, I'm Mr De Villier's solicitor.' He fumbles around in his briefcase and pulls out a business card and presents it to her. *Moyo and Chiripo, Solicitors, Lobengula Street, Bulawayo, Zimbabwe.* 'I understand from a nurse that the old man has just passed away – may God give him peace at last – and so I've missed him.' A wrinkle of anguish appears at the bridge of his nose.

'Can I help?'

'I sincerely hope you can. As Mr De Villier's legal agent I'm entrusted to manage his estate. Whilst in the UK I've been visiting clients who've emigrated from Zimbabwe and I've been looking for him all over. It's too bad that I'm too late. There are some papers that he may have entrusted to you for safekeeping.' He attempts to straighten his glasses without success.

Beth becomes aware of the weight of her bag. She tightens her grip. 'I'm just the doctor. You'll need to ask Matron. She'll put you in touch with social services. I believe they'll be managing his affairs.' Did she protest too much?

'Of course,' he says with nervous insistence, 'but I knew Mr De Villier well. You see he was… a secretive man. It's possible that he gave his papers to a friend or to someone like you, someone in a trusted position. He was reluctant to depend on anyone but those he knew well. In Zimbabwe many people lost everything through trusting institutions of state.'

Despite Robson's personal knowledge of her late patient, Beth feels disinclined to admit to having the deed. She should never have walked out of Twicare with it in her bag and, in any case, it would be foolish to hand it over to a man in a car park who she's never met before. 'I'm sure that Matron will be happy to help you. I'd better get on now. I've got other patients to see.' Presumably a locksmith will be called to open the safe. They'll find it empty – only she will know that her fingerprints are left inside.

Robson looks as if he is about to plead again, but then his expression becomes doleful. 'Of course. I'm so sorry to have troubled you. I hope he passed peacefully.'

'I think so,' Beth says.

'Please take my card and let me know if you have any news for me on this matter.'

Beth accepts his card uncertainly. As she walks to her car she thinks that perhaps she should have asked him if he knew of Selous's whereabouts and if he knew what had happened on Mr De Villier's farm, but no, it might have led to other questions and raised his suspicions. She should keep her dealings with the 'solicitor' at arm's length. Although, in one way, it's fortunate that she's met the man. It's brought her to her senses. She'll give the deed and the letter to Matron tomorrow to ensure that they are handed on to social services. To leave it any longer will be like persisting with a lie: it will only grow and become impossible to undo. Then she remembers Penelope's horoscope prediction that she would suffer a sense of loss and then meet a stranger who... she can't remember the rest. No matter.

When she arrives back home she deposits the papers in one of the unmarked files in Matt's office, the one holding the photos. She thinks she'll label it *Secrets File*.

Chapter 9

As Beth nears the end of her surgery the following morning, Brenda rings through. 'One of your refugee patients is here to see you,' Brenda says. 'They do love you, don't they?'

Hope comes in shyly, despite Beth's encouraging smile. She's bundled up against the winter chill in a thick woollen parka and polo-neck sweater. Hesitant, she takes her seat, folds her mittened hands snugly together on her lap and introduces herself by saying that she works at Twicare.

'I've seen you there,' Beth says, 'and Fortunate told me about you.'

'He did?' She catches Beth's words as if she's thrown a bouquet. 'That's who I've come about.' Then she huddles into her woollens again and says, 'I'm very worried about him.' A sprite of apprehension dances in Beth's chest. 'He's gone missing. I can't find him at his lodgings and he's not answering his phone.'

'Perhaps he's gone for a job interview somewhere or he's taking a holiday,' Beth suggests. Cripes, she hopes so.

'We Zimbabweans can't take holidays,' Hope replies with a flash of admonishment, 'and he likes his job at Twicare. Let me explain to you, Doctor, why I'm so concerned. There's this... man. He's in the Zimbabwe CIO. Central Intelligence Organisation. He calls me his girlfriend.' Beth remembers Hope's look of fear as she stepped into the BMW in the Twicare car park but now Hope speaks without emotion as if reading out an end of year company report. 'This Charlie Ten man... Charlie Ten is what we call the CIO... has been persuading me to send emails under false pretences to Fortunate.'

'Emails to Fortunate?' Beth finds herself blurting.

'Charlie Ten wishes to get some papers that he believes are in the safe in Mr De Villier's room. He asked me to find out the numbers for the lock for him but of course I told him no way could I do that. I said to him, why would Mr De Villier be willing to tell me the numbers? When I said that, Charlie Ten beat me.' She stops for a moment before going on as evenly as before. 'I told him that the only one Mr De Villier trusted was Fortunate – and you of course, Doctor. Then Charlie Ten came up with a new plan to get the papers. They're very clever these security services people.'

Beth gives Hope a knowing nod as if she meets them all the time.

'Fortunate met a woman at church here in the UK called Shungu. He loves her very much.' Hope falters and, briefly, there is a faraway look in her eyes. 'Shungu was only in the UK a short time and then, soon after Fortunate met her, she returned to Zimbabwe. Charlie Ten, he made me send emails to Fortunate as if they were from Shungu. The security services have help from the Chinese to do tricks with emails and other such things.'

'Oh yes, the Chinese.' Best not to admit to too much ignorance. 'You pretended to be Shungu, Fortunate's girlfriend?'

Hope says in a monotone, 'Yes. You see, he forced me.'

'Why didn't this Charlie Ten man just send the emails himself?'

'He needed a woman to say the right words, who knew how to speak to Fortunate's heart.'

Hope had done a perfect job on that. 'And what was in the emails?' Beth squirms, feigning ignorance like this.

'Shungu's first email was to ask him to prove that he was successful, that he'd made some money in the UK and so would be able to support her. We – that is *we* pretending to be Shungu – asked him to prove that he had a car. Charlie Ten thought that Fortunate would email her back to say he couldn't afford a car and then we were going to send another email to say, oh never mind, just get Mr De Villier's papers instead and then Shungu would definitely agree to marry him. Charlie Ten thought that Fortunate wouldn't want to refuse Shungu on two requests.'

'I see. Clever psychology,' Beth says, trying to stop her eyes widening. To think that she has a front row seat on something so theatrical, on such skulduggery.

'I knew that Fortunate would never steal the papers,' Hope says, 'but Charlie Ten believes that everyone can be corrupted, given enough incentive.' Beth frowns in disagreement – in principle – but Hope says, 'Believe me, the CIO people have ensnared many who you'd never have guessed could be trapped. There was even an archbishop.'

'So what happened next?' Beth says, hoping she sounds as if she doesn't know.

'Fortunate actually complied – in a manner of speaking – with the first email. He sent a picture of himself in front of a car. He was so desperate to please Shungu.'

'Unbelievable!' She is up on the theatre stage, unwittingly complicit. This will be in the papers. The broadsheet headline: *GP implicated in crime linked to foreign security services.* The tabloid headline: *Doctor 007.* 'Then what happened?'

'Charlie Ten was very amused and surprised when Fortunate complied with that first request. He made me send another email with another task for Fortunate. Something harder.' Don't tell me, it wouldn't have been a request to prove he had a farm, would it? 'Again Fortunate complied – so to speak. By this time Charlie Ten was becoming fascinated to see how far Fortunate would take it in going along with Shungu's requests. He then sent another email to Fortunate asking him to do an impossible thing.'

Beth finds herself reaching for the toy turtle on her desk and grips it.

'Charlie Ten said that we were then going to follow up this last email the next day, to say that this crazy request was just a joke and all Fortunate had to do now was to get Mr De Villier's papers and then Shungu would fly over from Zimbabwe to see him to discuss going to see her father to get his blessings on the marriage negotiations.'

'Wait a minute,' Beth says, 'why didn't this Charlie Ten man just order Fortunate to get the papers? I should imagine he could've threatened Fortunate in some way to make him steal them.'

Hope looks Beth in the eye. 'Fortunate's not a man to be intimidated. He would do nothing out of fear. But Charlie Ten understands one thing about Fortunate: that he will do anything for love.' Hope's small chin quivers and her emotions finally leak out as she becomes teary.

Beth hands Hope a tissue and when she recovers she asks: 'So do you have any idea what might have happened to Fortunate, where he might have gone to?'

Hope shrugs as she dabs the end of her nose with her mittened hand. 'Maybe he's hiding. I don't know whether he got the very last email we sent, asking him to steal Mr De Villier's papers. He may have realised that he'd been fooled. Or maybe he's gone to find Shungu in Victoria Falls to talk to her about these things, face to face.'

'What an astonishing situation,' Beth says.

'He thinks only of Shungu,' Hope adds dejectedly.

'You don't think Fortunate went to carry out the task he'd been set?'

'No, it was too stupid.'

'Do you mind if I ask what it was?'

Hope gives a dismissive sniff. 'It was so silly. Charlie Ten went too far. He was playing with Fortunate.'

'Tell me. I'm not going to laugh.'

Hope's lips crimp in derision and then she says, 'The request was for Fortunate to assassinate the President of Zimbabwe.'

'Assassinate? Wow! Now that *is* silly.'

'Charlie Ten also added some lies about Shungu's brother having been killed by the security services and Shungu wanting revenge so that her request would seem more believable but, even so, it was foolish.'

'Totally mad,' Beth agrees, frantically running through her last consultation with Fortunate.

'The next day Charlie Ten regretted sending that email. He hit the table with his fists and said that he'd lost an opportunity to get Mr De Villier's papers and that he'd have some answering to do if the Minister for State Security found out about the emails.'

'This is extraordinary, Hope. I'm not used to these sorts of goings on.' Then she wonders again if Matt already knows Charlie Ten. Could he be the man at the door? She and Hope sit in silent musing for a moment and then Beth says, 'Fortunate's a good nurse and a good person. I hope he turns up.'

Hope's eyes threaten to fill again but she holds the tears back with a few blinks and says, 'We'll just have to pray that he's all right.'

'But what about you?' Beth says, leaning towards her to place a hand on her arm and to look into her large, brown, child-like eyes. 'Your relationship with this Charlie Ten man doesn't sound too healthy.'

Hope stays silent so Beth says, 'If you feel threatened you should report it to the police. If he's been violent towards you then they might be able to prosecute him. If he hits you again, come and see me so that I can document any bruises.'

Hope looks at Beth as if what she's suggested is as unrealistic as an instruction to assassinate a president. Then she stands up to leave and says, 'Thanks for listening to me. It's been helpful to share this with someone, even if I know there's nothing that can be done.' Her shyness is falling away and Beth is glad to have, at least, gained her confidence. 'Oh and, Dr Jenkins, there's another thing. Charlie Ten forced me to give him the door code to Twicare.'

'Ooh, you'd better tell Matron about that straight away. She'll have to change the code.'

'I can't tell Matron about the CIO. She'll call the police and then, if Charlie Ten finds out, he'll make my life difficult or make very serious trouble for my grandmother in Zimbabwe.' She looks away from Beth, frowning. 'Maybe I'll just say that I was careless and left it on a piece of paper somewhere.'

After Hope has left, it takes Beth a while to feel ready to call for her next patient. She tries to reinterpret her last consultation with Fortunate but is none the wiser. She isn't particularly bothered at the Charlie Ten brute having access to Twicare. Mr De Villier is beyond harm's reach now and his papers are safely with her in Matt's office at home. It now looks risky to return them to Twicare.

She thinks she might ring the Medical Defence Society – to whom she pays three thousand pounds a year for legal protection – to ask what they think she should do. She rehearses what she'll say to them but it sounds as if she is making it all up. *I see, Dr Jenkins, just let me clarify what you're telling me: you're saying that the nurse told you that the Chinese are aiding* (and here the legal advisor barely bothers to suppress his incredulity) *a secret agent from Zimbabwe called Charlie in sending false emails to another nurse, whom you think the first nurse is in love with, in order to steal the title deed to land in Zimbabwe from a deceased patient of yours. But – correct me if I'm wrong here – I understand, from my reading of the newspapers, that the Zimbabwean government are redistributing land regardless of ownership of title deed. All land, I understand, has reverted to the State.*

However she tells the story, it seems highly improbable, if not a confabulation. The Medical Defence Society might suggest she 'see a colleague to discuss how you're feeling in yourself' or think her the sort of person that is high risk of using their services in future, and so up her premium. But they haven't had Mr De Villier's hand gripping their arm, or seen Hope's fear, or experienced Fortunate's passion and goodness.

The miniature Vesuvius of ash from a cremated body is forensically useless unless the patient died of an industrial dose of heavy metals or of radiation poisoning and so the law requires some extra safeguards before it permits incineration of evidence. Beth discussed Mr De Villier's death with the coroner who was happy that the cause of death could be noted as cancer of the lung and gave the go-ahead for a cremation. Two medically qualified persons must certify the cremation form: the first signatory a doctor who is the patient's regular medical attendant – but with no 'pecuniary interest' in the patient's death – and the second, a doctor not involved in the patient's care. Beth certified the first part of the form, the Part One, and then she asked Luke, a GP in a neighbouring practice, to act as the verifying doctor for the Part Two.

Luke rings her a few days later. 'Beth, would you do a Part Two for me? It's another nursing home resident. Died of lung cancer, like your Mr De Villier. By the way Twicare was a bit rough with Mr De Villier's body, or perhaps it was the funeral directors.'

'What do you mean?'

'It's difficult to do the external examination, isn't it? Especially when the body's stiff from the freezer, but when I picked up his hand to check that the wrist tag name was correct I noticed one of his fingernails was lifted. They must have caught it on something.'

A small stone of disquiet settles in Beth's throat.

'Sorry, expect you're busy,' Luke says. 'My patient's name was…'

Beth has to ask him to repeat everything because she is beating back a ghastly vision: Mr De Villier's large but weakened hands scrabbling against Charlie Ten's pinioning arms; Charlie Ten's full weight on the pillow over Mr De Villier's face. She can see him releasing Mr De Villier for a few seconds to ask again for the combination to the safe. Mr De Villier would never have given it.

'Got that?'

'Um – sorry, where's the body?'

It is at the same funeral director as Mr De Villier's body. She rings them straight away to tell them when she will be coming to do the Part Two and then says, as nonchalantly as she can, 'Has Mr De Villier been cremated yet?'

'We were given the go-ahead from the coroner yesterday and he was cremated this morning. Lonely man, wasn't he? Only people at the crematorium apart from us were a representative from Social Services and a nurse from Twicare. Hope was her name. Very nice of her to come. Anything you wanted to know, Doctor?'

'No thanks. I'm sorry I couldn't be there myself.' She calls off. The stone in her throat has grown to an obelisk. Poor Mr De Villier; and poor Luke and her, sitting side by side, in the GMC disciplinary hearing for having negligently allowed evidence to be incinerated. She pulls across a strand of her hair to nibble on it, something she doesn't remember doing since she was a child. But then it occurs to her, with a pride in having unearthed a forensic genius she's not known that she possesses, that there would have been blood on the sheets if Mr De Villier's finger nail had been lifted during a life and death struggle with Charlie Ten. She knows who to ask. She reaches for the phone again and rings Twicare.

She's relieved to hear Sean answer the phone – always so obliging, so easy going. When she asks to speak to Hope, he says, 'I'm sorry, Beth, but Matron's had to let her go.'

'What do you mean, let her go?'

'Those are Matron's words, not mine, darling.'

'Are you saying Hope's been sacked?'

'I'm sure Matron wouldn't like to use that expression. It's not in the policies,' he says dryly.

'I'm shocked. What did Hope do to deserve that?'

'I think you'd better ask the queen herself, you know what she's like. I could be let go myself if I divulged that sort of thing.'

Beth expects there's a protocol that specifies summary dismissal for carelessness with the key code. 'Do you have a contact phone number for her? I so need to speak to her.' She can sense Sean's hesitation. 'I promise I'll never say you gave it to me. It's very important.'

'Since it's you, sweetheart, I'll open her staff file but mum's the word.'

'Thanks. I'm very grateful.'

The number Sean gives her for Hope isn't answered although she tries six times over the next two days and leaves a message. Her Zimbabwean patients have all vanished: two missing and one dead. She feels she is as likely to meet Hope and Fortunate again as she is to bump into Mr De Villier. She often doesn't know how her patients' stories turn out and whether she's been helpful or not. But this time she's sure that her ignorance will haunt her.

CHAPTER 10

A package arrives for Beth in the post at work three days later. Standing by her desk she opens it and shakes out a DVD. It's likely to be a pharmaceutical-sponsored educational programme on a drug for erectile dysfunction or whatever is being heavily promoted before it comes off licence. On the cover is a target superimposed on the unmistakeable silhouette – kepi hat and Gallic nose – of Charles de Gaulle. The title, *The Day of the Jackal,* is in blood red. There is also a note.

Dear Dr Jenkins,
Thank-you for all your kind help. I shall never forget it.
Yours truly,
Fortunate

She wants to twirl around. But if only he'd let her know that he was all right. There is no return address. She stares at the DVD. As a gift it's unusual but she's become used to Fortunate's quirky ways. She doesn't open the DVD; it would require a pointy pair of scissors and several spare minutes to peel off the tight plastic wrapping and it's not her type of film. She prefers period costume dramas where the tension is generated by cryptic asides and smoky glances. She'll add *The Day of the Jackal* to Matt's collection, although it will be unlikely to compete successfully for his attention with *South Pacific*. There'll be no catchy songs to enthral him.

As she places the DVD in her bag, she finds herself hesitating. She lifts it up again and stares at the cover – at its stark, bold design. She turns it over and reads the blurb on the back.

Based on Frederick Forsyth's best-selling novel, The Day of the Jackal tells of a cold, suave assassin on a mission to kill General Charles de Gaulle.

She remembers Fortunate's sack-cloth-and-ashes mood when he came to see her; and then how his disposition changed to unruffled resolve. She sits down for support. Fortunate has returned to Zimbabwe to carry out that final quest, recounted to her by Hope, and set by 'Shungu'. It's mad, but merely to a different degree to the previous assignments that Fortunate had been happy to fulfil.

Fortunate is going to attempt to assassinate the President of Zimbabwe. His passion for Shungu knows no bounds. He'd try to slay dragons. Putting aside the inadvisability of such an act, it will be impossible. For a start, Fortunate is neither cold nor suave. He'll make a hopeless assassin. He's blundering, blindly lovesick, into danger and he'll be sure to come to a bad end. If Charlie Ten doesn't find him and smother him, then the President's security services will hunt him down. Beth taps her temple as if she can shake out an alternative explanation for this curious gift. Nothing rattles out.

She lies in bed that evening knowing she'll not be able to sleep. She considers ringing Alena to tell her what has happened but Alena will remind her not to waste too much empathy on the self-inflicted predicament and irresponsible behaviour of a patient. Christina will say something like, 'Hope he shoots the bastard dead: someone should've by now.' Preeti will say, 'Ooh,

Beth, let's speak another time; it's very late and Manesh is waiting for me in bed, you understand.'

Downstairs, Bruno is having his half hour howl on being locked up in the kitchen for the night. Penelope is on the phone in her bedroom, haranguing her publisher who must have hoped his day had ended, and Matt is out for the count beside her, mouth open and snoring. Mr De Villier's papers are still in Matt's office in the folder with the photos. She's continued to dither about what to do with the title deed. She's kept it far too long; it's too late to return it. Social Services would be right to question her judgment and the police would investigate whether she has a pecuniary interest in Mr De Villier's death – such as a two thousand hectare farm in Africa.

She looks over at Matt and at a small puncture wound in his cheek. She'd taken him that afternoon to the re-arranged dental appointment, arriving ten minutes late. The dentist had been tetchy, reminding Beth that Matt had now missed two booked appointments. As Beth sat in the waiting area avoiding the receptionist's scolding eye, she'd heard a shriek. The dental assistant came running out, pale as the walls, and fled through the door. Beth jumped up, dropped the *Easy Living* magazine she'd been flicking through (somewhat hopefully), and rushed into the dental room. She'd found Matt relaxed in the dental chair as if enjoying a spa treatment and the dentist pressing a swab to Matt's cheek.

'It looks like I've permanently lost my assistant,' the dentist said, giving Beth an exasperated look.

'I'm so sorry! What happened?'

'Your husband tried to grope her as she passed me the dental syringe. She dropped the syringe and the needle went clean through his cheek.'

'I do apologise.'

'I know he's got problems but can't you teach him some basic social skills?'

As Beth left the dental surgery, apologising again to the dentist, the assistant and the receptionist, Hector rang her to say that he'd like an answer to the partnership offer within the next twenty-four hours, 'or we'll have to advertise'.

Matt's snoring shakes the bed. She reaches for her *Poems From Around The World*. She has to concentrate when she reads poetry. To write poetry is a gift but it takes a genius to understand it. What does, *Like dastard Curres, that hauing at a bay, The saluage beast embost in wearie chace,* on first reading mean? If it doesn't mystify, it isn't poetry. She makes every effort to figure it out and finds it helps to treat a poem like a crossword puzzle: she can occasionally solve an incomprehensible line using clues from the lines that she's succeeded in deciphering.

Choosing a page at random, she reads a C P Cavafy poem titled *Che Fece... Il Gran Rifiuto*. As she reaches the last line, she sits herself up. She presses her hand to her chest. She understands it all. Every line makes perfect sense, is written for her, is meant to be read on that particular night by... yes, her: Bethan Jenkins, locum GP, rootless foster child, semi-bereaved wife. She reads it five times. Each time she feels a thrill and trepidation in equal measure.

For some people the day comes
when they have to declare the great Yes
or the great No. It's clear at once who has the Yes
ready within him; and saying it,

he goes from honor to honor, strong in his conviction.
He who refuses does not repent. Asked again,

he'd still say no. Yet that no — the right no —
drags him down all his life.

She runs her finger carefully and slowly under the words as if she's translating a sacred text: *The day comes when they have to declare the great Yes or the great No.... that no... drags him down all his life.*

Something gives way in her. A snapping stay. A crack in an ice field. She's falling into a white silence and in the vast quiet she makes her choice.

With a light and effortless movement as if she's taking to the air like Wendy in Peter Pan she leaves her bed and floats her way along the corridor to Matt's study. She slides out an atlas and by the light of the desk lamp surveys the page showing Africa — not the most detailed of maps but it's enough. Then she switches on the computer, logs in as herself, waits in a dream-like state for the nerdy display of its internal machinations to end and goes on-line. She books a flight to Victoria Falls.

Once in Victoria Falls she'll make enquiries, find someone she can trust to deliver Mr De Villier's papers to his son. She knows she can hardly justify that as reason enough to run away to Zimbabwe, but if she travels to Victoria Falls rather than Bulawayo she can look for Shungu and warn her that Charlie Ten has hijacked her identity and that Fortunate could be on a fatal errand on her behalf. Shungu might even know of Fortunate's whereabouts and then she'll find him. It will be a chance to put all her efforts into helping just one patient (free of Hector's fetish about time) instead of spreading herself thinly across the multitude. Stop! She grips the mouse tightly to tether herself. All this, she knows, is an excuse for creating a crack in the walls around her life. A way to break the frame. It's a *great Yes* thing to do. And then – and her heart leaps – of course, there is the riddle of Matt's photos. There'll be no harm in placing herself in a situation where she might find an answer to his silence.

After she clicks on *Confirm* on the web page, she finds herself taking long deep breaths as if the freshest air is breezing through the window. The oxygen of escape.

She returns to the bedroom still feeling as if she is borne on a surf of poetry. On the dresser she can make out, in the low light, the frame of a photo of Matt and herself taken on honeymoon by a beach on the Gower peninsular. She's not had the courage to look at it since Matt's stroke but now she cradles the photo and takes it to the window where she can see their features in what seems a gloaming light although it must be approaching midnight. Matt is in a dark blue gingham shirt, airy sunlight fluffing his chicly untidy hair. He has his arm around her, and her shoulder is snugged into his chest. Her upturned face glows, saying wordlessly *this, this, is home. Matt and me, the two of us, this is home.* Home for over two years, but now she knows she's on the move again.

She returns the photo to the dressing table and turns to look at the sleeping Matt. His hair is soft on the pillow. She kneels beside him and takes his hand. The hand of BC Matt. He doesn't wake although he quiets until the bedroom takes on that deep stillness that comes into the rooms of the recently dead – the same hush she'd experienced in Mr De Villier's room. She grieves for him; mourns her dead husband. She weeps for all the futures lost. She laments the children they will never have together, for that hoped-for family tree that is now not only cut off from above her (as a baby abandoned at night on the steps of a Swansea maternity hospital, a torn-off strip from a plastic bag tied around her messily severed umbilical cord – yes, she'd been all over the local papers and doesn't ever want to have fame again), but from below her as well.

She may have knelt there for hours, she has no idea. She finds herself drifting over Welsh hills until she descends through the open doors of a slate-roofed chapel set by an apple-green stream that flows over pebbles worn beautiful by time. All Matt's friends are in the old oak pews, some dressed for the sadness, others for the celebration of his life: his school mates; his university colleagues; many students (some red-eyed females, she notices); old Jack from the allotment; her friends; all six foster parents from her childhood; Penelope in a black dress, hat and veil; even Fortunate has attended, looking dapper in his spotless white shirt and pressed trousers. The small organ plays its reedy notes sounding strangely, wordlessly, expressive. The little preacher mounts the wooden pulpit and gives a passionate tribute. She can't make out his words but they give her solace and an undefined hope which acts, unexpectedly, as a final farewell. She hugs the guests and then finds herself on her own again by the brook below his allotment, unafraid of the nearby woods. She scatters his ashes into the water which then streams with light and colour, turning as wondrous as that apple-green stream in the Welsh hills. A sable appears noiselessly from the copse, powerful, bold and handsome, and crosses the stream to disappear into the distance.

Beth becomes aware of the breathing of AD Matt again. She lets BC Matt go.

She goes and lies in a spare room – a room some of their children might have grown up in. As she waits for first light, she forgives Penelope. She can see it now: a mother loves all the ages of her son: loves the baby before he becomes an infant; loves the infant before he becomes a child; loves the child before he becomes a man. Penelope can love the infant again. But a woman just loves the man.

It is Beth's day off so she has breakfast with Penelope while Matt sleeps on. Penelope is in a feathery white bathrobe (embossed discreetly on the sleeve in silk: *Raffles Hotel, Singapore)* and slippers as if about to have a session in a sauna. She pecks around the kitchen like a self-satisfied free-range chicken, preparing Matt's breakfast. She cuts his toast into fingers.

'Penelope, I've something to tell you,' Beth says, 'I'm going abroad.'

'I guess a holiday will do you good.' She seems to be making an attempt to look conspiratorially at Beth. 'You need to be refreshed when you start a family. Time your return for just before you ovulate. Keep a temperature chart.'

All the pretexts for Beth's departure – fulfilling a patient's last wish, rescuing Fortunate from his folly, finding an answer to the mystery of Matt's photos – collapse. She jettisons the thin excuses, the flimsy reasons. She should never come back. It floods her, like a breaking sun greening a dark and dreary landscape, that having said goodbye to Matt, she should start a new life; that for her, this is the meaning of the *great Yes,* the poem's true significance, its pull. There are millions of lives one can live and the one she finds herself in is simply the wrong one. It's not impossible to jump lives because it has happened to her before when her mother left her on the steps of the Swansea hospital. Perhaps her mother willed a happier life for her than she could offer to her herself; gave her child a new chance – made sure she was born again. It's a thought that makes her proud of her mother. And now, no longer a helpless infant, she should have the courage to make her own decision. Her story has become intolerably fixed; she is in a stuck plot. If she'd made up her own story, as she has for the people in the portraits on her walls, she'd diagnose herself as having writer's block. She has to create a new narrative.

She steels herself. 'I should explain, Penelope, I'm leaving.'

'They say you mustn't eat tofu when you're abroad; it solidifies the jelly in an English girl's cervix.'

'I'm Welsh,' Beth says half-heartedly.

Penelope eyes her through the narrowing slits of her false lashes. 'Did you say you're leaving?'

Beth nods.

Penelope's face turns the colour of red cabbage. 'So, you're running away!' Beth has a foggy thought that she is not – she is more... running towards something; but she says nothing. 'So, you're going to abandon Matthew just when he's on the road to recovery, just when he needs you most.' Penelope's upper lip tents in disgust. 'Are you having an affair? You are, aren't you? How could you? And after all the kindness, the house, the financial help, in fact every damned thing you've got.' She loses her breath and then her lips start to tremble as she looks down at Matt's toast fingers. 'What about my grandchildren?' she wails.

Beth leaves the table and runs upstairs, spraying tears all over the banisters and walls. She goes straight to the bathroom and splashes cold water on her face. She catches sight of her blotchy visage in the mirror. Strands of her hair cling to her cheeks, her eyes are red, her lips are puffy. She looks unhinged. After blotting herself dry with a towel, she hurries to Matt's study and rings Hector on his mobile to tell him that she's turning down the practice's offer of a partnership. When he fails to reply, she knows that he's dumbstruck. In between short breaths she thanks him for having thought of her, for the offer, and then, before he can gather his voice, she puts down the phone and goes to check that her passport is in date. It will be the first time she's ever used it. She parts the covers and stares at the blank pages. They are waiting to be stamped.

Chapter 11

eth's flight crash lands in Africa – or so goes her initial impression – but she is the only passenger who gives a yelp. She's arrived with a hard bump in Lusaka, capital of Zambia, but she has no previous experience of 'touchdowns' to compare this to. The woman sitting next to her, an Anglican deacon (on some rescue mission, like herself), says, 'My, that was a hard landing.' Beth is grateful that she's saved her from embarrassment.

From Lusaka she takes the connecting flight to Victoria Falls in Zimbabwe. This is a smaller aircraft whose four propellers set off a dentist's-drill-like vibration in her seatback tray. Not wanting to make a fool of herself again, she reads it as a sure sign of healthy engines and on this second flight doesn't take out a pen and paper to note down the safety instructions. Not that she feels particularly on edge – more a case of being habitually cautious. Apart from the hiccup of her first landing, she's been in a near comatose state from the moment she'd rung Hector to turn down the offer of a partnership to the final leg of her journey. Having made the decision to leave home whilst in a storm of sorrow and frustration, she's been emotionally limp, physically enervated, mentally paralysed.

The Captain announces their descent and suddenly it's as if a paramedic has slapped electric paddles on her chest and has pressed the 'shock' button. It's shame that surges through her, that causes her backbone to arch. She's over Africa, flying south of the equator (when previously she'd not even crossed the Greenwich Meridian) because she's run away from home at the age of twenty-eight and a half. Her ticket is only a return because it's as cheap as a single. What she's done cauterises itself on her conscience: she's abandoned her disabled husband, terminally upset her mother-in-law, thrown away her career and perplexed her closest friends. When she'd intimated to Alena that she was unlikely to return, and Alena saw that she was serious, Alena tried to coax her to cancel the flight, convinced that she was going through a dark night of the soul, or at least that she was particularly pre-menstrual. She suggested sweetly that they go away somewhere together – perhaps to Florence or Seville for a carefree girls' weekend. Her sister would look after her twins. At least, thinks Beth, she'd not made laughable excuses by telling Alena that she had stuff to do out here in Africa. That she was looking for a patient's girlfriend whose address and surname she doesn't have and hoping to deliver some papers to a patient's son – who is hiding somewhere in 'the bush'. She swallows hard.

When she'd told Christina she was leaving, Christina said, 'Zimbabwe? Zimbabwe! God, Bethan! What's wrong with Australia? Don't you want us to visit you?'

Preeti said, 'Manesh says his uncle was killed by a snake in Africa. His aunt said he deserved it.' She delivered her little joke dead pan, but Beth could see it was to hide something. She scores highly on those tests which ask for a match between a subtle facial expression and an emotion. Preeti was afraid for her.

Now she's sharing Preeti's alarm. For reassurance, she searches in her bag and pulls out the information sheet on her hotel that she'd printed off from their website. She'd booked in at an expensive place for three nights to give herself a chance to acclimatise before whatever happens next. She studies the colour print-out in detail for the first time.

The Zambezi River Hotel.
The last word in colonial chic.

The picture on the first sheet shows a waiter dressed in white with a maroon sash presenting a bottle of champagne to a voluptuously rich-looking couple at a silver-serviced table on a verdant lawn beside a blue river. The young woman wears a red evening gown and the man is in black tie, as if they are going to the opera. Beth studies them closely. None of the three looks at all worried that they are in Zimbabwe. That's calming. She turns to the second sheet and runs her eye over the photos: an impossibly colourful bird; a pale green sightseeing boat moored to a delightfully romantic wooden landing stage; a photo of a bedroom with a mosquito net suspended from the four-poster. How thrillingly exotic, while at the same time reassuring.

Beneath a map on the last sheet are the hotel's contact details including address. *Livingstone, Zambia.*

Zambia? Some mistake, surely.

She scrutinises the map. She finds the hotel right next to a drawing of Victoria Falls. That looks promising but the Zambezi River, whose waters pour over the Falls, marks an international border. There is Zambia on one side of the river and there is Zimbabwe on the other. The hotel has mistakenly been drawn on the Zambian side.

Her seat companion on this last flight is a gap year student, who's been sharing with Beth the higher frequencies of her music as they leak from her earphones. Beth says, 'Excuse me; we are going to Victoria Falls, aren't we?'

The student pulls out her earphones. 'Yah.'

'Is that Victoria Falls in Zimbabwe?'

'No way! It's Victoria Falls in Zambia. At least I hope so.'

'Oh ff... iddle!'

The student looks at Beth with widening eyes. 'Are we, like, on the wrong flight? Is this going to Zimbabwe?'

'I'm not sure.'

'Oh... My... God!' She cranes her neck to look for a flight attendant and says to Beth, 'I don't think anyone goes to Zimbabwe anymore. No one in their right mind anyway. I'm going to ask.'

She leans across the aisle where three Asian men – possibly Chinese and identically dressed in steel-grey trousers and checkered red shirts – are studying the in-flight safety sheets. Chinese! Perhaps the very ones who'd helped Charlie Ten on the technical side of impersonating Shungu in the emails. They'll certainly be going to Zimbabwe, won't they? A wafer of hope.

'Hi,' says the student, 'is this flight going to Zimbabwe?'

They nod affably but Beth doubts that they understand.

The student collapses back in her seat. 'This totally sucks,' she says loudly. 'We're on the wrong flight. What if they arrest us when we land? Daddy will be so pissed off, having to get me out of jail again. He had to fly all the way to Laos last time. At least this is slightly closer.'

The man behind them taps her on the shoulder and says, 'Excuse me. This plane's going to Livingstone in Zambia. It's the town on the Zambian side of Victoria Falls.'

'Oh cool, thanks,' says the student and giggles. 'For a moment I thought we were going to end up in the wrong country. How stupid was that?'

Quite. Beth stares at the hotel print-out. *Zambia* in black text. The wrong country. When she was a teenager she'd once found herself on a train going to Pembroke Dock instead of Bristol. She should've grown out of wrong country mistakes by now.

'They say they're amazing, Vic Falls,' the student says. 'They say they make Niagara look like a dripping tap. I did Niagara last year. Went with my parents – yawn! But now I'm going to have fun.' She tones it as a question.

Maybe this will all work out for the best. From this close, Zimbabwe looks far too dangerous. She's been saved from herself. She's barely heard of Zambia so guesses it must be peaceful; probably too safely dull to send reporters to. She should reinvent her escape as a holiday, a carer's vacation, instead of fooling herself she's on a foreign aid mission or can just walk away from home into a new life.

The student says, 'They say there aren't any fences or health and safety notices. You can just walk to the lip of the Falls and jump. Do you ever feel like you've just got to jump? Like you can't resist it? I think I'm going to stand back from the edge in case I get that feeling – and in case some nut pushes me.' She gives a nervous laugh.

Beth makes an effort to reassess her situation: her wrong country mistake has pulled her back from taking her own leap of danger. It's ironic. She's been saved by her stupidity. She nudges the student and says, 'You'd probably get a spectacular view of the Falls as you dropped.'

The student squeezes the tips of her fingers. 'Yeah, I guess so,' she says uncertainly. She puts her earphones back in and cycles rapidly through the menu on her music player. 'I'm going to do bungee jumping and white water rafting. I'm so totally up for that. They say Victoria Falls is the adventure capital of Africa. How cool is that?'

'Spare me,' Beth says to herself.

Beth's red-tiled hotel is even more charming than the brochure promised. 'It's modelled on the famous Victoria Falls Hotel over the border in Zimbabwe,' says the welcoming porter as if, even though Zimbabwe is out of bounds, she can at least make believe to be there. Deep green mango trees – hanging their fruit on long stems – frame the formal, colonial-style portico. Cream columns on square plinths line the way to a mahogany-panelled reception room and then on to a brick terrace. A fountain patters sparkling droplets onto red lilies in a pond. The ceiling fans in the reception area flap languidly like obliging captive birds. The only jarring notes are the stuffed animal heads on the walls – one of which is a sable whose expression, Beth notes, is one of considerable annoyance.

She wanders through to the lawns beyond the terrace and stands in the shade of an expansive tree bursting with flame-orange blossoms. Beyond, jutting out into the shimmering expanse of the Zambezi River, is the wooden jetty that she'd seen in the brochure. When she crosses the lawn to walk down to the water's edge, the chirruping of the cicadas is so loud that it's as if the blades of grass beneath her feet are a stringed ensemble. An Arabian-style tent shades a bar overlooking the water near the jetty. Having reassured herself that it is safe, she steps onto the jetty and looks downstream. A huge fire is blowing smoke across the river but when she hears a faint roar she sees she's looking at the lip of the waterfall whose spray rises hundreds of feet into the air. Beyond is Zimbabwe, veiled by vapour. She stands there and lets the bright colours, the warmth, the unfamiliar scents and the sound of the rumbling, rolling, river fill her.

After a lunch of ostrich salad, Beth books herself in for an activity. She stays clear of the *Ultimate Adrenaline Experience* (bungee jumping, bridge swinging and white water rafting 'two for the price of one, combo,' as if any survivors of the first and second could have a third chance to die at no extra cost), *Soar with the Angels* (helicopter sightseeing) and *Ultimate African Adventure* (walking with lions and riding on elephants – the reverse would have merited the adjective even more). She is certain that the high cost of each activity means that there is a fatality rate: each operator would have to make as much money as fast as possible before having to close down due to a death. She guesses they start up again under a different name: *Strolling with Snakes,* or just honest *Terminal Tours.*

She also dismisses the *Ultimate Swimming Experience*: a boat trip to Livingstone Island on the edge of the Falls, and then a swim in a natural infinity pool right on the brim of the Falls. 'You can lie in the pool whilst you look down over the lip of the waterfall.' She can imagine herself retching down the abyss with fright.

Instead she books a walking tour of the Falls and is taken the short distance in a tourist bus with three retired American couples. Their guide is a Zambian who says that the Falls speak for themselves so she will not overburden them with statistics unless they want to hear them, which neither Beth nor the other tourists leap at (it's hard to feel any emotion except a faint sense of ennui about how many cubic metres of water flow, unless one is a water utility engineer), but she does tell them that the Falls are a mile wide and that the border between Zambia and Zimbabwe divides its length. 'Of course the Zambian side is by far the best,' she says.

Beth sees from her map that the flow falls into a gorge from where it boils its way on down to the vast Lake Kariba in a series of zigzagging ravines. They take a path that runs through forest along the top of the sheer-walled peninsula that forms the first limb of the ravines. Soon they come out of the trees and there, opposite them, is Victoria Falls. How many ways can water drop? Like the silky waist-long hair of a platinum blonde, like a slow-motion detonation of glistening droplets, like steam exhaling from a boiling kettle, like waves of Hawaiian surf. Her poetry reading has paid off. She stands awed.

Further along the ridge they come to a metal footbridge spanning a knife-edge of rock although, with its high sides, it feels safer to stand on the bridge than the path. As the gap year student on the aeroplane intimated, the only barrier at the edge of the paths is the mental fence separating the imaginative urge to jump from dull reason. She turns away from the waterfall to look down the gorge and sees the historic iron bridge that links Zambia to Zimbabwe. A laden lorry is inching its way across. She is about to turn back when she sees something fall from the centre of the bridge. A sack from the lorry? Time slows as she sees that it's a person – a woman – her torso bucking, her arms flailing and thrashing about, as if she is trying to catch on to something to break her fall. Something in her build, her figure. No, it can't be! The gap year student.

Down she plunges, flaccid now, as if she's passed out.

'Oh, how awful!' Beth starts to exclaim. She bitterly repents her joke about the view as you fall. But, by whatever prayer the student has screamed as she drops, her fall is being checked, is slowing, as if time – at a precisely convenient moment for her – is going into reverse. Then Beth sees the rope attached to the student's ankles as it catches the sunlight. She comes to an undulating stop and stretches out her arms to slowly rotate a few feet above the water, getting an upside down outlook on her time-reversed world.

'Hey! Those bungee jumpers have got what it takes,' says one of Beth's tour companions, an American women whose red tracksuit top advertises *Tyler Tubes* over her pneumatic bosoms. 'They do it from a platform on the bridge. Say, we're from Arizona, and where are you from?'

'I'm from... Wales.'

'That's near England, right?'

'Yes, they're joined at the hip.'

'That's so cute. Love your accent. Is that Wales?'

'No, it's... from nowhere, or perhaps... anywhere. I haven't actually lived in Wales recently,' she admits.

'Not nearly as much water falling this end of the Falls as at the Zimbabwean end,' says the woman's companion from beneath his red baseball cap advertising *Tyler Pumps and Treads*. Mr and Mrs Tyler, Beth presumes. 'Apparently it's the wrong time of year; rains haven't fallen up-river yet so the water's low. We took a day trip to the Zimbabwean side yesterday. We didn't like to say this in front of our guide but we think the Falls are even more spectacular over there. You should go over. Gotta make the most of it all.'

'You did a day trip to Zimbabwe?' Beth says, tightening her grip on the rail of the footbridge.

'It was simple, we just fetched our passports, paid for a day-pass visa as we passed through customs, and there we were on the Zimbabwean side of Victoria Falls. We took a tour company bus – *Ultimate Zimbabwe Experience* – but you could just walk across. You sure get a different perspective of the Falls from over there.'

Beth stares across the gorge into Zimbabwe. It looks much

like Zambia: a few radio masts on the skyline and fine old trees greened by the mini-ecosystem created by the spray from the Falls. She can hear no gunfire, no riots and no one is throwing themselves off into the gorge. Zimbabwe looks as delightfully peaceful as Zambia.

Beth takes the hotel transport to the bridge after an early breakfast the next morning. She has her passport stamped at the bright-blue Zambian customs building and walks down the tar road – already radiating heat – towards the bridge. In her day pack she has the title deed, Mr De Villier's letter to Selous, the photos she had discovered in Matt's office, and expensive face cream brought in duty free – a present for Fortunate's girlfriend. She's set her chin against her fears and she's going to have a busy day, first trying to locate Shungu and then asking if anyone knows Selous. She hopes she'll find someone trustworthy who will deliver the papers to him.

The road cuts a curve down an embankment so that she can't see the bridge until she's almost upon it. She stops at its threshold. A railway line, a single track road and a footway cross the bridge. At the half way point there is a hut and platform for the bungee jumpers. At the far end a man holds a red and green Stop and Go sign for the occasional traffic that passes over. It's showing Stop. She still has time to turn back but when the man turns the sign to its green Go side, she sets out. The man must think her nuts, stopping and starting like that as if instructed by him, but she feels more confident pretending the decision to go through with her assignment is not up to her.

As soon as she steps onto the bridge, a fine spray cools her face out of the clear blue sky. Cecil Rhodes would have been pleased. Beth had read that he'd ordered the bridge to be situated

129

so that passengers travelling by train – on his dreamed-of Cape-to-Cairo railway line – would be wetted by the spray from the Falls.

As Beth reaches the end of the bridge, the man turns his sign to a red Stop again and, later, she wishes she'd taken notice. Rounding the curve of the road a short distance from the Zimbabwe side of the bridge, she sees the Zimbabwe customs buildings. It seems quiet although a few people mill aimlessly about, using their documents and papers as fans. Two uniformed customs officers are in conversation with someone hidden in a doorway. As she approaches, Beth sees an arm come into view – a male arm in a short-sleeved pale-pink shirt – as the man in the doorway moves a cigar to his lips. The shiny scar on his forearm winks at Beth in the sunshine. It's the tattoo of a human bite.

She can't remember crossing back over the bridge, passing the Stop-Go man, passing the bungee platform, passing the vendors of copper bangles who pleaded with her for a sale on her way across, but she does find herself stumbling as she climbs the step into the Zambian customs building. She hears herself gasping to the customs officer, 'Decided against!'

The custom's officer takes it in her stride. 'Don't worry; we have all you need here in Zambia. There's no need to go over there. It's not so safe there nowadays.'

Beth takes a grotesquely overpriced taxi back to the hotel and makes straight for the seclusion of her room. She sits on the bed, sweating as if she has malaria. Charlie Ten is in Victoria Falls. She might accept it as a coincidence, had Hope not lifted the paving slab on the goings-on of the Zimbabwean security services. She is being watched. Stalked. Charlie Ten is waiting to pick her up as soon as she crosses the border. He must know that she has Mr De Villier's title deed. A mosquito does an exploratory pass close to her ear. How had Charlie Ten known she had flown to Zambia? Why is there a mosquito about at this time of day? The two – Charlie Ten and the mosquito – seem linked in a grand, malevolent scheme which first showed its hand with Mr De Villier breathing 'Murder' at her in his room in Twicare.

She pulls down the mosquito netting and climbs underneath, sitting cross-legged on the bed. The mosquito settles on the netting, time on its side. She has a mind to ring room service: *What's this mosquito doing in my room?* She wonders if the hotel staff have a repertoire of mosquito-in-my-room jokes like those what's-this-fly-doing-in-my-soup ones. *Looks like it'll be doing very well. Thanks for enquiring, madam.* But she can't spin her thoughts off in a distraction for long and feels panicky so lies out on the bed practising the relaxation technique that she urges on her patients. It is, she discovers, ineffective. She is well beyond self-help. She needs a post-trauma therapist or, even better, a tranquiliser. Instead, she springs up and squashes the mosquito between folds of the netting. She feels a little easier until she sees it has tainted the netting with what she guesses is her own blood.

Flailing her arms she extracts herself from under the netting and takes Mr De Villier's papers from her day pack and stares at them. She's in possession of an object that is hotly desired by dark forces. They're attracting the wrong kind of company. Title deeds represent land, territory, the stuff of bitter disputes and wars. Perhaps she should destroy them, walk along the banks of the Zambezi through the forests – facing down horrible dangers – to the waterfall, to lean over the edge and throw them over. She puts her head in her hands. No, she's just a locum GP and she is never going to return to the waterfall. She's seen how dangerous it is under its smokescreen of beauty. The environs of the hotel are the safest place to be.

Her mobile receives a text. *manesh has slight cold. he asks should he stay in bed!! hope you having fun. xxx Preeti.*

Beth brings the display close, as if she can disappear into the phone and be teleported back next to Preeti. How she longs now to be with friends again. She finds herself missing AD Matt: his innocent puzzlement, his... just being there. She even misses Penelope with her take-that opinions. Bruno is the only one she hopes never to see again. She guesses she's coming to her senses. She texts Preeti back, *missing you. very hot and sultry here. see you soon. luv beth.*

She'll lie low and then use the return part of her ticket in another five days. She will have to extend her stay at the hotel, whatever the cost.

CHAPTER 12

The sun carries on shining and Beth spends the next two days on the white, cushioned recliners by the pool disguised under a wide-brimmed straw hat, an unrevealing one-piece black bathing costume (she has brought a barely decent white bikini as well but that now seems far too attention-seeking – even without Charlie Ten on her trail) and a cloak of factor fifty sun cream. She reads a so called 'misery memoir' novel in which an orphaned Irish girl grows up suffering every imaginable abuse, finally finding the love of her life, only to lose him to a falling tree. End of story. What a perfect read. It gloves in with her gloomy state of mind and affirms her pessimism.

She takes her meals at a single table facing away from the other guests. She hooks the *Do Not Disturb* sign on the door knob to her bedroom and wedges a chair against the door at night. She has a dream of being trapped on the lip of the great waterfall whilst Charlie Ten edges closer, coaxing her to hand over the deed, his scarred arm behind his back, ready to swing out and push her as soon as he gets a hold on what his Gollum-like eyes so desire. When he grabs the deed, she bites down hard on his forearm and they go over the waterfall together. She had not known, until then, that it's possible to have such mixed emotions in a dream.

The second evening arrives and she's becoming bored and so risks venturing into the bar. It heaves with tourists and tour operators boasting of their ultimate experiences. She doubts theirs is as frightening as hers. She buys a Nyami-Nyami cocktail (blue curacao, orange juice, cane spirit) and a lager, finds a table in a corner, and places the lager opposite her to make it look as if a companion is returning at any moment. She reads a book whilst pausing, from time to time, to catch snippets of conversation from the other tables.

'Did you hear about the six canoeists who set out in three canoes last Tuesday down the lower Zambezi? Only two and a quarter canoes have turned up at the camp and only four and a half canoeists… '

'The guide said it was a Senegal Coucal but I could see it was a Burchell's Coucal due to the faint barring on its rump…'

'It's really bad in Zim now; we got chased down the road by an axe-wielding mob.'

She wonders if she should loosen up a little and find people to talk to. She whispers to her invisible companion, 'Can I try your lager? That's kind. Thanks.' She takes a sip and replaces it opposite. She orders a David Livingstone (fresh mint leaves muddled with cloudy apple, honey and Irish whisky served on the rocks) and tries to pretend she is back in Tres Hermanas.

Late in the evening a man in his mid-forties, she guesses, and with a full term beer-belly under his heavily-pocketed safari shirt, comes into the bar with a tall, pallid, young woman who looks as if she's just arrived, like herself, from some dimly-illuminated town north of the English Channel. The tall woman grins vacuously at him as he drinks bottle after bottle. His voice grows louder and louder. He has taken her up in his sightseeing plane that afternoon. They are soon joined by a busty tour guide who says, as she bounces up to the pilot, 'Hey Croc, tell Rebecca 'bout your big escape, huh?'

He needs little persuasion and becomes impossible to ignore: '... four metres, probably more. My whole frickin' arm's in its mouth and I can hear my mate screaming, "The croc's got him! The croc's got Croc! He's a gonner, he's fish meat!" But that flat dog doesn't know who he's snapped on. He thinks he's got some rookie tourist, doesn't reckon on an old Rhodie, doesn't know we never die.' He slaps a note on the counter and shouts for another Mosi lager. 'So, he's got me skewered. All I can do is wiggle my fingers and tickle his tonsils. But that's enough for Crocodile Andee, girls. There's a flap, see, at the choke end of the reptile's throat. Stops the water flooding its lungs when it submerges. I get my fingers under the flap and leeeeft it. Should have seen the croc. Let's me go before you can say koeksisters. Then, you gotta believe this, man, I slap him hard on the tail as he gaps it so he never forgets me.'

'Wow! Awesome!' the tall woman says, her jaw going slack. The other woman presses against him with her bust and says, 'Show her the teeth marks, Croc.'

He bares a meaty, heavily-scoured shoulder. Beth is impressed, even from across the room.

Another man joins them saying, 'Hey, fly-boy, who you gonna fly in your luv-machine tomorrow?'

Beth turns her attention to her book and tries to blot out the noise. The women eventually excuse themselves, bored of the men's aviation talk. She doggedly turns the pages. This second novel of her 'holiday' explores the feelings of a mother whose infant was abducted from its buggy, but is written, Beth discovers towards the end of the book, by the abducted infant from the perspective of twenty years on. The mother commits suicide just before the abducted infant, now grown up, has tracked her down. It makes for a profoundly sad, unresolved, and therefore literary, ending. It's another novel to confirm her in her state of apprehension, although she's starting to wonder if she should try something different, something outside her comfort zone.

She picks up her third novel. Reading the back cover blurb she sees that *when Kirsty's husband goes off with Kirsty's mother, Kirsty finds herself on an emotional journey which will take her to a place no woman should find herself in. Exploring themes of cross-generational infidelity, Lolanta Schneider paints a disturbing portrait of a society whose conventions are crumbling and where there is no way back to the past.* It was recommended by Christina. Beth places it back in her bag, thinking that perhaps the writer should have taken it on herself to make the effort to think up a way back to the past. Or illuminate a path to the future if there really is no way back.

It's getting late and she sees that the pilots are drifting towards the door. Almost every other guest has gone and she can hear the bar staff fooling about in the kitchen at the end of their shift.

A text comes through. *I notice u taken ur keys. have changed locks. penelope.* Beth chucks her phone into her bag. She snatches up the novel she's just finished and pulls out the bookmark. It's a folded piece of paper on which she's written Cavafy's poem. She reads it again. *For some people the day comes when they have to declare the great Yes...*

Admit it: she has in no manner declared the *great Yes*. She's said *possibly, maybe,* and then, after seeing Charlie Ten at the border, *forget it.* She's merely taken an overnight flight to a hotel in the sun like thousands of others. What is so *great Yes* about that? She'll be going back home defeated. She looks up at the pilots. They've reached the door and are discussing arrangements for meeting the next day. This is the moment: *yes* or *no*? But if yes, she'll likely make it easy for Charlie Ten to get his hands on the title deed. The skin on her wrist prickles as she remembers Mr De Villier's grip as he'd hissed, 'The title deed was bought with blood.'

The title deed – it's just a couple of sheets of A4 paper. Surely there's a copy somewhere.

But… bought with blood. It must be worth the world, must represent much more than a postcode; more even than property – farm, garden or house. Perhaps it's so important because it represents… a home. Charlie Ten wants to rob Selous of his home, wants to strip him of his hearth. She's lost her home as well – for different reasons but she thinks she understands what it might be like for Selous.

She springs up and hurries over to the men. Now she's put on skates and has pushed herself out onto the thin ice of an unfamiliar lake. It's too late to turn back.

'Excuse me,' she says.

Croc turns to her, appraises her for a few seconds – reactions slowed by alcohol – and gives her a leery smile. 'Hey! What have we here? No need to say excuse me, Miss, it's my pleasure.'

He turns back to his friend who has hesitated in the doorway. 'Mushi, mushi, hey? Looks like my lucky night! I'll catch you up later.' He waves him away.

Beth regrets her tight skirt at the same time as feeling flattered – but ungrateful. Matt used to ask her how she could possibly have three emotions at once; she said that maybe women needed that ability in order to be capable of coping with the multiple needs of their children.

She plays it dead-pan with Croc. 'Sorry, I don't know your name, I'm Lynette.' She uses her middle name.

'Andy Bloemfontein, Croc to my friends, Crocodile Andee to my enemies!'

Beth thinks that she must have looked blank because he has to explain himself, which deflates his boastful announcement as sure as it would a joke. 'You know – that down-under Crocodile Dundee fellow. I'm the Zambezi version, but meaner and bigger in every way. Get my meaning, girl?'

She keeps pokerfaced. 'I couldn't help overhearing your stories. Are you a pilot?'

'That's me! Every day I get it up and keep it up.' He laughs conspiratorially with no one and places his hand up on the door frame, lolling there.

Beth glances over her shoulder. Apart from one man – small in an oversized black-leather jacket – on the opposite side of the bar who's fallen asleep in his chair, there is no one to eavesdrop. But she keeps her voice low. Now she's far from the lake edge and mustn't stop or the ice will give way. 'I want to get across into Zimbabwe.'

She can see that Croc is hearing her but not listening to her, is still showing off in front of some imaginary mate. 'I don't want to lose my cutest passenger but, to show I'm as honest as a man with an uncut diamond, I gotta tell you, Miss, that the easiest way to get to Zimbabwe is to walk across the bridge. Get your passport, stuff your handbag with US dollars, step out the door here and take a taxi.'

'I want to get in without going over the bridge. I want to avoid officials. I'll pay you to take me across in your plane.'

'For you, sweetheart, I'll do it for free.'

She's zipping along so effortlessly, so lightly on the ice. 'That's much appreciated, but I'll pay for fuel at the very least. When and where shall I meet you?'

Croc stops swaying on his supporting arm and looks at her long and hard. 'Jest over, huh?' She seems to have sobered him up. 'I do sight-seeing flights. Vic Falls from the air. Nothing illegal. Got my licence to protect. Got a business to run.'

Keep your eyes on the far shore, don't stop. Don't become emotional. 'It's really important I get into Zimbabwe – and I'll, ah, need picking up again.' She looks him earnestly in the eye. That appears to have little effect and she's tempted to flutter her eyelashes but he shakes his head slowly and says, 'You can't be real.'

'I beg your pardon?'

'*I beg your pardon*, she says, just like a Pom. Are you kidding, Miss? If we cross that border illegally… You some sort of journalist? They don't like journalists over there, chick. Their prisons are… let me put it this way: they strip you naked before you get to the cell door so you've got nothing to strangle yourself with. It's no place for a girl from England who says I beg your pardon.'

'I'm from… never mind. I'll take the risk. Like I said, I'll pay you well.'

Croc speaks slowly as if to a dullard, 'I don't frickin' care if you pay me with a sack of Krugerrands. I'm not flying over the border.' He turns towards the door.

Beth feels the ice crust splintering beneath her but she's far too far out to turn back. She doesn't raise her voice as she says, 'You're all swagger. Those scars on your arm look to me like a woman took a definite dislike to you. I'll find a pilot who's got the balls. What's the name of your friend?'

He stops. He's facing away from her but his head is moving about as if he's lost control of it.

She turns to go. '*All* swagger. I've met braver men clutching walking frames.'

She hears the door bang shut and feels him behind her. 'OK Lynette, I'll do it.' She faces him. 'You've asked for it,' he says. 'I hope you don't regret it.'

'Thank-you! You've restored my admiration for bare-handed crocodile killers.'

He doesn't smile. 'It'll have to be at night.'

'Whatever,' she says, but her stomach contracts.

'I'll pick you up at 3.45am just outside the hotel. I'll give the night watchmen a few kwachas to swear they saw nothing.'

'What? Tonight?'

'Yes – four hours' time. The moon will be touching the horizon and it's a clear night. Can't fly in the pitch black.'

Beth's stomach wrings itself dry. 'Are you... in a fit state tonight?'

He snorts. 'If I was in a fit state I wouldn't have agreed to fly you. Now don't say more or I'll change my mind. And one last thing: no luggage. And wear trousers and bring a jersey – the cabin windows leak.'

'Not a problem,' Beth says, and then the ice breaks and she knows herself to have plunged in up to her neck. Will someone please throw me a rope? 'If... perhaps... I'll only need to be there for a day. How will I get back?'

'I'll fix something.' With that, he is gone.

Beth has no sleep that she notices and gets up well before she needs to. She puts essentials in her day pack: a bottle of water, her sun cream, her mobile and the face cream for Shungu. The title deed, Mr De Villier's letter and the photos of the bodies are in a plastic folder which she has to bend to fit in. Her passport and US dollars are in her round-the-waist travel wallet. She slips her Zimbabwe travel guide – which has a map of the Zimbabwean side of the Falls – into a compact cloth shoulder bag, picks up her hat and leaves her room, clicking her door quietly shut. She slinks out of the hotel through the bar exit that opens onto the driveway so that she will not have to pass the reception desk. Outside she sees the glow from a cigarette. The two night watchmen move discreetly away as they see her. Croc's vehicle is waiting, engine quietly ticking over, at the end of the drive.

For a moment she hesitates. The GREAT YES, she tells herself. She walks to his vehicle.

'Hi!' she says, and is pleased to hear herself sounding as enthusiastic as a waiter in an American diner.

Croc grunts like a man with a hangover having to get up before dawn. 'You'll have to put your hat in your bag,' he says.

'I don't think it'll fit.'

'Leave it behind then.'

'What sort of plane are we going in?' she asks.

'It's no 747 and there's no in-flight video.'

Croc doesn't switch on the vehicle lights until they are on the road. They turn off before Livingstone which is Beth's first intimation that they aren't heading for the international airport. They drive along a bumpy track before turning again to end up in front of a metal mesh gate. Croc gets out to unlock it. Inside, their headlights illuminate a large sign on a small building. *Spray Wing Flights Ltd.* She can't see any planes. They park just beyond the building in the long moon-shadow of a clinker-built hangar.

'I'll need help getting her out,' Croc says.

He puts his back into sliding the hangar doors open along their runners. Beth follows him into the dark hangar. He shines his torch at what Beth takes to be the wing of a hang glider. It's angled steeply with the tip of one wing nearly touching the ground. She follows him around the wing.

'Here she is,' he says reverently, as if showing her Sleeping Beauty.

His torch illuminates the underside of the wing and four drooping wires, and then he swings the light down the slender pole that the wing balances on to a rectangular frame from which hangs a fabric hammock. Some of Beth's young-mother patients have buggies larger than this. Sewn into the hammock are two thin cushions, one behind the other. Behind the hammock is an engine the size of a rucksack with a plastic propeller sticking out from its back. On each side of the 'seats' are two foot rests suspended over… nothing.

'What's this?' she asks.

'It's a flexwing microlight. A small plane.'

'It hasn't even got doors or a roof. And the wing's all squiff. This isn't a plane!'

'Oh yeah? Well you're going to find out it's a bloody rocket. Now, if you'll get behind the engine and help me by pushing on the hub of the prop we'll get her out.'

He takes her shoulder bag and day pack and slings them in the hammock. She's left her hat in the car and now sees that taking it is out of the question.

She steps warily to the back of the contraption but says, 'I think I'm going to back out. It's not what I expected.'

'Don't push there, you'll break the prop.' He takes her hands and repositions them. 'You're not chickening out now. I've made the arrangements for you to be picked up. Jules is expecting you.' He levels the wing by pulling on a triangular frame and then commands, 'Push.' The whole contrivance moves forward on its toy wheels.

Once outside, Croc fits her with earphones and a helmet. He positions a microphone in front of her lips. 'Kiss that,' he says. He tells her to sit on the rear cushion and place her feet on the foot rests, then leans across her and fastens the seatbelt, pulling in yards of strap. 'Last passenger was a hundred kilos.' He presses her day pack and shoulder bag into her lap and says, 'Hold those bags tight. If you let go they'll fly back through the prop and then your packed lunch will fall like confetti over the Falls. Shortly after that we'll have to do an emergency landing in the dark. I don't want to join Jake underwater.'

'Jake?'

'A legendary pilot around here who just disappeared. Personally, I think he's at the bottom of the Zambezi. He used to fly with a long scarf around his neck and I suspect it got caught in the prop.'

Beth grips her bags as if they are being wrestled from her.

'Where are you going to sit?' she says.

'Now spread your legs.' He swings himself onto the cushion between her thighs. It's all very snug, as if he's giving her a piggy-back across the border. If she extends her head back to avoid pressing against his spine with the front of her helmet it only travels a few inches before colliding with the pole holding up the wing. She can hear Croc grunting and breathing over the intercom as he makes his checks. Before he starts the engine he shouts, 'Stand clear.' Surely unnecessary but, on the other hand, it is reassuring that he is going by a rule book.

The noise of the engine a couple of feet behind her head is deafening, despite her earphones. They lurch forward. She can't see where they are going because of the bulk of the pilot and is not aware they've taken off until she hears him shout through the intercom, 'Those are the lights of Livingstone down to our right.'

She opens her eyes and moves her head to look out. The slipstream catches her face, the air blowing in her cheek with its force. She takes shelter again behind Croc but has caught a glimpse of an island of light in an ocean of darkness.

'Where's Zimbabwe?' she says when she recovers her breath.

'Straight ahead where it's as black as night. Everyone who can has left the country, partly on account of a return to the dark ages. You can see one red light down there. That's a jamming transmitter just over the border in Zimbabwe, put up by the Chinese to stop outside broadcasts being beamed in.'

Beth's feet in her sandals are exposed to the slipstream. 'It's chilly up here,' she says.

'It's cold because I must have altitude. We'll soon be three thousand feet up. I want to cross the border high to avoid detection.'

When they level out Croc throttles back so that the engine noise becomes a low hum against the smooth rush of the airflow. Keeping her mouth firmly shut, Beth dares to look out and down again past her toes. The low moon illuminates the spray from the Falls which lie like a lacy veil over the inky course of the river. The lights of Livingstone look like those of a port on the edge of an ocean. Ahead is the blacked-out country of Zimbabwe. Even radio waves have been halted at the border. Her new world. It looks big – like it goes to the ends of the earth. She can get truly lost there; no one will find her; no one will risk it to come looking. She feels a flutter, a thrill, in her belly. She decides that a fugitive like her loves lawless, perilous, out of reach places. She's astonished not to feel terrified. Instead, her helmet can barely contain her growing elation. She's floating free from the earth, from gravity. She's cut the bonds of her first life, escaped its pull like a rocket blasted into space. A second life is out there on a different planet and in two hours the bright sun will rise and illuminate it. She almost gives Croc a squeeze with her thighs. This is what the *great YES* feels like. Anticipation. Excitement. Liberty. Independence. Nothing can beat the heady emotion of the *great YES*.

Then the engine cuts out.

For a moment it's so quiet that she can hear the stars twinkle. Then her stomach hits her tonsils as if the wings have hinged up. The machine tips sideways and they are falling and spinning, free as a sycamore leaf. The sleeves of her jumper are snatched and the strap of her helmet slaps her cheek as if trying to revive a drunk. The wind's low moan through the wires rises to a howl although she might be hearing her own shrieks. The lights of Livingstone orbit her. A bursting pain balloons in her ears. She grips her bags even harder as if they'll save her. Her legs clamp on Croc. Centrifugal forces are forcing her, bum first, through the hammock.

'What's going on?' she bawls into the cyclone. There is no reply. Her pilot has blacked out – or worse. She's on her own with her thrashing heart which will soon be ruptured and stilled. She waits for her life, her old life, to pass before her eyes but instead she has a bizarre, almost well-considered, thought: if she really is a heroic adventurer, like Captain Scott, she should breathe the last words of his diary, *It seems a pity*. She screams a great NO.

CHAPTER 13

Beth's head is thrown to the side and she sees that the machine has stopped spinning, although vertigo makes it seem that she's still turning in her seat. The intercom clicks. She hears Croc's voice. 'We're going to glide in without the engine. I don't want to attract any attention.'

Beth whimpers, 'I thought we were going to die.'

Croc chuckles. 'I had to lose two and a half thousand feet damn quick.'

She rests the front of her helmet on his back and closes her eyes. 'Have you ever done this before?' she says as they level off.

'An engine-off spiral dive and then a glide to touch down, yes; cross-border people trafficking, no.' He says it gleefully and she knows he will add this to his fund of daring-do stories for the girls in the bars. She can't begrudge him that.

They touch down lightly and roll to a rapid stop. Croc extracts himself and she follows, nearly dislocating her neck from the still plugged-in wire to her headphones. 'Easy, easy,' Croc says as he disconnects her and takes her helmet.

Beth sees that they've landed on a road. Croc says, 'Just off to the right up there you can see a telegraph pole. It may be the last pole in Zimbabwe that's not been chopped down for firewood. That's where Jules will be picking you up.' He looks at his watch. 'He'll be here in fifteen minutes sharp. He'll drop you back here at 4am tomorrow morning. If you're not here, you'll be on your own and have to find another way out of Zimbabwe. If anyone asks you how you got across the border, say you fell off a booze-cruise whilst drunk and landed up on the wrong side of the river.'

'How much do I owe you,' she says as he climbs into his hammock seat again.

'Forget it! If I'm caught, I don't want to appear to have benefited financially.' Then he shouts, 'Stand clear,' making her scurry away.

He starts the propeller, takes off with a roar and becomes a black moth, whirring above the silhouette of the trees. Soon Beth can no longer hear him. She turns and feels her feet on sure ground. She's reached the far shore of the perilous lake, crossed to the unexplored territory of a new life.

Beth expects that the African night will be singing with creatures but there is not a sound at this pre-dawn hour. She slips on her day pack and holds her shoulder bag in her hand in readiness to take out the guidebook and keep a finger on its map when Jules gives her a lift into the Victoria Falls village.

She starts walking towards the telegraph pole, feeling light on her feet. If Alena and the others could see her now! She's arrived in Zimbabwe. She's not just opened a crack in the walls around her life, she's pushed the walls down. She's going to do what she's come here for. Soon she'll find Shungu; soon she'll find someone who knows Selous. Safari Man! And then? There's no turning back now. She'll decline Jules's lift back to the temporary runway and ask him to get a message to Croc that she's staying in Zimbabwe. Perhaps she'll work in a hospital here and end up a cross between Albert Schweitzer, Mother Theresa and Bono and someone will eventually write a biography about her, finding the surprising secret of her past: her tragic home circumstance which caused her (in her youth) a moment of madness. This incident humanises her – claims her biographer. It shows that even the greatest doctor Africa has ever known had her demons 'but what a different, dull story, dear reader, this would have been if Dame Jenkins had not left her vegetative (sic) husband in the capable and willing hands of his adoring mother in order to dedicate her life to helping sick Africans.' She laughs out loud. It's just the grandiose and self-indulgent fantasising of a liberal Westerner who believes it might be possible to save the world in penance for her own personal failings. On the other hand… on the other hand… now she's said the *great YES,* anything seems achievable.

She keeps walking down the incline although the night thickens as the fingernail clip of moon is nibbled up by a cloud. She passes bushy shapes that line the road. One of the forms to her right, darker and denser than the others, moves. She hears a low crunching sound. She hurries her step, mouth as dry as Ryvita. What can it be at this time of night? Don't panic, don't run. Then she hears an engine start up and the shape resolves itself as a black limousine with tinted glass, its lights off. It rolls slowly, complacently, down the road towards her. She is certain that this is not Croc's friend Jules.

There is nowhere to run and so she stops and waits, her heart close to ventricular fibrillation. The vehicle coasts unhurriedly to a halt beside her. The rear passenger door opens quietly, leisurely, and a gorilla-dimensioned man, in a suit more black than any night, steps out, holds the door open and signals her to get in with his muscular finger. Again, she has no doubt that this is not Jules.

'Thank-you but I'm… waiting for someone else to give me a lift.' Her voice sounds as if she's inhaled helium. 'They'll be along shortly so, no thanks.'

The man winds into action. In two strides he is on her, unceremoniously gripping her around the lower chest with enormous hands and swinging her around and towards the car. Her shoulder bag goes flying. She squirms but the man is strong and she's soon on the back passenger seat and he is in beside her. He slaps her in the stomach. She doubles up, winded, unable to cry out. A hood is passed over her head. She fights for a breath.

The car starts off with the throbbing beat of a large engine. She finds her breath and groans. The man starts to pull her day pack from her shoulders. She does her best to make it difficult for him. 'I'm going to be sick.'

'Shut up!'

She retches.

The car stops abruptly and the driver speaks. 'Get the bitch out, you fool.' His voice is deeply creepy. Beth succumbs to waves of trembling. The man speaks again in his drum-throb voice. 'Let her do her sicking in the grass. Do you think we want the vehicle stinking for weeks?'

Her abductor abandons his attempt to wrench her pack off her, snatches off her hood, leans over her and pushes the door open from inside. She catches a glimpse of the front seat passenger. It's Robson, Mr De Villier's solicitor. She just has time to take in his anxious and apologetic look and to feel her limbs go to jelly and then spade-like hands are under her backside shovelling her out, all priority being given to preserving the velour. She's catapulted through the open door.

They'll be expecting her to fall to her knees 'sicking' but she kindles her limbs; wastes no time. The big fellow will be launching himself out behind her.

She runs.

The ground falls away. She expects to be floored immediately but finds herself doing an uncontrolled gallop down a steep slope before crashing into a forest. Wriggling and worming, she scours herself on sharp branches and furrowed bark. Foliage snares and fingers her in the deepest dark. She hears shouts behind but keeps pressing forward, like an insect scurrying blindly through dense vegetation. That lost-in-the-woods feeling from childhood envelopes her. An animal snorts and blunders away and she knows that whatever her own fears, to everything else she must now be the most terrifying beast in the forest. She scrabbles on until she notices a lighter area ahead. The trees thin and she finds she can run full tilt again. She trips and pitches forward to land full-frontal into water.

She'd thought that there's a reflex that makes you hold your breath when your head goes under water. It doesn't work for her: she screams. It comes out in a massive underwater gurgle like a torpedoed submarine, announcing herself, she's sure, to every crocodile for three miles up the Zambezi: 'Early breakfast'. She takes in a mouthful of Zambezi water. Stop panicking! Think! How she wishes she'd listened harder to Croc – how easy is it to find that epiglottal flap? And if she escapes those snapping jaws, she'll be swept down the abyssal drop of the Falls and, it still being night, she'll not even see the view. Why does she have ironic thoughts at moments of terror? *It seems a pity*. She surfaces in reeds with a whooping inhalation. Her thrashing about, she realises perhaps too late, is acting like a homing signal. She goes flaccid and scans around her. She has to find the bank fast.

The moon – out again like a forgiving guardian angel – illuminates her surroundings. Wherever she looks there is riverbank. The truth comes happily to mind: she is not in the treacherous Zambezi but in a small pond. She bends her knees and easily touches the muddy bottom with her knees. The water is less than three feet deep. She stands up, dripping slime like an emerging swamp creature, and finds that the pond is in an extensive lawn. It doesn't take her long to figure out she is on a golf course: bunkers and greens are visible down the fairway. In the trees nearby she hears grunts and urgent, bad-tempered voices. She slips herself down into the water again amongst the reeds. The voices soon fade to be replaced by the shuddering croak, right in her ear, of a king-size toad.

Her relief at not being discovered, and not being snatched by a flat dog in the Zambezi, soon gives way to other fears. She tries to recall what tropical diseases other than malaria (she has remembered to bring her antimalarials) can be caught from miasmic swamps set about with fever trees. She recalls musty books in the medical school library displaying names like dengue and chikungunya fever, infections too foreign to England's pleasant land to bother learning about. But she keeps herself half-submerged. It's safer to stay put for a little longer rather than risk blundering about.

Lying in a twisted position, supporting herself awkwardly with her hands and knees in the slippery mud, she forces herself to do some serious thinking on how a locum GP, with considerably more material comfort than most, not to mention a half-respectable role in an affluent society, could somehow arrive at such an appalling state of affairs: in a swampy pond in Africa with strands of rotting reeds tangled in her hair, pond-gloop down her cleavage, and with sinister officials scouring the night for her. She's been flying on her skates over ice and ignoring, not even hearing, the warning shouts from the shore. The *great Yes* has become the *big doh*. How is she going to explain all this to level-headed Alena?

Thinking of sitting in Tres Hermanas with Alena, Christina and Preeti makes her eyes go hot with self-pity. She wipes a soggy leaf from her lips and tastes mud. She tries to think straight. She has to reverse every impetuous decision she's made, step herself back to sanity: first return across the border, then reach the hotel and sit quietly in her hotel reading until her flight is due, then ingratiate herself to her mother-in-law, and finally ring Hector to say that she'd been too hasty in rejecting his very generous – no, humbling – offer of a partnership. The first step looks impossible. Should she try to swim the reptile-patrolled Zambezi? Unthinkable. Perhaps she should present herself to someone in uniform and ask to see the British Consul, demand to be treated under the Human Rights Act. But she doubts her pursuers will care much for procedure. The country is not run by the matron of Twicare. Hope's sinister 'boyfriend' is looking for her. She thinks it possible that his is the deep voice she'd heard in the car. He's closing in on the title deed. The title deed! It'll be soaked – destroyed along with Mr De Villier's letter to his son.

She extracts herself from the sucking mud, crawls up the bank and, kneeling on the grass, struggles off her day pack and opens it. Her mobile phone has drowned but the plastic folder in which she has placed the deed, letter and photo of the massacre site has kept their contents from a deep immersion. She lays each piece of paper out on the bank to dry off. She extracts her passport and money from the travel wallet around her waist and shakes and squeezes out the water. She considers submerging the cursed De Villier papers in the pond. But they've survived all that has happened so far, so perhaps they deserve better. Then she knows she should hang on to them in case she needs to exchange them for her life.

Baggage a little drier, she makes her squelchy, dripping way towards lights at the other end of the golf course, making little effort to keep to the shadows, succumbing to the easy option of letting things happen to her. She finds herself at the back of a hotel that opens out onto the green. Behind a low fence she sees a swimming pool with underwater lights. She rubs away mud from her eyelashes. Never has water looked so crystalline, so blue-rinse pure. There's no-one about. She has difficulty taking off her sandals; the water-logged leather has expanded. She lowers herself silently into the pool and wriggles out of her clothes, her cardigan now looking like it's been keeping a deformed rhino warm for a week. They sink, de-toxifying. She swims underwater to the other end of the pool, finds the in-pipe and scrubs her scalp in its powerful flow, rinsing away the muck and slime. The water is warm and it's easy to luxuriate in its caress. She'd like to stay there for hours but sees a light come on in one of the hotel's windows. Stars are disappearing as dawn approaches.

She fishes for her clothes, climbs out, redresses quickly, wrestling back into her wet jeans, but carries her water-heavy cardigan. She gives her sandals a rinse, feeling guilty at the grit and pond-flora clouding the water. The first guest in that day will think a hippo had blundered into the water in the night. Her list of crimes is lengthening. She goes to drip-dry by the trees that line the golf course. The light is returning. She has a moment of delicious hope: there will be boats by the river. She can borrow one and slip across. Where is the river? She regrets not hanging on harder to her shoulder bag which contained her guidebook and tries to recall the detail of the hotel brochure map although it had been drawn for the entertainment of guests rather than for aviators dropped behind enemy lines. She has a vague notion that Zimbabwe is south of Zambia; the sun rises in the east so she should keep it to her right to go north – or did the sun rise in the west south of the equator? She assumes not and walks along the edge of the golf course keeping the rising light to her right. Dry leaves crunch under her feet like empty snail shells and soon a burning sun bursts over the trees. She's drying out fast.

The trees became taller, denser and greener as she walks which she takes as a sign that she is nearing water. Sure enough she finds herself on the banks of the Zambezi; only a few watery yards from safety. At this dawn hour there's not a whisper of wind and a light mist swathes the trees across the river. It seems that a strip has been peeled off the pinky-blue sky and pasted out between the banks. Only the mother-of-pearl eddies around the stands of rushes that form small islands in the river give a hint of the water's deep flow beneath its radiant surface. The Zambian bank looks tantalisingly close as if she's found the river at its narrowest point. She thinks the scene simply too beautiful for there to be any danger. The bank where she stands is steep and so she moves a few yards further down. Perhaps she can swim after all. It will only take a few seconds. But from the new angle she discovers that what she thought was the Zambian bank is an island and on a sandy spit is a crocodile the length of a Canadian canoe, its yellow teeth spoiling its nonchalant, if not friendly, grin. She hears herself whimper. For a moment she fears she's about to lose that animal energy, that adrenaline-driven flight to safety that has propelled her this far.

A boat. All she has to do is find a boat. She returns to the higher bank and, gripping a tree, leans out as far as she dares to look up and down the river. Downriver she can see the spray of the Falls hanging like a no-smoke-without-fire warning in the morning light. Upriver there is no clinker-built rowing boat nestling on the bank with rowlocks and oars in place, a rope over a bough in readiness to be cast off, but there is a river-cruiser tied to a jetty. It's named *Cirrhosis of the River* and has benches on its canvas-canopied upper deck. A man is pouring buckets of water over the deck and then setting to with a mop.

She might be safer on board the boat. The security services will hardly expect the escapee to be taking a sightseeing river cruise. She must find someone to confide in. She rehearses what she might say to the boat's captain: 'Pardon me, I'm a doctor who should be about to start a morning surgery in England but I've got myself into a bit of difficulty. Please help me – please!' She sees herself sobbing uncontrollably.

A deckhand appears, loading crates of bottled drinks. Beth feels as thirsty as an undiagnosed diabetic and reaches in her bag for her water but finds the plastic bottle has ruptured in her headlong flight. She waits and watches until a barrel-bodied, sun-browned man, in his late forties she guesses, saunters to the rope across the gangplank up to the boat. He's wearing a white floppy bucket hat, a short-sleeved, chequered, blue cotton shirt and khaki shorts which are far too short. His ankles disappear, sockless, into dusty brushed-suede shoes. A tourist, she assumes, because he is white, although his outfit is not from any country she knows.

She has now dried out although her hair feels as if she's had an accident in one of Twicare's hood dryers. She's normally frizz-free even on high-humidity days. She approaches the jetty, trying to look as if she's just come from a breakfast of pink grapefruit, streaky bacon, eggs Benedict and morning pastries. The man turns and glances at her, surprised, she guesses, to see a fellow holidaymaker this side of the river.

'Hello, my name's Beth.'

'Uzzit, man? I'm Richard Douglas. Call me Dick.' His accent is South African although softer to the degree that Canadian American is to US American. She becomes hopeful that it indicates that he lives in Zimbabwe and is not a tourist. Surely he will tell her what she should do.

'I'm really sorry about this but I've no Zimbabwe dollars on me. Would you mind buying me a ticket and I'll pay you back later. I do have US dollars.'

He looks at her knowingly. 'I'm guessing you lost your Zim dollars in the swimming pool – I saw you from my hotel window before sunrise.' Beth feels her cheeks blush but he goes on, 'Look, there aren't many medicines left in this country but if you tell me what you need, I'll ask around.'

'Medicines?'

'I'll take you to a clinic. These border pharmacies can get anything.'

He's pretty astute: woman drops into pool before daybreak fully clothed, strips, washes her clothes, gets out naked, dresses herself back into her wet gear, disappears into the woods and reappears at the back of an early morning booze-cruise queue without any money. Quite mad. She offers him a blank, innocent, look.

'I don't know what your game is, man,' he says, 'but I could do with some company, so I'll treat you.'

He orders two shandys and an extra ticket from the Captain, paying for them with a brick-sized wad of notes. They sit opposite each other on benches with a table between – the other seating on board remains empty. Overwhelmed with thirst Beth drains the shandy in four long sucks. Dick lifts one end of his lip disapprovingly as she sets down the empty glass on the table. She would hardly call herself a ladette but he must be wondering. A mad bad ladette.

'Are you from here?' she asks, delicately dabbing her lips with the paper serviette that came with the shandy to restore a little etiquette.

'Born and bred in this country. Hanging on now by my fingerprints like everyone else who lives here. You're not from around here are you?'

'No, I'm very much not from around here. I… '

'Lucky you. I should have gapped it at Independence in 1980.'

'To be honest I'm in a bit of trouble… '

'Look at it this way: you're not alone. Every man, woman and child in this country is in the deep dambo.'

'The situation is that the Zimbabwe police are looking for me.'

Dick looks unimpressed. 'You're a foreign national; you've got nothing to get your broekies in a twist about. Not like me, all I've got is my Zim passport which entitles me to nothing but abuse.'

She feels desperation rise. 'Dick, I don't want to belittle your situation, but I entered the country illegally. I have to get back to Zambia. The CIO is after me.'

'The CIO?'

'Please believe me, Dick.'

His eyebrows arrow up like warning triangles. 'Are you sure? Charlie Ten are after you? Sheeet! You *are* in trouble, beeeg trouble.' Beth hopes he'll add, *But I'll see what I can do*, but instead he sucks on his teeth and says, 'You'll be picked up in no time after we get back to the jetty. The CIO is the only functioning organisation left in the country. Sheeeeet!' He scans the river bank with jittery eyes.

She stays silent, trying to reconcile herself again to her fate. The crew cast off and they chug out into the river, belching

157

smoke to pollute the otherwise pristine scene. They pass the island Beth had seen from the bank and she sees the crocodile slide effortlessly and silently under the water. 'Big one. Looks hungry, too,' Dick says, momentarily distracted from his gloomy prognosis on her situation.

A clicking sound comes from the speaker that's bolted to the frame of the awning followed by a watery noise like a digital radio trying to pick up a signal. Then it dies in what seems a terminal pop.

'Their commentary's not going to work, the PA system's *vrot*,' says Dick, 'No worries, I can do it.' He clears his throat, makes his fist into a cone, puts it to his lips and announces, 'The Zambezi is nearly four thousand kilometres long and runs through six countries but is only spanned by five bridges. The River Thames, a tenth of the length, has about two hundred bridges. Stop me if I'm boring you. This stretch above the Falls is where the Imperial Airways flying boat service stopped off on its way from Southampton to Cape Town. They called it Jungle Junction and—'

'Dick, sorry to interrupt but what am I to do?'

He lowers his cone. 'No point in jumping for it.' He points towards the Zambian bank. 'Too many snappers and crushers. You'd enter the food chain.' He clicks his tongue and shakes his head. 'You're in the isitshwala.'

'What?'

'Definitely in the rioolput.'

She's becoming convinced that she's going to have to engineer her own ideas. 'I… I know someone who might be able to help me.'

'Look, I would like to be able to help you but it's just… '

'There's a man I… kind of know, called Selous. Unfortunately, I don't know where he is right now.'

'Selous?'

She nods.

'There's only one Selous: Selous De Villier. It's a big country but there aren't many of us white guys left. I know of him.' Hope rises in Beth like a sunrise. 'No!' He shakes his head emphatically and squares his lower lip. 'Not a chance. Selous wouldn't want to see you. He hates company. He's the lowest profile oke in the world. Has to be, they say. In fact no one really knows Selous – and I'm sure he wants to keep it that way.'

Selous's introversion doesn't bother Beth at all. 'OK, I understand, but do you know where he is?'

'You could say I do,' he says.

'Oh, good!' Problem over! Surely Selous will find a way to smuggle her out of the country. She's imagined him as a bush-wise helpful guy and it's going to take good evidence to make her change her mind. Dick has to be mistaken. 'How would I get there then?'

Dick thinks for a long time. 'In different circumstances I'd take you to him in my bakkie, but – he'd kill me.' He looks at her with that no-hope expression again.

'What? Selous would actually murder you?'

'Yes, he doesn't like any company and what company he does keep is bad company – they say. I've heard he even has links to the CIO. Gets upset by uninvited guests. Goes berserk. He's supposed to be a good shot too.' He looks away from Beth down the river as if there is no more to be said or done but adds, as if to make sure there are no grounds for her misunderstanding him, 'Shame, real shame. Life's a bummer, huh?'

She refuses to believe that Selous will not see her. She's carrying his father's letter and the title deed to his land. 'Well, that's my last hope gone then.' She stands up. 'I'm going to have

to swim for it.' She starts to move along the rail. The other bank
– or is it an island? – is about two swimming pool lengths away
but there are hippos blowing like a pod of Moby Dicks between
the boat and the bank.

Dick leaps up after her. 'That would be very stupid, man,'
he hisses, and tentatively pinches the sleeve of her top. She moves
away and says, 'So what? I've been in a dumb mood for a long
time.'

She reaches a gap in the rail where a thin rope has been
strung across. She starts to undo the knot. She's embarrassing
herself at her highly manipulative behaviour but she is in the –
what is Dick's expression? – deep dambo. Anyway, she'll wake up
soon and go and prepare Matt's breakfast. Since his stroke, he
likes Coco Pops. She might even try to make up with Bruno by
giving him a rasher of bacon – at the end of a long fork.

Dick grips the knot. 'Jeez! You're crazy! You do need
medication.' She makes to move to the next gap in the rail and
Dick holds his hands up. 'Look, I can make a plan. Let me see.'
He blows out through puckered lips. Then he rubs his heavy
chin. Then he nods. 'I'll give you a lift. You can come with me.'

She nearly lets herself fall into his arms.

'It's a five hour drive. I'll have to conceal you. Sheesh, it's
bloody risky. We'll just have to hope Selous's not in a hot mood.'

CHAPTER 14

There are no secret policemen waiting on the jetty when they return. Dick tells Beth to stand off to the side amongst the trees while he drives back to his hotel to pack and check out. He'll be about an hour. While she waits for the sound of his return, she finds a branch to sit on, hidden from the road and overlooking the river. She thinks about what Dick has told her about Selous. What if he is right? What if Selous is mad? A psychotic who's not on medication because there's none in the pharmacies. What an irony: both she and Safari Man are insane.

Time passes, minute by pregnant minute. After two hours she's convinced herself that Dick is not coming back. Why should he? He's already a tour ticket and two Zambezi shandys out of pocket. But just as she's re-examining the swimming option, he returns.

'The police are everywhere,' he says, breathless and flushed. 'My bakkie was taken apart. We'll go back the same way and hope they won't bother to search it again. But look, we must be quick. They'll soon find out you were on the boat and shortly after that they'll find out that I was with you. We'll both be wanted men.'

He taps the lid of a large metal box behind the front seat of his vehicle. 'I'm going to have to put you in here with the puff adders.'

Beth shrinks back. He lifts the heavy lid. 'It's OK, that's just the name for the fat worms I use for fishing.' He takes out a brace of fishing gear, including nets and a lidded plastic container marked *puff adders*. 'Please climb in.'

She's hit by a stench of motor oil and fish, or is it oily fish? 'Look, you've been incredibly kind but I think I should give myself up. I couldn't live with myself if I got you into trouble.'

He snorts. 'Trouble? Don't fret; we're all in trouble. Everyone in this bleeding country's in trouble. What's a little more? Everyone has to help each other.' He moves the sacking on the floor of the box and points out a drain hole in the corner. 'That's your air-hole. Tap the side if you've got something life or death to say, otherwise keep stum. I'll let you out when it's safe. Quick now.'

She has to lie in a foetal position to fit and uses her still damp cardigan as a pillow. He drapes the nets over her and then she feels the tackle, the rods, her day pack and the box of worms dumped on top. He tells her he'll have to close the lid until they get out of town. It becomes as dark as the inside of a crocodile. The stench is overwhelming. There's no end to the humiliation, the degradation.

They bump down the untarred road. Beth is sure she can't last long. Then the vehicle draws to a stop.

'So you are back this way again, sir.'

'Yes, I've found my hat,' Dick says.

'God is gracious.'

'Where's your boss?'

'He's over there, relieving his bladder.'

'Tell me then. What's going on? I've never seen so many policemen.'

'Do you have cigarettes?'

'Sure. Let me see... here.'

'Thank-you, sir.' Beth hears Dick light the policeman's cigarette. 'We're looking for a fugitive. She's a white woman. She entered the country illegally on a sabotage mission.'

'Sabotage?' Dick says.

'Yes, she's on an assignment to wreck the economy.'

There is a pregnant pause and then they both laugh.

'What I wish to know,' says the policeman, 'is why anyone wants to take the risk to enter the country illegally when everyone else is trying to get out by whatever means.' They both laugh again.

'Hmm, how would I recognise her?' Dick says.

The policeman coughs as if to restore gravitas and says, 'They say that she's quite short, thin, and has dark hair. They say that she's very clever and very crazy.'

'Is she dangerous?' Dick says. 'Is she carrying weapons? A rocket launcher? Surface-to-air missiles?'

Beth is worried that Dick has overstepped the mark but the policeman chuckles again and then says quietly. 'If so, then I hope she's on her way to the President's residence.' Beth hears another vehicle draw up behind them. 'You may go. Have a good day, sir.'

'Bye,' Dick says. '*Sala kuhle.*'

They move off again and are soon on a smoother road, so that instead of being in pain Beth is merely uncomfortable. They've been going for about fifteen minutes and she is about to push up the lid to breathe fresher air when Dick says, 'There's another road block.'

The policeman here is less congenial, ordering Dick to turn off the engine.

'What's going on?' Dick says.

'I'm going to search your vehicle. Open the door.'

'By the way,' Dick says, 'I saw a white woman crossing the road, going west, about three miles back from here next to that big baobab. I don't know what she was doing out here in the bush. I hope she's all right. I should have stopped.'

'What did she look like?' orders the policeman.

'She was quite short, slim, and had dark hair.'

'Not fat and with black hair? Are you sure?' says the policeman.

'Yes, and I don't like to be judgmental but I thought she had a look about her which made me think that maybe… maybe she was not quite right in the mind… a bit crazy. I really should have asked her if she was OK.'

The policeman shouts to his colleagues. Beth hears him run off and then hears slamming doors and engines revving and then vehicles heading back up the road in a cacophony of crashing gears.

Dick sets off again at a leisurely pace, whistling to himself. Then he says, 'Yes, I'd definitely say she was crazy. No wonder I didn't stop.'

Dick will not allow Beth out of the box but he wedges the lid open to save her from suffocation. She closes her eyes and just has time to think that she's failed to find Shungu and is unlikely to be able to return to Victoria Falls to look for her when exhaustion overcomes her.

When she wakes she's desperate to change position and tries to wriggle over. The tackle on top of her shifts and she has a bad premonition. She lies very still. A trickle of cold water runs down her neck and then she feels something squirming on her cheek. She tries to move her hand to wipe away the worm but her fingers are trapped in the net. The whole writhing gloop lands on her face. The worms thrash and buck as if each one is being pinched by the tail. She cries out.

She hears Dick say, 'For Pete's sake, be quiet. We've reached Bulawayo. Just take it easy and we'll be there soon.'

When she has to snort to stop a worm entering her nostril, she can bear it no longer and pushes up the lid. She sits up, disentangles herself from the net and picks off the worms, gagging as she does so.

'Sorry Dick,' she says, faint and nauseated. 'I've spilled your puff adders.'

'Agh, shame man! Not all of them, surely?'

'I'm really sorry.'

'Look, never mind, my fishing trip's over anyway.'

'I can't stay inside the box anymore, Dick. I'm a mess.'

'It's OK now, there's no one about and we're nearly there. Had a good zizz, hey?'

'Yes, I suppose I did.' She clambers – all elbows and knees – out of the box, her limbs stiff and hip tender. 'I'm in a mess, Dick. I stink of fish and oil and my hair's soaked in worm slime. Can we stop so I can sort myself out? I can't meet Selous like this.'

'Ugh, look man, it's too late to go to Selous's place today. He's way out of town. You can stay at my place tonight, get yourself all dolled up, and I'll take you tomorrow.'

Beth feels better, being in bright light again. They are travelling down a wide residential street lined with magnificent purple-blossomed trees – jacarandas, she learns later – whose petals carpet the road. The afternoon sun casts a warm blush. White bougainvillea spill over the walls of the properties to hint at luxuriant gardens under the iris-blue sky. She temporarily forgets her dishevelled state. She's emerged from her box to find herself in a privileged world. Bulawayo seems a town of millionaires.

Then she catches a glimpse through a chain mesh gate of what lies behind the high walls. The property, a substantial bungalow, is surrounded by dry stands of maize like a house on a prairie. Long-legged chickens scratch in the dust-blown drive that leads to the cement front steps. In the next property a cow is trying to drink from the green water in the swimming pool, its front legs down on the first step.

'Did you see that, Dick? There was a cow in there! The gardens are like little farms.'

'It's subsistence farming in the city now,' Dick says. 'Every patch of land is an opportunity to grow food – particularly for the blacks that have moved into the suburbs. Maybe it'll be like that in every part of the world one day. The supermarket shelves are empty. The kids in government introduced price controls a few months back to try to crush the soaring inflation – but of course all it's done is bankrupt the retailers.'

Beth looks at the street with a new eye. Tufts of severed wires – like the clumped legs of dead spiders – sprout from the white insulators of the telegraph poles, the bellies of the glass in the lamp-posts are broken and the fittings hang out like guts, the culverts are collapsing and the grass verges grow untended. A pool of what might be sewage lies in a ditch. They pass a metal gate, heavy enough for an ambassador's residence, but a cardboard placard planted next to it says in finger-painted lettering:

Flornt with Stile. Hair cuts.

Natural weeve, Deva, Fingercuts, Selebrity

They turn into Dick's house. There is no fence at the front of his property although spiky cacti mark the boundary. 'My mother hates to be walled in,' Dick says when Beth comments. She thinks she might be a woman after her own heart. 'We've been burgled three times but there's really not much else to steal now and we don't bother to ring the police anymore because they tell us that they'll only come out to investigate if we can come and collect them. They've no fuel for their vehicles.'

Dick's house has a thatched roof which extends down to the ground. There are deep cut-outs for the windows and front door. He unlocks the yellowwood door and they enter a large open-plan living area with the thatch high above them. They cross a polished black-stone floor towards French doors that open on to a wide red-brick veranda. Apart from the plainness of its furnishings – solid dark-wood armchairs with square, beet-red cushions, a couple of large leather pouffes – it's like being in a safari lodge.

'Come out on the stoep and meet my mother,' Dick says. 'It's four o'clock sharp so she'll be having tea.'

Beth asks for the bathroom first to clean herself up and comb the worms out of her hair. Dick doesn't seem to notice that she's looking like a survivor from a worst-animal-nightmare experience.

'Why of course. But just one thing: there's no reliable piped water anymore. We've got a borehole but the water table's low so leave the water in the bath. We use it in the garden.' Then he says happily, 'Us Zimbabweans, we always make a plan, no matter what happens.'

Through the partially open bathroom window Beth can see two women, each approaching eighty she guesses, both as sun-ripened as Mr De Villier. One has hair as fluffy and white as cotton bolls and the other has thin, grey strands covering her small head and hollow temples. They are sitting in the shade at a table on the veranda, near to her window. The thatch has been cut high this side of the house but a fig tree abuts the veranda, forming a thick green canopy, a balm to the eyes from the still achingly-bright garden beyond. A maid sporting a bright red woolly hat (as if it's minus five degrees), a baggy green cardigan, and a tired blue dress, is pouring hot water from a flask into a teapot. The tea service is bone china but few of the pieces match and the flower prints on the lace-edged tablecloth are faded. The handle of a silver spoon curls from a chipped Denby sugar bowl. White paint flakes off the rusting table legs. The scene looks like the last gasp of colonial living.

'Thank-you, Nombeko, you can go off duty now,' says the woman with the fluffy white hair, whom Beth takes to be Dick's mother.

'Good afternoon, Madam,' Nombeko says, and softly claps her hands before padding off in dust-stained plimsolls, treading lightly along the fringes of her employers' lives.

'Deidre, I meant to say your succulents are just splendid,' says the other woman. Her voice is weak and her knitted shawl can't hide a frame that gives a nod towards emaciation. Her cup shakes and clinks in her hand as she lifts it from the saucer to bring it to her lips. Senile ecchymoses blotch her forearms.

'Thank-you, Judith. I do try,' Deidre says. 'They really are the only plants that will make a garden look like a garden since we stopped having rain.'

'Oh, rain!' Judith says. 'How long is it since we had rain? I think we haven't had rain since… since we became Zimbabwe. Not proper drenching rains. Ah, those sweet rains.' She draws in a sighing breath and Beth sees that her lips are dry and fissured. 'And those sweet, sweet days. Do you remember, Deidre?'

'Of course,' Deidre says, softly.

Judith's eyes are sunk far back in their sockets but light flickers there like a distant star. 'Remember those concerts in City Hall? All the women in their summer dresses, the men in their best, come off the farms or from surveying the railways or building the dams. We were building a modern nation. All we wanted was to live in a civilised country. And remember those picnics by Hillside Dams, and shopping in Haddon and Sly, and coffee and cake in the City Gallery, and ice cream at Eskimo Hut.'

Deidre looks up sharply. 'Quite unlike you to reminisce, Judith, you're always telling me off for saying *when we this* and *when we that.* But now you've given me the excuse, I'll take it. Yes, those lovely Rhodesian days. And we thought they'd go on forever.'

'A thousand years!' says Judith. 'That's what Smithy promised.'

They are silent for a while.

'Do have another peanut biscuit,' Deidre offers.

'Oh can I?' Judith reaches for it with an urgent hand and puts it whole in her mouth. She places her fingers to hide her lips while she chews and then helps it down with sips of tea.

'Have another, Judith,' Dick's mother says. 'They're there for eating.'

'I think I will. So delicious. Where did you find flour?'

'Dick's always on the look-out.' She leans forward. 'Are you getting enough to eat, Judith?'

'I manage. Do you remember my maid, Thando? She visited me yesterday and gave me an egg.'

'An egg? Is that all you had all day?'

Judith hangs her head, takes a tissue from her lap and holds it with a trembling hand on her lips. 'All week, Deidre, all week.' She closes her eyes.

'Oh Judith,' Dick's mother says. 'I hadn't realised. You're starving. You should've told me.'

Beth sees Judith dab the corner of her eye. 'Blacks and whites, we're all poor together now,' she says. 'I suppose we all deserve it. Every one of us.'

'I'm so sorry. I should've realised, should've noticed. You're terribly, terribly thin.'

'You're so lucky having a good son like Dick,' Judith says. 'How I wish more than ever that George and I had had children. They would've looked after me, sent me something to live on. George put all our savings into the pension. At Independence I remember George running through to me in the kitchen, excited, to say that he'd just been listening to the news and no one was to be deprived of their pension rights. But now the pension won't buy an egg. At night I dream of boerewors and bobotie, of melktert and orange mousse. The blacks know best: your child's your pension, and the more you have, the richer you are. Who else is there to look after you between Cape Town and Cairo but your own kin?'

'Please, Judith, don't upset yourself,' says Deidre.

'We tried to be Edinburgh-on-Limpopo. Look at the names of our suburbs: Glencoe, Glengarry, Burnside. All we wanted were pensions and lights and drains and running water. I'm glad George is gone, Deidre. He would've died of shame.'

Deidre reaches her hand across and rests it on Judith's stick-like wrist. 'I wonder – why don't you move in with us? Come and stay with Dick and me. The spare room's quite comfortable and you can bring your things, make it your own.'

'That's kind, but no I couldn't, Deidre. You see I said to George I'd never leave the house he built me and I'll not break my word. It's all I've got left now, that promise I made. It's because people don't keep their promises that we're in the state we're in. Prime Minister Smithy and President Bob, they never stuck to their promises.'

Beth pulls herself away from the window. She bathes in a centimetre of water and rinses her hair sparingly with the cup on the bathroom shelf. Her own hunger pangs seem self-indulgent.

Dick and his mother invite Judith to join them for a 'braai' on the stoep that evening. Dick stokes up a cooking heat in the brick barbecue on the edge of the stoep. Whatever the state of the supermarket shelves, Dick has sourced plenty of meat and beer. Deidre makes a potato and bean salad and, although Judith only manages a small strip of steak, she sits and eats the salad whilst she talks quietly with Deidre.

Dick, waving a lager in one hand and braai utensils in the other, talks loudly at Beth. 'You always think things can't get any worse. That we've reached the bed rock. Then the politicians start digging again and it does get worse.' He snakes a long boerewors sausage onto the grill. It uncoils in the heat. 'Really, they should kill this before they sell it.' He sprays water from a bottle over the too hot charcoal. 'Where will we be in five years? In the bloody ground, I think. Dead of medieval diseases like cholera and sleeping sickness.' He turns the chicken legs. 'The next election's already decided.' He reaches for another can, pops its tag and sprinkles beer on the meat. 'Always will be while the big chief's alive.'

'Why've you stayed here, Dick?' Beth says, as Dick pauses to wipe the sweat off his brow. 'Why don't you emigrate?'

'I was born here, man. I've got a Zim passport and I can't stop thinking of myself as indigenous, although I'm told by the ruling Party that I'm not. Unfortunately, my skin colour shouts the colonial and settler past. We're all tarred now with the same white brush, if that's the way to put it. But how would I fit in if I left to go to a foreign country? I'm non-indigenous everywhere. How could I wear my vellies in London?' He points to his stained and battered bush shoes. He has a point, Beth thinks. He is also still in his too short shorts. 'And anyway, the fishing's bloody good here.'

He splashes a juicy steak onto the grill. 'I survive.' He wipes his forehead again with the back of his hand. 'I've got mining interests: gold, tantalum, chromite, lithium. I'm getting out what I can, while I can. I should've been in platinum but that needs complex processing and capital investment.' He flips the steak which sizzles and drips. 'And I've branched into black granite. Fetches six hundred US a square metre for a polished slice.'

Beth nods, trying to show interest.

'But, that's nothing. Over the other side of the country they've found a massive diamond field – second biggest in the world, I'm told. The army have taken that over on behalf of certain members of the ruling Party. In Harare they're building themselves huge concrete palaces in the grotesque style. And the diamonds will provide them with the weapons to keep them in power forever.'

When they turn in for the night, Dick finds an unused toothbrush for Beth and she finds a large T-shirt in a drawer to wear as a nightie. As she climbs into bed and blows out the candle on the bed table, the room light comes on. A power cut has ended. She climbs out of bed again to turn off the light switch and notices that the bookshelf is bursting with thrillers. She sees De Gaulle's unmistakeably Gallic silhouette on the spine of one and reaches across to pull it out. *The Day of the Jackal.* She reads it in bed, wondering where Fortunate is at that moment.

She tries to put herself in Fortunate's place and imagines him studying the text to pick up tips on carrying out an assassination, learning how to model himself on the assassin named the Jackal. She thinks that Fortunate will have been far more diligent in his attention to detail than her but she is soon engrossed. The Jackal, she discovers, is a tall blond Englishman whose emotions are shuttered behind cold blue eyes. She hopes that Fortunate will have immediately seen the difference and stopped right there. However when she reads the line delivered by a member of the shadowy group of ex-servicemen seeking De Gaulle's demise – *There is no man in the world who is proof against an assassin's bullet* – she fears that Fortunate might, at that point, have been encouraged to read on, to give it a go.

On the other hand, as Fortunate turned the pages he'd have seen that the assassin's task involved meticulous and fiendishly complicated preparations. He'd have to get his hands on the President's schedule and then stake out the site of the assassination attempt in order to work out such intricacies as angles of fire, the sun's position at the chosen moment, the likely whereabouts of the President's security men, and the escape route. If he followed the Jackal's example, he'd have to find an expert gunsmith to make the weapon and then practise firing it at a target to ensure the sights were not off-centre. The Jackal had practised in a forest, aiming at a melon that he suspended from a tree in a string bag. Fortunate might also need forged papers and have to change his appearance. He'd have to ruthlessly eliminate anyone who got in his way. Beth hopes that by the time Fortunate had reached page one hundred, he'd have concluded that Shungu was just asking too much. When she's finished – a speed read – it's very late and she lies back aware that her speculation on Fortunate's intentions is laughable as well as insulting. He might be love-sick but he's no fool.

CHAPTER 15

Despite the risk of running into the CIO, they drive into central Bulawayo first thing the next morning so that Beth can buy spare clothes and toiletries. Dick's mother might have found something retro for Beth in a drawer but Beth has not confessed to her that she has no luggage, to avoid having to divulge to her that she's an illegal immigrant. Beth has a vague notion that the less Deidre knows the better, in case the CIO raid and think Deidre complicit. This fugitive life is complicated and restricting.

The wide streets of Bulawayo seem built for the droving of great herds of cattle to market and for grand processions in a country where land, at the city's founding, must have looked boundless. It has an air of resigned contentment, comfortable with its mix of red-tiled, settler-era buildings and recessed storefronts with their shaded walkways. The traffic lights are broken and a few aging cars edge across the junctions, mingling with pedestrians who stroll languidly in the sun.

They park on the slope of a huge storm drain on a back street and Beth follows Dick to a shop called *Bulawayo Boutique*. It has a 'Closed Until Further Notice' sign in the window. Dick knocks on a side door and it opens a crack before the proprietor, a woman in a '50s floral dress, lets them in. Dick leaves Beth with the woman so that she can look through the shop's selection of tops, skirts, trousers and underwear. She takes some time to decide on a new top and safari-style long shorts, feeling she must be well turned-out to meet Selous. It isn't so much that she feels she needs to impress the man, she tells herself, but that the occasion is auspicious, a consequence of – dare she speculate: even the culmination of – having said the *great Yes*. She pays in US dollars and makes her way back to Dick in the car.

Beth buys toiletries from a pharmacy via another back door and buys flowers for Dick's mother from a vendor on the street, and then they return to Dick's house. She gives Deidre an envelope of US dollars for Judith and then exchanges a few US dollars with Dick for a shoe box of Zimbabwe dollars. He generously transacts at 'next week's likely black-market exchange rate' so that the notes will not be immediately worthless.

'The exchange rate's so unrealistic that you'll be throwing your money away if you go through official channels,' says Dick. 'The official rate's just the regime's way of amassing vast wealth by exchanging Zimbabwe dollars – they print them in greedy haste – for hard currency at an unrealistic exchange rate from the Reserve Bank. The Reserve Bank's the personal bank account of the regime's top brass. They're all acting outside the law so shouldn't expect anyone else to bother with the law either.'

They travel out of Bulawayo, Dick and Beth, along an empty road that crosses a wide and gently undulating landscape whose horizons – alternately receding then advancing with the lie of the road – are softened by a uniform mantle of short sun-fried trees. Wispy clouds melt in the thick blue sky. Dick is pensive and quiet, not in a mood to talk, which is fine by Beth. She's happy to be on the last leg of her journey to find Selous and glad to be able to sit on a seat rather than curled up inside a box. Her hair is glossy and smooth after another wash – she's controlled the frizz – and she's wearing the loose cobalt-blue blouse that she bought in Bulawayo. She allows herself to dabble a moment in shallow thinking: she's all ready to meet Safari Man.

After half an hour the road finds gullies and watercourses. Angular outcrops of rock fracture the skyline and the trees become taller and well-leafed. They take a narrow side road with a strip of tar just wide enough for one vehicle.

Dick's nose shines with sweat and the hairs on his arms are sodden despite the air-conditioning being on chill. She asks if he's all right.

'Just hot,' he says. Then, a little later, 'Sheesh, man. This place! Gives me the creeps.'

'What do you mean?'

'All the people buried here. It's a cemetery. Mzilikazi, Cecil Rhodes, British soldiers, impis, settlers. Been lots of skirmishes and fighting. They say you can still find pools of blood amongst the rocks. And then there are all the ancestors and their shrines. At night they say you can hear voices echoing from rock to rock. It's spooky.'

Beth looks out at the scenery, trying to see what Dick sees, but it all seems benign and pretty. She's nearing her destination and feels confident and at ease. She's sure that the most traumatic stage of her journey is over.

They draw up next to a dirt track but Dick does not turn off the engine. Without looking at her he says, 'It's been a pleasure to meet you, Beth.'

'This is it?'

'Selous lives down there.' He jerks his head to indicate the side road, although his gaze remains fixed ahead as if he's lost the use of his ocular muscles.

The track leads towards a jumble of rocks arising from a tangle of forest. Two crumbling brick pillars about five feet tall stand either side of the entrance to the track. The remains of a metal gate hang from a twisted hinge as if a vehicle has crashed through.

'I just go down… ' Beth says.

'Yes, walk down there until you find his house. I believe it's only a k.'

'You're not sure?'

'Pretty sure, yah.'

'A kilometre?'

'Can't drive you nearer as he might hear the vehicle.'

'So it's safer for me to walk?'

Dick wipes his forehead with the back of his hand. 'That's my opinion.'

'OK.' She puts out her hand to shake his. 'Thank-you so much for all your trouble. I'm sorry to have put you out.'

He winces, although she's meant it sincerely, and gives her hand a quick squeeze. 'Sorry I can't take you further. Here, have my cell, it's an old spare.' He hands her his mobile phone. 'Later this morning I'm going out to the mine and am staying over for three days but if Selous's not in, then come back here, give me a call, and I'll arrange for you to be picked up. My number's in there – although reception's *vrot*.'

'That's kind. No really, I'm so grateful. I'll be in touch, let you know how I got on.' She gives him a confident smile. She doesn't want him to feel bad; he's already gone the second mile for her.

He doesn't smile back. 'Better get going, huh? Soon be dark.'

'Of course. Bye, Dick.' There are at least four hours to sunset.

She steps out, closes the door and waves to him. He glances at her then with apprehensive eyes before grinding into gear and making a noisy, urgent, three point turn.

She waits for the sound of his vehicle to fade and then turns to face the track. Although the place is remote, untamed and wooded – just what she would ordinarily have shunned – the light is so all suffusing that even the shadows are cool and welcoming. She is only a few footsteps from her goal. There are many shameful reasons for leaving home but there is at least one noble aspiration: to deliver Mr De Villier's letter and deed to his son. Against the odds, and despite a few lapses of good judgment on her part, she's close to achieving that one thing. Charlie Ten hasn't found her. She will soon be rid of the deed. Dick is terrified of Selous but she distrusts Dick's judgment. He has a worst-case outlook: sees calamity and pools of blood everywhere. She knows that at least one person had loved Selous: his father. So he can't be all bad. Now that she's put aside the fantasy of a magazine-model man, she guesses him to be a fiery, complicated character, or socially inept, perhaps suffering from Asperger's syndrome. He's simply misunderstood. She remembers the boy in the picture: open faced, relaxed and happy in his world. He has become something of a therapeutic challenge. She fancies she'll try some Talking Therapy.

She sets out resolutely, following the twin sandy ribbons of the track as it wends its way, fringed by sprays of soft grasses through light-limbed trees whose delicate leaves – in colours of chestnut, plum, lemon and every shade of green – dance in the sunlight. If these are not God's favourite colours then he doesn't exist. She finds she's acquired a clarity of vision so that she can see in pin-sharp detail, under the intense indigo-blue sky, every bud, fruit, nut and bower in that bountiful arboretum.

The track soon skirts rocks and becomes overhung by larger trees, whose back-lit leaves are as luminous as stained glass. Birds sing with organ-pipe purity. She crushes small yellow fruit under foot, freeing their citrus incense. She soon feels the caress of the sun on her shoulders again as the track breaks out onto a flat grassy valley that runs straight as a causeway in a parted sea. Colossal blocks of stone, stacked in tight articulation, rim the valley and lichens stream down their faces in colours of rust, brilliant yellow and powder blue, as if an artist has poured down poster paints. Fairy castles of stone. She finds her purposeful pace has slowed to an amble, undone by the splendour, giddy and euphoric. Her fingers trail in the soft sea of grass heads by the edge of the track. She is alone in the woods but unafraid. Her dread of forests and nature-in-the-raw (nature not safely behind the glass of the TV screen, not on her Gorilla Rescue leaflets) has been charmed away. She's happy to trip on, exploring and luxuriating in the carefree sensation that has come over her and that she's not felt since before Matt's stroke. Perhaps Matt walked along here once, had gone hunting for rock art here. She finds herself looking for his footprints in the white dust of the track.

At the end of the valley the track dips into a depression running with clear water under dappled shade. She slips off her sandals and paddles into the cool water. The sandy riverbed cushions the soles of her feet so that she feels light, buoyant. She's leaving the bonds of earth as if back in Croc's 'rocket' but this time she's borne up by nature.

She steps out of the brook and her eye is caught by a dark form ahead. Standing amongst fresh grass is a sable, just like the one on the wall in Matt's office. The sable is motionless and tranquil, black coat glossy and flecked with rainbow colours in the sunlight, its horns arcing long over the golden haze of its mane. She couldn't have been more enchanted if she'd come across an ebony unicorn. Sables must be terribly rare, an endangered species, she thinks, and she is one of the last people to see one. How she's bursting to share with someone what it is to be alive in such a place. One day she'll say to Alena and the others, 'I once saw a sable in those hills,' and they won't believe her. She'll double the direct debit to her animal charities.

As she looks into the well-like depths of the creature's eye, she remembers how, when she'd dreamt of his funeral, Matt's spirit had taken the form of a sable. Now here he is again, strong and free amongst the rocks. The thought makes her tearful, a mix of joy and sadness. She'll forever hold this moment, quietly treasure it. It will stay with her, as sacred and mysterious as the love that she has lost. She feels weightless and finds herself drawn forward as if the sable will lead her deep into an enchanted land.

The sable startles and two things happen simultaneously: a terrifying crack, like a rock splitting asunder, and blood sprays from the sable's nostrils. Its head is thrown back as if its horns are yanked by an invisible hand. A spasm travels like lightning down its flanks and it drops onto its belly as its legs crumple. Its mouth smacks a rock, smearing an epitaph in blood as its head comes to rest. All this she sees with the clarity of vision that place has given her, although her gaze remains on the sable's eye. Where she'd looked into its placid depths, a dark jelly oozes and runs down its cheek like a tear.

She cries out. Her legs give way. She falls to her knees in the shallow water. The world becomes distant; her hearing fades as she's wrenched away from the land of make-believe and knows herself to be returning to the country of men.

Then someone is lifting her, pulling her up strongly, if not roughly, by her arm. 'What the hell are you doing here? You nearly screwed up my client's shot.'

She knows before she looks around that this is Selous, and that Dick has been right to fear him. She can't tear her eyes from the dead sable. Dead Matt.

Rage fires her. She hates this man as deeply as... as she'd loved her husband.

She turns and slaps him.

He takes a step back. 'Steady!' he says. For a moment they glare at each other. The intensity of his look is reminiscent of his father's but while his father's eyes had been a clear blue in which she'd once glimpsed far-sightedness, Selous's dark eyes are unreadable.

'You're trespassing,' he says as he picks up her sandals and takes her by the arm again to march her away from the stream. She doesn't resist because she wants to get away, wants to escape this place of killing. She stumbles in front of Selous, getting flashbacks to the murder of the sable, seeing how all magic, all dreams, are an illusion. She hears and feels again the slap of the bullet and the slump of the sable's body. She sees Matt falling when he had his stroke. That comment on the student's website: *He fell like a cedar.*

She's pushed down a path which winds its way through trees until they come to another track. There is a topless four-wheel drive parked in the middle of the road, its doors missing, its grey paint blanched and scratched.

Selous throws her sandals in the vehicle. 'Jump in there and stay there.'

'You don't have to point your gun at me,' she says, but he has turned and is gone.

She stands by the vehicle, thinking she should find her way back to the road, and then she remembers that she has Dick's mobile. She fumbles it on. No signal. Reception is *vrot*.

Selous returns within a couple of minutes and, without a glance at her, says, 'We're going.' He vaults up behind the wheel and she pulls herself up into the passenger seat. He fires the engine and they are off before she has time to sit herself down. She falls hard against the back of the thin seat, bruising herself on its frame.

'You're bloody discourteous,' she says as she straightens up and presses the small of her back. She scowls at him but he takes no notice. With some reluctance she admits to herself that, in one respect, the daydream she had about him in Twicare was correct. He is Safari Man. He's got it all: the khaki kit, the bronzed outdoorsy physique, the leather-banded suede hat that shades his keen eyes, the well-forged jaw that looks right for pressing to the stock of a rifle. But he cuts no ice with her – he's merely a poster boy for savagery.

She has to grip the seat edge to prevent herself from being thrown clear out of the vehicle as they swing at speed down the road. They arrive at another broken gate. Beth's eyes are drawn to a wooden board nailed to the trunk of a large tree whose python-sized branches reach for them over the road. On the board, in crudely painted black lettering, is written:

KEEP OUT. WAR VETS.

War Vets: veterans of the liberation war which had ended twenty-seven years before, now spearheading the violent invasion of white-owned farms. She might have laughed at this, as if the sign reads KEEP OUT. SUPERANNUATED SOLDIERS, had Dick not disabused her the previous evening: 'Chancers and youth militias. Weren't even born in the war. Bob's mob, Gooks, Green Bombers. Trained to maim and kill.'

It doesn't put Selous off. They drive straight on. So this is it. She's found the reason Dick fears him: he's crossed over, joined the dark side, lost all moral bearing. Selous does not look left or right as they come into a farm compound that's like a scene from a ravaged country; the Huns have passed through. Everywhere there is evidence of fire and abandonment: blackened store sheds, derelict animal pens, soot-caked outbuildings stripped of doors and window frames. A little further on they pass a substantial house with a Cape gable frontage. The awnings above the covered veranda are torn and the wall is pocked with bullet strikes. On the croquet-flat lawn, dried brown, two men sit on stools around the remains of a fire. One has a blanket covering his head and leans forward as if cold whilst the other, in soldier's fatigues, fondles a rifle on his lap. They take no notice of the vehicle as it passes.

They do not slow but keep going until a few hundred yards further on from the house they come to a small unmolested cottage shaded by handsome trees and supporting flowering climbers. It's a dramatic contrast to what they've just driven through and the scene would have been pretty, was Beth in the mood for it. An old white Mercedes lurks under a carport next to the cottage. Its chrome trim has dulled like tarnished family silver. It remembers better days.

They come to a halt. Selous says, 'Get out and wait here.'

Beth steps down and doesn't look back. His wheels spit gravel against her legs as he pulls away.

She's not going to make herself at home in the cottage – he's not had the civility to offer it – but she wanders towards the carport to lean against the vehicle in the shade. A small rat, or perhaps it's an enormous mouse, is scurrying about on the red leather seat inside. She shudders but opens the door to let it out. It disappears through a hole in the leather, declining freedom. The keys are dangling in the ignition, a bullet cartridge as a key fob. She feels nauseated and goes to sit on the bonnet, seeing again, in vivid images, the brutal, bloody, pointless killing of the sable. Dick had been right: Selous De Villier is deranged. Those unreadable eyes. A creepy feeling grows. She knows nothing about what has happened on this land. The burnt out buildings, the war vets, the murder that Mr De Villier had spoken of. The place smells of anarchy and danger. A hell in what should be paradise.

Selous's vehicle speeds past again and now he's accompanied by two men in bright orange workers' overalls. She guesses they are going to collect the sable or hack off the head or saw off the horns or whatever they do. She waits, sitting on the bonnet of the Mercedes with her head in her hands, sinking in exhaustion.

When Selous returns much later it's with his client, who has difficulty manoeuvring his fat red knees out of the vehicle to climb down. He's about fifty: a plethoric schoolboy in shorts who has never grown up. He waves at her in a smug way and shouts, 'Hello, my name is Daaf. I'm from Holland.'

Selous encourages Daaf into the cottage, ignoring Beth.

After a few minutes Selous comes out again. 'You'd better come in now.'

She follows him through the door and can hear Daaf having a shower. Making an effort to get a hold of herself, she takes in the room as she would the room of one of her nursing home patients. She wants to find clues to Selous's life. She's already sure there'll be no photos, nothing to suggest a web of human relationships. She startles as she sees the rock art, a large canvas reproduction: a hunter, in the colours of the earth, spare in form, naked, forever running across an invisible landscape. Matt would have been interested but now she's seen a 'hunt' she thinks the painting merely represents the bloody past. But she is wrong about the photographs. There is one. It's small and almost lost in a wide wooden frame on a dark wood sideboard. She recognises it. A man, a woman and a boy in front of a tower of balancing rocks.

She turns to face Selous. He's opening a small fridge with a gas cylinder beside it in the corner of the room. She's come a long way and she has to finish the task. 'I've seen that photo before,' she says.

He half turns. 'Why are you here?' he says abruptly.

Why is she there? So many possible answers and all not enough on their own: I'm running away from difficult home circumstances; I'm looking for a patient's girlfriend to warn her that her boyfriend's in danger; I'm looking for a new life; I thought you would help me escape the country; I was your father's doctor. And, of course, there is the deed and the letter. But no, he doesn't deserve them yet, has not yet earned them.

'It's too complicated,' she says. 'You wouldn't believe it.'

He takes a jug from the fridge and fetches a glass and pours her water. 'Try me.'

'I entered the country illegally. Now I'm looking for some help to get out.'

He places the glass on the table. She flops into a chair and drinks, suddenly parched.

'I'm not the welfare state,' he says.

She splutters on her drink. 'I don't expect you to be.' Bloody hell!

He returns to the fridge, splits a Castle lager from a pack, pops off the top with a glancing strike against the edge of the sink, pulls a glass from a shelf and deftly arranges them all on a carved wood tray. His client will soon be finished showering.

When it seems that he'll say no more, she says, 'I don't want

185

to be here anymore than you want me here, but if you'll extend me the courtesy of telling me how I can get back to Bulawayo, I'll leave.' She drains her glass. 'Alternatively, you could shoot me.'

She sees the corners of his eyes crease a little as if she's amused him and then he stops for a couple of seconds as if thinking over both options. He says, 'You shouldn't have come here. It's dangerous.' Yes, that's obvious, she thinks: all the bloodthirsty oafs with guns. He can read her. 'It's much more dangerous than you think.' He's silent and then says, 'How did you get here?'

'I got a taxi.'

He shoots her a disbelieving look. 'However you got here, he'll know you're here.' He looks out of the window as if 'he' is likely to have arrived already. 'I'm going to have to hide you immediately. He'll come.' There's not a flicker of emotion in his expression.

'Who'll come?' Beth's stomach tightens.

'It's too complicated. You wouldn't believe it,' he says quietly.

She sees it now: he's playing with her, trying to frighten her. She's about to stand up, reach into her bag, chuck his father's deed and letter on the table and then set off to the main road to find reception and ring Dick. But the Dutchman has reappeared. He has a red V of sunburn on his upper chest, is hairy-shouldered and naked except for a red towel wrapped low around his hips. His belly hangs over his towel like a white sack.

Selous says, 'Daaf, I'm giving this woman a lift. Help yourself to the beer on the tray and relax on the recliner on the stoep. I'll be back in about an hour.'

'No problems,' Daaf says, 'I'm ready for a siesta after felling that sable.' And then to Beth, 'Nice to meet you. Your name? Where are you from?'

Selous signals to Beth with his hand, ordering her, she thinks, to keep her mouth shut.

Damn him, she's not going to join his game. She forces a sugary smile at Daaf and says, 'I'm one of Selous's call girls.'

She immediately regrets opening her mouth. How could she have blurted that out? She feels herself blushing.

'Yah?' Daaf smiles broadly at Selous. 'Good! Good! This is a great country!'

Selous's laugh lines threaten to form again and Beth is sure she's being patronised by both men. Then Selous says to her, 'Wait in the vehicle. I'll be a few minutes.'

She does as he says but sits on the hard seat with her arms firmly folded. When Selous comes out of the cottage he's carrying a large, battered, army-green holdall. He has a short-handled axe in a sheath on his belt. They drive off but have not gone far up the track when he swerves off into the trees picking a route that takes them well away from the road. Then, without warning, he pulls up unnecessarily sharply. He jumps down, collects the holdall, adjusts his axe in his belt, takes his gun from the back and orders, 'Come with me.'

Beth steps out but then freezes. He's not looked her in the eye since they glared at each other when they first met – the sign of a man who has no wish to get emotionally involved with his victim. He's unstable, unable to integrate with normal society, unhinged by whatever has happened here. What if he's going to take her to a quiet spot, shoot her and bury her under branches? She steps back so that the vehicle is between them. 'I'm not coming.' She sets a grim and resolved expression. 'Where are you taking me?'

He shrugs. 'Please yourself, I've got my client to look after.' He dumps the holdall on the ground, springs behind the wheel again and says, 'There are some rocks to hide amongst about five hundred metres in that direction. In the bag you'll find all you need for the night. Don't come back to the cottage under any circumstances.' By his standards it's a long speech. He starts the vehicle and then as an aside says, 'Keep a look out for leopards. Talk to yourself as you walk, you don't want to surprise one.'

Beth rushes forward and puts her hands on the bonnet. 'OK! You've made your point!'

He doesn't even glance at her. He steps out again, picks up the holdall and walks into the bush. She follows like his poodle. Earlier that day she'd walked through the same landscape and found it enchanting. Now it's prickly and eerie; less open; here and there are scattered boulders, partially concealed by shrubbery and gripped by green snake-like roots that pipe across the rocks. Selous's silence somehow makes her step stumbling and she finds herself unable to avoid the long thorns which snag her sleeves. He's about to abandon her out here. She must do something. She says to his back, 'I knew your father.'

She's used to his long silences by now and waits patiently. Eventually he says, 'It's better to keep it to yourself.'

'How could you say that? He was your father!'

Another long silence. 'My father and I were estranged.'

Putting aside everything she'd learnt about how to break bad news to patients, she says, 'He's dead.'

Selous's step never falters. She can't see his face to see if any shadows cross. His head bows but better, she thinks, to watch his step in the grass than from emotion.

The bushes are thicker now, pressing in. It's easy to lose sight of Selous. Perhaps he's trying to lose her. 'I have a letter for you from your father and also the title deed to his land. That's why I'm here.'

They reach a towering dome of rock whose base is protected by a thicket of trees and bushes. 'Here we are,' he says, as if she hasn't spoken. He bends down and worms his way into the tangle of branches. Beth hesitates and then follows, fearful of losing sight of him. And then she finds she has lost sight of him. Her lost-in-the-woods-experience as a five-year-old grips her like the bite of a wolf. She stops to listen. There's a scuffing noise above her and she sees Selous's boots on the rock above her head. She follows him, fingers hunting for the sharp crenulations of the rock to pull herself up the steep face, thinking as she goes of the irony of having risked everything to get the papers to Selous and then finding him uninterested.

They climb until she's breathless and then they follow the contour. The face becomes steeper and she is about to say she can't go on when they reach an edifice of balancing rocks. She thinks they will have to clamber up beside it but instead they drop down a little to a cleft in the rock. Selous turns himself sideways to squeeze himself through. She follows, anxious not to lose sight of him again. The cleft is only a metre deep but is angled so that only when she's through can she see that it opens out onto a flat platform about two metres deep and a little more wide. Below the platform the rock falls precipitously away into the trees whose heavy-branched canopy hides the platform from any outside view. Ahead is a dead end of rock. Apart from the cleft they have squeezed through there's no other route to the platform. She moves towards the rock face away from the drop and is going to put her hand on it to steady herself when she sees the art on the rock. There are strings of deer-like creatures and those long-legged hunters again, running after their prey for ever.

Beth finds herself saying, 'My husband, he's – he was – an archaeologist. He specialised in these. He worked here in Zimbabwe for a year.'

Selous has put down the holdall but is looking at the rock face. For such a trigger-happy numbskull he wears an almost contemplative expression. 'He'll not have seen these. The only white man who's ever seen these, is myself.'

'That must make me the only white woman.'

He nods slowly, still eyeing the paintings. Beth guesses he regrets revealing to her this secret place. Turning suddenly he squats to unzip the holdall. Taking out slender poles he slots them together to make a frame while she looks on incredulously. He pulls out mosquito netting and stretches it over the frame to form a tent. When he's satisfied himself that it's taut and that the zip works he stands up and points his chin at the holdall. 'There's bedding and a foam mattress in there, also a torch, water and biscuits. Don't move from here.'

'For pity's sake! You're going to leave me here?'

He's already disappeared through the cleft. She hears him moving down the rock and then there is the sound of an axe on wood. He comes back and wedges a heavy branch in the crack. He takes it out again and turns it through one hundred and eighty degrees, wedging it again, hammering it in with the blunt side of the head of his axe. Satisfied that it's tight, he leaves, gone without another word, leaving her a prisoner in a wild land.

She becomes aware of the absence of sound: not a whisper of wind or the faint whoosh of traffic or the buzz of a farm machine or the hum of a computer. In outer space it would signify desolation but on her rock hideaway it feels heavy with anticipation: a trap about to be sprung; a beast preparing to pounce; a snake readying to strike. When the sounds come they are dry sounds: snick, patter, snap. Delicate as a timepiece. Is that the fracture of a desiccated leaf under the supple paw of a leopard? They climb trees, they climb rocks, don't they? She looks at the paintings, thinking they will calm her, but immediately thinks of Matt's secret photos. The bodies, the bones, in front of the paintings. Her own situation mirrored. Perhaps she will be discovered in a few months' time, or never; her dismembered skeleton scattered on the platform. She begins to fear the photo of the bodies has been imagined, that it is some prescient trick of her mind. Oh Matt, what happened?

She busies herself, laying out the foam in the tent, making a bed with the sheets and blanket. Selous has thrown in a pillow as well. Weak and thirsty she drinks water from the flask that Selous has left her, eats four oat biscuits (she's surprised to find that they are homemade and palatable), and then she wonders where she will pee. She tries to shift the wedged branch, thinking she at least needs the option of running (screaming like a banshee) back to the cottage. It's just as likely she will find herself running for ever, like the hunters on the rock, eternally lost. The wood will not budge and she's now glad not to have the choice.

The night comes down with uncompromising density, as if she has a retinal detachment. She's naked against the dark and rummages blindly in the holdall for the torch. When she finds it she hears herself whimper with relief and clutches it so hard that her knuckles show ghostly-white in the gloom. Retreating into the tent she tucks the netting firmly under the mattress, lies out flat and covers herself with the sheet, pulling it up to the bridge of her nose and then stares up, saucer-eyed, at the sky. Starlight pricks through the netting. A bird sounds a long melodious, if doleful, note. Warmth radiates off the rocks from the heat of the day and the air is clean and fragrant. In other circumstances it would all have been beautiful – and romantic. She thinks of Matt as he used to be, his lean but strong arms, his ready chat, and feels how his presence would have transformed everything. She wonders if he'd camped out here in these hills when he was searching for rock art. His experiences in the bush must have numbered amongst the most intense in his life; and she hadn't been there to share them with him. And he had not wanted to tell her about them. Perhaps words failed him.

She follows the line of rock above to where it meets the sky. In a dip on the skyline there's an object with a fuzzy outline, head sized. She looks back at the stars determined not to succumb to her imaginings. The fuzzy thing moves. Peripheral vision is very sensitive to motion, she knows. But the mind plays tricks: did it stir or not? She thrusts her torch towards it in a threatening gesture although it takes a few seconds for the switch to respond to her trembling jabs. The light spends itself on the netting. When she turns off the torch and her eyes dark adapt again she sees the outline is still there. She notices other fuzzy shapes. She has to admit it; she's surrounded by the bloody things, all watching her. They are, surely, clumps of grass overhanging the rock. 'Well, stare if you want,' she says out loud.

She turns on her side, pulls the pillow over her head and curls into a ball. She prays for sudden oblivion.

CHAPTER 16

Beth is snapped out of sleep by a noise: a single crack that would accompany a lightning bolt. Now all is quiet and she thinks that maybe she's dreamt it. Then she remembers the sound the gun made when the sable was shot. The sharp violence. Is Selous on a night hunt? What beautiful creature is bleeding now? Her fear ratchets up: *who* is bleeding now? A profound silence follows the gunshot, as if every living thing has been slaughtered. She lies still, waiting, listening. Another shot follows about a minute later. Perhaps he's making sure that whatever he's pierced is dead, putting it out of its misery. She hears nothing more and can only lie there, straining her ears. The shapes above her still watch her. Mute time passes and sleep is stealing up on her again when there's a noise close by: the scuffing of feet on rock, followed by suppressed sobs. She sits up and tugs at the netting to free it from under the mattress.

Selous's voice is as low and monosyllabic as ever. 'Stand there.' He's removing the barricade from the crack.

Beth worms her way out from the netting and stands with her back pressed against the rock. She shines the torch at the crack. She will blind him.

The face that shows is not Selous's. She bangs her skull on the rock as she recoils in shock.

'Hope!' she breaths. 'How the… ?'

Hope's cheeks shine with tears. She closes her eyes against Beth's light.

'Hope?'

Hope collapses on the ledge and sobs.

Beth kneels down beside her. 'It's me, Beth, Dr Jenkins.'

Hope shakes her head.

Beth puts an arm around her. 'It's OK, it's OK.' She's vaguely aware of Selous wedging the branch into the crack in the rock again and then leaving.

'What's happening, Hope? Why are you here?'

Hope pants and tries to control herself. 'We were trying to find you.' She dissolves in sobs again.

Beth waits, her arm tight around Hope's shoulders, and then says, 'Who's *we*, Hope?'

Hope turns her head. Her face is all lip, blubbery, wet, like a young child's. 'He's dead.'

'Who's dead, Hope? Tell me. We're just on our own here together. It's OK.'

Hope props herself up and wipes her eyes with her fingers. She lets her head droop and then says in a hot snuffly stream, 'The one who's dead is Fortunate... he was shot by that man... we were coming to find you... Fortunate says you maybe came here to this place but that man shot him... we were just walking... we ran and that man... he shot... he fell... he is dead... he is dead...'

'Stop! You mean Fortunate? Fortunate's dead?'

'Fortunate, the same who you know.'

Beth's arm falls off Hope's shoulders. They squat, dumb, except for the panting of Hope's breaths. It's all too surreal, too damned impossible. Gentle Fortunate, kind Fortunate, Fortunate who she's got to... got to love. Beth stands up and presses her fingers hard into the rock face to try to connect with something solid and real. As she does so it's her heart that hardens: they can't afford to wallow in sorrow. Not yet. The mourning and recriminations will follow. She turns and says, 'Are you absolutely certain that it was the man who brought you here who killed Fortunate?'

'He's the one.'

'Why were you here, in this place, on his land?'

'We were looking for you. After you left, Fortunate contacted me. He told me that Charlie Ten had confronted him and ordered him to steal the title deed from Mr De Villier. So he went into hiding.' Hope's words squirt over Beth like a bleeding artery. 'Then Mr De Villier died and you left and he was worried for you. He went to your house and asked your mother-in-law. She told us you'd gone to Zimbabwe – she said, *she's gone off to Africa with her lover*. But Fortunate was sure that you'd come here to the old man's farm. But Fortunate said that Charlie Ten would also guess the same and you'd be in danger. That's why we came here. Fortunate said that we must find you quick.'

The horrible irony passes through Beth like a skewer. They'd both been trying to rescue each other. 'Are you absolutely sure he's dead?' she asks.

'He fell hard. He's dead.' Hope lifts her head and says flatly, 'I loved him,' and then, after a pause, 'but he loved Shungu.' She drops her head again and quietly weeps.

A desperate solution presents itself. Beth tugs on her sandals, picks up her day pack, strides to the cleft and sets at the branch like she's kicking something to death. It shifts in millimetre increments and then falls away. 'Hope, please get up.' She takes her hand, helps her to her feet and leads her out, away from their shelter and back down the granite.

The granite has an other-worldly luminosity – as if lit by the Milky Way – aiding their descent to the foot of the rock. Beth is stern with Hope, who remains absorbed in her grief, cajoling her to keep close behind her and to watch every step. Briers reach for them and each footfall crackles. They come across the track and then walk in what Beth hopes is the right direction back towards the cottage. The overhanging branches are so black that the sky appears rent by spreading fractures. When the outline of the car porch comes into view she takes Hope's hand and they circle behind the low building. She asks Hope to wait and finds her way to Selous's four-wheel drive. She takes the cap off one of the front tubes. Her nail has only just enough unbroken curve to press the nipple. The hiss of the deflating tyre sounds deafening. When she returns, Hope is hugging herself as if freezing.

'There's a car in the car port and I think Selous leaves the keys in the ignition. I'm going to go and check. Stay here. If the keys are there I'll start the engine. If you hear the engine running then quickly jump in beside me. If it won't start then, I'm sorry, you'll have to run and find somewhere to hide.'

'What will you do, Beth?'

'I don't know.'

Beth starts forward but Hope grabs her arm. 'I can't do this. I'm not coming with you… I'm going to go and find where Fortunate lies. I can't leave him. I never said goodbye.'

'That's crazy. Don't risk it, Hope. We've got to get away. There's nothing we can do for him now.'

Hope lets go of Beth and slips away into the night. Beth starts out after her but almost immediately is snagged by wire lying behind the car port. By the time she extracts herself she knows it's too late. She has to find her way back to Bulawayo, has to summon help, although Dick will still be away at his mine.

She rounds the back wall of the car port and, stepping onto the concrete floor, she bends forward to steal along the side of the vehicle. The old Mercedes door is heavy but opens with a quiet click. A rodent, presumably the large mouse she'd seen before, leaps out of the door and through her feet, abandoning ship. She tries not to take that as a bad omen as she suppresses a scream. The key with the bullet cartridge key fob is still in the ignition. She lowers herself onto the leather seat and places her hands on the wheel. She immediately has a good feeling about the car – it has the demeanour of a dependable old battleship. She names her Bismarck. They are going to escape and find their way to Bulawayo. There are civilised people in cities – that's why most people live there. Surely it will be possible to get some men together, send out a posse or something. She hunts with her feet for the pedals, pressing them in turn: clutch, brake, throttle. She finds the handbrake. She even locates the light switch. She does not find the gear stick. It isn't where it should be. Automatic? No, there is a clutch. A stalk is sticking out of the steering column. She pulls and pushes on it. It swings around like a flailing arm. She moves it until it feels like it's in neutral – its most floppy position. There might be markings on the gear knob but she can't see them in the dark. She will just have to hope for the best.

She turns the ignition one increment and the dashboard lights wink on. This is the moment. She narrows her eyes and turns the key hard. The car lurches backwards as if it has touched a hot plate. They hit the shelving at the back of the car porch and stall. There's a second of silence and then the thud of falling cans, heavy with oil or paint, and the tinkle of breaking glass. She sees a light flare in the house. She presses her foot hard down on the clutch, throws the gear shift in another direction and turns the ignition again. The engine fires easily. Exhaust smoke billows past the windows. She releases the clutch. Bismarck staggers forward. She swings the wheel to pass the cottage. The front door yawns open and there is Selous running out in front of her. He is stark, hairy, naked; his eyes dark shadows in his face. He has a gun and starts to raise it but she hunches her shoulders and Bismarck lumbers up speed. She will not forget Selous's look as he recognises her at the wheel: shock, wonder and, best of all, awe. She catches him with the edge of the wing as he tries to spin out of the way. Her last view of him is his torso passing her window. Nice butt.

She turns on the lights and drives as fast as she can in whatever gear she is in – probably first judging by the howling of the engine. The lights illuminate the twin ribbons of dirt track either side of the grassy-Mohican in the middle of the road. White ribbons to safety. She will soon be at the main road and then she'll search for another gear and will drive like Schumacher to Bulawayo and get help for Hope. She loosens her grip on the wheel as her hands are hurting.

Just before the junction with the tar road, her lights pick out a stationary saloon facing her way. Its lights come on – high beam – as soon as she's seen it. There's no room to manoeuvre past. She stops, although Bismarck's brakes are not as effective as she'd have liked so that only a few feet separate the vehicles. She plays with the stick in the vain hope of finding reverse again. The driver's door opens and a police officer steps out. He leans into his vehicle again to fetch his cap, places it on his head, adjusts it carefully as if attending a parade and comes to her window. She lowers the glass, fixing him a frozen grimace.

'Good evening, madam, you're up very late, can I help you?'

Beth feels very small inside Bismarck's bulk. Small and vulnerable. 'Thank-you for asking. I'm a tourist,' she says.

'Tourists are very welcome in Zimbabwe.' He beams at her. 'I'm from the Zimbabwe Republic Police and I'm at your total service. Perhaps I can escort you to your destination. Which hotel are you staying in?' Beth sees now that he has a friendly face.

'Er... that one in Bulawayo... escapes me, the name.' She forces a furrow in her brow.

'Southern Star?' he suggests.

'Yes... yes, that's the one.'

He becomes distracted by the tax disc. His face falls. 'Unfortunately, I see that your tax disc is not in order.'

Snared by Selous. His incapability of being a law abiding citizen. 'Oh dear! I'm sorry about that. You see, it's a borrowed car.'

The policeman's frown dissolves and he breaks into a playful smile. 'I have some good news for you: at present you're not breaking the law as you are on a private road.'

'Oh, that's great,' Beth says, thinking honest police officers in foreign places should be given gold stripes on their epaulets.

'Madam, let me escort you back to Bulawayo.'

'Will you really?'

She must have looked as if she would kiss him for he smiles magnanimously and says, 'Madam, today it's the policy of the government to welcome tourists.'

'Thank God I'm here on the right day.'

The policeman laughs loudly but then, as quickly, sobers. 'But, Madam, there's a little problem. You see, we've run out of fuel.'

'Ah.'

There is a pause as he looks at her expectantly. He helps her out. 'Maybe you could give us a lift back to Bulawayo. We'll arrange for the police vehicle to be picked up tomorrow.'

'Of course. But what about the tax disc?'

'Under these exceptional circumstances, whilst the car is under the jurisdiction of the ZRP, there'll be no fine.'

'And how are we going to get past your car?'

'You'll be able to drive over the grass there.'

Now, in the company of this delightful official, Beth draws breath to tell him what has happened on the farm but he says, 'Excuse me, one moment,' and returns to his car. He speaks to someone inside. The door opens and a man steps out. It's Robson.

CHAPTER 17

Beth quashes a reflexive flailing for the door handle. Two miraculous escapes have been granted her but hoping for a third is too greedy. The policeman makes himself comfortable in the back and Robson helps himself to the passenger seat beside Beth.

'Please don't worry, Dr Jenkins.' Robson sits forward in his seat with his hands pressed together as if in prayer, eyes round as a rabbit's behind his squiffy, wire-frame glasses. 'I'm very glad to have found you safe. Such a relief for me.' Beth stays silent. 'You misunderstood our intentions in Victoria Falls. We were only wishing to protect you.'

Beth finds her voice. 'The punch your henchman dealt me gave me an alternative impression.'

'Not my employee, I can assure you, but I'm so sorry about that. Let's go – you can go over there to get around our vehicle.'

'It's unforgiveable. It was a violent assault.'

He turns his head to glance anxiously back up the track. 'Too heavy handed with a woman, that's true. It's best to go now.'

Beth turns onto the verge and bumps her way around the police vehicle. 'Well I'm going to take it further,' she says, and then thinks how stupid she's sounding. There'll be no complaints unit. And she's an illegal alien.

'Let it go, Dr Jenkins. He's already been punished.'

'Punished?'

'Beaten.'

'For letting me escape?'

'Severely beaten. I hope that satisfies you.'

'Is he all right?'

'I've not made enquiries. It's not my department. I'm only a solicitor.' He fidgets impatiently. 'Dr Jenkins, please hear me. I'm trying to help you. Believe me, I'm risking myself for you in coming to this place. There are many things that you don't understand.' They are back on the track and Beth can see the broken gate where the track meets the tar road ahead. 'Let me explain everything. When you crossed the border the security services were concerned for your safety. That's why they picked you up.'

Beth finds herself laughing. 'I was perfectly happy and safe before you abducted and assaulted me. Why were you looking for me in the first place?'

He turns to her with an urgent and solemn expression. 'You'll find that what I'm to tell you is difficult to believe – as I said, there are many things that you don't understand. In the UK you were in contact with a man named Fortunate Mukumbi. Unfortunately… ' he pauses to give her time to appreciate his word play, '… he has a criminal record.'

Fortunate! A criminal record! That hardly seems plausible. Her face must be shouting *I don't believe you,* even in the dark, because he goes on quickly, 'Yes, as I said, it's truly surprising and it's disappointing news for you. Interpol, with the help of the Zimbabwean authorities, have been keeping him under surveillance and they saw that he'd tried to become your friend. They were concerned that maybe he'd asked you to carry something into the country for him. Something illegal perhaps.'

'I thought you were a solicitor, not a customs officer,' she says.

'I'm a man of the law, but the same surveillance people who were watching Fortunate saw me meeting you in the car park at Twicare Nursing Home. They insisted – as I'd met you in the UK – that I came with them when they picked you up for questioning in Victoria Falls. They wanted you to have legal representation.' He lowers his voice. 'You see, it's the CIO – state security – who detained you. They are hard people but they didn't wish to create an international incident. I'll admit it's unusual for them to care too much about that but they have their reasons.'

Beth stays silent.

'Believe me,' says Robson, a note of desperation in his voice, 'I hate those CIO guys myself but when I refused to co-operate they beat me up. It's still painful for me to breathe. How could I decline their request? The other man in the car that night cannot be refused.'

Beth swallows as she remembers the other man's voice.

'They intercepted the phone call that your pilot made to the man named Jules who was scheduled to pick you up. They encouraged him with persuasive methods to tell them the location of the rendezvous. So, you see, they are infallible.' He nods agreement to himself.

'Except I got away,' Beth says.

'Very lucky but regrettably you have stamped on the leopard's tail.'

'I'm in the deep dambo, then,' Beth says to herself.

'Don't worry at all, I'll help you. That's why I've been looking for you. I learnt, through independent means, that you came to this dangerous place. The CIO man doesn't know that I'm here

– at least, I hope not! Dr Jenkins, I'm so very relieved to see that you're safe.'

'What's the danger?'

'That man on the farm – Mr Selous De Villier – he's not a good man.'

'What do you mean?'

Robson shakes his head. 'It's beyond believing.'

'You can tell me. I'd like to know.'

'It's too terrible.' He shakes his head again.

'Look, I–'

'What sort of man kills his own mother?' Robson says in a strained whisper. Beth's mouth goes sandy. 'Yes, it's true. It's well known. That's why everyone stays away from him. His own dear father, a man of good standing, a kind man, had to flee the country of his birth in his old age to escape from his own son.'

She thinks of the murder that Mr De Villier had intimated, the horror that he could not utter. She hardly registers Robson saying, 'I'm sure he's killed others. Many others.'

'Why did he kill his mother?'

'The devil got into him; or the madness of syphilis perhaps. As a doctor, you'd know more about these things than me. It's not my department – I'm a solicitor.'

'Yes, you said.'

Beth is overcome by nervous exhaustion and has a sudden vivid vision of Fortunate dead in the forest, his kind face smeared in the dirt like the sable's. 'Why don't you have him arrested?'

Robson nods curtly as if it's a natural enough question – but naïve. 'That's a delicate matter.' He moves his hands in front of him as if trying to manipulate a recalcitrant object into shape, something difficult to mould to his satisfaction. 'You see, Dr Jenkins, I'm just an unassuming man serving the law, but in this country there are far greater powers than the law. The law here is only for little men like you and me. Selous is protected by some big guys. Powerful people.'

She must be looking aghast, for he smooths his imaginary object with pulpy fingers and says, 'Don't let this worry you. One day he'll be brought to justice. But, for now, he's useful to some…' he leans over, 'Party people.'

'Party people?'

Robson places a finger to his lips and glances back at the policeman but Beth can see in the mirror that the policeman is asleep his head back on the seat, mouth open. Robson manoeuvres himself close to her so that his breath tickles her ear. 'ZANU-PF.'

The PF feels like a blown kiss. She pulls her head away but he's returned to his place again.

It's all too much like the script of a tragic circus set in a police state. She has to reach for the droll. 'Zanu Pief? No relation of Edith?' she says.

'What?'

'French singer – never mind. Little joke.'

Robson slaps his hands on his knees and relaxes for the first time. 'Hah, hah, hah! Dr Jenkins, you're fast. Yes, those ZANU people, *ils ne regrettent rien.*' He looks for a hint of smile from her and gets it. 'Aaaah… ' He carries on chuckling to himself, hangs one arm from the grab handle above the window and spreads out his other hand on his thigh. 'That's better, Dr Jenkins. We're singing the same songs now.'

They are now on the main tar road again but outside not a single light shines to indicate a human presence. It is just her, Robson and a comatose policeman in what must look from space, appropriately, like a black hole in the ground of Africa.

'You know, Dr Jenkins, I knew Mr De Villier well. He trusted me.'

'Uh huh.'

'That's why I must do the right thing.'

She makes an attempt to reassess Robson. Her misgivings are starting to look like prejudice. She doubts he's the model of an upright solicitor but she has to recognise that there can be good people – or at least ordinary people – having to live in bad institutions, in police states. People having to earn a living, trying to feed their families, being as decent as they can within the constraints of a corrupt and violent system. Who is she to judge him?

'We'll soon drop you off at your hotel,' he says. He yawns and looks ready to go to bed himself.

'That's very kind. I'm wondering though how I'm going to get back to Britain? Am I going to be arrested?'

'Don't worry, Dr Jenkins. I'll work something out. As your white friends say: we'll make a plan.' He sounds like Dick at his best.

Curiosity needles her and she says, 'You asked me about Mr De Villier's papers when we met outside Twicare. Did you ever find them?'

'Regrettably, they seem to have gone with him to his grave but let me give you some confidential information. I know that I can trust you, Doctor.' He clears his throat. 'Mr De Villier confided in me that he wished his farm to go to his grandchild.'

'Grandchild!' She makes a correction to her steering as Bismarck wobbles off line.

'Yes, Selous De Villier's daughter.'

'That man has a daughter? Selous has a daughter?'

Robson meets her eye and they share a profound sorrow for the child. 'She's in South Africa, in an orphanage in Cape Town.' He tuts, shaking his head slowly. 'It's one of the saddest situations I've come across in all my years in my profession.'

'What happened to the child's mother?'

'Oh, that was very terrible. She died while holidaying in South Africa. She was the victim of a car highjacking. They shot her. Poof! Just so!' Casually, he pulls an imaginary trigger.

'How appalling,' Beth gasps. 'So why is his daughter in an orphanage? Why isn't Selous De Villier looking after his own daughter?'

Robson shakes his head again. 'He only considers himself.'

How can evil run so unchecked through a human heart? He'd killed his mother, abandoned his daughter, and even shot sables.

'Although Mr De Villier – the old man – wanted his farm to be inherited by his granddaughter,' Robson says, 'he always told me that he would have to follow the custom and give it to his son. In many respects, he was a man of principle.' He adds grandly, 'It was a privilege to have known him.'

'What does it matter? Hasn't the land been taken by the war vets anyway?' Beth asks.

'No, not quite. You see this land is different. There are some farms that are owned by Dutch citizens. There was a bilateral agreement between the Dutch government and the Zimbabwe government concerning farms owned by Dutch passport holders. These were in place before the land invasions by the war vets in two thousand. Mr De Villier was such a man. Even if the land is taken now, there'll come a time when the rule of law must be restored. Then either the land will revert to the legal owner or compensation must be paid. These international agreements can make life difficult for ZANU people. They have to be mindful of the future.'

'So Selous – or Mr De Villier's granddaughter – could receive something eventually, when all this comes to an end?'

'I believe so, but it would be a shame if the land goes to Selous. I would much prefer to follow the desires of the old man's heart and arrange for his granddaughter to receive the deed in trust. I would like to do this for my old deceased friend, Mr De Villier.'

Beth's fights her distrustful heart. 'Don't you have a copy of the title deed?'

'Mr De Villier kept his documents to himself. Of course there's a copy with the Registrar of Deeds in Harare but it's best to have the original that does not have a big stamp on it saying *This property now vests in the President of Zimbabwe* to show to an international court if these matters are resolved in future. It will help to show that the deed was handed over personally. Unfortunately, Mr De Villier was a man who found it difficult to trust others. That's what's caused all these complications after his death.'

That fits like a slipper with Beth's own impression of Mr De Villier. Who is she to stand in the way of his granddaughter receiving her rightful inheritance? She's thankful she's not left the title deed with Selous. It's looking as if things might work out for the best. She imagines herself, a mysterious visitor from Britain, taking Mr De Villier's granddaughter out of her high-walled orphanage in a tatty suburb in Cape Town to a cafe overlooking the sea, buying her a frothy pink milk-shake and whatever cake her child's enormous eyes rest upon. She tries to picture what she looks like. Does she have Selous's bold tracings or is she a little replica of her dead mother who she imagines, for some reason, had been a sun-kissed blonde – perhaps because she herself is the opposite of that – and who did as she was told. It's astonishing: the man had actually had a wife. How had she put up with his insults, his taciturn behaviour? What could she have possibly seen in him? Beth's feelings cartwheel unexpectedly into an atavistic emotion which, embarrassingly and inexplicably, seems close to physical desire. She puts it down to exhaustion.

She thinks of the abandoned little girl again. The two of them sitting on light-blue chairs by a sunlit window overlooking the sea, their table pretty with a chequered yellow table cloth and a pink flower in a vase. There she is telling the little girl (as the child opens her mouth to its limit to engulf an icing-smothered bun) that her grandfather has left her some land. Beautiful land with rocks and streams and paper-bark trees in a country far away. There are still sable (she hopes – if her father hasn't shot them all) amongst the trees. The little girl is concentrating on her straw, making loud sucking noises as she clears the bottom of her glass. Beth wants to adopt her.

'Dr Jenkins?' Robson is looking sideways at her.

Still, her instincts lean towards caution. 'Do you have a letter or something to prove that you were his solicitor, that he wished you to enact his will?'

'Yes, I have a letter, of course. You're right to ask these things. I'll fetch it from the office and show you tomorrow morning.'

Beth looks Robson in the eye. He doesn't return her gaze but he is as relaxed as she would expect of a man telling the truth.

'All right,' she says, 'if you can bring the letter tomorrow morning I'll see what I can do. You never know, I might be able to help in some way.'

Robson turns to look at her, a broad smile breaking out. 'Dr Jenkins, you're a truly remarkable woman! Thank the Lord! It would be good to discharge my duty to God and Mr De Villier so that his granddaughter can receive her inheritance, the land of her ancestor. That's most important.'

Beth feels a warm wave of relief. At last she'll be getting rid of the bloody title deed. Right now she has more important concerns. Her thoughts turn again to Fortunate. A criminal record? She can hardly imagine him involved in something Interpol would be interested in like drug smuggling or assassination attempts. After all, he'd passed Matron's Criminal Records Bureau check. Matron would be horrified if she'd found he'd slipped through with a felonious past. Then she remembers his *The Day of the Jackal* gift and frets that there might have been more to Fortunate than she can imagine. But now he is dead and Hope is in danger. Even so, she can't bring herself to mention Fortunate and Hope to Robson.

She keeps it generic. 'I'd better tell you something. I was driving away from Selous's place because someone has been shot on the farm.' The lights on the dashboard swim. She looks away from Robson.

Robson mutters, 'Terrible, terrible. But it happens all the time.' And then, 'We can do nothing. That man is protected by the Party.'

'There's a woman there who was with the man who was shot,' Beth says. 'She's still there, hiding on the farm. Can you send the police to rescue her?'

He shakes his head and says emphatically, 'It's not possible. It would not be fair to ask the police to take such a risk and anyway they couldn't do so without permission from the Party people.'

Beth tries not to speculate where Hope is now and what has happened to her. She's left Hope to fend for herself while she escapes to safety in Bismarck. The thin line of the horizon remains featureless – like her ideas on what to do to help Hope. Dick will know, surely. She no longer trusts her own judgment. Those she thought were good people are not, and vice versa. Do countries in turmoil sort the wheat from the chaff, stress-test character, lay bare each citizen's true nature which at home is modified and constrained by a functioning judiciary and a living income? She's overcome with weariness. With Fortunate dead and Selous shown to be a murderous felon, the excuses for being in Zimbabwe have evaporated.

She says, 'You kindly mentioned you might be able to help me leave the country.'

'Have no worries – I've been giving it some thought. There's an airport here in Bulawayo. I'll buy you a ticket and will bring it to the hotel tomorrow morning.'

'That's very kind but I don't think I've got enough cash to pay you.'

'Again, no need to worry – you can make a transfer to my account when you get back to the UK.'

Robson trusts her and she is grateful, but there is still the problem of her illegal status. 'But won't I be arrested when I go through passport control? I don't have a visa.'

'Leave it to me. There are a few officials in immigration who owe me favours. I'll meet you at the airport and will ensure that they regularise your passport.'

'Will I have to pay a bribe?'

'Please, Dr Jenkins! That's corruption! We're not a banana republic.'

'Your help is much appreciated. I'm sorry I've caused difficulties.'

'Don't mention it. You see, I'm just fulfilling my obligations.'

As they enter Bulawayo, Robson suggests she drop them off at the police station. They will give her instructions on finding the Southern Star from there. They drive through a medieval night of dark, deserted streets. Even the police station is unlit.

'See you tomorrow at 11 o'clock,' Robson says. He shakes the policeman awake who says, 'Goodnight madam, enjoy your stay in Zimbabwe. Tourists are always very welcome.'

They are forlorn at the gate. Beth guesses that they envy her going to a hotel. She finds the Southern Star without difficulty and parks the vehicle at the back, out of sight of the road. It is 3.30am. She falls asleep behind the wheel.

She wakes sweating with the sun hot on her face. The car is not in the shade and she is being slow cooked. It's just after 8am. She winds down the window to get air and then uses the driver's mirror to make herself look respectable using the brush she'd bought at Dick's pharmacy. She finds a twig and a dead spider in her hair.

The receptionist, a young woman alone behind the counter, looks surprised to see Beth and keeps glancing over Beth's shoulder as if waiting for a male companion to appear. They have a room. In fact she offers her the choice of any of their sixteen rooms. She tells Beth dejectedly that she is their only guest.

'Can I have breakfast?' Beth asks. 'A cup of tea?'

The receptionist looks at the clock on the wall behind her. 'Unfortunately we've just finished serving breakfast.'

'But you have no guests.'

'I'm so sorry.'

Beth stands there silent, washed over again with the memory of what has happened to Fortunate and wondering what has become of Hope.

'You see, our cook's not in.' Then, as if she interprets Beth's distraction as stubbornness she gets up with an excessively laboured movement and says, 'I'll ask.' She goes through a door at the back of reception. After several minutes, during which Beth thinks she's forgotten about her, she returns and says, 'Have you US dollars?'

Beth nods.

'We're able to serve you breakfast for thirty US dollars.'

'I think I'll just have tea.'

'Ten US?'

Beth's room smells faintly of creosote from the poles supporting the thatched roof but the bed is comfortable. She leaves her limited possessions and goes to sit in the breakfast room. She adds four cubes of sugar to her tea. She tries to ring Dick on the mobile he'd given her but there is no reply. He's probably deep inside a mine somewhere. He'd warned her about Selous and he'd been proved right. There's no one to help Hope. She'll have to have faith that Hope will find her way off Selous's land, perhaps by retracing the route she and Fortunate took to enter the farm.

When she returns to her room, she takes out the title deed and smooths out its creases. The deed is a little worse for wear but Mr De Villier's letter to Selous is still sealed safely in its envelope. She wishes she'd finally discharged her obligation to Mr De Villier by abandoning them in Selous's car port for Selous to find later. She takes the letter in her hand and turns it over, tempted to tear the flap open. Then she thinks that she should not intrude on such an intensely personal message and, in deference to her deceased patient, she places it back in her bag. She'll leave it in Bismarck at the airport.

The room telephone rings at 11 o'clock. 'There's a gentleman in reception wishing to see you,' the receptionist says in a languid voice, as if not having anything to do makes any task that does crop up seem Herculean.

As Beth makes her way to meet Robson, she has a momentary worry that she'll be faced with Selous, or Charlie Ten bearing his scar, but it is the solicitor – looking smart-casual in his brown leather jacket and an open-collared pink shirt – who comes towards her as she enters the room.

'Ah, Dr Jenkins, I hope you've slept beautifully. Let me give you your ticket straight away.' He passes her a packet. 'It's an Air Zimbabwe flight from Bulawayo to Harare tomorrow morning and then you'll transfer to the London Gatwick service.' He hands her a piece of paper on which he's written his bank account details so that she can pay him when she arrives back in the UK. 'And here's a letter from Mr De Villier to myself – just to confirm my credentials.'

'Let's sit down,' Beth says and invites Robson to one of the coffee tables. When they are seated, she unfolds the letter.

Dear Mr Chiripo,

Following our last meeting, this is to inform you that I do not ever wish to see you again. You call yourself a solicitor! No, you are a snake and a crook.

Goodbye and good riddance,
De Villier

Beth can't tear her eyes from it. 'But Robson, this letter certainly confirms he knew you but... that's all. He's not exactly complimentary is he?'

'Don't worry yourself,' he says. She looks up at him. He's unabashed. 'I didn't take offence. You know what a hard time he had, God rest his soul. It made him short tempered at times. But

214

as you can see, I've got nothing to hide from you – it confirms to you that I was his solicitor.'

She finds her gaze resting on her ticket which she's placed on the smoked glass table top between them. Robson adds, 'After this letter he rang me and was very apologetic. To be honest, Dr Jenkins, this was always happening. He sacked me many times but always rescinded later. He was that sort of man.' He shakes his head and smiles, fondly recalling his difficult but characterful client.

'Don't you have a copy of his will? Isn't there something to confirm he wished you to act for him?'

'Of course I have that documentation but it's in our head office in Harare. I can arrange for a copy to be sent to you when you return to the UK if that's necessary. It's up to you.'

Looking past Robson through the window, unsure what to do, Beth sees a topless four-wheel drive flying past, travelling out of town along the road outside the hotel. At the wheel is Selous, a determined expression on his face. The previous night's terrors circle her head like a creeping leopard.

She hears Robson say, 'It's not a problem. I'd rather you were two hundred per cent contented.'

She reaches into her bag, takes out the title deed and places it on the table. 'There you are, Mr De Villier's title deed.'

Robson's eyes gleam and he opens his hands in a gesture of wonderment before reaching out to stroke the papers with the tips of his fingers. 'Oh, Dr Jenkins, you have surprised me! Yes, you're a surprising woman. I thought the deed was lost.'

Breathing out her relief, Beth says, 'Well, it's a long tale, but it looks like this chapter of the story, at least, will have a happy ending.'

'When Mr De Villier's granddaughter is of age, I'll make sure she knows of your part in all this.'

A lump swells in Beth's throat – something good has come

out of the devastation. Her efforts have not been completely wasted. She's salvaged a puppy from the bomb site.

Robson explains that he'll meet her at the airport to oil her passage though passport control. He also produces a letter signed, he says, by an 'important person' which will excuse the absent tax disc when she has to stop at the police checkpoint on the way to the airport. 'Just show them this letter, and see them step back and salute you,' he says with a chuckle. He gives her a map and talks her through the route to the airport. She tells him that she's taken Selous's car without permission.

'Oh, Dr Jenkins! More surprises! You're driving a stolen vehicle? It's fortunate for you that you have me as your solicitor.' He is all chuckles and smiles.

'I had to take it to escape from Selous.'

'Of course, of course, you were lucky to get away unharmed.'

'I suppose I'm just going to have to abandon it at the airport. What will happen to it? Will someone be able to let Selous know that it's there?'

Robson shrugs. 'I'm sure Selous will hear of it and come to collect the vehicle. It would be too dangerous for anyone to return it to him.' He stands up and extends his hand. 'I'll see you at the airport tomorrow, Dr Jenkins. I'm going early to make arrangements for your VIP treatment.'

Later, Beth sits bent over her lap on her bed and lets her tears flow. Tears of relief, tears for Hope, tears for Fortunate. Then she tries Dick again on her phone but gets a continuous tone. She sits herself up straight, then goes and dries her face. She'll risk it and drive to his house, if she can find it. If he's not there, at least she can say goodbye to his mother and leave a message for Dick about Hope.

CHAPTER 18

Central Bulawayo and its immediate suburbs, Beth discovers, are laid out in a grid, like Manhattan: First Avenue, Second Avenue and on right up to Fifteenth and then, in an adjoining suburb, First Street, Second Street and on up to Ninth. Each avenue and street is so long and similar that, after half an hour, she loses hope of finding Dick's house again. She is about to return to the hotel when she sees a blistered sign saying 'Museum of History and Antiquities'. There is still plenty of time before night falls so she turns into the empty car park and stops Bismarck out of sight of the road, under a gigantic jacaranda tree. There is a pleasing popping sound as she drives over the carpet of fallen lilac-blue flowers. She hopes Bismarck will be garlanded by the time she returns. She deserves to be, the dependable old rescue ship.

Despite the surrounding shaggy gardens, the museum itself is striking: a steel-framed, mirrored-glass, two storey building. It's a little dusty but the jacaranda bloom reflects in the glass. It would not have taken more than a hose down to shine like the Guggenheim. Through the smoked-glass entrance door, Beth finds herself in the dark, or so it seems, contrasted with the outdoors. Three paraffin lamps on a wood reception counter cast a dull, carroty glow.

There is a man behind the counter in a thick jersey despite the stuffy atmosphere. Perhaps the building is normally air-conditioned. 'Good afternoon,' he says with an air of surprise, 'Can I help you?'

'I'd like to look around the museum please.'

'I'm sorry but we've just closed. There's a power cut.'

'How long will it last?'

'Maybe an hour, maybe until I pass.' He laughs apologetically.

'I'd love to see your exhibits. Can I not borrow a lamp?'

He looks doubtful.

'You see, I'm a tourist.'

'A tourist, here in Bulawayo?' He looks at her intently as if she's a museum exhibit. 'OK, if you wish, you can take a lamp. The entrance fee is five hundred dollars.'

She checks her money. She only has notes with a face value of two hundred thousand dollars which Dick has told her are each worth less than ten pence. With inflation of at least fifteen thousand per cent they will be worthless by the end of the week.

'Five hundred dollars? That seems very cheap.'

'We've not updated our prices for months. We've had no instructions from Harare.'

She gives him a two hundred thousand dollar note and he starts fumbling with a wad of cash. 'I'm sorry, I've no change,' he says eventually.

'Keep that note then. It'll look in the books like you had a few hundred visitors today.'

He smiles and hands her a lamp.

She carries her light high, as if about to enter the cave of Tutankhamen, and pushes open the opaque-glass door marked *To the exhibits.* It closes silently behind her and she finds herself in a long tunnel of a room whose walls and ceiling are painted black. She guesses the glass-panelled displays sunk into both walls down the length of the room would be dramatically lit were the power on. Instead, her lamp casts a dim glow on a geological display of metal ores; it's as if she's a miner searching for treasure deep underground. The next room focuses on the treasure hunters of the late eighteen hundreds: colonial era exhibits, including a saddle bag, a medal from a campaign as forgotten as its wearer, and monochrome photographs of handlebar-moustached men sitting on wooden trunks with their boy-servants standing off to the side. Then comes a picture of a chief named Lobengula who – with a BMI of at least thirty-five – is brought to her attention by his wearing little more than a thong and a feather. He has an intelligent and benevolent face. There is a quote from the king in a caption beneath his picture:

The chameleon gets behind the fly, remains motionless for some time, then he advances very slowly and gently, first putting forward one leg and then another. At last, when well within reach, he darts his tongue and the fly disappears. England is the chameleon and I am that fly.

Pages from a treaty are displayed underneath. *I Lobengula, King of the amaNdebele Nation, and of the Makalaka, Mashona, and Surrounding Territories, send Greeting: Whereas I have granted a Concession in respect of...* the writing becomes too small to read easily in the dim light but Beth guesses that this treaty represented the strike of the chameleon and also a new chapter in the region's long, deadly battles over land.

There's a connecting passageway before the next exhibit hall and, as Beth passes through, she sees a pale, orange light leaking under a door and hears the sound of a mechanical typewriter. Then the light disappears and she hears an exasperated 'Aarsh!'. There's the harsh scrape of a chair being drawn back. The door opens and a young woman comes out, holding her dead paraffin lamp. She is neatly dressed in a breast-pocketed white shirt, a wide hip belt and hip-hugging, cream jeans. Her hair extensions are contained in a pink hair-scrunchy. Their eyes meet and Beth says, 'Hello'.

'Hi,' says the woman, and then, with barely disguised exasperation, 'My lamp's run out of fuel. How can anyone work in this place?' She hurries on past Beth, on her way to reception.

'Excuse me,' Beth says after her. 'Do you want to use my lamp? I'm going now.'

The woman stops and turns to look at Beth, frowning severely as if Beth has presented her with an appalling dilemma. She says uncertainly, 'If it's OK?' And then, somewhat desperately, 'You see, I need to finish my work.'

They swap their lamps. 'I'm so grateful,' says the woman.

Beth asks what she's working on.

'Come in and see.'

'Oh no, I don't want to disturb you.'

'Please – I'd like to show you.'

'I'm Beth, by the way.'

'My name's Lindiwe, although people call me Lindi.' She smiles warmly at Beth and Beth wants to hug her. Here is someone kind-hearted, a normal woman in this country of lawless men.

Beth follows her into her room. Stacks of paper and an ancient typewriter with circular metal keys sit on a large Formica-top table. A half-typed page and backing carbon are positioned in the roller. Sheets of drawing paper are heaped on deep-racked shelving on the opposite wall.

'I'm writing a monograph,' Lindi says eagerly, with a gesture to the table. 'I'm trying to record every rock art site in the Matobo Hills. I note each site's details, such as its surroundings and the compass direction of the rock face, along with its map reference and GPS co-ordinates. Then I list each drawing at the site. The drawings are cross-referenced to the reproductions on the big sheets over there.' She points to the shelving.

Beth's heart leaps. Could Lindi have met Matt, or at least know of him? Her lungs overfill as if a fresh breeze has burst through the window. 'Are you connected to a university?' she says.

'The University of Zimbabwe, yes, but that's hardly functioning now. The lecturers are not paid and the students are always on strike. My funding's from the UK. Professor Harman of Cambridge University has raised a research grant for this project. It's part of my doctorate.' She smiles proudly at Beth. 'Do you want to see the drawings?'

Beth suppresses her question about Matt. 'I'd love to.'

Lindi pulls a sheet off the shelving and lays it out on the table on top of the papers. The sheet is densely covered in exquisitely-rendered pencil reproductions of rock art: antelope, hunters and indeterminate shapes. 'That's a lot of work,' Beth says, impressed.

'An artist comes up twice a year from Durban to draw the paintings. I take her out to the sites and she sketches the paintings and then takes photos. We project the slides onto the wall here and then she traces each illustration onto the paper from the slides, using the photos and sketches as a reference. Many of the sites we go to are unknown and there are hundreds of them. Sometimes I think my work will never end.' She adds, with a note of excitement, 'They may not have been seen by anyone else for thousands of years.'

'How old are the paintings?' Beth says, remembering Matt's Henri Breuil lecture.

'African rock art was painted on surfaces that are exposed to the weather so they generally go back no more than ten thousand years, unlike in Europe where the paintings are often down deep caves, protected from the environment. At Chauvet, in France, they date back at least thirty thousand years.' Lindi suddenly looks riled and says, 'Some don't accept that reason for the relatively young age of rock art in Africa and say that the African's powers of imagination took longer to develop.'

'That's ridiculous,' Beth says. 'My husband would have had something to say about that. I wonder if you knew him; you might have met him. He's published a lot on the rock art of southern Africa and was here a few years ago.'

Lindi raises her eyebrows expectantly.

'His name's Matt Hallam.'

'Matt... Ha...?' Lindi breathes. She looks away from Beth. There is something complicated about her reaction. It's not the response of someone who's never heard of him, or what Beth would expect had Lindi just known Matt's name as an expert in his field. Lindi clears her throat and looks in an unfocused way at the opposite wall. 'Hallam?' She furrows her brow. 'Matt Hallam... he publishes?'

'A lot... used to,' Beth says, feeling distant. 'I thought for a moment that you knew him.'

Lindi frowns at her typewriter.

'He used to work out here in Zimbabwe,' Beth says. 'I'm sure he must have gone out many times to the Matobo Hills.'

'I must have... missed him. I'm sorry.'

Beth stands there, dumb. There's a raw silence before Lindi snaps into motion, returning the sheet of drawings to the shelf, saying, 'I'd better get on before this lamp dies like the last one. Let me show you out.'

Lindi ushers Beth politely, but firmly, through the door and then leads the way to reception. Lindi's silence is heavy in front of her.

'Good-bye,' Lindi says quietly when they reach the reception area. 'Thanks again for letting me use your light.'

Beth watches Lindi disappear into the museum. She leaves hesitantly, stopping for a while just outside the door before returning to Bismarck. She looks up at the windows of the museum but can't see through its mirrored glass. By contrast, the sky above is a clear, late afternoon blue and speaks of transparency. Lindi is certainly too young to be an old flame of Matt's. But even if she were, why is it necessary to be embarrassed? She lets herself into Bismarck but sits there strumming on the steering wheel. She's found someone who knew Matt, she's sure of it – a stroke of luck, although she guesses that Matt would have frequented the museum. It will be an uncomfortable experience to return to Lindi's room and confront her. But she's come thousands of miles and tomorrow she'll be gone, unlikely ever to return.

She takes the photos of the cave out of her bag, steps out of the car and returns to the museum. There is no one at the ticket desk so she helps herself to the remaining functioning lamp and goes straight through the museum to knock on Lindi's door.

'Who is it? I'm working,' Lindi calls.

'It's Mrs Hallam – Beth. I'm sorry but I have to ask you something before I leave. I have something I'd like to show you.'

She hears Lindi's chair move and Lindi opens the door but doesn't invite Beth in. Lindi stands there, looking at Beth with slightly raised eyebrows – an expression that shouts that Beth needs to be quick.

'I'd like to show you a photograph,' Beth says. Lindi folds her arms defensively in front of her chest. Beth lifts a photo towards her. 'I believe my husband took this. I'm trying to find out about it – the circumstances in which it was taken.'

Lindi stares at it, moving a little to let the light of her lamp fall on it, giving nothing away. Beth holds her ground. Eventually Lindi says, 'What do you wish from me?'

Beth says, 'My husband is severely disabled. He's had a stroke. I'd very much like to talk about him with you. I won't keep you long.'

'Your husband, Mr Hallam?'

Beth nods.

'A stroke? Is he… in a wheelchair?' Her eyes widen, alabaster white ringing her soft brown irises.

'No, but he's lost all his memory and will never regain it. He can't remember a thing – he hardly knows me, his wife.'

'Oh, I'm so sorry.' Lindi shutters down for a moment. Then she says, 'You'd better come in.' She offers Beth the chair but Beth declines and so they both stand, uncertain.

'My husband remembers nothing about his time here in Zimbabwe,' Beth says. 'He doesn't even remember that he's an archaeologist. I want to see where he worked and understand what he did and, of course, there's this photo.'

'A terrible pity,' Lindi says distractedly.

'You knew Matt, didn't you?'

Lindi gives Beth a discomposed glance. 'Yes, I did. I'm sorry.'

'That's OK.' It's going to be slow, this peeling away of Lindi's reticence. She touches the picture. 'Can you tell me anything about this? Why he might have had this photo?'

'He never told you?'

'No – and I don't know why. It's distressing me, Lindi. We were very close. We loved each other and yet he never told me about this.'

Lindi meets Beth's eyes and Beth can see that Lindi is

warming to her frankness. 'Men forget to tell us the important things,' Lindi says with a shrug. She looks down at her typewriter and smooths the edge of the paper in the roller. 'I was just out of school and used to help at the museum here. Those were the days when we had power and light. I became Mr Hallam's assistant, writing up his field notes, sometimes accompanying him on his field trips.'

'You accompanied him? Were you there with him when he took this picture?'

'No, I wasn't.' She hesitates and then, all of sudden decisive, says, 'He came to me one day. He was very shocked. He told me he'd been taken to a cave where there were many bodies – skeletons.'

Beth indicates the photo. Lindi nods. 'He was taken there? Who took him?'

'His maid,' Lindi says.

'His maid?'

'Yes, you would call her his cleaner. She was the only survivor of a massacre.'

'A massacre?' Beth grips the frame of the door.

'There was a time we call Gukurahundi. It was soon after Independence in the early eighties. The President's forces were sent here to Matabeleland to suppress a rebellion, but they were brutal and tortured and killed thousands of innocent people. His maid was only five at the time but she was rounded up with her parents and some others. She was left for dead in the massacre but after the killers had gone, she escaped.'

'How terrible.'

'She was found wandering amongst the trees and was cared for by her grandmother. She was the one who took Mr Hallam to the cave.'

'And he took this picture.'

Lindi nods again. 'He came to tell me about it, that he was going to report it to the authorities straight away but,' she stops, draws breath, and says, 'I advised him not to.'

'Oh, you did? Why was that?'

'I feared that his maid would be at risk. I thought she might lose her life. You see, those who carried out the massacre were the ones in power. They wouldn't want living witnesses and she would've been the only witness, the only one who knew who was responsible. And I was certain Mr Hallam would be kicked out of the country.'

'So what happened?'

'Mr Hallam had difficulty believing me.'

'And?'

'He went to the authorities.'

'And?

'Yes.'

Beth stares at the photo. Bones, more bones. She can't meet Lindi's eye.

CHAPTER 19

Beth stands in front of Lindi imagining Matt's reaction to knowing that he'd been responsible for his maid's death. It would have devastated him. But now at last she has a possible explanation for Matt's silence on the photos, about this episode in his life, although it was disappointing that he'd not shared it with her. She could have understood, talked it through with him. And what of Lindi's reaction at Matt's rejection of her warning? She probably blames him for the consequences. The naïve do-gooding foreigner. No wonder Lindi doesn't want to admit to knowing him.

Then she has a prick of impatience. She says, 'Perhaps these things shouldn't be kept secret. Matt, I'm sure, was trying to ensure that justice was done. He didn't want to collude in a hideous crime. Keeping quiet makes it as if the massacre never happened – erases it from memory.'

'Maybe it didn't happen,' Lindi says quietly.

'What do you mean? Here's the evidence.' Beth thrusts the photo under Lindi's nose, the firmness of her action belying a sudden doubt. The evidence to hand is laughably slim: a photo at an unknown location by a man who's lost his memory and the only other witness is dead.

Lindi speaks slowly, deliberating as she goes, careful to find the right words. 'Mrs Hallam, there's no one to investigate it. The perpetrators are in power and the police and officers of the law are only in their jobs courtesy of those in power. Many of the judges and magistrates serve their masters, not the law. They've been rewarded with land and properties. For the rest of us, we have to live. For now we just wish to survive, we can only look to the future, not into the past. Not yet. It's not over yet – I don't know whether it'll ever be over. You see, we're on our own. The only government with the power to help us has sealed its lips, has even accepted garlands. We have to carry on our lives as best we can. It's not easy for us here, Mrs Hallam.'

To carry on our lives as best we can... Robson had said the same. Beth almost blurts *I've run away from mine*, but does not.

'I'm so sorry about Mr Hallam's stroke,' Lindi says. 'He was a very fine man.'

The light outside is rapidly dying away. She'd better get back to the hotel before nightfall. She makes to leave, saying, 'I do appreciate you telling me. I'm as good as widowed and it's been distressing to have unanswered questions about him, so this has been helpful.'

Lindi smiles with a quick movement of her lips and follows Beth out and back to the entrance. Beth leaves her lamp on the reception desk.

As they part, Beth says, 'I'm very sorry about what happened to the maid after Matt reported the site. Matt must've been appalled.'

'The maid?' Lindi says, looking puzzled.

'You said the maid had been... murdered.'

'Murdered? Oh! No, you misunderstood. Mr Hallam was discreet about how he'd found the cave. He didn't mention his maid. The only consequence as far as I know of him going to the authorities was that he himself was expelled from the country. That was what I meant.'

'That's such a relief!'

Lindi turns to leave but Beth reaches out her hand to touch Lindi's arm. 'I'd love to meet her, Matt's maid. Do you know her name? Do you know where she lives?'

Lindi shrugs. 'I didn't know her and we're scattered now, us Zimbabweans. She might have left the country to find work. If so, she's almost certainly in South Africa – perhaps illegally. It would be impossible to find her.'

As Beth drives back to the hotel, she finds her relief that Matt's maid was not harmed is replaced by the cutting awareness that she still has no convincing reason for Matt's silence. She'd thought she'd been lucky enough to find herself shining a torch into the black hole of Matt's past but finds there is no bottom to the pit. The beam has spent itself in the abyssal depth. For a moment she thinks she should try to look for the site where the photos were taken, if it still exists. To descend the pit. But she has a flight to catch, amends to make and relationships to repair. She has, in the end, only one life to live.

The letter that Robson gave Beth, signed by some bigwig, induces the grovelling effect he'd predicted at the police road blocks on the way out of Bulawayo the next morning and soon she is on a long straight road which will take her to the turn off to Joshua Mqabuko Nkomo International Airport. She wonders when Shungu will hear the sad news about Fortunate. She guesses she might never know. Her ticket is on the seat next to her and her flight will leave in two hours' time. She's entered the same anaesthetised state that had visited her before her flight to Africa. She'll have plenty of time over the next few years to contemplate – perhaps under therapy – why she'd run away from home to become an illegal alien on the run.

The road is free of traffic except for one vehicle, a long way behind her, visible in her mirror like a small boat floating in a mirage. Ten minutes later and she can see her junction far ahead down the road. The vehicle behind has gained on her. As it nears she sees that it's a topless and battered four-wheel drive. At the wheel, is Selous.

Bismarck's far-side wheels rumble along the verge as Beth momentarily loses control. She squashes Bismarck's accelerator into the foot well and Bismarck gathers speed as ponderously as a heavy lorry. But a wider gap develops. If she can reach the airport she'll come under Robson's protection. There is the airport sign now, imprinted with an aeroplane silhouette. She eases off a little in readiness to turn. Selous gains on her again. Her eyes flick between the mirror and the junction. God help me! Mustn't slow down too early. At the last moment she brakes hard. But Bismarck's brakes have little bite. She is far too fast to take the junction. The sign flashes past. Selous is on her bumper, waving at her to pull over.

She stands her foot on the throttle again. What to do? Weaving like a boat negotiating a shipping channel, she fumbles in her bag for Dick's mobile. She waits for a straight stretch of road, steadies her driving, and manages to ring his number but there is no reply. Bismarck's top speed seems slightly faster than Selous's vehicle and ever so slowly, Selous drops behind. She takes measured breaths to stop the tingling that's creeping up her fingers. She's been blowing off carbon dioxide. 'Don't you know there's global warming?' she finds herself saying out loud in a panicked voice.

Selous takes longer and longer to reappear in the mirror (looking like the dark head of a bird of prey on the grey body of his topless vehicle) at the occasional curves in the road until it's at least ten minutes since she's last seen him. She presses on, Bismarck at full steam, trying to put as much distance between them as possible. The tar turns to dirt and dust puffs up behind her, as if Bismarck is topped with smoking funnels. On she surges, looking for a road that will take her to the right or left, hoping to circle around and back to the airport but, apart from tracks to abandoned farm homesteads, there is nothing.

She dares to slow down to try Dick's mobile again but is now beyond the reach of a signal. She dithers as to whether she should turn around but thinks Selous is not the sort to quit. She glances at her watch. It will now be impossible to make her flight. She looks every now and then for a signal on Dick's phone. She passes a cart pulled by donkeys and the occasional figure squatting under a tree in the middle of nowhere, doing what there, she can't guess. A child holds up oval objects like large seed pods, wanting her to stop and buy them but she leaves him in her dust cloud. She passes a long green bus named *Special Express* turning on flat ground by the road beside a sign saying *Terminus*. She hopes it isn't prophetic. After another hour she comes across a small village near a hill with a mast and sees she has reception. She pulls to the side of the road and tastes her dust as it wafts through the windows. She rings Dick.

'Ja? Dick, here.'

'Oh Dick.' She suppresses a sob. 'I'm so relieved to hear your voice. Thank God I've got hold of you at last. I'm lost. I'll try to explain. Terrible things happened at Selous's and I had to escape by stealing his car.'

'Could you repeat that? You stole Selous's car?'

'Yes,' she replies, 'it's a long story but I had to, to escape.'

She hears him swear.

'Anyway I was on my way to the airport this morning and I got chased by Selous and now I'm… I really don't know where I am. All I know is that it's too late to get back to the airport.'

'Chased by Selous? Streuth! OK, talk me through the route you've taken.'

Beth does her best and Dick punctuates her description with cursing but eventually he says, 'OK, I think I know where you are. You're heading towards Lake Kariba. How's your fuel situation?'

'I found a petrol station with fuel in Bulawayo. You have to leave the tank full when you rent.' She hears herself laugh nervously.

Dick painstakingly gives her instructions whilst she scribbles them down. He finishes with, 'You'll see a sign saying Hippo Heights. It's a hotel overlooking Lake Kariba. Check yourself in there. I'm going Tiger fishing on the lake in a week and I'll come and pick you up from the hotel in my houseboat. Then we'll make another plan, hey? Zambia's on the other side of the lake. You'll be able to see the shore from the hotel.'

'Only if you were going fishing anyway, Dick. I don't at all want you to go out of your way for me. A week? I'll be waiting for you. Oh Dick, thank-you!'

'You're sure Selous's not following you?'

She looks in the mirror. 'I don't think so, but how would I know?'

'You'd better get going again, man. That oke doesn't give up.'

When Beth puts down the mobile she sees there are four little faces at her window, staring at her. They don't smile back. One offers her an upturned hand as if cupping a little bird and then points to her mouth with the other. Beth can see their village behind – a few thatched huts beside hot, unploughed fields.

Empty pots and pans lie on a raised wooden platform in the sun and a brown dog – all ribs and skin – is collapsed in its shade.

Although she has a bottle of water she has no food with her but opens the glove compartment to find half a packet of Marie biscuits that have escaped Bismarck's resident rodent. She hands them to the children and they fight over them. A young woman comes hurrying over from the village and crossly tells the children to leave. She says to Beth, 'You'd better move on. The youth militia are in the village and they'll not tolerate the children speaking to you. The government's preparing for the elections next year so the militia have taken over the primary school. They're educating us.'

'Educating you?'

'How we should vote.' She leans forward to speak quietly although there is no one else to overhear. 'They say that they'll know if we've voted for the opposition Party. If we vote for the opposition, then they'll ask us whether we want a long sleeve or a short sleeve on the arm that we've used to cast our vote.' She makes a cutting motion on her wrist and then does the same above her elbow.

Beth stares at the woman's impassive face. The sky has gone from blue to a bruised purple. 'But why are the children so hungry?'

'We normally eat well here,' the woman says, 'but those families they suspect of supporting the opposition, they prevent them from ploughing and growing their own food. So their children eat beetles.'

Beth looks beyond the woman and sees men – more boys, than men – in green uniforms filing out of the only tin-roofed building in the village. She guesses it to be the school. The woman glances back and then turns without another word and walks back to the village. Beth drives away but loses concentration, skidding on a corner and scraping Bismarck's side on a fallen tree that's spilled onto the road. She feels like she did when she saw the emaciated Judith, sorry at her self-absorption in behaving like a character in one of her misery-lit novels, whilst around her people starve and risk having their arms amputated.

The road narrows and becomes riven with erosion gullies. The country becomes wilder and hotter. Stone shards cut at Bismarck's tyres. She keeps going for another three gruelling hours following her hastily written instructions from Dick. The fuel gauge needle approaches the empty mark. She is far out of mobile signal range here and has no idea what she'll do if she breaks down. She wonders if she can drink the radiator water if she runs out of fuel and is stuck for days. Then, just as a warning light comes on under the fuel gauge, she crests a rise and the hotel appears in front of her, bright as a pilgrim's celestial city.

She'd imagined Hippo Heights as another thatched safari lodge but it's an adobe style building with thick white walls, deep sunk windows and wooden vigas protruding through the upper walls. The road terminates in a gravelled car park covered in dead leaves. Old trees dangle sparsely-leaved twigs from knuckled branches. The hotel at the end of the world. There are no other vehicles. When she turns off the engine, Bismarck hiccups and makes a metallic ping noise as if she is also at the end of her road.

Beth picks up the mobile again, hoping for a signal so that she can let Dick know that she's arrived. It gives a beep and then dies, out of charge. When she steps out she's struck by the silence. Her crackling footfall on the leafy gravel seems to be that of an explorer arriving in a long-lost jungle ruin of a long-extinct civilisation. The solid wood door is locked and an insect has made its nest over the crack. She knocks hard but receives no answer so circles the walls until they step down to reveal the complex of buildings beyond.

She shouts 'Hello, anyone here?' but there is no reply. She steps over the wall where it becomes a low boundary marker and follows a dirty terracotta stone path running between the silent buildings. She comes out onto a wide, flat, untended lawn bordered by untamed shrubs. To one side is a swimming pool behind a low wooden fence covered in rampant honeysuckle. The pool is empty apart from a couple of inches of green water in which frogs float like lime bubbles. A worry grows that the place has been abandoned a long time ago and now predatory animals make it their lair.

Beyond the lawn, the view opens up over the lake. It's such a beautiful sight that she ignores her apprehension and makes for the edge. The forested ground drops sharply away and then opens out onto a flat strip of lushly-grassed shoreline. At the water's edge a herd of elephants graze, pulling up the grass with ease in their supple trunks, swishing the bundle about in the water as if washing their salad. Cormorants perch blackly on the white bones of trees, their wings fanned out to dry. The sun is low and its light runs a crimson sash down the body of the still lake. Oval islands string the water like drops of honey on glass. On the opposite shore the slopes of the Zambian escarpment rise into a cloudless sky. Somewhere an eagle cuts the crystal air with a spine-tingling call.

She keeps her guard. She's become intoxicated by ravishing landscapes since arriving in Africa but there's an ominous pattern developing. Whenever her fears are charmed away – for instance by the mesmerising flow of water over Victoria Falls or the crisp light of the Matobo Hills – it turns out to be a harbinger of danger, if not disaster. Here is another Elysian scene.

She hears a movement behind her. She jumps, a cry escaping her lips as she swings around. A tall skinny man in a dark blue and black striped dressing gown hurries towards her while he ties a knot in the cord around his waist. His legs are bare and his long feet are in a pair of pink flip flops a couple of sizes too small for him.

'Can I help you?' he asks.

'Oh please, yes.' She hears herself whimper with relief. 'My name's Lynette. I'd like to book in to the hotel.'

'I'm Johnson, the hotel manager.' He holds out a long bony hand. 'You want to stay here? You want to have a room?' His eyes fill with astonishment.

'Yes, I'm hoping to have a holiday here for a few days.'

'Is the President deceased?'

She gives him a puzzled look.

'I thought that perhaps the situation has changed,' he says, 'and you're the first of the many tourists we're expecting when–'

'As far as I know the President's fine. I'm just… passing through.'

'You're very welcome but as you can see I've got up late today on account of there being no guests. We only have a skeleton staff.'

On cue Beth sees two distinctly thin people, a man and a woman in matching grey and green hotel uniforms, standing watching her and Johnson from the steps of the hotel terrace.

'Is the hotel closed?' she asks.

'Not exactly but it's so long since we've had a guest that you've surprised us. But don't worry; we're pleased to serve you.' He waves instructions to his staff.

'Perhaps I'd better just check out the room rates first,' she says.

'Are you a foreign national?'

'Yes, very foreign.'

'Then it'll be four hundred and twenty US per night. That's full board, of course. There's nowhere else to dine around here.'

'That seems steep! That's a five star price but, if you don't mind me saying, look at your pool and the gardens here. It's more like a derelict hostel.'

Johnson looks mildly apologetic but says, 'The room rate is set by Karkroski Hotels International so the price is beyond my control. Hippo Heights is designated as five star and until I receive instructions otherwise I have to charge that price.'

'Is there somewhere else I can stay nearby?' It seems a rhetorical question.

He looks to the sky, as if an angel will reveal it, and then says, 'The closest place is Kariba Town but that's a four hour drive around the lake.'

At that price she's going to have to move on, but it's far too late in the day to set out again and she's hungry. She says, 'I'll have to stay one night and then I'll need to fill up my tank. Do you have fuel? I'm down to my last drop.'

Johnson shakes his head. 'The nearest place for fuel is Kariba Town.'

'I'm stuck here then. I'll have to sleep in my car.'

'Ah, I don't think that would be permitted,' Johnson says, 'and it would be inadvisable on account of the night animals. There are hippos and lions.'

'What am I going to do then? This is very awkward. I simply can't afford it.'

Johnson studies the sky again and then, animated all of a sudden, says, 'Maybe if you tell me you're a Zimbabwean resident we can charge you the local rate. It'll be five hundred thousand Zim dollars per night, full board.'

On the unofficial exchange rate that is almost too small a sum to compute. 'Well, thank-you. I suppose I have become a *de facto* Zimbabwe resident.' On account of not being able to leave, she nearly adds.

'Good, now I can charge you local. This'll actually be more conducive and convenient for me and my staff as we cannot guarantee an international service due to the prevailing conditions.'

'That's fine by me. Please, just treat me as a local.' She guesses that, like the museum, Johnson has not had instruction to put up the local rate to keep up with inflation. Some can live in Zimbabwe like kings, whilst others starve.

Despite Beth's downgrading, as they reach the steps to the terrace, one of Johnson's staff presents her with a hot damp flannel, lifting it from its silver platter with a pair of hallmarked tongs. Beth wipes her face and hands and is embarrassed to see that the flannel has turned road-red.

She asks Johnson if the hotel has a phone so that she can ring Dick to let him know she's arrived but he says the telephone wires have been stolen somewhere down the line and his own mobile is flat. There is no fuel for the generator so there is no chance of recharging it. Fortunately they still have gas for cooking. He says he'll have her bags brought up and is surprised when she lifts her day pack and says, 'These *are* my bags.'

Her room – the honeymoon suite – overlooks the lawn and the lake. Johnson says she will have to move out if a honeymoon couple happen to book. Fat chance. When he leaves her to 'unpack' she goes to the large window and looks over the tatty grounds and to the lake beyond. So here she is, the sole guest of Hippo Heights, a resort that must have been spectacular in its time but is now being nibbled away by nature. A luxury hotel with a manager who has long given up bothering to get out of his pyjamas.

She falls into a routine. Before breakfast she walks to the edge of the lawn to see the world painted afresh like an oil painting brushed with thick bold strokes: streaks of cerulean blue on the lake, viridian green on the lake shore, burnt sienna on the hills and bands of cobalt blue in the sky. She has breakfast of black tea and a scrambled or boiled egg with toast on the terrace (they make bread in their gas oven and keep four hens in a walled hen house). Then she strolls around the ragged grounds being careful not to stray into the wilds. Before lunch she reads by the frog-infested pool (they have a library of salacious paperbacks from the seventies). Lunch is on the terrace again: salami, a salad from their high-walled vegetable garden, and sometimes freshly baked bread and jam. After lunch, as the heat makes her limbs heavy, she takes a long siesta in her room and then has tea on the terrace. When the sun is low she takes a warm gin and tonic (the fridge has broken down but they are well stocked with G and T) down to the lounger on the edge of the lawn overlooking the lake. After dark the Zambian escarpment becomes a sharp-edged silhouette against the star-teeming sky. In the evening, Jekuche, the cook, concocts dinner from tinned food although asks her after a few days if she'd like fresh chicken – or whether she'd prefer to carry on having eggs.

The staff – five have stayed on, hopeful of better days – give her space and she keeps herself to herself. She doesn't want to have to answer questions such as what she is doing in Zimbabwe and where she is going next.

As the days pass she witnesses the hotel's inexorable dismantling. One evening an elephant walks in a straight line through the grounds with no regard to there being a hotel there, as if it's an army tank, flattening a stretch of breeze-block boundary wall near the staff quarters. Ants form nests around the paths in the spreading cracks. A woodpecker works patiently on a protruding viga. At night, hippos munch and crush the lawn like a herd of fat, short-legged cows.

Boats pass far out on the lake and occasionally multi-storeyed houseboats moor on the shore, but not near the hotel, and none stops at the hotel's jetty. There's nothing to stop for. After dark, lights dot the lake from the black-painted fishing boats – more platforms than boats – that catch the sardine-like kapenta fish by attracting the shoals with a lamp suspended over the water.

When the week is up, Beth keeps an eye out for Dick and his houseboat. At the end of the ninth day she becomes uneasy but he'd not told her which end of his fishing week he will pick her up. Perhaps he doesn't want his fishing holiday ruined, as she had his last one. On the fifteenth day her heart tells her that Dick isn't going to turn up.

She hopes nothing serious has happened to him. Perhaps his mother has died. She feels guilty that he'll be worried about her or will be frustrated at being unable to make contact. Not that she is otherwise particularly perturbed by her extending stay at Hippo Heights. The truth is that she feels safe here. She believes herself to be out of reach of Selous De Villier and Charlie Ten. The desperate scene at the village on her journey from Bulawayo is also never far from her mind. Hippo Heights seems far from such a brutal world. She guesses the lack of voters in and around the hotel makes it unlikely to attract the attention of the militia. But it isn't only external peril that she's avoiding; she is also safe from her own blundering. Whilst she's at the hotel she can't bring mishap on herself. She can't end up in ponds, in hot metal trunks or on precarious rock ledges. As soon as she leaves the hotel, she knows it will all start again and she is not yet ready for it.

She tries not to think of Matt. Whenever he comes to mind (a sudden unease: is he all right, does he know she's gone, is he hurt by her absence?) she leaps up and walks briskly about or counts boats on the lake or picks up her novel to become someone else.

She calculates that her Zimbabwe dollars, on the unofficial exchange rate with the US dollar, might allow her to stay at Hippo Heights until she's forty, or, if hyperinflation continues, indefinitely.

CHAPTER 20

bout a week later, Beth wakes from her siesta to find a stack of Zimbabwean newspapers in reception. Jekuche says that the back copies have been dropped off by boat, along with a few supplies. 'Now I can cook you some fine food,' he promises.

'You should've woken me,' Beth says. She's missed an opportunity to hitch a lift to Kariba Town.

'I'm sorry, but they didn't want to linger. They think it has become too wild here.'

Beth has had her fill of forgettable paperbacks and so takes the newspapers to her lounger and reads them through. 'Imperialist treachery', 'capitalist machinations' spew the columnists as if every nostalgic Cold War ideologue has been welcomed onto the newspaper's payroll. The opposition Party is described as 'a proxy of the British government', 'American puppets' or 'imperialist agents'. 'We will not go back to being a colony', reads the title of a main editorial. The President features frequently and is described as 'an object of cynosure, held in both reverence and veneration'. Beth is becoming bored when her eye is caught by a small piece on the fourth page under *International News*.

Missing tourist suspected swept over Victoria Falls.
Twenty-eight year old UK doctor, Bethan Jenkins, was holidaying in Livingstone, Zambia, when she disappeared from her hotel. Mr

Bishonga, a spokesperson for the Zambian police said, 'On the evening prior to her disappearance, Dr Jenkins was seen reading in the bar. The hotel management reported her missing the following day. An extensive search has been carried out but there's no trace of the missing person. We're proceeding to investigate her disappearance and are co-operating with the Zimbabwean authorities in case she lost her footing and fell over the Falls.'

Mr Bishonga intimated that, if this was the case, it was unlikely that her body would ever be recovered. The Zambezi is infested with crocodiles.

Riveted as to her fate, Beth hunts through the papers until five days on she comes across an update.

Missing tourist's bag found in Zambezi.

A bag belonging to missing UK doctor, Bethan Jenkins, who is believed to have lost her footing and fallen over Victoria Falls a week ago, has been found in the Zambezi by a member of a white water rafting team.

British gap year student, Emma James, from Godalming in the UK said, 'The rafting was awesome. I was thrown out of the boat and got swept onto a rocky ledge and in this crack I saw the bag. Inside the bag was a soggy guidebook with her name written in it. What was so amazing was that I sat next to Dr Jenkins on the flight to Livingstone and she told me how terrified she was of falling over the Falls. It's totally tragic that her worst fears came true.'

Zambian police spokesperson, Mr Bishonga, said, 'This wraps up the case.'

How had her shoulder bag ended up in the river? No matter how, the truth is that she's officially dead. No one has any expectation of finding her body. She's been devoured and her atoms are now loosely reorganised in the shape of a crocodile. If anyone cares to think of where she is now they can imagine her as living a new life as a reptile – not what she had in mind when she went looking for a fresh start. She might then have ended up as a crocodile skin handbag, the sort of item that Christina would buy. She looks out over the lake, the moat separating her from her previous life. If she truly wishes to assume a new identity she can now do so. The *great Yes* has been astonishingly effective in giving her the opportunity. She would never have guessed the power of poetry.

About a week later – she now no longer bothers to count the days – she is in her room in the afternoon when she hears shouting. She crosses the floor to look out of her window. Uniformed officers – police or perhaps some sort of security unit – swarm over the gardens like an invasion of army ants. So this is it, they've caught up with her. Her non-appearance at the airport will have seemed suspicious to Robson. The illegal immigrant is on the run again and she can't blame him for alerting the authorities. She looks beyond to the Zambian escarpment with a nostalgic longing, a feeling of *Hiraeth*, the Welsh version of homesickness.

There is little she can do but wait for a knock on the door, although she doubts that they will be so polite. It surprises her, how calm she feels. She guesses she's known all along that, sooner or later, her suspended state has to come to an end. Her boat is not going to come in and there seems no other way out than to be escorted away.

As she watches, into the swarm comes a man with no neck and broad shoulders. His wide-based gait takes ownership of the ground he crushes. Oversized gold cufflinks bling the sleeves of his pale blue shirt. Johnson follows closely in his wake, wearing his dressing gown and pink flip flops. The visitor's voice is loud and assertive. 'This place is falling apart. What sort of manager are you? You couldn't run a plastic bag stall in Mbiro market.'

'Sir, very sorry, but there's no income. There are no tourists, sir, to generate revenue,' pleads Johnson.

The man swings around to face Johnson. His eyes are slits between puffy eyelids as if he has an allergic oedema. His heavy jowls drag his lips into a leaden scowl. 'This was the topmost hotel on Kariba. Our Comrade President will not tolerate unpatriotic behaviour. You will bring the Party into disrepute.'

Johnson shrinks back. 'When's the date of his arrival, sir?'

'That's classified. Expect him anytime, like the return of our Lord.'

Johnson opens his hands in a gesture of despair. 'Sir?'

'You have workers. They're idle. They can shape the bushes. They can cut and comb the grass. They can get off their beds and go and scrub the pool and fill it with water.'

'The pool water is pumped from the lake but the pump's broken, sir.'

'Then use buckets. What's wrong with you? Or do you have holes in your buckets?'

'No sir. We can use buckets of course.'

'Do you have any guests?'

'Only one, sir.'

'When does your guest leave?'

'That is uncertain, sir.'

'You'll have to dispose of him.'

'Dispose! Sir? Please?'

'Don't be stupid. You'll tell your guest he must leave. Get me a Sprite.'

'We don't have any Sprite. And sir, we have no food for the President's party.'

The man turns to a side-kick. 'Nelson, fetch a Sprite from the vehicle. And Johnson, get out of your night clothes or I'll have you strangled by the cord around your waist.'

'Of course, sir.' Johnson hurries away, hugging himself, leaving the loud-mouthed man to march around the grounds peering over walls and around fences.

Soon Beth hears an unfamiliar sound: the deep-throated hum of a generator. It seems a metaphor. The engine is returning to the life of the hotel: they are being powered up, life is in forward gear again. That's fine because she's ready to face the future, to step on board. Staying here is not a new life, it's suspended animation. Just a sabbatical. She decides not to break her routine of watching the sun set over the lake. It might be the last opportunity she has to do so. She makes for her recliner at the edge of the lawn. As always she scans the lake for a boat heading for the Hippo Heights jetty and, as always, the boats pass by, miles out on the lake. She ignores the security men who are still poking about, giving the hotel and its surroundings a thorough reconnoitre before the President's visit.

It's not long before the man who admonished Johnson walks over to her. He holds his bottle of Sprite tightly by its neck as if he's throttling a green parrot. 'I'm Mr Madzwaya, a security chief from the President's office. I hope that you're enjoying your stay.' He speaks with an urbane civility in a deep voice.

'It's a lovely spot,' Beth says, feeling apprehensive as his voice rolls over her and his shadow falls on her.

He looks out over the water. The sun bleeds its day-end reds down the length of the lake and the elephants graze in the grasses of the shoreline. 'A pretty place for you,' he says, although he himself seems scornful. She wonders what the sight means to him. Are perceptions of landscape culturally determined? Does he see the scene quite differently: a threatening wilderness perhaps, or a potential gold mine of tourist revenue? Or has he lost his forefathers' awareness of the land, which Beth guesses as being rich in stories. He turns to her. 'Can I join you?' He points at a chair next to her lounger. She nods.

He sits down – making the chair groan – and deposits his Sprite on the small table between them. He stretches out, rests his head back on his clasped hands, and says, 'Ah, it's good to have some R and R. A man in my position never gets a chance to sit down.' Beth offers him a sympathetic nod. 'But let me introduce myself properly. You can call me *Bonifuss* – spelt Boniface. Boniface Madzwaya.' He grins expansively although his eyes are coldly watchful. 'My mother considered me pretty.' He seems to be inviting her to comment.

She smiles weakly. 'I'm Lynette.'

'Lynette? I see. What a pleasure to meet you. I'm sorry if you've found standards are not what they should be. At this time in our history we are struggling. You see, we're suffering under Western sanctions.' He speaks calmly, in the voice of a reasonable man refusing to be provoked by dastardly schemes. 'It's crippling our economy but, let me tell you, it'll never crush our spirit.'

'I see.'

'You're from the UK.' It's a statement, not a question, but she nods. 'That's acceptable. You're a tourist.' He smirks teasingly and then lowers his voice as if letting her in on a secret. 'You're the sort of white we like. Take it from me that the whites living here are no good – they're all colonists. They're like the jacaranda trees, they're not indigenous. Frankly, they should all be uprooted and sent packing to their home countries.'

'Um… are you from this area?' Beth asks.

He guffaws. 'No, no, this place is for animals… and tourists.' She fears she's insulted him but he goes on, 'I was born a long way from here in a village the other side of Harare.'

'Must have been nice, growing up in a village,' she says, trying to keep to small talk, and then remembers the village that was being re-educated.

'Yes, I'm a child of the soil, of the land,' Boniface says. 'You see, I'm Zimbabwean. This is our country, our land.' There is now a menacing edge to his voice. 'It can never be taken from us. Never!'

'I see.'

'Zimbabwe for Zimbabweans and England for the English!' He looks at her expectantly.

'Actually, I'm Welsh!'

'Wales for the Welsh!' There's a cynical edge to his laugh. 'If you wish some advice on revolutionary de-colonisation then you're speaking to the right man. You see my father was a hero of the second Chimurenga.'

'Chimurenga?'

'The war of liberation against the racist Rhodesian regime. Yes, my father was a revolutionary.'

'You must be… er… proud of him.'

'Of course.' He takes a swig of his Sprite. 'So you see, I don't drink beer. My father was a hero but he had a liking for beer, for *chibuku*. That's why I'm teetotal.' He exhales a satisfied breath and then says in a matter of fact manner, 'He used to beat us, especially my mother. Hmm, particularly my mother.'

'Oh, I'm sorry,' Beth says. 'Are your parents still living?'

'No, my father's buried in Heroes' Acre outside Harare as is befitting for a national hero. The President spoke at his funeral. Yes, my father was a great man.'

'Wow. And your mother?'

'My mother was beaten to death,' he says without emotion.

'Your father? He beat your mother to death?'

'No, no, my father beat her, but never to death; she was hit by Rhodesian soldiers. They came to the village and accused her of hiding what they called *gooks*, of giving protection to freedom fighters. Then they hit her with a rifle butt. She fell dead.'

'How terrible.'

Boniface sits silent for a moment and Beth can see that his mood has thickened. 'I learnt two things from my father. Number one: liberation comes through the barrel of a gun.' Then, with a sudden thrusting movement, he raises a fist in the air and shouts, '*Pamberi nehondo*, Zimbabwe for Zimbabweans!' Beth shrinks back but then he breaks out into singing in a surprisingly melodious bass voice in his language and some nearby officers join in. When he's finished he turns to Beth and says, 'I like to sing the liberation songs.'

'It was... tuneful.'

He relaxes back in his chair again. 'I'm sure you've the same in Wales.'

'Perhaps... I'm not really sure about that.' Then, 'Oh, they... we... do have *Hen Wlad Fy Nhadau* – Land of my Fathers.'

'Good, good,' he says in a non-interested way.

'And number two?' she says.

'Number two?'

'You said you learnt two things from your father.'

'Yes, yes, number two: leave the alcohol alone!' He chortles deeply.

'And you? Were you a... freedom fighter?'

'Yes, I am right now a freedom fighter. This is the third Chimurenga.' His eyes bulge and his voice becomes accusatory. 'What you, Lynette, have to understand is this: the land is our

249

spiritual nexus. Our ancestors are buried here – they are like roots under the soil and we are new shoots growing from those roots.' He leans towards her and points a finger at her. 'So we'll not rest until we own every centimetre of the land.' He rolls back into his chair and sounds suddenly tired as he says, 'But only some of us have earned that right. I'm referring, of course, to those of us who belong to the liberating Party. You see, we are the only ones who've spilt our blood for the sake of the land. Therefore the land belongs to us.'

One of Boniface's men interrupts them. 'Excuse me, sir. There's a call on the radio for you.'

Boniface struggles out of his chair with a grunt of displeasure but turns to Beth and says, 'We'll speak again later.' Then he smiles slyly. 'It's been such a pleasure, as mutually oppressed peoples, to share our philosophies.'

Beth sits there a little longer looking out over the darkening lake, Boniface's voice resonating in her like a rumbling night train. The mosquitoes float silently, pretending to be as innocent as dandelion heads. She finds a film of sweat has formed on her forehead.

When she returns to reception it's ablaze with light. Johnson – now appropriately dressed for a hotel manager in pressed black trousers and a white shirt – is in conversation with one of Boniface's officers. As she enters, he breaks off and signals her into a corner. He speaks in a furtive voice. 'I'm very sorry but we're going to be closing soon for guests. With special regret, I have to inform you that we must terminate our hospitality.'

'What's happening?'

He looks around and, seeing there is nobody near, says, 'There's to be a grand party here for the President and his security chiefs.'

Beth feigns ignorance. 'The President? Will the President be here?'

Johnson taps a finger on his lips and looks around again before answering. 'Yes, it's his birthday in February and, as part of the preparatory events leading up to the celebrated day, he's holding a private party here in which he'll be giving out medals to the highest ranking officers in the CIO. So, most unfortunately, we must request that you check out.'

'Johnson, although I've appreciated the way you've looked after me, if I'd been able to leave I would've left a long time ago. How am I going to get away?'

'The security services have brought a fuel bowser with them,' he says. 'I've asked them to fill your tank. We also have fuel for the generator so you can charge your cell. Now is the day when you can contact your friends.'

'Oh wow!' Beth's heart races. 'But my mobile – my cell – got wet and I don't have a charger for the one a friend lent me.'

'Take mine for the time being,' Johnson says. 'Try your sim in it.'

She runs up to her room. When she opens her own mobile to remove the sim card she finds the battery has leaked a sticky residue. She extracts the battery and then takes out the sim and wipes it. She fiddles it into Johnson's mobile and turns it on. *Welcome to Econet.* One uncertain bar of reception shows on Johnson's mobile but texts and multiple notifications of missed calls keep popping up on the display as a reminder that things have happened in the outside world whilst she's been away. Her previous life has tried to find her.

The first text is dated three days after she'd left home and is from Alena: *Hope you having fabulous time. Come back refreshed. Matt OK. x.*

The next, three days later, is again from Alena: *Frantic with worry. Please text. x.*

A day after that is another from Alena. It says simply: *Beth. Please text.*

Two days later there is a long message from Preeti, fully punctuated: *Bethan, I'm so sorry if I ever irritated you. You were my best friend and I never told you and now it's too late. It's awful and I don't think I will ever be completely happy again.*

Then comes Christina's text: *lifes a bitch cant believe u gone tell us u r not.*

Beth walks in rapid circles around her room. Perhaps they've had her funeral by now. Or did they need a body? Their dilemma will have had parallels to hers with Matt. An absent body in her case and an absent mind in Matt's. But before she rings, she slides Dick's sim card into Johnson's phone. Dick has tried to contact her. There are several missed calls and then one text: *big problem. govt minister wishes to help himself to my mine. been called to investors meeting in joburg. unable to go fishing. suggest drive to kariba town. ring when you there.*

Using her own sim card again she tries to ring Alena, still pacing her room to ease the pressure of her excitement. The call is barred. *Please enter code to enable outgoing international calls.* Code?

She jabs out a text. *am alive and well. so much to tell. please ring. cant ring out.*

While she waits for Alena to ring back she stands by the window in the hope of finding better reception. The Zambian escarpment has come closer. Why, she can almost touch it. The call comes a couple of minutes later: a crackly ringtone appropriate for a place almost off the end of the world.

'Beth! Oh, Beth!' Alena – unflappable, calm and collected,

Alena – is sobbing. 'We've just returned from your funeral! We're in Tres Hermanas. Am I drunk? Is that really you?'

'I'm fine, really I'm fine. The reception's terrible. Can you hear me?'

She hears cries in the background and Alena saying, 'Wait, keep quiet,' to the others. 'Say again, Beth.'

'I'm in this defunct hotel called Hippo Heights in Zimbabwe.'

She only hears the last part of what Alena says next, '… you escaped from the river?'

'I was never in the river. I was in a slimy pond on a golf course.'

'What? I don't understand. They found your bag in the river.'

Beth loses her. The phone crackles. '… but Beth, before you go any further… ' then the line cuts out. It rings again but when she answers she can't hear Alena. She sends a text: *will try to move to better reception.* Then, wanting to take a step at a time, she adds, *dont tell anyone but you three am alive until weve spoken again.*

She hurries downstairs clutching both functioning phones to go to the edge of the lawn in the hope of finding a signal. She almost runs through the hotel lobby but is stopped by a security man.

He holds out his hand. 'Give me your phones,' he says in an unfriendly fashion. 'We're now locked down. No one's permitted to ring out.'

Beth grips the phones tightly to her chest. 'I'm waiting for a phone call. It's very important.'

'I have my orders. We're not police, we're state security. No one refuses us. You must give them to me now.'

'Well, I can't! This is an emergency.' Her hands cramp.

He scowls and raises his voice. 'You think because you're white, you can dictate to me?' He turns and signals to another officer to come over. 'Arrest this woman.'

The other officer goes to hold her arm but she is already releasing her lifelines. The man snatches them and then waves away his junior.

'When will I get them back?'

'When it's permitted.' He turns and marches away.

CHAPTER 21

Each step up to Beth's room is a mountain of disappointment. She goes and sits hunched on her bed and looks out of the window towards Zambia. The escarpment is far away, as hazy as an almost-lost memory.

It is not long before Beth hears a knock on her door. She turns and says, 'Come in.'

It's Johnson. He's fidgety, appears frantic to speak with her. 'Lynette, my sincerest apologies for inconveniencing you but I have important news for you.'

She stands up, alarmed. 'What is it?'

'Mr Madzwaya has informed me that you can stay in residence for the President's party. In fact he wants you to be a guest of the President. This is a great honour for you. Mr Madzwaya says that you're a special friend of Zimbabwe. I'm sorry; I'd no idea who you were.'

'What do you mean? Who does he say I am? Who am I?' Her words echo in her head, *who am I?*

'He's not said exactly, but to be invited to the President's party, well… it's as if you're a heroine of the liberation!' Johnson shakes his head in wonder.

'I don't want to be a heroine. I just want to leave, Johnson. I really, really, want to check out. It's been over six weeks now. Christmas has come and gone. You've been very kind but I need to go.' She drops herself down on her bed again.

Johnson reaches his hands out to her in alarm. 'Please,

Lynette, it would be inadvisable to decline an invitation from Mr Madzwaya. He's a big man; when he visits Bulawayo in his official capacity his motorcade is a kilometre long.'

'I don't care. He'd be an insignificant man, probably having to get about by foot, in the sort of world I want to live in. I don't trust him.'

Johnson's eyes are pleading. 'It'll not delay you long. After the President's party you'll be able to depart when it pleases you.' She starts to shake her head again. He looks sheepish and says, 'I've been instructed by Mr Madzwaya to disable your car.' He pulls an electric cable out of his pocket and stares at it sorrowfully. 'I do apologise most sincerely. Mr Madzwaya doesn't like to be refused.'

Over the following days, trucks and boats carrying large crates – supplies for the President's party – come and go and a camp of tents is erected for the soldiers tasked with transforming Hippo Heights back to its former magnificence. The swimming pool pump is mended, the terracotta paths are scrubbed with soap and water, dead foliage is pruned from the shrubs and the dust hosed off every leaf. Rainbows arch in the sprinklers on the lawns. The walls are painted a dazzling white and the thick wooden doors polished to a deep lustre. Beth tries to keep out of the way, avoiding the curious glances of the soldiers. A member of staff is instructed to stand by the swimming pool all day with a net to keep it bug-free. A helipad is cleared in the bush.

Beth doesn't see Boniface Madzwaya again after he'd introduced himself. Johnson tells her that he's returned to Harare, leaving a deputy to oversee the preparations. There is nothing to do but wait.

She's reading on the terrace one morning when she hears a shot ring out and hears shouts from the jetty below. A soldier is pointing his rifle in the air whilst others are waving away the boat that is heading for the jetty. It seems to be a gate crasher, and an ugly one at that. The boat has the look of an oil rig from a tropical delta: a rust-eroded, box-like shape, three decks high, holed by effluent pipes, each drooling a stain like a long black beard. It floats on black oil drums. The top deck is open and topped by a patched, sun bleached, green-canvas awning. This cannot be a delivery of party poppers.

The warning shot has its desired effect: the water around the boat churns; thick exhaust spews out like burning oil as the engines are put full astern. But the structure keeps coming forward under its momentum. The soldier levels his gun at the window on the face of the vessel nearest the shore. Beth can see someone in a red baseball cap behind the window – perhaps the Captain – desperately waving his innocence. She can also see a woman in a blue silk top and white cargos coming down the ladder from the upper deck to a small platform just above the waterline. Beth recognises her instantly. When the woman reaches the platform she also holds up her hands to the soldiers.

Beth runs down the path shouting, 'Alena!'

The soldiers turn towards Beth and one holds up his hand to signal her to stop but she's soon past him and up on the jetty. The houseboat edges away. Alena is leaning over the hand rail shouting, 'Beth!' and then she is shouting up at the wheelhouse, 'Wait!' There are only twenty feet of water between them but the gap is widening. Beth dives in. When she breaks the surface the boat seems to be moving away too fast for her to catch it. She hears a soldier shout, 'Dangerous! Dangerous! Crocodiles!' She submerges her head and recruits every muscle for a frantic crawl. When she lifts her head again, Alena's hand is there. She grips it and then has a hold on the boat's platform. Alena helps her out and then she is in her embrace.

They are speechless for a few moments and then Beth says, 'You've come to rescue me. I can't believe it. I love you!'

Alena says, in a matter-of-fact tone, 'The line was terrible but I heard the name of your hotel and we had a little help from a friend of yours and so here we are.'

'Where are your twins?'

'With my sister.'

'But first, is Matt OK?'

'He's fine.'

Beth embraces Alena tightly again but Alena holds her with a light touch and Beth remembers that Alena has never been one for displays of emotion. She prefers to save her energy for tidying up and sorting out a mess. The worse the better. Good Alena; it's hard to imagine anyone else who could have arranged and accomplished her rescue.

There's a squeal from above. Preeti is coming gingerly down the ladder in silver wedges. Alena and Beth hold their breaths until Preeti is on the platform. After they've hugged, Preeti says, 'Manesh thinks I'm at my mother's for a week. He won't ring the land line because he won't want to accidentally get his mother-in-law on the phone. Today I texted him to say that we were having a nice day looking at saris in south London. Oh Beth, you look so well!'

'Where's Christina?' Beth says, 'Did she come too?'

'She's being sick,' Alena says.

'Really? The lake's dead calm. Poor thing.'

'Let's go to the upper deck,' Alena says, 'we've got drinks and snacks all ready. Do you want to change first? You can borrow my clothes.'

'No, I feel cool and refreshed – I'll soon dry out.' Preeti gives her a towel from the handrail.

Alena leads Beth through a metal door that opens onto a stairway up to the top deck. Christina is there waiting and is with Beth in a couple of long strides. She holds Beth desperately and Beth is enveloped in Fendi Palazzo perfume and long blonde curls. 'I thought you were dead, Bethan Jenkins. How could you do that to me? Don't ever, ever, do that again.' She releases Beth but then places her hands on Beth's shoulders and leans forward and presses her forehead against Beth's forehead and closes her eyes. Beth feels now the depth of the pain she's caused; and is appalled.

Then Preeti tugs on Beth's hand. 'Come, let's sit down,' she says as she pulls her towards a table. Beth sees that the shoreline is receding but doesn't care that, once again, she's in possession of only the sodden clothes that cling to her. She takes a seat and attacks her wet hair with the towel to make sure that all this – Alena, Preeti and Christina out here on a blue, shimmering lake in the middle of Africa – can't be rubbed away. On the table are flowering grasses; there's a jug of iced water and sodas; there are drinking glasses that sparkle, one acting as a vase for a spray of delicate pink flowers. Polished wooden bowls – positioned on a shiny red ribbon that runs the length of the table – brim with macadamias, pistachios and peanuts. Each end of the ribbon is tied in a bow. This is the homecoming party and her friends have been preparing it for hours. She drops her towel to her lap. Alena, Christina and Preeti stand in an embracing circle, staring at her with silly smiles on their faces. Beth knows that her own smile (framed by the damp tangle of her hair) is crooked with guilt. These are her friends, but she'd betrayed them, visited them with anguish. She'd acted as if her life was her own; as if it was entirely hers to choose what she did with it. That had always seemed a given. But now she has, she thinks, become a little wiser.

'Would you like to be the resurrected Jesus: cast out a net and then cook fish for us?' Christina says dryly.

Alena lifts her hands. 'OK, just hold it.' She goes to the top of the stairs and waves to someone to come up. Then, all smiles, she says, 'Beth, there's someone else on board. The day after you rang, Hope came to your house and I bumped into her as she was coming out. We couldn't have got here without her advice and help.'

Hope comes into view and then, light on her feet, runs to Beth. Beth stands and feels a burden roll away. 'This is perfect,' she breathes.

They kiss and Hope says, 'I have to tell you straight away that I have good news for you. Fortunate's alive!' Beth leans back and searches Hope's excited eyes. 'Fortunate wasn't shot at by Selous. It was a member of the security services who tried to kill him. They'd been following you, and also Fortunate and me, hoping to get their hands on Mr De Villier's title deed. His bullet hit a book in Fortunate's rucksack and knocked him down, but he wasn't harmed.'

'You're kidding me!'

'No, no, I'm not!' Tears sparkle on Hope's eyelashes.

'So what happened next? How did you escape?'

'We didn't escape – Selous found us. Oh, Dr Jenkins – may I call you Beth? – I was so mistaken about him. Selous came out of his cottage when he heard the shot and fired at the man who tried to kill Fortunate so that the man had to run off. Then Selous wanted to hide me with you because of the danger to us.'

Beth thinks this is improbable, after all she's heard about Selous. Hope has been duped. She doesn't know that Selous killed his own mother; doesn't know that he's left his daughter in an orphanage. But she will not disabuse Hope straight away in case she spoils this happy moment. 'That's so wonderful that Fortunate's OK. Where's he now?'

'I left him with Selous.'

'He stayed with Selous?'

'Selous was very kind to us.'

'You said.'

'Yes, he looked after us. Fortunate wished to stay with him.'

Preeti is bursting to interrupt. 'Come and sit down and tell us everything, Beth, right from the beginning, and don't leave anything out.'

Despite Preeti's plea, Beth judges that there are some things she should keep to herself, at least until she has understood more. In the end she confesses to almost everything: her impulsive decision to leave home; her desire to deliver Mr De Villier's deed and the letter to his son (she leaves out any mention of Shungu and the ridiculous worry that Fortunate was going to assassinate the President); her illegal entry by microlight into Zimbabwe (at that point Preeti, jaw loose, looks as if she's going to pass out. Even Alena exclaims, 'My God, Beth!'); her rough treatment at the hands of Selous (she exaggerates a little); and her escape from the farm in Selous's car ('You're bloody kidding, Bethan Jenkins!' Christina says). She doesn't tell them that she's given the title deed to Mr De Villier's solicitor. An uncertainty plays on her, now that Hope has come to Selous's defence, that she's made a terrible error. She tells them that she became very lost on her way to the airport and ended up at the hotel. She finishes by saying, 'I think I must've been having some sort of mental breakdown to have left home like that.' She doesn't try to explain the *great Yes*.

There's a prolonged silence when she's finished as if Alena, Preeti and Christina are having to relive the weeks she's been away in the new knowledge that she'd been alive all the time. They're recalling what they were doing – and what stage of worry or grief they were in – at the turning points of Beth's story. She apologises for the trouble she's caused and for the heartache she's made them suffer.

Preeti drains an ice cube from her glass to her mouth and then says, juggling the cold lump from cheek to cheek, 'I think we'd be a teeny bit angry with you, Beth, if it wasn't for the fact that you've done the perfect – the decent – thing by becoming alive again.'

'Your poor old foster-parents had a memorial service for you,' says Alena. 'We all went of course, even though we didn't want to believe it until your body was found. Even Dr Moncrieff was there. And Penelope. She was surprisingly upset! Said you would have made a good mother. I've brought the order of service with me and a copy of the eulogy I gave. I guess it's an opportunity for you to correct it for next time. Actually, now you've told us all this, I don't think I really knew you, so there's a lot of correcting to do.'

'Does everyone know now that I'm alive?' Beth says.

'You said not to tell anyone anything yet,' Alena says, 'so we didn't.'

'Oh yes, so I did.'

They tell Beth how they'd hired the boat in Kariba Town at very short notice from a boat yard mechanic who doubles as captain and whose two younger brothers cook and act as deck hands. Hope negotiated the price down from extortionate to eye-watering. The cabins are metal-walled boxes, Gas Mark 9 in the day and not much better at night so they sleep on mattresses on the top deck.

Beth takes in her surroundings. Despite the tattered awning and the corroded state of the rest of the boat, the upper deck has the style of a handsome Victorian pier with its long wooden floor, elaborately wrought railings and even a lamppost with a gas lamp. Cushioned recliners look out on the lake. They've left the shore a long way behind now, and Hippo Heights looks like a dazzling white Spanish village on a hill. She remembers that she's going to miss the President's party. She'd almost started to look forward to it, despite being anxious at not having a party dress. She fills her lungs with the warm easy air. How good that she's not going to have to meet the slyly menacing Mr Madzwaya again. But what has she left in her room? Not much. Her passport. Oh well, she's got by without it so far. And Mr De Villier's letter to Selous. Still in her day pack. But all that business now seems a long time ago. An aberrant other life. A mistake.

Christina has been unusually quiet, sipping frequently at a glass of water and sucking sticks of biltong – the salty cured meat popular in Zimbabwe. Now Beth catches her signalling to the others with her eyes. Alena says, 'I'm just going to take some washing-up down to our crew.' Preeti and Hope jump up to help.

'I'm sorry, I gather you're seasick,' Beth says to Christina when the others have gone.

'Sick, yes. Some of it might be the clumpy *sadza* porridge they give us for breakfast but some of it isn't.' She clears her throat. 'This is bloody awkward.' She coughs. It occurs to Beth then that Christina has not lit up a cigarette.

'I'm pregnant,' Christina says.

'Pregnant? Pregnant! Wow! That's fabulous, Christina!' She jumps up to put her arms around her. She'd always thought Christina needed the ballast of a child in her life although she believed that the man would happen first.

Christina coughs heavily again and looks away from Beth out over the water. Beth sits down. 'Isn't it? I mean not that I'd think ill of you if you've decided to... '

Christina looks increasingly bilious and pale. 'I'm carrying Matt's child.'

'I don't think I've met him. Matt?'

'For God's sake, Beth! I'm carrying your husband's child. Matt's baby.'

'Matt's baby?' Beth finds herself looking down at their conversation from a height, out of body. She feels no emotion. The woman with the tangled dark hair and wet clothes is asking, 'How can you possibly be carrying… ?' The blonde woman doesn't reply. 'I don't get it,' the dark one says dumbly and Beth can hear her thinking: artificial insemination, some form of remote control mechanism? Or is the blonde one uttering a profound but incomprehensible metaphor for a momentous psychological transformation?

Beth is opposite Christina again, looking her in the face, and Christina is saying, 'Look Beth, when you ran off and died, I helped out a bit at your house. We took it in turns keeping an eye on Matt when your mother-in-law went off on one of her spa weekends.'

'Did he… rape you?' Matt's baby. His child.

'I thought you were dead.'

'What, it just happened?' Beth stares at Christina.

'For God's sake, Beth! Of course it didn't just happen. I was bloody torn to shreds by your death. I've known you since we were schoolgirls. The one reliable person in my life. You were my… my mooring. And then you disappeared.' She takes a hungry breath and then controls herself. 'It was like I was… don't take this wrong… fucking you, bringing you back to me.' She starts to cry silently.

Beth finds herself at the rail. Just take it slowly, step through it. She doesn't look back at Christina, keeps her voice flat. 'Matt's severely mentally disabled.'

Christina mumbles, 'I thought you were dead,' and then gives a loud sob and blurts, 'Mentally, yes, but only mentally.'

Beth grips the rail as if she can crush it.

'I thought I was infertile. I've got PID,' says Christina, quiet again. 'That's why I'm dumped by my boyfriends when it gets to talking with them about our future. At least… I think it is.' She starts sobbing again.

'I should imagine that you could be prosecuted. Taking advantage of a man with… a learning disability. Raping him!'

'That'll be up to you.' Christina's voice is now almost too low to hear. 'But I didn't force myself on him.'

'And my side of the bed was hardly cold.' Beth can see it now: an amorous advance from Matt, his hands on Christina, her hesitation, and then, flushed, Christina fumbling for his belt… it got too painful to imagine further. In the kitchen? They'd done it there once themselves – uncomfortable. On the sitting room sofa? Twice – a little better. Or did Christina lead Matt up to their bedroom?

A gust of heated air sears Beth's face. 'Does Penelope know?'

'Yeah. She certainly does.' Christina blows into a tissue. 'She came back unexpectedly and found us… '

'Oh please! And?'

'She was thrilled to bits. Then she wouldn't stop phoning until she was sure I'd missed my period although I told her that was impossible. When I did miss, she frogmarched me to the chemist for the pregnancy test. She insisted on taking the strip, then when she saw I was pregnant she went mad, screamed the turban off the pharmacist and shouted, *Look, it's a grandchild!*

'What's going to happen, Christina? A child is for life you know.'

Christina blows loudly into her tissue again.

Beth says, 'You're going to keep the baby?'

'Of course.'

Matt's baby. She sees Matt as she first saw him, remembers that – even in her floaty infatuation – there was the sober female intuition that she'd like her children to have him as their father. Beth forms it on her lips. A baby. The tears burst from her eyes and fall like rain over the side of the boat. It should have been her having Matt's child. If he had to make someone pregnant, it should've been her. She should've listened to Penelope. Matt will live on, a memory of him in flesh and blood, but there'll be nothing of her, nothing of them together, in the child.

She becomes aware of Christina standing beside her at the rail. 'Beth, if you want me to terminate, I'll give it some thought.'

'No! No, I don't.'

'Good, 'cos I couldn't do it.' Then, after a while, she says, 'I've always wanted a baby.'

Beth dries her eyes. 'Are you going to move in with Matt or something?'

'You're talking as if I've consummated a relationship.'

The sun burns the back of Beth's hands. She walks to the end of the rail and descends the stairs. She hears Christina say after her, 'I'm sorry, Beth. At the time I didn't believe in the resurrection of the dead.'

Beth stands on the platform over the water. It's midday and the boat is wallowing on the still lake with the engine off. Although it's calm, the surface of the lake is silvery and alive, like the skin of a fish, a soundless shimmering that invites her in. She wants to be on her own again, to feel washed of what she's been told. She strips to her undies and lowers herself down, then pushes herself out and swims with languid strokes away from the boat. The water tastes clean and pure and is at body temperature so that she has little sense of immersion, just suspension. A haze makes the shore all but invisible. Above her is an infinitely high sky and below, what feels to be a bottomless depth of water. It comes to her that, if she keeps going, she'll eventually reach Hippo Heights. She floats between diffracted colours, on a boundary between the lives she can live.

CHAPTER 22

Beth swims on in a numb state, the water smooth around her, until she becomes aware of Christina's voice coming from far over the water. 'Beth! Beth!' She turns herself about and sees the boat, a distant charcoal blot in the white light. Christina is standing alone at the rail, forlorn and frail as if she is the one about to drift away, to dissolve in the haze. Minutes pass and still Christina waits, her figure alternately fading and forming. Beth hangs motionless in the vast tranquillity of the lake. Then, in slow but resolute strokes, she starts back to the boat, her shock and outrage melting away like a bath salt. By leaving home she's created a crack in the walls around her life but that fissure, that chink through which she'd seen the light of escape, has brought down the whole house. She is as much to blame as Christina – maybe even more so.

Now there are going to be four of them – five if she counts Penelope – in what is looking likely to be one of those alternative family arrangements she'd read about in the Family section of the Saturday *Guardian*. She sees that Christina's pregnancy changes little in practical terms for the situation at home. She remains Matt's legal wife and is entitled to live with him, even if Penelope has changed the locks to the house. She still has a responsibility to Matt which, recently, she's not fulfilled. It's pointless to rage. She will want contact with the child, as painful as that might be at first, and she doesn't want to burn bridges with Christina in case it breaks apart their small sisterhood. And she thinks that, whilst they had all made no small effort to come out to Zimbabwe to rescue her, Christina had perhaps made the most.

She recalls what Christina said to her after revealing that she was pregnant. Christina had called her 'my mooring'. It was unexpected, but maybe the bereaved find that they can only distil in a single sentiment what a person really meant to them, after they are gone.

Alena appears on the platform of the boat in a red bikini and dives slickly into the water, creating hardly a disturbance in the skin of the lake. She swims towards Beth. What do they think? That she's going to drown herself? They must be wondering. When Alena reaches Beth, a little breathless from her energetic breast stroke, she says, 'I'm so sorry for you. You must be mad at her. Preeti and I are. I meant to warn you when we spoke on the phone.'

Beth turns on her back and paddles with her feet as she looks up at the sky – a blue vent in the haze. She is warm, caressed and supported as she flows. She wants Alena to swim beside her, cutting the water, slipping along like a dolphin. She wants Preeti to be there, splashing about, an untidy paddle. And she wants Christina sitting in a punt nearby in a long flowery dress dipping her fingers in the water, saying, 'I'm bloody well not going to get my hair wet. I've just washed it.'

She says, 'I'm not going to fume at Christina for long. She's not the only one to do something unexpected. And she's got her reasons.'

'But what she did is a… betrayal,' Alena says.

'I don't know,' Beth says. 'Maybe it is if I look on Matt as BC Matt. But just think, I'm no longer going to have to endure the pressure from Penelope to act as a test tube for her grandchild.'

When they reach the boat, Beth can hear Christina retching in the toilet off the stairwell. It must be horribly hot and airless in there.

In the afternoon they moor on a small island. They lean against the rail, absorbed in their thoughts whilst they watch the crew lash the boat to two trees and secure a gangplank across to the shore. Beth has not said anything to Christina but earlier she'd given her a short, wordless hug and Christina said, 'Oh God, thanks Beth,' before bursting into tears.

Christina, Preeti and Alena go for a walk on the island under the grey-green canopy of the leadwood trees but Beth stays behind with Hope. They go and lie on the loungers and look out over the lake while they sip cream sodas through long pink straws.

Beth is glad to have Hope to herself without the crisis and urgency of the previous occasions they'd met. Here on the houseboat, Hope has been composed, has been listening to their conversations and – if not joining in – has smiled when they've laughed and been appreciative of Christina's and Preeti's attentiveness to her. Beth guesses that Hope's dream is not yet extinguished. Fortunate is alive. The fire still burns. She has seen Hope go to the rail and gaze out towards the Zimbabwean shore. Somewhere out there, over the horizon…

But Beth has Fortunate on her mind as well and wants to douse smouldering speculation. She asks, 'Do you mind telling me about Fortunate? How much do you know about his background? Where he came from? His family?'

Hope hesitates before saying, 'To be honest, he doesn't talk about himself much so there's very little to tell you. He just likes to go on about Shungu.' She gives *Shungu* a bitter inflection and then sucks hard on her straw.

Hope's ignorance is not reassuring. Beth says, 'You'll think it a strange question, but is it possible that Fortunate has a criminal record?'

Hope, still sucking on her straw, turns her face towards Beth so abruptly that the straw fractures on the rim of her glass. She pulls it from her lips. 'No, I cannot imagine that! Who would say such a thing?'

'But you just said that you don't know much about his past.'

'It's true, but I'm sure he's in no way the criminal type.'

'But where's Fortunate now? What did he do after you left Selous's place?'

'He stayed on with Selous.'

'Did he go hunting with Selous whilst you were there?'

'No, but Selous showed Fortunate how to shoot. They hung a melon from a tree and Fortunate practised shooting it.'

Beth jerks up to a sitting position. 'That's like in *The Day of the Jackal*! It's as if he's following the book. Hope, this is going to sound outlandish but I'm worried that Fortunate's going to carry out that last task he was set by Shungu – by Charlie Ten, I mean. He sent me the DVD of *The Day of the Jackal* after he left Twicare. It's about an assassin who tries to kill General De Gaulle. The assassin sets out on his own. No one knows his background. He practises his shooting on a melon – just like Fortunate. You don't think Fortunate's actually planning on carrying through that last task?' Hope looks unconvinced but Beth asks, 'Did you tell him that the emails he was receiving weren't from Shungu?'

Hope touches her forehead with the back of her hand as if Beth's question has caused her a fever. 'No, I was going to but... it wasn't the right time... I wasn't the right person...' Beth sees that, besotted by Fortunate as Hope is, she would have had difficulty in admitting to him that she'd been used by Charlie

Ten to deceive him. Hope says, 'So you're worried that Fortunate is actually going to attempt it – to assassinate the President?'

Spilling her drink as she waves her arm, Beth says, 'The assassin in the book gets close to De Gaulle by disguising himself as a disabled old man and tries to shoot De Gaulle as he's giving medals to war veterans.' She puts down her drink and wipes the sticky drips from her bare legs. 'The thing is, there's going to be a party for the President at Hippo Heights and the President's going to be giving out medals to officers of the security service. It'd be an ideal chance for an assassin to kill the President.'

Hope says nothing. Beth tidies her limbs. She sounds foolish.

'Even so,' Hope says, 'I don't think that Fortunate would actually do that.'

'But he was infatuated with Shungu,' says Beth. Hope winces. 'Remember the other tasks that Charlie Ten set him that he was so desperate to fulfil. They weren't rational requests but that didn't seem to worry him or to stop him acting on them.'

'That's true,' Hope says. Beth sees a wash of doubt in Hope's eyes. 'He's a passionate man.' Her chest rises in a silent sigh as she look looks out over the lake. Then she says, 'The strange thing is that Fortunate did disguise himself as an old man when we were on our way to find you at Selous's place.'

'Really?' Beth exclaims. 'It's not impossible then, is it?'

Hope mulls it over whilst she tries to straighten her broken straw. Then she says determinedly, 'No, I don't believe he could do such a thing. He never mentioned this to me and I just know that he's not like that.'

Hope's certainty seems final and Beth's bubble of speculation bursts. 'You're right, Hope, it's a silly thought.'

That evening Hope says she'll sleep downstairs as she doesn't like the wind that blows at night over the top deck. Beth goes down to see Hope's cabin and (after they've agreed that its metal-walled functionality needs softening with walnut panelling and a floral curtain over the porthole) Hope asks Beth to sit down beside her.

When Beth has settled herself, Hope takes a deep breath and says, 'With everything that's happened I think I'd better tell you something.'

Beth is tired and deeply weary of shocking revelations so says with involuntary sharpness, 'You're not pregnant, are you?'

A momentary look of surprise crosses Hope's face and then she says quietly, 'I owe a lot to your husband.'

Beth stops breathing. The cabin seems to judder.

'Before he had his stroke,' Hope says, 'he was my guarantor when I applied for a visa to work in the UK. It's no coincidence that I work at Twicare. Mr Hallam recommended I apply for a job there. He said he'd heard you say that they employ people from other countries.'

Beth jumps to her feet. 'And I'm the last to know about it all! Why do you think he never told me about you? You must have corresponded a lot over the visa and the job.'

Hope hesitates.

'I'm sorry, Hope,' Beth says, and plonks herself down on Hope's bed again. 'I'm over-sensitive about what my husband didn't tell me. But I'm OK, please go on.'

'You see I knew him in Zimbabwe.'

'Uh, huh.'

'I was his maid.'

'His *maid*? Hope!' The cabin lurches again. Hope is looking down at her lap, her face giving away no emotion. Beth looks at Hope: this is the woman Lindi has told her about. She isn't a nameless peasant who has disappeared into a grinding rural life or died of HIV in a township slum in South Africa. Her life has already become entwined in Beth's. Hope had known Matt before she did and had told him about the most important and painful event in her life. Beth says, 'I'm not sure I can cope with all this but you'd better tell me everything. We've a lot to talk about. Matt and I were very close. At least, I thought we were. I don't understand why he kept quiet about you, why he never talked about his time in Zimbabwe. He knew I was capable of keeping secrets. It doesn't make sense.' She has the disturbing thought that Matt had been suspicious that she'd spill his beans to her friends in Tres Hermanas. She guesses it's a nagging worry for any man, that his partner will tell his secrets to her female friends as if those friends sit – by biological principle – within the chambers of a woman's heart.

Hope says gently, 'Maybe he didn't want you to worry.'

'What would I have to worry about? Were you having an affair?' She knows she sounds cross and shrill.

Hope stays even-voiced. 'No, there was never anything like that. Let me tell you, please. When I was his maid I took him to a place in the Matobo Hills near Bulawayo where there were the bones of several massacre victims. These were innocent people killed because of their ethnicity and because they lived in the wrong place. You see, I was the only one that remembered them, who knew what they'd suffered.' She stops speaking and holds herself still.

'And why did you choose to tell Matt? Why take Matt to the site?'

'I wanted to tell him because I thought that if something were to happen to me, the memory of that... thing... would be lost. No one would ever remember. It would be as if it never happened.

That is what the perpetrators want.' A fire burns briefly in her eyes. 'So far, they've been permitted to forget. But there's also another reason. It had become too much for me to hold this memory, this... hurt, alone. Of course, Almighty God knows, but we're just people and God is God. I needed someone else to share it with.'

'But why did you share it with Matt and not one of your friends or a relative?'

'My grandmother knew but she was becoming an old woman. Mr Hallam was an outsider; he had no local connections, no baggage of blame or guilt. He had no hatred or love to defend. He would keep the memory and then one day, maybe one day, he would know what to do with that memory.'

'And what happened after you took him there?'

'He reported the site to the police superintendent in Bulawayo. Then he was deported from the country.'

It's what Beth already knows. 'Did he ask your advice before reporting it?'

Hope shakes her head. 'It surprised me. Sometimes I feel he acted correctly, and sometimes... I don't know.'

'Why are you sharing this with me?' Beth asks.

'Because Mr Hallam no longer remembers; and so the time has come for you, his best friend, to hold his memories. To keep them.' Someone starts hammering on metal nearby, perhaps on a pipe in the nearby engine room, but Hope shows no sign of having heard it.

The hammering stops and the boat becomes as silent as the *Mary Celeste*. Beth speaks softly as she says, 'Is there anything else you want me to remember?'

Hope tells Beth then, in a quiet steely voice, of her parents who were both primary school teachers working in a rural area – of the day they were herded together with other villagers, crushed into a pickup truck and marched through the bush at gunpoint; then there was the man who cut them down with bullets, shouting, 'Sell-outs! Cockroaches!' And then the long night, before she struggled from under her dead parents and wandered in a daze, away from the site.

Beth holds Hope's small hand whilst she cries. After a while Beth says, 'What do you want me to do, Hope? Should we report it to an organisation that logs this sort of thing?'

Hope turns to her, her delicate gentle face melting Beth's heart. 'For me, it's enough that you know. That brings me some peace. Someday it may be that justice will come but now is not the time. This is a type of justice: that we remember.'

Beth squeezes Hope's hand. 'I won't forget.' She has a conviction that Hope's story will one day be told. Someone will write about it. She'll ask someone to write about it. Words in print will speak against the silence of the perpetrators, and shift power from executioner to victim, robbing the men of violence of their authority.

She thinks of the images of the massacre victims, still in her bag at Hippo Heights. Should she tell Hope that she's been in possession of the photos? Of course not. It's not the right moment, if it ever will be. She stands up to let Hope sleep but Hope says, 'You were saying how you didn't understand why Mr Hallam said nothing about all this. You must understand that the man who carried out the massacre is very dangerous. He's still feared. Maybe your husband didn't wish to put you in any danger.'

Beth isn't convinced that's adequate reason for Matt's silence. The sharp fact is that no one knows why, not even Hope. Then she recalls Matt's fear at the man who came to the door and she says, 'And where's he now, that man who carried out the massacre?'

'In fact I've told you about him before, when I was in the

UK,' Hope says. 'He was the man who wished me to be his girlfriend. He doesn't know that he tried to kill me when I was four.'

'Oh, Hope. Charlie Ten?'

Hope bows her head and Beth can hardly hear her say, 'It's him.'

Beth takes it all in: the man who tried to murder Hope as a child has now used her for his own scheming purposes, presumably unaware of who she is. It's incredible, but then she thinks it's not: the trajectory of life can run like a path over an invisible landscape of time and place which is shared with others. The valleys and ridges of that mutual landscape can incline and channel those paths, to lead people to collide again with each other years later.

Hope says, 'This is the same man who perpetrated the massacre, and it is the same man who your husband reported the massacre to. He was the police superintendent at the time.'

'And now he's in the CIO?'

'Yes, he's very senior in the security services. A very powerful man. He's close to the President.'

'What's his name, Hope?' Beth asks, although she already knows it.

'His name is Mr Madzwaya. Boniface Madzwaya.'

CHAPTER 23

I t's late, but when Beth returns to her mattress on the top deck, she finds Alena, Christina and Preeti chatting like young girls on a sleepover, Alena updating them on the latest films and theatre productions, which she and Martin try never to miss. Christina is giving her blunt opinions and making libellous declarations on leading actors and actresses whilst Preeti says she can't go to films with Manesh because he's always so exhausted from his work re-plumbing hearts that he falls asleep immediately and snores. Beth is glad of their talk, thankful to have distraction from what Hope has told her.

As the conversation dies, Beth stares up to the heavens. The stars are dense – they seem to have been thrown across the marble-black night sky like handfuls of salt. She'd like another rocket, Croc's rocket, to take her up and away again.

She finds that she has slept and, although it is still dark, there is just a hint of pre-dawn light in the east. She's had a dream-free night but knows something deeper than dreams has been at work. She sits herself up. A low moon casts a path of light across the water, leading a way to the far shore. She's no doubt what she has to do. She dresses, steals downstairs and knocks on the Captain's door. He emerges with a towel around his waist, smelling of spirits. Beth tells him that they need to be under way as soon as possible. She wants to be dropped back at Hippo Heights. When he looks reluctant to be persuaded, she informs him that she's expected there by the President. She also shows him her dollars.

When Beth returns to the deck, Alena whispers sleepily from her mattress, 'What's happening?'

'Do you have a frock I can borrow?' Beth asks. 'I'm going to the President's party. We're going back to Hippo Heights.'

'But we've just rescued you!' Alena exclaims.

Beth sits on Alena's mattress and fills her in on her unfinished business. She explains everything and ends with, 'So you see I'm obsessed. I have to find answers. And I want to help Hope. I have to speak to Boniface Madzwaya, and he's going to be at the party. I have an invitation and, if I don't take this chance, I doubt I'll ever get it again.'

'So you're just going to walk in and ask him?' Alena asks, one eyebrow elevated.

'I'll have to pick my moment.' She gives Alena a twisted smile. 'Boniface is teetotal. Perhaps I can get him drunk.'

Later, when they are well under way, Christina begs Beth to let them join her at the party but Beth tells them that she is the only one with an invitation – the only one who is a heroine of the revolution.

'Why *are* you a heroine of the liberation?' Preeti asks.

Beth laughs. 'It's a thing the hotel manager made up. He misjudged the reason for my being invited to the party. I think the chief of security wants to impress me, or maybe he just wants a harmless, token, white.'

'Pity,' Christina says.

'I hope you're right,' Preeti says.

They arrive at Hippo Heights mid-afternoon and receive a hostile reception from the Presidential guard as they approach the jetty.

The Captain holds off. Beth can see the shine on the soldiers' boots and knows that this must be the day. She stands at the top deck rail and shouts to the soldiers to fetch Johnson. She can't make herself understood but then sees Johnson's lanky frame coming down from the hotel. As soon as he steps onto the jetty, Beth yells to him that she's come back to honour the kind invitation given her by Mr Madzwaya.

Johnson argues in a spirited fashion with one of the soldiers and in the end they are waved forward. Preeti, Alena and Christina join her on the boat's platform as the Captain nudges the oily beast forward against the tyres protecting the jetty. Johnson, dressed in a black suit and bright red tie, welcomes Beth with a warm smile and his bony hand. 'We must be quick as the President will arrive soon and all protocol must be observed.'

Beth explains, 'On reflection, I thought it would be very rude of me not to accept Mr Madzwaya's kind invitation to attend the party. My friends will come back for me tomorrow.'

'You're looking very fine,' Johnson says as they climb the path to the hotel.

'Oh, thank-you! I have to look my best for the President.' She's wearing Alena's red, tie-front, drape dress and her tights and she's in Christina's black court shoes (with a knot on the vamp). She's used Preeti's mascara and her Guerlain lipstick. All she's missing is a matching clutch bag. Her shoes are a size too big but she doubts anyone will notice. She wonders if she'll be the only woman at the party.

'You'll find it's been a great honour for you,' Johnson says.

'Is Mr Madzwaya here?' Beth asks.

'He's here. Everything's ready.'

And so is she.

An enormous silk marquee with flying pennants has been erected on the lawn, open at the front to give a view of the lake. A red carpet flows like an issue of blood across the terrace, down the stairs to the lawn and disappears into the back of the marquee. Johnson says, in a low voice, that Beth has saved him some trouble by returning and then takes her to find Boniface but he's preoccupied with his duties, hardly looking at her as he snaps, 'You're almost late, but at least you're here.' He receives a call on his radio phone and turns away from her to talk, before striding off into the hotel. Beth fears she may not get a chance to confront him.

Military men stand around in cliques on the lawn, their uniforms spangled with colourful ribbon bars and party-poppered with gold braids, tassels and lanyards. Jekuche is filling their crystal glasses with Moët et Chandon champagne. A small group of women strut and shimmer near the edge of the lawn in their fashion-house dresses. She's pleased that she can hold her own in Alena's Chanel piece. That's what you can slip into if you can borrow from a friend who's married to a futures trader. Johnson brings her a fresh orange juice but then hurries off on his duties. She is about to pluck up courage to drift over towards the women when she hears the buzz of a helicopter. It flies low overhead, its blades chopping the air with a harsh thwack thwack, making the silk of the marquee sink and flow. Excited chatter erupts from the guests as the muscular machine disappears behind the hotel. 'The President,' boasts a man near Beth as he reaches for the knot of his tie, whether to check it is straight or as an involuntary gesture to protect his neck, she can't tell.

Ten minutes after the helicopter lands, the President appears on the terrace and walks down the carpet with a jaunty gait. He's smaller than Beth expected; he compensates with dinner-plate glasses. He raises a hand graciously to acknowledge the prolonged applause. Boniface escorts him into the marquee. The guests are lined up by a master of ceremonies and ushered forward to be introduced in order of importance to the President. Beth is third from last with two overawed-looking men behind her. They are the only ones not sporting medals on their uniforms. The President's eyes are almost closed and he stands unmoving as Boniface introduces each guest. How will Boniface introduce her, she having told him her name was Lynette? But she mustn't miss any opportunity to ask him about Matt.

When it's her turn, she whispers to Boniface, 'I've got to talk to you afterwards.'

Boniface just has time to hiss, 'There's no chance of that,' before they are in front of the President. 'Your Excellency, this is comrade Doctor Bethan Jenkins,' Boniface announces.

The President is uninterested.

'She's a very... er... useful friend of the Party – and she's Welsh.' The President remains unmoved; totally preoccupied it seems with affairs of state, or asleep on his feet.

'In fact, your Excellency,' Boniface says loudly, 'she's a good friend of the Prince of Wales.'

'Ah!' The President's filmy eyes widen and gleam like an attentive owl. He looks at Beth and smiles faintly, saying with a cultured and precise voice, 'Indeed? Pass on my good wishes to my friend, the Prince. Let him know that it's my sincere wish that we'll meet again when he's King. I very much hope that by then your Prime Minister and his clique of gays and neo-colonial adventurers are no longer attempting to re-colonise us.' He chuckles deeply.

Although nervous – perhaps because she is nervous – Beth finds herself smiling awkwardly back, but there's no time to deny royal connections or to dissent. Boniface has pushed her on and is ushering forward the next guest. The President returns to his stony state.

Inside, Beth is seated between the two men who'd taken up the rear of the queue. The tables have been laid for a banquet and she can't help but say, 'Wow!'

The man on her right chuckles and leans towards her. 'The roses and crane lilies were flown in yesterday from Kenya whilst, of course, the tulips came from Holland. The lobsters, crab, crayfish and mussels are from France but the duck and king prawn are from China. Beef is from Argentina. The pawpaw, mango, and dragon fruit you see in the fruit salad arrived fresh only this morning from Malaysia. Do you like crème-chantilly? It's from Paris. Ferrero Rocher? They're from Italy. Me, I like it all and I'll finish the banquet with Johnny Walker Blue Label.'

Beth remembers the starving children on her way to the hotel but it seems a futile gesture to refuse to eat so she tucks in as heartily as anyone whilst she watches for an opportunity to speak to Boniface. Her seat mate says little more during the meal although leans across soon after they start eating to tell her, 'We're at one of the President's most important functions this year but the media aren't allowed near. Many of the guests are being decorated for top secret services to the state.' Secret services? More like accidental services in her case, she thinks. She feels nauseous.

When everyone is satiated, they are ushered out – burping shamelessly – whilst the mountains of golden sweet wrappers and crustacean remains are cleared and the furniture re-arranged. Beth tries to catch Boniface's attention but he's instructing his security team and ignores her. Half an hour later they are invited back into the marquee. The tables have gone and the chairs are now in two sets of rows that face each other. The deeper set of five rows faces away from the open front of the marquee whilst the opposing set of two rows, raised on a low plinth, looks out onto the lake. There is a green-leather armchair for the President in the centre of the first of the two rows to give him a good view over the water, although the last blush of pink is decaying to purple as the sun falls away.

Beth makes for the furthest of the five rows by the open front of the marquee but feels a firm hand on her shoulder. It's Boniface. 'Dr Jenkins, come this way. I've reserved a place for you in the second row over there behind the President. It's a great honour for you.'

She protests but he's insistent. And so she finds herself almost directly behind the Presidential armchair. Boniface leaves her there between the two men that she'd sat next to at the meal. He strides to the open end of the marquee and looks out at the lake. The light is fading rapidly but Beth can see three black kapenta boats far out in the bay, fishing lights not yet lit and nets raised on their booms like dark wasp nests. A patrol boat stirs up tar-black eddies from the bituminous depths of the lake as it draws alongside the nearest kapenta boat – presumably the security services giving them a look over. Boniface turns around. His eyes squint and he moves a couple of steps each way, looking back at the President's chair from different angles. Then he returns and orders the man sitting on Beth's right, 'Swap places with Dr Jenkins.' The man jumps up to do so but Beth looks at Boniface, puzzled.

'It's protocol, Dr Jenkins.'

'It's very important I speak to you afterwards,' Beth says, remaining stubbornly in her seat as if that will persuade him to acquiesce.

'If there's an afterwards, you can see me then,' Boniface says darkly. Taken aback, Beth swaps places.

Back Boniface goes to the front of the marquee before turning to inspect the seating arrangement again. Beth has the impression that he's lining her up in some way. She is now almost directly behind the President's chair. A disquieting thought comes to her. She remembers *The Day of the Jackal*. She'll be in the line of fire of any assassination attempt from the mouth of the marquee. She checks herself. The heat is turning her into a conspiracy theorist. The President could not be safer: security men swarm about like hornets. The cream of the CIO are present. What can possibly go wrong?

But what would stop an assassin? Obvious: to see a friend in the line of fire. She finds herself crossing her hands in front of her chest. Does Boniface suspect that Fortunate is going to make an attempt on the President's life? Does he believe what Hope dismissed as ridiculous? Is he betting that Fortunate will not shoot if she's behind the President? Of course he won't shoot. She rests her hands on her lap.

But what if there's another assassin out in there in the wilds? Someone cold and suave. The security services are taking elaborate precautions. There must be a reason. She stares, feeling as pop-eyed as a thyrotoxic, towards the half-lit lawn and the now dark lake. In her red dress she must look like a bull's-eye in a target. Beside her, she realises, are two lowly, expendable men.

Whilst she tries not to think that there is only going to be the Head of State between herself and an assassin's bullet, the President enters to loud applause to take his seat in front of her. They all stand. No sooner has the President arrived at his chair than he turns to her and hands her an envelope. He says that it's a private message for Prince Charles and would she deliver it at her earliest convenience? He turns back, giving her no chance to deny a friendship with the Prince. She finds she's tightly clutching

285

the envelope. She's becoming a transcontinental courier; this has to stop.

Johnson appears through the flaps at the side of the marquee, carrying two great bunches of gold and lilac balloons. The guests clap again as he makes his way to present them to the President. Beth can't see the President's face but his little fidgets tell her that he's as pleased as the birthday child who opens the final wrapping on the pass-the-parcel. The two security men on the lawn either side of the entrance have turned their attention from scanning the shadows at the edge of the lawn and the black expanse of the lake and are looking into the marquee although they remain poker-faced. She hopes they aren't getting distracted. She thinks of the Jackal firing his high-powered rifle at the melon. She remembers Frederick Forsyth's description of the melon exploding, leaving just the hanging remains of the string bag that contained it. The melon connection is macabrely appropriate, the way they've all been stuffing themselves with fruit at the banquet.

The President takes the balloons. He raises his arms theatrically – sycophantic laughter babbles from the guests – and then holds them aloft without releasing them. The security men have turned their attention to undoing the knots that hold the rolled-up flap of the marquee as if they've decided it's too much of a risk to leave it open now that night has fallen. The roll loosens and drops a little as the first knot at one end is undone. A sudden movement of sultry air from the lake agitates the balloons. Beth sees something move in one of the bushes at the end of the lawn. She pulls in her shoulders and catches her breath. The man at the other end of the flap is having difficulty with his knot. For heaven's sake, what's wrong with you, man? Give it to me; let me do it. Get that roll down fast. He succeeds in pulling out one loop.

That's when it happens: a cracking retort, so loud and close that she thinks the assassin is next to her. She chokes on her heart. The security men swivel, knees bent, reaching for their handguns.

The guests in front of the President retract their necks. A collective gasp sucks the air from the marquee, followed by the briefest moment of dead quiet. But the President is still standing, his head intact, and Beth sees that there is no dark stain spreading on her dress. A piece of lilac balloon lands at the President's feet. A large moth flies in a crazed arc from the bush on the edge of the lawn.

The marquee erupts in hee-hawing laughter. Beth swallows her heart again and chuckles with the rest, exchanging a how-silly-we-were look with the men next to her. Even the President turns from side to side, smiling, still holding the balloons aloft. Then he releases them and they float merrily to the top of the marquee trailing their silver ribbons while everyone claps with sweet relief.

Beth sees the security man at the mouth of the marquee return to his knot, exchanging smiles with another official – he's momentarily off guard. The night outside thickens, a cloaking opacity. She can no longer see the surface of the lake. She finds herself apprehensive again whilst all around is good-humoured murmuring. Out of the inky dark, from the direction of the lake, she sees a single flash of explosive light.

CHAPTER 24

Above the clapping Beth hears nothing, but Boniface – standing to the side at the end of a row of chairs – slumps forward onto the powdered bosom of a large woman. Embarrassed, she pushes him off. Then she screams. Everyone turns to look. She lifts her hand out in front of her as if it's not her own. It drips blood.

Pandemonium breaks out. Security men throw themselves at the President, the scrum upending Beth and her chair. Guests dive to the floor or scurry out, bent double. The ruck with the President somewhere inside disappears through the back of the marquee. Beth lies still, cheek pressed to the unyielding planking of the floor. Outside she can hear firing and catches glimpses of panicked soldiers running about on the lawn. She's trampled as the remaining guests escape. No one takes any notice of Boniface who lies still, face up. She hears vehicles revving in the car park. Shouting and shooting continue. She's facing the front of the marquee, where the flash came from, but there is nothing to see out there. Amid further shouting, she hears vehicles racing off, and then the whine of a helicopter starting up and the thundering of its blades as it escapes from the killer whose bullet has found its way past the elite guardians of the Party. She lies there and waits for her heart rate to subside. Before long there is not a sound except the low throb of a boat engine, way out on the water. Then she hears a desperate groan.

Getting shakily to her feet Beth picks her way through the upended chairs to Boniface. They are the only ones left in the marquee and the silence suggests they are the only ones left at the hotel.

'Mr Madzwaya, it's Dr Jenkins.'

His chest heaves and he lifts a clawing hand to his throat. Blood stains the right side of his jacket. Beth fumbles his buttons undone and yanks his jacket apart. His shirt is ripped, revealing a bloody furrow along the side of his chest. A bubble of blood glistens like a reptilian eye in the wound.

Boniface's eyes find Beth, fixing her with an imploring stare. He can't speak through his struggle to breathe. She examines his chest, drumming it out with her fingers, watching the rise and fall, feeling his trachea. He has a tension pneumothorax. Air is being sucked in through a hole between his ribs when he breathes in but the puncture is acting as a valve, preventing air from escaping when he breathes out so that, with each breath, more and more air is being trapped between the chest wall and his right lung. The lung will be squeezed down to the size of a grapefruit and the pressure will be pushing his heart over to the left, crushing the lung on the other side as well. The act of breathing is suffocating him to death.

She needs a hollow tube. She can see nothing suitable in the marquee but then she reaches into Boniface's jacket pocket and finds a ballpoint pen. Boniface's eyes are starting to lose their focus on her and his fingers have loosened their grip on his throat. His lips go black. She pulls out the innards of the pen and presses a fingernail under the end plug to pop it out. Boniface's fingers slide off his neck. Gritting her teeth, she thrusts the pen through the hole in his chest. A blood-stained mist hisses out under pressure. Boniface starts gasping hungrily and his lips colour. Beth puts her thumb over the end of the tube when he breathes in and releases it when he breathes out to help re-inflate his lung. He groans.

She shouts, 'Anyone there? I need help.' No one answers. She looks at Boniface, helpless under her thumb. Her digit is the only thing keeping him alive. She's been on automatic, doing what she's been trained to do – thank God she'd worked six months in A & E – but now she goes weak, feels her concentration drifting. She imagines herself waking, as if from an Alice-in-Wonderland-type dream, and finding herself on the upper deck of the houseboat.

Boniface groans again. She must focus, she must stick fiercely to the task. Here under her thumb is the last person on earth, as far as she is aware, who knows why Matt never told her about the massacre. She has to keep him alive. But what would Hope think she should do? Would it not be a form of justice to let him die? It would be as secret in its execution as the crimes he'd committed.

She isn't sure whether her head overrules her heart or it's the other way around, but she says, 'No one seems to care about you, but I do. I'm going to help you survive.'

She shouts for assistance again. She hears scuffling and Johnson comes through the flap of the marquee.

'Oh, Oh, Oh! What's to happen?' Johnson looks down at the scene with an expression of raw horror.

'Everything's OK.' How has that come out? 'We've got to get Mr Madzwaya to hospital.'

'Everyone's departed! There's no one here. The President's party have driven off in their cavalcade. My staff have run off into the bush although it's notably dangerous there at night because of the animals.'

Johnson tells Beth that the nearest hospital is in Kariba Town. She asks him to fetch a mobile phone and, looking overjoyed to have something to do, he hurries off. She reassesses her patient, whose life is being sustained by the crudest of life support, checking his pulse and respiratory rate. He has stabilised, his breaths quieter, although he stares with fearful concentration at the roof of the marquee.

Johnson returns and Beth asks him to take over pen-duty, showing him what to do, wrapping a tissue around the pen to make it less messy. She pours water on her hand from the one vase still standing in the marquee and uses a nearby paper serviette to wipe off Boniface's blood. Then she rings Alena. It takes three attempts to get a connection.

'Alena?'

'Hi Beth! Have you had a fantastic time?'

'No time to chat. There's a man here with a tension pneumothorax. He needs to be in hospital. Can you bring the boat across?'

For a moment Beth thinks she's lost the connection but then Alena says, 'It's dark, Beth. I don't know whether it's possible. I'll ask.'

'It's really urgent. There's no other way. Ring me back.'

The phone attempts to ring several times but keeps disconnecting. Then there's a text: *capt wants xtr cash but on way.*

While she waits, Johnson appears with Jekuche and a stretcher from a store room in the hotel. They have even found an emergency medical kit which has a needle and syringe and an ampoule of diamorphine, only moderately out-of-date. Beth reluctantly gives Boniface his pain-relief.

She sees the houseboat's lights from a long way off but it seems hours before it reaches the jetty. She sends a text to Alena:

tell hope patient name boniface madzwaya. Two more members of staff materialise and help to carry Boniface down to the jetty.

As soon as the houseboat gangway is secured, Alena hurries down and takes over pen-duty to give Johnson and Beth a break. Preeti and Christina look on with ill-disguised disgust from the top deck, a lantern casting a morbid light. Hope is nowhere to be seen.

In a feat of strength and balance on the part of the hotel staff, Boniface is lifted upstairs to the deck but he remains subdued and motionless as he is manoeuvred. They place him on a cushioned locker next to the rail but his eyes start rolling about and he becomes agitated.

'His lung might be collapsing down again,' Alena says, checking the pen is still in position, but Boniface gasps, 'This is a dangerous place. The assassin might still be out there. Where are all my men?'

Beth can see how – well-lit on the top deck – he will make a tempting tableau. She lowers the canvas blind although Boniface will still be visible from the other three sides.

Preeti finds sticking plaster which they use to secure the makeshift chest drain. Alena and Beth debate trying to construct an underwater-seal drain – to relieve them of their duty with the pen – by using hosing from the boat's plumbing.

Preeti suggests they ring Manesh for advice but Alena agrees with Beth that it's best not to try to be too clever and find themselves being instructed on some elaborate procedure by a cardiac surgeon who might not be able to imagine their situation a long way away from a room full of bypass machines and ventilator equipment. It will also be too complicated to try to explain Preeti's deception in the same conversation.

When they are under way, Beth says she'd like to have a private conversation with the patient. She takes over from Alena, sitting herself on a chair beside Boniface. He is the first to speak, saying in a strained whisper, 'Someone would prefer to kill me, rather than the President.' A haughty expression puffs up his face. It's he, Boniface Madzwaya, not the President, who is now the country's most hated man, the preferred target of assassins.

'You don't think that they were aiming for the President and hit you by mistake?' Beth says, unable to resist raining on his parade.

He shakes his head and scowls. 'That was a true professional and he may know that I'm not yet dead. I think you should mount a guard on the deck.'

A guard? Preeti and Christina perhaps? Beth says, 'Who would want you dead?' Surely not Fortunate?

Boniface forgets his precarious state of health and spits, 'Counter-revolutionaries! Reactionary elements! Sell-outs!' then chokes. When he's caught his breath again he says, 'But you've saved my life, Dr Jenkins. How can I repay you?'

For a second Beth is tempted to tell him how odious she finds him, how sad and twisted, how it is not her that needs repaying, but Hope. Then she controls herself and takes the opportunity he's given her. 'Since you ask, there are a couple of things.'

'Huh?' His eyes swivel to find her.

'There's... some information I want from you.'

'Information? Information! Why, of course!'

'I happen to be the wife of an archaeologist called Matt Hallam. He was working here in Zimbabwe in 1999 but was expelled from the country.'

Boniface continues staring up at the canopy although his respiratory rate increases.

'I know that you know him,' she says. 'It was you that had him expelled.'

Boniface hisses, 'That's a silly notion, Dr Jenkins.'

'I also know about the place with the bones that my husband found.'

Now Boniface speaks with a surprisingly strong voice. 'You should terminate this discussion. It's not helpful to you.'

It can't be deliberate, her hand is tiring, but she moves the pen. He flinches. She says, 'For your own reasons, you didn't wish my husband to talk to anyone about it. One of the pieces of information that you can give me is to tell me exactly what you said to him?'

'You're his wife. Ask him! I'm sure he'll tell you that you're mistaken.'

'Mr Madzwaya, he never did talk about what happened and now, because of his medical condition, he's not in a position to tell me. Whatever threat you made to him has become irrelevant but, for entirely personal reasons, what you said to him is important to me.'

'This is such silly talk. Let me give you a gift, Dr Jenkins. I can pay your hotel bill. It must run into millions of dollars. You were pampered in that five star place for a long time.'

'We can speak plainly, Mr Madzwaya. I've no pressing personal interest in the history and politics of this country, or your part in it. In fact I've had enough of it. I never wanted to be part of a revolution gone rancid, a liberation war that substitutes one injustice for another. I'm not a detective or a lawyer from a human rights organisation and I'm not in a position to change the past. What I'm asking you relates to a private matter.'

Boniface stays silent for some time and when he speaks again he sounds tired. 'Very well, you want to know what I said to your husband. I'll tell you.' Beth prepares herself to be told a lie. What she is sure of is that if he does lie, she will know it. 'It's very simple,' Boniface says, 'Mr Hallam came to me when I was a police superintendent in Bulawayo. He told me that he'd found the place of the skeletons in the Matobo Hills. Close by, he found paintings on a hidden rock face.'

'Paintings, you say? Rock art?'

'Yes, bushman paintings.'

'So?'

'I said I would destroy those paintings if he talked about the skeletons that he'd found.'

'Why was that?'

'The bones were an internal security matter. They had nothing to do with Mr Hallam.'

'Is that all you threatened him with?'

'He was crazy about the scribbles on the rock, your husband.'

Boniface is making sense. 'What were they like, those paintings?'

'I don't know. I never looked. They were painted by primitive people. They don't interest me. We've moved on. But I guessed, from the way your husband spoke about them, that he wouldn't want them vandalised.'

Paintings. Had Matt judged the preservation of the paintings as more important than seeking justice for the dead, decided that justice could wait or be subsumed by a higher cause, that art that had survived millennia should not be sacrificed through impatience for justice for some bones that had lain there for just a few years? But Lindi had said that there were hundreds of rock art sites. Is each site as precious as any other? Or were the paintings Matt had discovered so extraordinary, so unique, that he decided he shouldn't do anything to compromise their preservation?

'Are the paintings still there?'

'I assume so.'

Beth stares forward over the front of the boat, out at the lake. Pricks of light are popping out of the dark as the kapenta boats start fishing. She believes Boniface to have told her the truth. Matt, with his passion for rock art, would have agonised over the matter. There's a logic to what Boniface has said. She can see a dim glow at the bottom of the pit of Matt's secrecy. But to see clearly she knows this: the answer lies at the site. It has to, perhaps with the paintings themselves. She will have to find the place.

But first there are other matters to clear up with Boniface. 'Did you ever visit my husband in the UK?'

A small smile plays on Boniface's lips as if she's reminded him of a seedy joke. He says, 'I might have wished to remind him of his obligations.'

Beth remembers Matt's fear of the man at the door. 'Obligations! You mean of your threat. He wouldn't have remembered you but he must've found you particularly creepy.'

Boniface rotates his hand in a take-it-or-leave-it gesture. 'I discovered anyway that he's now a cretin, an imbecile.'

He might as well have punched her in the stomach. She can't speak. When she recovers she says through a stiff jaw, 'And Mr De Villier? Did you murder him?'

'I've answered your personal question, Bethan Lynette Jenkins.' He stops to pant. 'I've repaid my debt – although you're just another white and so I owe you nothing. But to show my mercy, I'll arrange your safe passage out of the country.' He grunts and pauses for a moment, as if exhausted. 'You've tested my patience to the limit. I believe I already bought you a ticket out of Bulawayo but you didn't accept my generosity.'

A ticket out of Bulawayo? Her means of escape from the country. So it was a trade. A ticket in exchange for her patient's title deed. Beth has a sudden hallucination: she sees the flick of a leopard's tail and then a blur of movement, then feels the crunch of its teeth in her skull and the puncturing of her lungs with its claws.

'It's high time you quit my country. When we get to Kariba Town, wait there and as soon as I'm able, I'll arrange your deportation. The Zambian border is close enough to throw you across.'

Beth calls for Alena to take over – and finds her voice comes out in a tortured wail – and then she goes and sits on a low locker near the prow and stares unseeing into the void of the night. Robson, who gave her the ticket, her safe passage out of Zimbabwe, is Boniface's lackey. There's no doubt: she's given away Mr De Villier's farm to Boniface.

Perhaps someone out there on the lake will shoot her dead.

After the Kariba Hospital ambulance has disappeared up the road from the harbour, Beth descends the stairs to Hope's cabin. She finds Hope sitting still as a frightened baby bird on her berth, red-eyed. She sits down beside her and waits there, disinclined to speak, her arms heavy on her lap. After a long time, she says, 'I'm so sorry Hope. I may have saved Boniface's life. Did I do wrong?'

Hope shrugs. They stay silent. Eventually Hope says, 'I've been thinking about Fortunate. Maybe you're right; maybe Fortunate lives a double life. And who is Shungu anyway? I only saw her once, when she attended church.'

They sit in silence again until Beth all of a sudden finds that she has an urgent need to talk, to tell Hope what she's done. 'Does Fortunate know Boniface?'

Hope shrugs again. 'He never mentioned him. But let me tell you, there are many who have suffered because of that man, there are many who hate him, who would wish him dead.'

'What are you going to do next?' Beth says. 'Are you going back to England?'

'Yes, I need to earn. I have to send money to my old grandmother so she can feed herself. Will you be flying back with us, Beth?'

'No. I think I've made a terrible mistake and I'm going to have to find Selous and apologise.' She tells Hope how she'd come to give the title deed to Robson after he'd told her that Selous killed his mother, but that now she knows she's been duped. Well and truly stung.

Hope shakes her head slowly and sorrowfully and says, 'You weren't to know.' Then she says, 'Selous's workers told me what happened on the farm.' Beth hardly breathes as Hope says, 'They said that when Selous's father was still living on the farm, Boniface wanted to take the land. One day he came to serve Mr De Villier with eviction papers. They shouted at each other. When Boniface left, the old man went into his house – he was on crutches as his legs were very diseased – took a gun and shot at Boniface's vehicle as he was driving away. About a week later Boniface's men came and burnt the place. They tied up Mr Dr Villier and beat him. Then they abducted Mrs De Villier.'

'Abducted her?'

'Boniface informed Mr De Villier that if he wanted to see his wife alive again he must hand over to him the original title deed to his farm.'

Beth remembers Robson telling her how Mr De Villier was a Dutch passport holder and that the land was subject to an international agreement between the Dutch government and the

Zimbabwean government. It came to her that if Boniface had the deed he could forge a letter from Mr De Villier to say that Mr De Villier had willingly handed over the land and here – voila! – is the original title deed to prove it. Boniface might not feel secure in his holding of the land without that piece of paper. She asks, 'So what happened next?'

'Mr De Villier said that he couldn't sacrifice his son's future for his wife's life. It was his sacred duty to pass on the land to the next generation. The truth, he said, was that lives come and go, but land remains.'

'And Selous? What did he think?'

'The men told me that Selous knelt at his father's feet and begged him to change his mind, but he would not. Maybe Mr De Villier didn't believe that Boniface would carry out his threat.' Beth sits very still, waiting for Hope to tell what she already expects. Perhaps, if she doesn't move, she can undo or retrospectively prevent what happened next. 'Later,' Hope says, in little more than a whisper as if such things should not be verbalised, 'Mrs De Villier's body was found in the forest.' Beth feels the thump of falling bodies. 'Then the old man fled to the UK.'

'And to think that I gave Mr De Villier's title deed – the document that he refused to swap for his wife – to Boniface.' Beth hangs her head.

'You weren't to know,' repeats Hope.

'But why's Selous still on the land? Why hasn't Boniface thrown him off?'

'One of Selous's men told me that Selous may be making payments to Boniface from the profits of his hunting business, but I don't know if that's true.'

'Selous pays money to the man who murdered his mother?'

'That's what the man thought but... I don't know.' Hope has a couple of false starts to what she wants to say next as if trying to find the least painful way to spell it out. 'Perhaps Boniface was hoping that if he let Selous stay on the land then the title deed would find its way back to him – and then he could snatch it.'

'Which is exactly what happened,' Beth says, her head heavy.

'They're very smart, these CIO people,' Hope says.

A minute passes as Beth faces up to her status as a kapenta minnow in a lake of tiger fish. She tries to fathom out Selous again, recalling their brief, tense, unhappy meeting: his unreadable eyes, the cruelty of his sport, his taciturn behaviour. But she also remembers the laugh lines that formed fleetingly at the sides of his eyes and in crescents on his cheeks. They hinted at an earlier, happier Selous. She guesses he'd not had much to smile about for a long time.

'There's just one more question, Hope. Why does Boniface want that land? What's so special about it? It's a beautiful place but it's not really much of a farm with all those rocks and trees. You couldn't grow much there. Apart from hunting, it seems unproductive.'

'I don't know for sure – Mr De Villier kept a small herd of cattle – but I think that Boniface wishes to control access to the place of the massacre. He does not want any investigators.'

'You mean the massacre site is on De Villier's land?'

'Yes, I do.'

Beth jumps up. 'Oh my, Hope. Look, could you take me there? You see I've got to see the paintings. I must see what Matt saw.'

Hope looks away. Beth sits down again and says hastily, 'Sorry, that was a very insensitive suggestion, of course not.'

'I'm returning to the UK now,' Hope says, 'to earn money so that I can look after the future.'

'Of course you must.'

For a moment Beth imagines herself doing the same, following Hope's example, getting back to her responsibilities, looking after Matt, earning a wage before her savings disappear. But coming so close to making a decision to return home confirms her against it. She has to face her guilt, she has to have the courage to look Selous in the eye and apologise for giving away his title deed. She also has to give him his father's letter, still in her bag at Hippo Heights. And she must return Bismarck. Then, somehow, whatever it takes, she will find the site of the massacre and the paintings.

She says, 'Is there anyone else apart from Boniface who knows where the site is?'

Hope frowns. 'I don't think so.'

'What about Selous, do you think he'd know?'

'I doubt it. It's in a hidden place. I don't even know if I could find it again myself.'

Alena is taking last photos of the lake from the upper deck when Beth finds her. 'Alena, I'll have to ask the Captain to take me back to Hippo Heights. I must drive the car back to Selous.'

Beth waits for Alena to dissuade her and come up with an alternative idea for returning the vehicle, a more level-headed solution, but Alena thinks for a moment, then says, 'We're coming with you.'

'Isn't your flight… ?'

'We've got another three days. Should be able to make it back to Harare in time if we go back with you via Bulawayo.'

'Are you sure?'

'Dead sure. I don't want you disappearing again or getting into any more scrapes.'

When they tell Preeti and Christina, they are happy that the decision has been made and are up for the ride. The Captain is persuaded again with the promise of further hard currency. Beth expects he'll be able to retire at the end of their voyage.

As they approach the jetty of Hippo Heights, Johnson shouts to Beth, 'You can't come in. The forensic people are here.'

Beth shouts back, 'We're just going to take the car and go.'

Johnson waves them forward and – having said goodbye to Hope – they disembark. Johnson brings Beth the meagre possessions she'd left in her room including her day pack and also says he's put in an envelope marked 'His Royal Highness The Prince of Wales, by hand' that she'd left in the marquee. They gather around Bismarck as Johnson opens the bonnet and replaces the wire that he'd removed at Boniface's instruction. Christina looks on with undisguised disgust at the oily, dusty, transport. Beth shakes hands with all the staff, thanking them for their hospitality and wishing them many guests sometime soon.

At first, Bismarck will not start. 'Oh, this is bloody great,' Christina says. But the staff push and – coughing up black phlegm – the Mercedes fires and they are on their way.

Beth is reminded how rough the road is. Christina, sitting beside her, clutches her belly and scowls as if Beth is trying to bounce her baby out of her. The journey passes quickly as Beth preoccupies herself with what she'll say to Selous and the others are absorbed in watching the scenery. Beth doesn't even notice passing through the village that's being re-educated. She thinks that Selous will be perfectly justified to shoot her on sight. She tries to invent some way to recompense him for the loss of the title deed. She considers offering him Matt's allotment and then thinks how insulting that would be: a paltry cabbage patch in exchange for hundreds of acres of hills and forests. You'd hardly be able to keep a goat on the allotment. They arrive in Bulawayo just after dark and find their way to the Southern Star.

Beth rises early the next morning having not slept well and leaves a note for Alena. Then she leaves the hotel on her own and drives out to Selous's farm. Her heart pounds in synch with the beat of Bismarck's engine as she comes to the track to his cottage but she finds that there are stones blocking the way. Two men sit by the broken gate, one young and wearing a T-shirt printed with the face of the President, and the other older and in the orange overalls that Beth had seen Selous's men wearing. As she stops they stand up and come over. The younger has a stout stick. She winds down two inches of glass and keeps the engine running.

'What do you want? This isn't your place,' says the younger man threateningly.

'I'm sorry but I'm looking for Selous De Villier.'

He sneers. 'De Villier? Devil! He's gone.'

'Oh, do you know where he is?'

'He's no longer here.'

'He doesn't live here anymore?'

'No, the land's been totally liberated.'

Looking beyond the young man, the land appears to Beth just the same as before, as if it is not that fussed about its new freedom.

'Do you know where he's staying now?'

'No one cares. Maybe he's gone back to his home country.' He waves his stick vaguely in the air as if indicating another world, another planet where Selous's race should be banished to.

Beth slips Bismarck into gear to leave and the young man turns away but the older man leans down and whispers to her, 'My name's Tulani. If you see Selous, give him my good wishes. Tell him that now I have no work.'

The road is long and desolate on the way back to Bulawayo. Beth is about to turn into the Southern Star when she changes her mind and drives straight to the museum.

'Back again?' the receptionist says as she enters. 'The price is still five hundred!'

She leaves him a high denomination note and walks through to Lindi's room. The lights are on this time.

'Oh, Beth! I'd not expected to see you again,' Lindi says, jumping up from her desk and giving Beth the same warm smile she gave her at their first meeting. 'I'm so glad you've come back. I've been feeling so guilty at how impolite I was last time.' They hug lightly.

'I shocked you,' Beth says, 'and now I'm going to shock you again! I've borrowed a car from a man named Selous De Villier who lives out in the Matobo Hills. I need to return it to him but when I went to his farm I found he'd been chased away by war vets. You don't know him do you? How I could find him?'

Lindi smiles. 'Where are you staying?'

'The Southern Star.'

'Come and stay with me and I'll see what I can do.' She smiles again.

'The only thing is, I've got three friends with me.'

'Doesn't matter. Bring them as well.'

They follow Lindi in her rusty yellow Datsun – trailing smoke as if she's cooking in it – along the same road out of Bulawayo that led to Selous's farm but they turn off some distance beyond his broken gate onto a dirt road.

Preeti, sitting beside Beth in the front passenger seat, says, 'There's no mobile reception so there's no way Manesh would come here.' She waves her phone about outside the window. 'His sense of security is directly related to the strength of the signal. He won't go into the third bedroom at home because you can't get reception in there.'

There has been overnight rain and Bismarck slews and slithers in the dips and turns of the road as they head further into what Beth remembers Fortunate referring to as the communal lands. Giant, white cloud-heads tower in the royal blue sky. Women call to each other in voices that carry far as they work in the freshly greened fields beneath the turrets of granite. There's grandeur to this land.

'Where the hell are we going?' Christina asks. She looks pasty and leans her head out of the window to catch the air. She's been otherwise quiet since telling Beth of her pregnancy.

'I've no idea,' Beth says.

The track levels and they pass cattle – softly coloured in maroon, chestnut and dove grey – grazing beneath the kopjes.

Lindi turns off through a gap in a fence, elaborately constructed of layered branches, and they follow. She parks in the shade under a tree. They've reached their destination. Lindi's place.

Christina gasps. 'Holy cow, Bethan Jenkins, was this your idea?'

In front of a wall of high rocks are four thatched huts each belted in colourful geometric patterns. Their thatching is neatly trimmed – one in a layered design. They step out of the car into dappled shade. Goat and cow-bells tinkle mysteriously from every direction as if sounding from the rocks. The air is pure and warm and a bird sings in enthusiastic welcome. Beth is charmed.

An old woman emerges from the nearest hut. She is bent at the waist, supporting herself on a gnarled stick, and looks at them with rheumy eyes beneath her yellow head scarf.

'That's my gogo – my grandmother,' Lindi says. 'Gogo MaNyoni.'

They are introduced. Christina first.

'Sakubona,' says Gogo MaNyoni.

'I'm sure, and hello to you too,' Christina says.

'She said, *I see you*,' says Lindi. 'You reply, Yebo, sakubona.'

'Yeah, boosackoobona,' tries Christina. Gogo MaNyoni breaks into a gummy smile and Lindi corrects Christina again. Gogo MaNyoni then greets each of her guests as they are introduced so that by the time she reaches her, Beth feels that she is on her first step to becoming a fluent isiNdebele speaker.

Other family members appear and Beth loses track of who is related to whom. Lindi is called Auntie by two small children but later Lindi tells her that they are orphans, both by HIV, and that her family has adopted them.

They eat 'sadza and relish' – a maize meal mash and beef casserole – around a fire in the dining hut that evening. The atmosphere is a little formal and conversation is stilted until Christina throws her plate on the floor. Christina's hair, the lightest object in the hut, attracts insects. They crash into her without inhibition. The first, a beetle the size of a large marble, hits the side of her plate with a hard ping sound and then, its wings motoring madly, shifts itself upside down to become glued in her sadza. The plate lands food-down on the floor. Gogo MaNyoni, sitting next to Christina, finds this side-splittingly funny, but Christina is on her feet, dancing about, her blonde hair flying as she tries to rid it of a long-winged insect. Lindi lends her a dark shawl to wrap around her head.

After the main dish they help themselves from a bowl of small brown fruit which have the texture of biscuits but the taste of dates. It's a fruit of the forest, unknown on the shelves of supermarkets. Outside, the cicadas sing a tireless note. Gogo MaNyoni leans down and wraps her old hand around Christina's ankle.

'She says you're lucky; you have fat ankles,' Lindi says.

Alena uncharacteristically sprays a mouthful of her drink of water laughing. Christina, going as pale as her hair, says, 'Tell her she's made my day.' She leans down to hold one of Gogo MaNyoni's spindly ankles which her fingers easily encircle. 'Chicken's legs,' she retorts.

Beth sees Alena shoot Christina a disapproving look. Such disrespect to a venerable old lady. But when Lindi translates, Gogo MaNyoni flaps her hands in amusement.

'Are mine fat?' Preeti says, presenting a leg to the old lady, who gives her ankle a squeeze before pronouncing.

'Yours are chubby,' translates Lindi.

'Oh my word, that's exactly what Manesh says about me,' Preeti says.

'And mine?' Alena says.

'Very smooth,' is Gogo MaNyoni's verdict, to Alena's satisfaction.

'And mine?' Beth says.

'Good for running far.'

That night, after the others have fallen asleep, Beth stands outside the doorway of their hut to watch a lightning storm play on the horizon like some far off war. Lindi joins her and they chat. Beth comes around to asking her about the Chimurenga – the war that led to Independence and that changed Rhodesia into Zimbabwe.

'It's best to ask Gogo MaNyoni about that,' Lindi says. 'I was very young at Independence but Gogo goes on about it a lot. Her father was expelled from his land just north of here but the deepest hurt to her was the humiliation: as a young black woman, she wasn't permitted into the department stores in Bulawayo but had to choose her skirts from the window and signal which she wanted to the shop assistant on the other side of the glass. So she loves to talk about that day in 1979 when all sides put down their weapons and the freedom fighters, both men and women, came in from the hills in their combat fatigues. She says they had a faraway look in their eyes. They had become strangers to a settled life. They found it impossible to talk of their experiences in the bush, how they'd lived for years off their wits, all the secret ways they knew, how to make a bed of leaves, how the frames of their living quarters were the trees of the forests. Some couldn't get used to eating again in a room with a table, chairs and a stove but went to find food in the forests as they had in the war.' Lindi chuckles softly as she says, 'Gogo MaNyoni slept with some of those men as if, by doing so, she could take full possession of the freedom they'd won.'

Sheet lightning turns the rocks into an incongruous, alien, Antarctic landscape of ice blocks, snow domes and crevasses.

'You have to live at a time of war to experience such things,' says Lindi, 'but perhaps we all want to have our own Day of Independence; a moment when we can believe our future is free of the past and that anything is possible.'

After the lightning, the night darkens as if a hand has reached out across the sky. Lindi says strongly, 'But now Gogo MaNyoni's furious because our leaders have trampled on our liberation. She says they've eaten their own legacy. At Heroes' Acre near Harare, where our liberating fathers and mothers are laid to rest, they now give a hero's farewell to those who've tortured and murdered to further the rule of the regime, to tighten the grip of the Party.' Thunder cracks like colliding rocks. 'Beth, we are not yet fully liberated.' They stand there in silence, hearing an on-going rumble. 'Freedom has always to wait for tomorrow. This is why we live as best we can with whatever freedoms we have today.'

Beth has only just got dressed the next morning when Lindi comes into the hut and says, 'Beth, there's someone here to see you. Shall I invite him in?'

'To see me?' If it's Robson Chiripo she's going to kill him. An ascaricide will be the most appropriate poison for that worm. 'I'll come out.'

She steps out with busy hips but there, standing in the already bright sun, is Selous. He's taken his suede hat off and holds it in front of his belly, like a cowboy at a funeral. Her heart lurches. She was hoping to find him but he has found her. She isn't ready, hasn't got her mea-maxima-culpa speech at the starting gate. She's not put on her make-up.

'Mrs Jenkins, excuse me,' he says, 'I owe you an apology. And I guess I could do with having my car back.'

She's paralysed by his statement of contrition and his lightly-delivered remark on her theft of Bismarck. Her tongue glues to her palate. After a few moments she says with an involuntary lisp, 'It's the other way around... the apology... I've behaved terribly... the car and... ' she can't bring herself to finish... *your farm as well*. She can't spit it out, not with Lindi standing there.

Selous returns his hat to his head. 'It's really not necessary for you to say more. The truth is that I upset you. In fact I was less than courteous when you came to the farm.' Beth was not able to read Selous's eyes when they first met but they are perfectly readable now, even in the shadow of his hat. Sincere is the word.

Christina appears at Beth's side and puts an arm around her shoulders. Beth can tell by Christina's silky movements and her face turned up to show her perfect neck that she's taken one look at Selous and got the hots for him. 'Hi, I'm Beth's friend, Christina.' Christina! What does she want? A stepfather for her baby?

'Selous.' He proffers his hand to shake hers.

Christina minces forward, takes it with a stroking motion and then lets her fingers trail on his as she lets go. 'Selous. That's a great name. How did you get it?'

'My mother gave it me,' Selous says, deadpan.

'Very droll,' Christina says and giggles.

'Selous was a famous hunter but I think she just liked the name,' he adds.

'And do you hunt?'

'Yes.'

'Awesome, a real white hunter! If you need someone to keep you company when you have your sundowners in camp, just let me know. Although don't expect me to cook for you.'

There's a hint of a smile from Selous. 'The hunting's more of a necessity than an adventure,' he says, 'although we've always done it around here.'

Beth recalls the rock paintings depicting hunters from thousands of years ago. But that's just the sort of excuse people give for bull fighting and female genital mutilation. *We've always done it that way around here.* She scolds herself: right now, it's she who is the guilty party.

Christina and she must look an incongruous pair: her straight Celtic-black hair against Christina's golden streams.

Christina, bubbly and pouting, almost dancing on her feet; herself, repentant, embarrassed and standing slightly stooped from the weight of her guilt.

Beth turns to Lindi. 'Do you and Mr De Villier know each other?'

'Oh yes, from a long time,' Lindi says. 'My older brother used to work on old man De Villier's farm. He managed the cattle side of the business – before Mr De Villier's herd was slaughtered by the war vets. Now my brother's in South Africa selling soapstone carvings on the streets of Johannesburg.'

'Sorry,' Selous says in a low quiet voice, as if it were he that banished Lindi's brother.

'Like to come in?' says Christina, forgetting they are themselves guests.

Beth tries to wrest control from Christina. 'Let me get your keys first and show you some damage I've done to your car.'

Leaving Selous with Christina to fetch the keys gives Beth an inexplicable throb of anxiety. She checks herself: Selous is a looker, true, but he's also in a business partnership with the man who'd killed his mother – not to mention that he exterminates beautiful animals. She must make amends for what she's done but will not be blind to his unsavoury life style choices.

She picks up the letter from Selous's father with the car keys. Back outside, Christina is in intimate – although almost one-way – conversation with Selous. She has her hand on her hip and is lolling seductively as she tries to find a way past his polite formality.

'So you get clients from all over the world. That must be so fascinating.'

'Not always,' Selous says.

'Do you get celebrities?'

'I wouldn't like to judge.'

'Amazing! What a life!'

Beth interrupts. 'Can I, um, show you a scrape on the car? I'll pay, of course, and for the wear and tear.'

She sets off towards Bismarck, hoping to have Selous to herself to say what she needs to say, but Christina is walking him over, having entwined her arm in his as if she's coming down the aisle. Lindi follows behind the happy couple. Selous looks to be taking it in good humour, although Beth feels disconcertingly pleased to see that he's not giving Christina explicit encouragement.

Selous rescues her. 'I'm going to give the car a little run. Perhaps, Mrs Jenkins, you could come with me and we can have a chat while we drive.'

'I've just made you some tea,' says Lindi to Christina. Bless, thinks Beth.

Selous and Beth are in the car before Christina has time to refuse. Selous deftly tames the flailing gear stick and they pull away.

Beth says nothing for a while and Selous seems in no hurry to talk either. Eventually she says, 'I've done a terrible thing.' She takes a deep breath to spill it all out but he says, 'I doubt it.'

How she wishes he was half right. 'You see, not only did I steal your car, but I gave the title deed to your land to a man called Robson who claimed he was your father's solicitor. Robson's working for a man called Boniface Madzwaya who's someone senior in the CIO.'

Selous changes gear but there is no force, no anger, in his movement. 'I guessed.'

'You guessed?'

'I've been kicked off the farm – Boniface set his war vets on me. They've beaten up my employees. They've burnt down my cottage.'

'Oh, that's just… I can't tell you how… '

'Boniface doesn't need me anymore. Not now that he has the title deed.' He speaks in a matter of fact way without accusation.

'It's all my fault,' Beth says. 'I badly misjudged you. You see, I was told lies, although that's not an excuse. I shouldn't have let myself be prejudiced by… the sable.'

'And my rudeness to you?' Selous says. 'I think your anger was what my mother used to call, in the old fashioned sense, righteous anger.'

A condolence to him on his mother's death is on the tip of Beth's tongue but he says, 'She goes well, doesn't she?' He gives the steering wheel an affectionate tap. Bismarck seems to be purring, as if she knows she is back with her rightful owner. 'Probably did her good to get a long run.'

'I can't tell you what a fool I feel,' Beth says. 'Is there any way I can undo what I've done? I'll do absolutely anything to help you get your title deed back.'

Selous replies, 'I want to show you something. Do you mind if we take a longer drive?'

They follow the road for over half an hour, Selous occasionally pointing out features of the landscape: balancing rock formations, a pair of black eagles perched high on a kopje, a sacred hill where rain ceremonies are carried out and voices speak from cracks in the rock. They pass a sign saying Matopos National Park and then, after a twisting route through flat grassy valleys, he draws off by the side of the road.

'It's a short walk up the kopje,' he says.

They leave the car and Selous leads the way. Soon they are climbing a bare granite slope to the top of a hill scattered with

314

spherical boulders taller than Selous. Beth is surprised to find a grave on the summit. It has a brass plate set on a raised rectangular stone base on which are the simple words, *Here lie the remains of Cecil John Rhodes.*

Selous doesn't give it a glance but says, 'As you may know, Rhodes was a British entrepreneur at the height of empire in the late 1800s. He owned vast tracts of land in southern Africa and had grandiose ambitions that were only thwarted by his death. But, of all the land Rhodes owned and had seen, he stipulated in his will that he should be buried here. He called it *The View of the World.*' Selous is looking out over the hills and Beth follows his gaze. He asks, 'How would you describe what you see?'

Beth sees a sea of kopjes in every direction: choppy crests and billowing domes in deep-ocean greens, sprays of yellow and red, washes of granite grey. In the troughs between the peaks she knows there to be secret grassy vleis, clear streams and pockets of forest. Beneath their feet, lichen patterns the rocks like maps of the land.

'I see a very pretty view,' she says.

'It's certainly that,' Selous says, 'but it's also much more. There are places on this earth from which one can see further horizons, so perhaps Rhodes wasn't referring to the distance one's eye can travel from here when he called it a view of the world. I'm guessing he meant it gives an impression of the intricacies of the world: its complexities, its possibilities and secrets. But not in the sense of a striking landscape, a pretty view. You could think of it this way: the land we're looking at is a sea of stories.' He pauses and adjusts his hat. Beth thinks for a moment that he's said what he wants to say, is going to let her guess what she is to infer from *sea of stories,* but he goes on, 'Can I give you a short history lesson?'

She nods, the scenery around her fading away.

'Millennia ago, hunter-gatherers painted their art on the rocks here and came and went at will but over the last few hundred years these valleys became home to farmers keeping cattle, growing crops, and consulting the oracles in their cave shrines. Then about one hundred and seventy years ago the Matabele arrived here from south of the Limpopo, conquered the farmers and settled. But they didn't have long before they were in turn overpowered by the British with their Maxim guns.

'Now the land is again changing hands by force, as has been the pattern around here for a couple of centuries. Everyone wants to hold the title to the land. But then, when they have their hands on the title, they find it's not enough. They want more. It's like they've captured a girl, but now they want her to freely give them her love. They want her soul. But then, even that's not enough. They want to become her soul. This rock that Rhodes is buried in has an isiNdebele name meaning *dwelling place of the spirits.* Rudyard Kipling understood what Rhodes craved when he wrote a poem for the occasion of Rhodes's burial. It ends:

Living he was the land, and dead,
His soul shall be her soul!'

Beth aches to think how well Matt might have got on with Selous, him having verse on the tip of his tongue like that.

'He was not the only one,' Selous continues. 'There's a memorial to the Matabele king, Mzilikazi, not far from here. He also lays claim to the spirit of the land.'

'What do you mean by the spirit of the land?' Beth says apprehensively. The way Selous's history lesson is going it looks like she's given away much more than his property rights. She's handed over his soul to that gangster, Boniface Madzwaya.

Without hesitation Selous says, 'It's the human stories that have been played out here; you could say – if you were being poetic – that those stories are like spirits drifting amongst the rocks, taking possession of them. Sure, it looks from here like an empty wilderness but it's soaked in human history, both collective and personal. So what I've been coming around to saying is that my father's title deed is not the land itself, it's not the spirit of the land. Out there, I've got my own story. So, in the only sense that really matters to me, I'll never lose the land. It now holds my story, no matter who takes the title deed.'

'But your story here was dependent on your father having the title deed,' Beth says.

'Yes, you're right, it gave me a slice of time here and I'm grateful.' He's been looking out over the view as he speaks, thumbs in his belt and arms relaxed, but now he turns to Beth and says, 'To be frank, there's another reason it doesn't bother me. I've had my fill of cattle ranching and hunting but mostly I'm done with all the envy and greed displayed here in our lust for land.'

'If you're done with all that, why did you stay after your father fled?'

'I've asked myself that and I'm not sure – perhaps I wanted to close off my story here under my own terms. I was pushing my luck in that respect. Not everyone's had the opportunity – our farm employees, for example – and, in the end, nor did I. But it gave me a little more time to walk with my memories.'

They tread back down the hill to Bismarck in silence. Beth thinks of the stories she's heard whilst in Zimbabwe: stories from angst-ridden Dick, from starving Judith, from ideologue Boniface, from traumatised Hope, and now from Selous. She will ask Lindi more of her story later. It strikes her that the land has far too many conflicting stories. Stories that allow for no one else's. They cut across each other, are incompatible fixed stories of victimhood, hurt and entitlement that run from generation to generation. It seems that Selous sees all of that and wants to break free and make a new narrative.

When they sit down again in the car Beth takes out the letter she's long carried in her bag and hands it to Selous. She's embarrassed at how scuffed and creased it has become from its tortuous journey. 'This is the letter from your father. Please take it. I don't want to have to carry it anymore.'

Selous hesitates but then accepts it, excuses himself, opens the door and steps out again. She turns to see him walk at a slow pace down the road as he reads the letter. Then she sees him fold it again and carry on walking, the letter gripped in his hand. Beth closes her eyes and waits.

When Selous returns he says nothing, just sits behind the wheel, lost in thought.

'Are you all right?' Beth says.

He nods slowly although his eyes are still far away.

'If you want to tell me what your father wrote... I'll listen,' she says.

He hands her the letter. 'You're welcome to read it but there's no need to find it upsetting – as I said, I don't care for the title deed.'

She reads the letter that has somehow survived every accident of her journey.

Dear Son,

You may never receive this but if you ever hold it in your hand it will be thanks to my doctor, Dr Jenkins, who took the trouble to fulfil an old man's last wish. The title deed to our land is also in the safe keeping of the doctor. I've kept it from that snake Boniface Madzwaya and his partner in crime, Robson Chiripo.

Beth drops the letter to her lap. It is her patient, Mr De Villier, not Selous, that she's most betrayed. She chokes again with what she's done, spells it out to herself in all its severe truth: she's given away the land that Mr De Villier had bought with his wife's life. Bought with her blood.

'It's OK,' Selous says quietly. 'When I said I don't care for the deed, please believe me. And as for my father and mother, they'll always possess the land, although not in the way my father dreamed of.'

Beth reads on, still not quite believing.

Son, I hope you live long on the land and may your memories of me be from happier times – you, me and your incomparable mother – for those are the times that have filled my thoughts in these, my last days.

Your father.

There is an additional note at the bottom of the page.

There is a nurse who has shown me kindness. Should you still not wish to hold the title deed (you're a stubborn oke, like your father) then it should go to my nurse. His name is Fortunate Mukumbi. Dr Jenkins will tell you how to contact him. This note, written by my own hand, is my last will and testament.

He'd signed and dated it two days before his death.

'That's the Fortunate Mukumbi you know,' Beth says. 'Now, because of what I've done, even he can't inherit the land.'

Selous has turned to look out of the window, his head cocked, listening. 'There's a sable nearby.'

Beth looks out. 'I can't see it.'

'You won't see him; he's walking amongst the trees. But I can hear him.'

Beth listens, but apart from birdsong hears nothing.

Selous starts the car and they drive off, the kopjes like living things, watching them pass.

'Boniface was shot three days ago,' Beth says.

'So I understand.'

'You heard!'

'News travels as fast as a bullet here – particularly that sort of news.'

Especially if you fired the bullet, thinks Beth. Selous has ample motive even if he doesn't care what has become of the title deed. Boniface had killed his mother. She's sure he would have no trouble felling a man at several hundred yards.

'But he's going to live,' she says. 'Boniface will survive. He's in hospital in Kariba.'

Selous glances at her then and she senses she's surprised him – knowing detail like that. She tells him what happened, trying to judge whether his reactions are compatible with being the one who pulled the trigger, but he gives nothing away. When she's finished he says, 'It would have changed nothing if he'd died.'

'It might have changed something for me,' Beth says. She tells him about Matt, about the site and the massacre that Matt had kept secret from her, of Boniface's threat to Matt, of her need to see the paintings, her hunch that she might find the reason for Matt's silence there. Selous listens attentively. She finds her voice threatening to fracture when she tells him about Matt's stroke but he says quietly, 'I understand,' and she gets through it. She ends with, 'So I'm guessing Boniface is the only one who knows where the paintings are, the only one who could take me there. But I don't know what to do. Should I go back to Kariba and somehow persuade him to take me when he's better? I think he'll just boot me out of the country.'

Selous mulls it over, although she guesses he thinks her suggestion foolish but wants to find a polite way of saying so. Eventually he asks, 'Your friend, Hope, said the site is on my father's land?'

'Yes, that's what she said.'

'I know almost every inch of the farm, and I've never come across it but… there is one place… a place I've never explored as it's hard to get to and I avoided it as a child as I found it a bit spooky. If the cave is anywhere on the farm then that's where it'll be. But we'll have to find a route that avoids the war vets.'

'You'll take me there?'

He nods once. 'We'll go one morning, first thing.'

'You don't have to, Selous. I'm a bad penny for you.'

'I don't think so,' he says and turns to her, his eyes steady on hers. For a moment she thinks the creases on his face might deepen into a smile. Emotions bubble up in her: regret, confusion, uncertainty. Those compound emotions again. But the most cloying is of loneliness. She feels loneliness stretch out like an infinite road ahead of her. She has friends, but no family. She is married, but alone.

She spikes her self-pity and says, 'Where do you stay now that you can't go back to your farm?'

'Close,' he says as they draw up at Lindi's place. 'One of Lindi's uncles has lent me a room. It's a few minutes' walk from here.'

They step out of the car and he says, 'Tomorrow I'm going

to give your friends a lift to the airport. The next day I'll knock on your window at 5.15am. We'll go to the site together.'

'We will? Thank-you.'

Selous turns and walks off down a track that winds between the rocks but dangles the car keys from his hand and says, 'I'm keeping the keys with me this time.'

She calls after him, 'Oh, I've not shown you the scratches on the door or sorted out the hire.' But he is gone. She'd also forgotten to ask him where he thought Fortunate went to after he'd left the farm. Who is Fortunate, anyway? Does Selous have any better idea than she does? Appearing and disappearing at critical moments, intentions unreadable. A muse? A secret helper? Playing some dangerous game of his own? She remembers how the Jackal's identity remains a mystery beyond the last page of Forsyth's novel.

Beth holds back her tears as she says goodbye to Alena and the others the next day although they all protest that they will see each other again before long. She asks them not to tell anyone else yet that she is alive. She's not quite done with the *great Yes*.

Christina hugs Gogo MaNyoni. 'Hey, I wish I had a grandmother like you. Lala kuhle.'

'That's goodnight,' Lindi says.

'I know,' Christina says. 'I just love it! Lala. Isn't that beautiful?'

'Hamba kuhle,' Gogo MaNyoni says.

'Go well,' Lindi translates.

'Oh, hamba kuhle, sala huhle, lala kuhle. Isn't that just fucking divine?'

They all wave madly through the windows of Bismarck as Selous drives them off. Lindi and Beth wait for the sound of Bismarck's engine to fade.

Back at the house, Lindi points to the red light on the socket above the electric hob and says excitedly, 'Look, we've got power! Let's cook!'

She chops beans and Beth washes potatoes in a metal bucket. Beth apologises for disrupting Lindi's week but Lindi dismisses it with a shrug and asks, 'Was everything OK yesterday with Selous? You sorted out the car?'

'Selous was so understanding,' Beth says, 'but I must tell you this, he thinks he knows where the site is, the place of the massacre that Matt's maid took him to. He's going to take me there tomorrow.'

Lindi stops chopping and turns to her. 'You shouldn't go,' she says firmly.

'Really?' Beth says. 'Look, it's kind of you to be concerned... I'm going to be affected by it... but I'll cope. And anyway it's not the bones I want to see. Matt found special paintings nearby. I'm going to look for them. I have to see what Matt saw.'

'What Mr Hallam saw?' Beth thinks she sees alarm in Lindi's eyes. 'The painting? But Beth, that's not necessary.'

'Not necessary?'

'If you want to see the painting I have a drawing, a tracing of the painting. You can come to my office at the museum and I'll be pleased to show you.'

'You're saying you know about the paintings – the *painting*, you say?'

Lindi turns away and takes another handful of beans from a sack and drops them on the chopping board. 'Mr Hallam didn't want anyone else to know about it.'

'Lindi, I'm stunned. I didn't know you'd been there – although I guess I never asked.'

Lindi shuffles the beans to line up their ends and starts topping them. 'Yes, I visited the site. How could I not, with my interest in rock art? So, there's no need for you to go. Come to the museum and see it for yourself.'

She has a cheerful tone but Beth thinks that it's forced and wants to take Lindi by her shoulders, shake her and beg her to spill out every secret she holds.

Controlling her voice, Beth asks, 'Did you go with Matt?'

'No, I went on my own. It was about a month after he was expelled. It wasn't easy to find but he'd given me directions. When I found it... ' Lindi shakes her head. 'I stayed there all day just staring.'

'And what was it like?' Beth imagines a life-size hunter or a strange symbol, never seen before in rock art.

'You can come and see the drawing. Then you'll understand why Mr Hallam was so excited.' Lindi gathers the cut beans and rinses them in a bucket. 'But at the same time, of course, he was troubled. It was as if he'd opened the chamber of Tutankhamen but then had walked away; left it for vandals to scratch or spray with graffiti. What to do? I can still see him pacing up and down the corridor at the museum.'

Beth can too. 'And then what?' she asks. She realises that she's been stupidly holding a potato in her wet hands for over a minute now.

Lindi glances again at the light on the socket switch. 'My lucky day! The power's still on.' She drops the beans into a pan and then uses a ladle to fill the pan with water from another bucket. 'After he reported the bodies we never communicated again because he was expelled. But maybe he wrote something, wrote a draft paper about his discovery, filed it away, waiting for the right time to publish. It would cause a sensation in archaeological circles – maybe in the wider world as well.' She half turns to Beth. 'Have you looked at his papers? Maybe there's something on his computer?'

'But what do *you* think, Lindi? What are your theories?'

Lindi places the pan on the hob of the old yellow stove. 'I have my ideas of course but I wanted to speak again with Mr Hallam… I was hoping that one day… ' She shrugs sadly.

'So you saw the skeletons as well. And is the site on the De Villier farm?' Beth says, remembering what Hope had told her.

There's an indifferent tone in Lindi's voice as she says, 'I don't really know where his farm ends but the place is in that general area so, yes, maybe.'

'I'd really like to go there, Lindi.'

Lindi turns on the stove's knob.

Beth wonders if Lindi has heard her. She says, 'Visiting the site is important to me.'

Lindi places a hand lightly on the hob. 'Yes! It's heating.' She turns to Beth again. 'It's a hidden place. I really don't remember exactly where it was – it's so long ago and in those days we had no GPS. I don't have the coordinates. But I do remember that there were warning symbols – painted creatures – on the rocks nearby. They guard the place.'

Beth is silent.

'You and I may not believe in them,' says Lindi, 'but they make you feel uneasy, as if it makes no difference to their power whether you believe in them or not.'

Beth thinks she can smell electrical burning, then there's a popping sound.

'Oh, tits!' says Lindi. 'Excuse my English.' She turns the stove off and groans. 'The cooker has blown again. Just when I've got power for the first time in four days.' Then she says absently,

'Look, Beth, it's not necessary and remember that the war vets have taken over the land. It's much too dangerous.'

'Uh huh.' Beth joins Lindi at the hot plate. 'Sorry about your stove. Can I do anything to help?'

'No, I'm going to go and fetch my brother. He'll fix it. I'll see you in about half an hour.' Lindi hurries out the door.

Beth is left standing in the acrid air, still holding the potato. She drops it on the worktop, goes to the door and looks out at the great rocks that surround the homestead and finds her gaze drawn to their overhangs, shadows and clefts. It does seem unwise to venture in there. There must be thousands of hidden places and it would be easy to feel spooked by coming across some symbol of a spectre on a rock. She remembers the threatening war vet at the entrance to Selous's farm. She remembers Dick's fear of the area. And what if she's putting Selous in danger? The rock art reproductions she's seen in Lindi's office are almost as good as the real thing, so why risk it?

CHAPTER 27

awn is just a thinning of the night as Beth and Selous set out in Bismarck along small tracks that wind for miles past castle kopjes slumbering between feathery trees. Beth has left a note for Lindi to say that she has to do this. She has to visit the site, see the painting. She'd not taken long to come to a decision. After all, finding the site is what she'd stayed in Zimbabwe to do.

They come to a place where they drive over exposed rock. Selous negotiates a careful path and then turns off sharply before stopping at a place hidden from view of the track. As he gets out Selous asks Beth to close her door quietly, then he picks dry grass and walks back along their path to the track, brushing the few patches of sand where their tyres have left an impression. Then he signals her to follow him.

Leaves and tall grasses burst into a mosaic of colour as the sun breaks the horizon. They walk softly across what seems virgin land although the artists who painted the picture they are on their way to find would have trodden the same ground millennia ago, and others too: small groups on hunting expeditions; then cattle herders looking for fresh pasture; and then Boniface with a line of stumbling terrified people. Beth remembers Matt telling her that scenes depicting violence are extraordinarily rare in rock art (and in the one that came to mind, he said, there was something else significant about it: elements of the landscape had been depicted). But then, at those times, land did not need defending; it was wide enough to offer its gifts freely.

Selous stops and points out a small figure the colour of old blood painted on a beak-like overhang of rock. The figure has been pecked by time but its long sinuous tail, strong arms and clawed hands convey a menacing power. Selous says under his breath, 'It's an isituhwane. A ghost. Amongst other things it's feared as a sign of bad luck.'

Beth feels uneasy, has a sense of being watched. 'Lindi told me about these.'

Selous says, 'There's no need to believe it. Things only take on the meaning we choose to give them. It's like the land; it takes on any significance we claim for it. If you look on the land as the home of your ancestors it becomes sacred; if it's a pretty view, you want it preserved; if it's going to feed you or make you money, you set boundary markers to keep others out and then you plough it or dig it.'

They move on and come to a long spine of rock. Beth clambers up after Selous. They find themselves looking out over a tree canopy contained by a high circle of granite to make a forested bowl perhaps three hundred metres across. This is a darker place, the trees dense with rubbery leaves, a green pungency, the air heavy and still. On the opposite side of the bowl the trees rim the base of a great dome of naked granite.

'Matobo means *bald headed*,' Selous says, looking at the dome. 'My guess is that it's over there.' He points to the foot of the rock. Then he waits, listening. Eventually he nods and they descend into the bile-green shade of the trees.

Beth keeps close to Selous as he negotiates his way through curtains of vines and latticed tunnels of fig roots. He stoops and points to black droppings. 'Leopard,' he whispers. They skirt tumbled blocks of granite cloaked in creepers. She wonders whether Hope and Matt took the same route and how Matt's trepidation must have grown as they travelled deeper and deeper into that forest guarded by the isituhwane and weighted with what they are about to see. She can only guess at Hope's courage as she returned to her parents' grave with Matt. How could she have been so insensitive to suggest that Hope show her the place as if it was a picnic spot?

When they reach the foot of the granite they find that the rock doesn't curve smoothly into the soil but is broken off to make a high, vertical face. Selous makes a flipping-a-coin gesture and then they make their way to the right. The trees thin and the sunlight on the lip of the granite picks out slate-blue lichens and shallow, sharply-etched gullies cut over millennia by flash floods. After a few minutes of walking, the rock takes on a shallower slope and it seems unlikely they'll find a cave. Selous turns and they retrace their steps and then follow the rock to the left. Beth is starting to lose hope when they come to a corner where the rock angles away from the light. Around this corner Beth sees Selous hesitate and then step through a crack in the granite, wide at the base and narrow at the top. She waits outside.

After a few seconds Selous comes back out. He nods. 'It's in there, the rock art that your husband found.'

Beth can't move.

'Do you want me to come in with you?' Selous says.

He waits, patient, until she says, 'No, I think I can do it.'

'You'll be fine, shout if you want me to join you. I'll be outside and perhaps follow the wall around a little further.'

'Thanks so much.'

She steps forward and finds herself in a wide cave-like crevice with almost vertical walls that rise high above her before angling in at the vault although they do not quite meet. Light falls softly like a hanging veil. Then she sees it, startled. There on the rock face is the painting of the sable, the original of the photograph that hangs in Matt's study.

She presses a hand to her lips. The photograph in Matt's study is flat, untextured and colourless in comparison to the original. Here the sable surges from the rock as if trying to break free, eyes on a distant horizon, mane flying, flank taut. She has an urge to reach out and run her fingers through its bristling fur or to take hold of its tapering horn. The artist has captured the living creature. Then it blazes in her – warm and luminous – that Matt has been here, has stood under the same lineaments of light, on the same grains of earth, in front of this canvas of rock that melds the past and the present, actuality and art, substance and its meanings. She's suddenly overwhelmed by a sense of Matt's presence, she can feel him near: his breath, the texture and warmth of his skin, the hair on the nape of his neck and the pressure of his body against hers. She closes her eyes.

The solidity of the sensation as quickly dissolves; Matt is no longer near, and she opens her eyes again and calls to Selous to join her. When he comes beside her, she says, 'Matt had a photo of this in his study at home and I never knew that he'd taken that picture here. He never told me it was from Zimbabwe and of course Mrs Incurious never asked.'

'It's astonishing,' Selous says. 'I've never seen anything like it. The archaeologists will fall on their knees when they see this.'

As she stands there, Beth finds the thrill of their discovery is, little by little, replaced by something else. A small hollow feeling which grows until she can put a name to it: disappointment. There's something missing. What was she expecting? That everything would fall into place? That Matt had written his own message to her on the wall?

Behind her she senses Selous shifting his weight. He says, 'I've found the site of the massacre.'

Beth braces herself. 'I think I'd better see it.'

'There's nothing to see. It's been cleared.'

She follows Selous around the rock across heavily-leafed ground. Close by they come to a place where the granite dome seems to have been scooped out with an enormous spoon making a shallow wide-mouthed cave. She recognises the crack in the back of the rock from Matt's photographs. The floor is unnaturally flat and smooth as if it has been levelled and scoured, although a generous scattering of blown seed pods, dead leaves and twigs indicate that time has passed since its clearing; there is not a trace of the skeletons or clothing. The place has a cold silence to it. Not a bird sings in the forest behind them.

Selous is examining the walls which are covered in a red wash. 'Whoever removed the bodies also cleaned down the rock. Look, there used to be San paintings here. You can see the ochre's been scrubbed away.'

Beth can just make out the faint remaining shapes of the paintings: hunters and animals, all figures common to rock art sites. 'Someone's destroyed them?' she asks.

'Sometimes you find this – the paintings rubbed away by the hides of cattle if the place was once used as a shelter for livestock – but look, even the paintings up there, above cattle height, have been erased.' The cave has lost all its voices, ancient and modern. 'If this is the site of the massacre then it's been well sanitised,' Selous says. 'Looks like a lot of care's been taken to remove evidence. Everything's been washed down to ensure no fibres of clothing or spots of blood remain.'

Beth guesses that Boniface and all others like him follow the trials of men like Slobodan Milosevic, listening intently to the forensic evidence, and know that a trace of DNA can corroborate a witness's story, can find them facing justice many years after their crime.

'Where would Boniface have taken the bones?'

'There are plenty of abandoned mine shafts around here. You could lose anything down them.'

They walk quietly back through the trees, Beth lost in her thoughts. She's found the same archaeological treasure that Matt found, although she has seen it many times before in his office at home. She's discovered – as if she couldn't have guessed – that Boniface has erased the forensic evidence of the massacre. Boniface has thought nothing of destroying the art in the cave where the skeletons lay but she remembers he'd told her that he'd not even bothered to look at the painting that Matt had been so anxious should be preserved. It occurs to her that there is now no reason for Lindi to remain silent on the find. Lindi can write her paper, announce it to the world, establish her name, become famous even. All those years of silence were unnecessary.

On their drive back to Lindi's place, Selous doesn't ask questions and Beth is grateful not to have to talk. She is moved by his sensitive assistance. He'd let her be when she wanted space to herself but taken matters in hand when she needed assistance and help, as if he could read her better than herself. She becomes aware of his sure hands guiding the wheel, whilst every now and then he slots the gear lever smoothly home. She finds herself wishing that he'd stop the car, lean across her, hold the outer curve of her hip in his hand, and kiss her. She sees herself running her fingers along the laugh lines on his cheeks, as if that will coax him to smile. Her want of a kiss, she tells herself, has little to do with it being a long time since that has happened, or to a sudden falling for Selous – that would be absurd, not to mention far too complicating. It's simply to quash, just for a moment, her sudden loneliness which has settled on her like a crushing weight.

But Selous drives on.

Nearing Lindi's place Beth sees a young child walking by the side of the road. She finds herself giving a small huffing, emotion-releasing laugh – seeing the girl reminds her of Robson's lie. 'Robson told me that you had a daughter. He said you'd left her in an orphanage in South Africa.'

'And what did Robson say had happened to my wife?' Selous says evenly.

'That she'd been shot in South Africa. Robson said, *Poof! Just so!* Beth squirms to remember how she'd so readily swallowed Robson's ridiculous yarn.

Selous says quietly, 'That much is true.' He returns Beth's appalled gaze with a steady eye.

'I'm so sorry, I didn't know,' she blurts.

'*Poof. Just so,*' he says without parody. 'Like your Matt, I guess.'

'Yes,' she says eventually.

'Sasha,' he says, as if breathing a prayer. 'She was five months pregnant. I was told we would have had a girl.'

Selous drops Beth at Lindi's whilst he drives on to do 'business' in Bulawayo. She needs to be on her own and takes a walk down the road. Cow-bells gong, someone is chopping wood, farmers call to each other across a field, a woman dries her washing on the frame of a bush. She's encircled by domesticity. She thinks of

Selous, grieving for his wife, his mother, his unborn child and she guesses he might in time grieve for his father. In all that, he'd tried to protect her when she'd gatecrashed his farm, had saved Fortunate's life, and had forgiven her prejudice and her theft of his property – both car and farm. She feels her face go hot with shame at her needy yearning for a kiss from a man who is still in shock and grief.

When she returns, she finds Lindi is at home and – eager now to tell her about the cave – she bursts in on her. 'There are no skeletons there, Lindi! They've all been removed.'

Lindi looks up from her table where she's writing. 'I'm relieved you're back safely and yes, I know, I didn't find them either.' She has a matter of fact voice.

'You didn't? You looked at the cave when you went to see the painting?'

Lindi puts down her pen. 'I found nothing. It was hard to believe that anything had happened there. Very difficult to believe.'

Beth steps back. 'You think Matt made it up? You think that that time in the eighties you call Gukurahundi never happened?'

'Gukurahundi happened, of course.'

'But this incident, this instance was, you think, somehow made up?'

Lindi looks at her a little wearily and says, 'To get justice against a man, there must be evidence. Good evidence. Where is that evidence?'

Should she tell her that she knows Matt's maid, Hope? That Hope has told her everything? Then a new thought lurks, as if it has emerged from a dark crack in the rocks outside. Has Hope built an elaborate story? Did Matt and Hope collude in some way for some reason still lost to her?

334

It will be less disturbing to talk about the painting. 'I know very little about rock art but the painting of the sable looked fabulous. You said yesterday that it's very unusual?'

Lindi brightens. 'To an archaeologist with an interest in rock art it's the find of the century. Mr Hallam thought it might predate all the other rock art in Africa. Often I get out the drawing and look again, cross-checking it with the literature, trying to find out if anyone else has come across anything similar in any other part of the world. But it's unique.'

'But Lindi, if you knew that there was no trace of the massacre site next door to the painting why didn't you tell your colleagues about it? Speak to your PhD supervisor?'

Lindi shakes her head. 'You don't know Boniface Madzwaya. Even without the bodies he might look on me as another witness and investigate how I knew about the site. He expelled your husband, a foreigner. What would he have done to me, a national? The time was not right.'

'But it's OK now, surely? Now it's such a long time ago.'

Lindi puckers her forehead as if Beth has touched a deep uncertainty. She says, 'I'd hoped it would be Mr Hallam that would publish one day, maybe a joint paper. That would've been so nice.'

'But to Boniface, that would link you with Matt?'

'Yes.'

'It's not going to happen now. Matt can hardly write his name, let alone publish a paper.'

Over the next two weeks Beth helps the nurse in the local clinic on an informal basis – Lindi says that since Beth has no licence to practise medicine in Zimbabwe she must keep a low profile. She also helps at the primary school, playing games such as tug of war and a variant on *What's the time Mr Wolf?* with a fierce Mr Lion taking the place of Mr Wolf.

Selous comes and goes, greeting her politely but letting her be, although she very much wishes he wouldn't let her be. She can't help herself. She puts it down to wanting to somehow help him smile again, despite her knowing that her past behaviour, and her own neglected responsibilities to Matt, disqualify her from being the one to do that. And yet it is because of Selous that she feels relaxed about her continuing illegal status, confident that Selous would find a way to get her out of the country if that were needed. On a kapenta boat perhaps.

She doesn't trouble Dick again although sends him a text message, on a mobile that Alena left with her, to thank him for his help and – not to add to his worries – says that everything has 'worked out all right'. His return text indicates that he's still in the thick of problems at the mine but pleased he'd been of some help.

Some nights she frets that Selous and Christina might be in contact with each other, might have something going between them. She has a notion that that will somehow add insult to injury. First, she sleeps with my husband and then she sleeps with… who?

Matt is on her mind as well. She resigns herself to knowing that there will always be a fracture running through her remembrance of BC Matt. She'll just have to live with it. By coming out here, finding Lindi and discovering Hope's connection to Matt, she'd built a bridge to his past, but when she'd walked across that bridge she'd collided with the rock face of his inexplicable secrecy.

The mobile signal is poor around Lindi's house although she can get reception in the nearby clinic or if she climbs the granite whale-back behind her house. So she keeps in touch by text with her friends, reassuring them that everything is just fine. But about two weeks after they leave, she receives a text from Alena.

Penelope told me that there's a man taking Matt out to the allotment. It's Fortunate! Matt seems to be loving it.

Fortunate. What a friend he is to Matt. The only friend that Matt has made AD. Matt has lost the companionship he used to have with her before his stroke but he's gained another's.

That night, Beth lies in her bed imagining Matt working on the allotment with Fortunate. She remembers Matt's contentment when he was with him – his new pal. Fortunate has found a way through to him. Perhaps, perhaps, she can do the same. Maybe she should find it in herself to learn from Fortunate.

A single star is framed in the window of the pitch dark room. It draws her from her bed and she finds herself standing by the opening, looking out into the night. Southern constellations pepper the huge sky above the faint forms of the hills. It's so beautiful. Beautiful… but; but it's not home. And there's the catch: she's run away from the life she'd found herself in – the place, the circumstance, her house, her husband – but she can't truly escape. The life that she's cut herself loose from is what made her who she is. Its mesh of memories, for better, for worse, forms the ground of her being and is entwined through her every thought. It's her DNA. It is herself. She should have known it. To become someone else in a new life, in a new land, she'd have to have become like Matt: someone with no memory.

CHAPTER 28

Early the next morning, when Beth knows that Alena will not yet have left for work, she climbs the rock behind the house and rings her to say that she's coming home and to ask her to break the 'bad news' to Penelope that she is alive. Then she watches the sun rise, plating the rocks with a brassy light for as far as she can see. In the rifts and seams of the golden granite, stories flow and intermingle. She'll so miss this land and fancies that her own story here, brief and embarrassing as it is, is becoming a spirit of the place, even if there are grander or more worthy stories out there. The stories of Mzilikazi, Lobengula, Rhodes, Selous, Boniface, Lindi, Hope, and thousands of others who ghost the hills.

She's about to descend the rock again when her mobile rings. It's Penelope. Beth stands rigid, and lets it ring. She can hear her mother-in-law saying *what the hell have you been playing at?* And she'd be right.

She tries to ignore the noise but it swamps down the granite slope, infiltrates the quiet valleys, invades the hills. She shuts it up by answering.

'Have you heard? I'm having a grandchild,' Penelope says excitedly.

Beth finds herself smiling. Of course, Christina to the rescue. 'I'm delighted for you,' she says, and is surprised to feel an uncomplicated pleasure in sharing in Penelope's joy.

Beth hears Penelope say something offline and then Penelope says to her, 'I think Matthew wants to speak with you.'

There's a fumbling on the handset. Beth's heart leaps and she has to lower herself to her knees, and then holds the phone to her ear with both hands. 'Matt? It's Beth here.'

There's a long silence although she can hear the faint sound of his breath on the mouthpiece.

'Hello Matt, can you hear me?'

Then she hears him say, 'When are you coming home?'

She can't speak and bends her head. The granite is dissolving. Then she hears Penelope ask Matt to give her back the phone. 'No, stay on the line, Matt. I'm coming back soon.' She can't keep her voice from wavering.

She thinks he is going to ask her the same again but he says, 'What's wrong?'

'It's OK, I'm OK. What about you?'

He says, 'I miss… '

She waits but when he says no more, she says, 'What do you miss, Matt?'

'I miss… you,' he says.

She grips her mobile as if it were Matt's hand and imagines him standing there, several thousand miles away, and a million miles from who he was before, but there is a link between them, a rickety little bridge. She'd thought it was all one way, the only thing connecting them being her own memories of what he used to be and her efforts (lately abandoned) to do her duty towards him, but now it is Matt who has – with what she can hear is agonised effort – tried to throw a rope back to her. 'I miss you too, Matt,' she says. She's spoken so softly that she's worried that he's not heard her, so says it again.

There is a scuffling noise and Penelope's voice comes loud

and imposing over the line, 'I'm going to bring Matthew out to see you.' Before Beth can say that she thinks that's not a good idea, that she is returning home, Penelope says in a stiff tone, 'I'm not succeeding with him.'

'Has he changed?' Beth asks. 'He seems to know I've been away.'

Penelope doesn't answer immediately and when she speaks again her voice is nasal and faltering. 'No, he's just the same. If anything he's worse. Nothing's working. All my affirmative thinking, my yes-he-can attitude. No one could've been more positive than I've been, could they?' She ends in a whimper. Beth hears her sob.

'I don't think you could have tried harder,' Beth says. Penelope is silent. 'It's all been too much for us both, hasn't it?'

'I've treated you terribly,' says Penelope in a barely audible voice and then sobs again.

Beth wants to hold Penelope, wrap her arms around the thin tree of her body, stand with her against the storm. Penelope quietens as if she has her head on Beth's shoulder. Beth waits, her own breaths are long and silent. Then Penelope blows her nose and says in a fast stream, 'I'm booking a flight as soon as possible. I'll send you a text from the airport when we arrive. Look forward to seeing you.'

'But Penelope… ' Beth's mobile makes a continuous buzzing. Penelope has put the phone down.

Beth hears from Lindi that Boniface Madzwaya is on the De Villier farm, living there now, convalescing from his injury. Beth decides that before she troubles Selous again to ask his help in leaving the country, she should first go and pay her patient a home visit to call in what she hopes he still feels he owes her: a safe passage out of Zimbabwe. If Penelope is to come out with Matt then she'll return home with them both.

She needs transport to go out to the farm and when she asks Selous if she can borrow his car one last time, he says, 'Of course, but one last time?'

For a moment she thinks he's teasing her about her theft of his car and then she realises he's asking if she's leaving. 'I guess I need to go home soon to look after Matt.'

Is there disappointment in his eyes, or is that just wishful thinking? He nods and says, 'Please don't disappear without saying goodbye. If you need a lift to the airport, just ask.'

There are no war vets at the entrance to the De Villier land and Beth is soon approaching the main homestead of the farm. Sitting beside a low table on the lawn in the shadow of a tree in front of the damaged Cape gable frontage of the main house, is Boniface. His chair is reclined back a little but he rests an arm on the table. Beside him a young woman, arms weighted with gold bangles, sits straight-backed. They turn to look at Beth as she approaches. Beth sees Boniface reach out and give the woman a shove. The woman comes over as Beth stops a short distance away. Leaning down at Beth's open window, the woman examines Beth disdainfully, exposing more than Beth wishes to see of her soufflé-like breasts above her low cut dress. Perfume steams up from her cleavage.

Her pink-glossed lips quiver hotly. 'What are you doing here? You're trespassing.'

'I've come to see Boniface Madzwaya. We know each other.'

'In your dreams,' the woman says. 'This is the white colonialist's car; why don't you *ftsek*?'

'If you'll excuse me.' Beth opens the door determinedly, so that the woman has to step back.

Beth hears a weak shout from Boniface. He's waving her over. 'You're in big trouble now,' warns the woman.

Boniface's table is strewn with bottles: Bols brandy, Jameson whisky, Gordon's gin, Amurula liquor, Van Der Hum. It looks like the entire contents of someone's drinks cabinet. Mr De Villier's, she guesses. Boniface is clutching a bottle of Bohlingers beer.

'Well, well, my old friend Dr Jenkins.' Boniface's speech is slurred and his eyes have the shifting, unfocussed look of the drunk. 'This is the exact woman who saved my life!' he says to his friend.

'Oh, I didn't know!' the woman says, switching from a gutter vernacular to Queen's English. 'Dr Jenkins, it's such a pleasure to welcome you. Mr Madzwaya has told me so much about you. Please know that I'm delighted to meet you. It was a case of mistaken identity just now. Please sit down and make yourself comfortable. I'll call the maid. Would you like a cup of tea?'

Beth shakes her head, still staring at Boniface. He starts to move his beer bottle towards his mouth and then thinks better of it and pours it into a glass. Froth spills over onto the table. Beth stands silent. 'As you know, I'm teetotal,' Boniface says, 'but a man in my position must have some R and R.'

Beth takes the chair Boniface's woman was sitting in. Boniface waves his hand in the woman's general direction in a perfunctory manner and says, 'That's my fiancé. She's from Victoria Falls. I believe you dropped in there.' He chuckles to himself and then winces. 'Ah, I keep forgetting my injury.' He twists his heavy torso to make himself more comfortable. 'We're a very modern romance,' he boasts. 'We met on-line when I was in the UK a few weeks ago. She's my internet date!'

'Internet date?'

'Her name is Shungu.'

Beth's bag slips to the ground as her hands go weak. 'Shungu?' Nausea wells. She stares at Shungu long and unswervingly. She has difficulty guessing her age; she might be twenty-five or thirty-five. Perhaps she is whatever age her lovers wish her to be. Her face is intelligent, knowing, and startlingly beautiful now that she isn't scowling at her. Beth has experienced the cunning beneath but she guesses Shungu can conceal it well. With her silky charms, Beth sees why Fortunate fell for her.

'So, it's kind of you to pay me a visit,' Boniface says in a louder-than-necessary voice, 'but perhaps it wasn't to pass the time of day?'

Beth hesitates, still stunned to find Shungu there, thinking what a lucky escape Fortunate has had, but knowing also that he'll be devastated, if he doesn't already know.

Boniface, apparently taking Beth's silence to indicate she wants to speak privately, turns to Shungu and says, 'Leave us, woman. I must talk to my doctor.' Shungu leaves demurely.

Beth collects herself and says, 'Have they found the assassin? The man who tried to kill you?'

Boniface hiccups and then grimaces before saying, 'We found the culprit. A soldier on a patrol boat on the lake accidentally discharged his weapon.'

She can't tell whether he's telling the truth. 'Oh, so no one wanted to kill you!'

'Not that one, no.'

'Unlucky for the soldier, I guess.'

'Very, very, unlucky for him,' Boniface says, sobering up for a moment. He swaps his beer for his glass of spirits and downs it. He closes his eyes and looks as if he is going to nod off.

Beth leans over and says, 'Mr Madzwaya, it's time for me to

343

go home. I'm hoping you can arrange my passage through passport control at the airport. You said you would do that for me.'

Boniface screws up his eyes as if he has photophobia. 'I'm getting plenty tired of your escapades. Every time I wish to help you, you disappear. Are you serious about leaving this time?'

'I am. I'm going back to look after my husband.'

Boniface returns to his beer and then wipes froth off his chin with the back of his hand. He asks, 'Do you have that letter that my man gave you to show at the police roadblocks?'

'You mean your man, Robson Chiripo? Yes, I do.'

'It'll work at the airport as well.' Then, with some effort against his pain, Boniface stretches both arms out wide as if to encompass his land, and well beyond, and says, 'You're fortunate to know me, to have the privilege. One day that letter could have you saluted everywhere on this continent. That's how I see things developing as we liberate ourselves from the hypocritical ambitions of the West. But we must stay alert: the monster of imperialism is lurking in the bush awaiting a more favourable opportunity to devour our national sovereignty.' He hiccups again and winces. 'But first we'll have to deal with reactionary elements.'

Beth picks up her bag and places it on her lap, ready to go.

Boniface throws an arm towards her as if trying to lay hold of her but she is too far away and he lets it fall heavily on the table and grimaces. 'You know, Dr Jenkins, Dr Lynette, Dr Bethen, yes, Bethen. I must tell you something since you're such a very good friend of mine. Since you're such a fine friend of the struggle, a heroine in aiding the indigenous peoples such as myself to get back their land.' He belches freely. 'I must tell you this: your husband, he didn't want to leave anything to chance.

I think he didn't trust me.' He raises his glass to himself and titters.

'What do you mean?'

'He came with me in my *bakkie* to give me some help. It was too big a job for one man. Oh, your husband, he worked hard. That load was surprisingly heavy. I could never have done it on my own. Yes, he worked like… what's the white man's saying?… he worked like a black!'

'Done what on your own?' Beth asks, although the answer presents itself as menacingly as a meningitis rash. Her vision tunnels. All she can see is Boniface's leering face.

'Ah yes.' He starts giggling but eventually says, 'You see, Bethy, we did it together.'

'He helped you remove the bodies? Is that what you mean?'

Boniface's hand goes to his side. 'Ah, maybe you should check my wound.'

'My husband helped you clear the massacre site? What are you trying to say?'

Boniface suddenly goes cold and his voice resonates with menace. 'Oh Lynette, what site? What are you talking about?'

'You must have forced him!'

'Force him? No, no, Bethoh, it was he who suggested it! I think he would have shot those sell-outs himself, if he thought it would protect the scribbling on the rock. Such a helpful man, such a very good man!' He takes a swig from another bottle and dribbles down his chin. 'But you know my father? He was a freedom fighter, and me, I am too.'

He lets his weight subside into his chair and closes his eyes. But as soon they shut he opens them again and looks wide-eyed at Beth. 'Tell me, as you are a learned doctor, is it true that an invisible speck of blood can land a liberation hero in The Hague?'

He grunts and sinks back again, letting his arm drop to rest his bottle on the scarified grass.

It seems now that he's losing awareness that she is there. 'Some people whisper that I killed my father… but why would I do such a thing?… he was a liberator, a hero, I could never have betrayed him… I cannot imagine doing that… it's not possible… even if he'd been going soft… had lost his fire… but the liberation must go on… we cannot afford to be sentimental… I was young, zealous… ' He releases his bottle, pulls up his arm to rest it on his lap and rubs his bite-shaped scar as if he could erase it. 'Do you know a good plastic surgeon?'

Beth hooks her bag on her shoulder, stands up and walks to the car. She sees Boniface for the last time as she turns Bismarck. He's slid down his chair, bottle now held on his belly, and is looking out at the land through puffy half-closed eyes, having his slice of time there, making his own story. She drives slowly through the wreckage of the farm: the burnt out cattle sheds, the smashed water tank, a vandalised borehole pump. She lets Bismarck find her way along the twin ribbons of track back to the road, the grasses either side silently flaming. The sun has fallen behind the upper trunks of a row of tall trees. Alternating bands of light and shadow sweep across her hands on the wheel. Oh Matt. Now at last, she understands. Perhaps he'd hoped that a memory not shared could unmake what he'd done. As if it never happened. But the truth is this: he'd not shared his secret with her; he had kept his lips sealed even in their closest embrace – for shame.

CHAPTER 29

Beth is in the clinic three days later and has just finished tending to a child's burns when she receives a call on her mobile.

'Is that Dr Jenkins? I'm calling from Joshua Nkomo Airport, Bulawayo.'

It's a male voice, no one she recognises. 'Yes, it's Beth Jenkins.'

'I have your husband here with me.'

'Oh! Who are you? Where's Mrs Hallam?'

'Mrs Hallam stayed in the UK but she's sent out your husband.' Penelope! But she can hardly complain with her own abandonment of Matt. 'I was assigned to look after him on the flight from Harare to Bulawayo. Can you come and pick him up?'

Beth has no transport and the airport is the other side of Bulawayo. Lindi is at the museum. Selous is… she doesn't know where. She tells the escort that she'll ring him back and calls Lindi who leaps at the chance to collect Matt although Beth warns her that although he will look very much as she remembers him, he will not recognise her.

Three hours later Lindi's lopsided Datsun draws up outside her house. For the past hour Beth has been waiting under the shade of a tree. So much has happened to her that it's impossible not to believe that momentous things have happened to Matt as well. She can't believe he'll not be different. But in what way, she can't imagine.

She goes to Matt's door and opens it. He hardly looks at her as he steps out and he says nothing. As he stands there, more interested it seems in the surroundings than her, she hugs him and then can't let go. It's his form, the firm physicality of Matt, that she holds. She buries her face in his chest. His shirt becomes wet. She thought that she'd said goodbye just before she'd left for Zimbabwe. Will this grieving, this longing, never end?

When she opens Matt's suitcase, she finds a note from Penelope. *Bethan, here's Matthew. Unable to come as too much to do preparing for the arrival of my grandchild. Maybe you'll do better with Matthew than I have.*

Beth can't find Matt's medication in his luggage. He was on three different pills for his blood pressure. Penelope always grumbled about them, saying that they'd be counteracting each other and damaging his immune system. She guesses that Penelope has stopped them. She'll have to try to find a new prescription in Bulawayo as soon as possible.

In Lindi's extended family there is a place for Matt. He's taken under the wing of Lindi's youngest brother, who leads him out to the fields in the renewed light of each morning, where Matt works with the farmers as contentedly as he had on the allotment with Fortunate. He exhibits no embarrassing behaviours. Beth walks out to him each day with a snack and a flask of tea.

They sit together, mostly silent, in the shadow of a kopje, out of the heat of the sun. Several times she is on the cusp of asking him whether he remembers what he'd done with Boniface at the massacre site. She wants to understand, she's willing to see his point of view, how he came to feel that he must do it.

One day she has to stop herself pummelling on his chest in frustration at his on-going silence. He must sense her exasperation because he stands up suddenly and walks away around the side of the kopje. She follows, heart heavy. He stops in front of a rock face and looks into it as if staring into nothing, into blankness. She comes near and puts a hand on his shoulder. 'I'm so sorry Matt. You knew I was irritated with you didn't you? I shouldn't be like that.'

But Matt is studying the granite. Rock art figures climb the wall, faded and pocked, not the best examples, but he's captivated. He steps a little closer to the wall and reaches out so he almost touches them. It's remarkable that he's so content, standing still, absorbed. It's out of character for AD Matt. Apart from when he's gardening, or watching South Pacific, or working on the land, she's not seen anything hold his attention in the same way.

At first she pushes away the idea that comes to her. It's unwise, possibly cruel, certainly risky. Matt remains relaxed in front of the paintings, tilting his head as if there are aspects to what he sees that require deep thought. She knows now what she must do. Why else is she in Zimbabwe with Matt?

'I'm going to take you to see a very special painting, Matt.'

She thinks Selous might warn that it's inadvisable when she says that she wants to take Matt on her own to see the painting, but he accepts without protest and drops them at the same spot that he and she had set off from before. He will wait for them. He gives her a compass and explains how to follow a bearing that will take them to the rocky spine that overlooks the trees in front of the site and another bearing from the rock that will take them to the foot of the granite dome at approximately the right place.

It's a fresh blue-sky morning giving the same clarity of vision that she'd known on that day she'd first walked to Selous's farm before the sable was shot. It has rained in the night and the air is humid and scented: wet-straw, peppery leaves, sweet fruit. The rocks stream their lichen colours.

Matt follows her with no apparent anxiety and is surprisingly sure-footed in what must be a confusing environment for him, although perhaps the outdoors, the natural world, isn't as perplexing to him as an urban landscape with its harsh angles, instructing signs and mechanical noises that require so much to be learnt and processed for their interpretation. Perhaps in the great outdoors, memory-independent instincts step in.

When they arrive at the spine of granite, Beth stops and suggests to Matt that they sit down for a moment. They rest their legs on the warm slope of the rock and look across the trees to the huge bald head of stone on the other side. If it were a bald head, then it would contain a mind. She thinks of the painting inside the rock and remembers Matt's comment in his Henri Breuil lecture about the universe imagining itself in the mind of the artist.

'There's a beautiful painting over there, Matt,' she says. 'It was very special to you once.' Matt looks disinterestedly over the trees, as if his mind is encased in granite. He has a hand on the rock, supporting himself, and Beth leans across and places her hand on his. As she feels the heat and familiarity of his hand under hers, she thinks of Fortunate's acceptance of the way Matt is now, of his engagement with him, free of the memory of who he used to be. She finds herself rephrasing what she's said. 'The painting is very special to you, Matt. It means a lot to me as well. We're going to go and see it together. It's our painting.' Matt's gaze moves from the distance and settles on her hand on his.

'Matt?' She tries to find him, to reach him. 'Here we are, the two of us; it's just you and me, here and now. We're doing this amazing thing together.' Matt looks up at her with no trace of the restless, barren expression that he's had since his haemorrhage. A feeling as light as the stroke of a paintbrush touches her heart, and she says, 'I love you, Matt.'

It's the first time she's told him since his stroke.

He surprises her. Standing up he holds out his hand to her. She puts her hand in his and he lifts her assuredly to her feet.

They walk together down into the trees. She holds her compass in her other hand but has little need of it. Matt seems to know the direction to take. They move in an easy silence and she's overcome with the feeling that BC Matt is back with her again; but then it seems that it is not that Matt has become miraculously restored, or has somehow remembered that he is her husband, but that it is she who's found a crack in his skull, a way through to his mind. She sees that she's stepped through by way of his perpetual present. She's put aside the harsh narrative within which she's become trapped: its gloomy back pages of loss and disappointment, its forward trajectory to a misery lit ending. Right then, as she walks with him, they have no need of memory. The now, the moment, is sufficient, is where they can know each other again. It's the only place Matt can find her, and therefore it's the only place that she can find Matt.

When they reach the rock face and come across the cleft that leads to the painting, she grips Matt's hand tighter in case he reacts adversely, apprehensive that the place might spark a buried vision of the nearby massacre site. But he releases her grip and steps forward to pass through to the painting. She follows him. A wash of bone-white sunlight high on the opposite wall casts an indirect light on the sable. They are inside the skull. Matt exclaims, 'Look!' when he sees the painting and then stands perfectly still, engrossed. After a while he turns to her and reaches his hand towards the painting, inviting her to share it with him. She sees that there is joy in his eyes.

She comes beside him and puts her arm around his waist whilst she looks at the painting anew. She's never considered herself susceptible to hypnosis: she is far too precious about handing over control of her mind to someone else. But in front of the sable and next to Matt she becomes aware of entering something close to a trance-like state. It is not so much a hallucinatory experience but a deep sense of calm, like a still pool at the end of a race of white water. Journey's end.

If only that moment between Matt and her could go on forever; for them to stay becalmed there with no current of time carrying them on. But she knows, even as she remains bewitched, that the here-and-now, the eternal present, is more like a wave on the sea rather than a pool of quiet water. It does not travel alone but is bisected by other waves, is spattered with rain storms, crashes on shores.

She's only dimly aware of the sharp barks of baboons nearby. They fail to distract Matt. Eventually he looks down at her and for the first time since his stroke, he smiles at her. She's caught in the same vivid blue gaze that stopped her heart when she first met him. Then he says, 'You... ' and his brow furrows. He's fighting to catch a wispy sentiment, a soon-to-have-escaped notion. 'You... you... ' She stays motionless, holding her breath, lightly embracing him. 'You've come home.'

She squeezes him tightly and feels him tentatively move his arm across her back, folding her close with a tender touch. She smiles up at him and places her head on his chest and he lifts his hand and lightly strokes her hair. 'I've come home to you at last, Matt.'

The baboons bark again, louder now. Beth hears the swing and rustle of branches as if the creatures have been disturbed. She breaks away from Matt and turns back to the entrance and steps through. Matt starts to follow. Heavy boots trample dry leaf-fall. She stops and waits, her hands across the entrance to protect Matt. Where has this courage, this composure, come from? Three men, hard-eyed and boss-headed, stride into view. They carry staves.

'What are you doing here? Get out! Get out!' one shouts. They lift their weapons.

'It's OK, we're going,' she says.

But the men halt and stare behind her. She turns to take Matt's hand but he is no longer standing there. He's fallen noiselessly back into the cavern. The light falls like a gentle rain on his still form in the cradle of the rock.

She knows before she bends down to hold his head that he's dead, that another bud in his brain has burst, perhaps by a sudden rise in blood pressure when he saw the men. He'd started, that morning, the antihypertensives she'd tracked down the day before in Bulawayo. Perhaps it'd been too late.

She finds herself on her knees beside him and strokes his thick fair hair, beds her fingers in the hollow under his cheek bones then lightly traces her fingers up to the dent in his nose, across his brow, to his ear, and down his jaw to press the swell of his lips. She bends to kiss him. His features swim ever softer through her tears as if he's sinking beneath the surface of their still pool to be fluxed away into the river of time. She is aware of the men shuffling closer to look, hesitant and silent. Then she forgets they are there.

When she turns around at last, they've gone.

Her gaze falls on the painting again. It will eventually be analysed and argued over by the experts but she doubts they will ever experience what Matt experienced. Having no knowledge of the stories of the painter's era, no one will ever know what culturally-rooted symbolism the painter wished to convey but the artist's imaginative creation has burst away from its own time. The art's ageless beauty, like the surrounding natural world, has spoken directly to Matt, a man without memory. That was why she'd seen a flush of joy on his face. He'd heard a voice from the rock, from an all-powerful spirit in the land whose story is the mother story, from the mind of the universe.

Left alone with Matt's body, Beth eventually lifts herself up to go and find Selous, but before she does so she feels compelled to see once more the cleared massacre site. The notion that she should return to the site has, she thinks, come to her in her trance whilst she'd been standing in front of the painting with Matt.

It is as cold and voiceless on the sanitised ground as before. Matt, what am I missing? Is this all? Are you as silent in death as you were in life? She sees the angular fissure in the rock behind the cleared floor. It looks like a crooked mouth. She walks over to it and weights a foot on a small projection on the rock and hoists herself up towards the fissure. She manages one more step by wedging the toe of her trainer into a crack. She puts her face to the crevice and waits for her eyes to adapt to the dark. There is little space in there but enough for what she sees: at least one item of dark blue clothing and a bone. A jawbone. The site still speaks.

She lowers herself down again and looks back up. It would not have been difficult for Matt to have reached up and placed a few items in there, perhaps when Boniface was temporarily away from the site whilst they cleared it.

She takes Matt's photos out of her day pack and studies them again. There are the bones and clothes (some dark blue) on the floor of the site; there is the out-of-focus fissure in the rock face. She turns over the photo that Matt annotated on the back. Above his writing there is the symbol of a cross, an RIP. It seems out of character for him to have made that mark; he was not one for that sort of gesture, religious or otherwise. On a hunch she turns the photo over again and holds it up to the light. The centre of the cross is exactly over the point in the crack of the rock where she'd peered in. Now she sees that Matt pressed hard with his pen so that the mark is faintly embossed on the front of the photo. An imprint to anchor the memory, a defence against forgetting; until the time comes to excavate the evidence like a fossil. Until then, the mind in the rock – in the land – holds fast the memory.

POSTSCRIPT

B eth came to me, an author, three years later, to ask if I
would write about Hope and what had happened to her.
'As a way of keeping the memory,' Beth said, 'and as a
kind of small justice against those who wish what they've done
to be forgotten – as if it never happened.'

But as I listened to Beth, I found Hope's story, Selous's story,
Matt's story and all the others were like a confluence of rivers,
whose currents twisted most tightly, most strongly, around the
undertow of Beth's story. As for Fortunate, Beth's favourite
patient, his river runs through many human hearts.

Having discussed the book with Hope, Beth asked me to use
fictitious names on the page for the sake of Hope's safety and
that of Fortunate. I've done so, although their pseudonyms,
Hope and Fortunate, hold something of the meaning of their
real names.

Change has come to Zimbabwe's political landscape. At the
time of writing there is a 'government of national unity' imposed
on the regime by the country's neighbours. But Beth says it's as
if the elected Italian government has been ordered by the
European Union to share power with the mafia and been content
for the ministries of justice, police and defence to be entrusted
into the Godfather's portfolio. The perpetrators of political
violence remain above the law.

After Matt's death, Selous took Beth to the airport to

accompany Matt's body back to the UK. As he said goodbye to her in his quiet, mindful way, he gave her an envelope addressed to Fortunate Mukumbi. In the envelope, he told her, was the title deed to his land, a copy of his father's letter and a letter from himself to Fortunate in which he gave his blessing to his father's land going to his father's nurse. As I write, Fortunate is not yet on his farm, although it might be that when you, the reader, have this story in your hand, Fortunate is on his 'too beautiful' land, having his time there, making his own story to become another spirit amongst the rocks.

For now, Hope and Fortunate continue to work at Twicare. Matron took them back with little protest and updated them both on her latest protocols including a *Safe Policy*. Mr De Villier's safe had been opened by a locksmith. 'Would you believe it, Dr Jenkins?' Matron said. 'It was empty! All that fuss for nothing.'

As for the allotment, Beth persuaded Fortunate to take it and he and Jack work on it together at weekends.

Beth took an opportunity to ask Fortunate why he had sent her the DVD, *The Day of Jackal*. 'What DVD, Dr Jenkins? I never sent you a DVD.'

'Clever, those state security people,' Beth said dryly when she told me this.

Hope knows that for her, justice in a court of law might never come. Beth told her what Matt had done, how he'd helped Boniface erase the evidence, but that she believed Matt to have hidden a few remains that might be useful to a prosecution at some future date. Hope said simply, 'My mother and father named me Hope. They named me well.' When Beth told her that Boniface was on the farm but had taken to the bottle, she shrugged and quoted from her bible, 'Evil men will be cut off, but those who hope in the Lord will inherit the land.'

A paper was published in the *International Archaeological Journal* two years after Beth left Zimbabwe. It made headlines across the world. The paper was entitled *Early upper Palaeolithic rock art in Matobo Hills, Zimbabwe,* but the news channels were more colourful: *Astonishing Rock Art find overturns theories.* The publication's principal author was Dr Lindiwe Dlamini. Before the introduction to the paper there was a dedication to the late Matthew Hallam who, it stated without elaboration, had discovered the painting. The art had been dated and was declared the oldest rock painting in Africa, matching in age the thirty-thousand-year-old paintings of Chauvet in France. It had been protected in its secluded location by a benign microclimate which had prevented its destruction from the abrasions of time suffered by Africa's other rock art. The ancient date confirmed if anyone doubted it – and some did – that the imaginative mind of ancient Africans equalled that of their European cousins. The paper's authors suggested that other art in the cave (elliptical forms, snake-like creatures, fish, giraffes and zoomorphic figures) gave clues as to why there was a unity of symbolic concepts and style over the ages. Beth says it'll keep the researchers busy and happy for centuries.

At the same time as Lindi's paper was published, Beth returned to Bulawayo to attend Hope's wedding to Fortunate. Matron had allowed protocol to be breached, permitting them to take simultaneous leave from Twicare for a week. After the wedding service there was a photo session in the gardens of Bulawayo Centenary Park. The sun shone brightly and the flamboyant trees were in full flame under the bold blue sky. Beth saw Selous making his way towards her through the crowd, nodding a brief acknowledgement to others as they greeted him, but intent on reaching her. She was overcome once more by that crushing loneliness that had lurked, angina-like, in her breast since Matt's stroke and death. He looked younger than she remembered, perhaps because he was clean shaven and had dressed in a well-cut suit for the wedding.

They were shy at first and exchanged pleasantries, him asking her about her work (a locum in a different practice), her friends (still meeting at Tres Hermanas) and her house (now renting a flat).

'Have you still got Bismarck?' Beth asked.

'I'm not sure I should tell you,' Selous said, smiling widely and making Beth's head swim. She relaxed, knowing that time had not turned bitter his memory of their fiery first meeting and its consequences. 'Not yet, anyway.' Not yet?

'By the way,' he said, 'Fortunate told me you'd be coming to the wedding.'

'And Fortunate told me you'd be here as well,' she replied. They were both, she wanted to suppose, having the same thought, but now it seemed they circled each other in their talk.

'Who is Fortunate anyway?' Selous said, with an expression of light-hearted puzzlement. 'Where did he come from? Even after attending his wedding, I'm none the wiser.'

'I've no idea either,' she said. 'But I guess it doesn't really matter. Hope seems to know who he is and it's plain he loves her.' She remembered the first time she'd met Fortunate, overhearing him say to Mr De Villier in Twicare, 'I'm so sorry, sir; I'm a long way from home myself.' If she'd not met Fortunate, she'd never have come home to Matt. But that all seemed a long time ago, now that she was standing there with Selous.

'Are we, do you think?' she said.

Selous turned his head quizzically.

'Fortunate, I mean.'

He smiled enigmatically. 'Can we talk in the shade over there?' They walked together towards a jacaranda tree, away from the crowd. A gust of balmy air blew across the park showering them with the tree's last blooms as they came under its canopy. There was a scent of gardenia from a nearby flower border. Without saying a further word, Selous pulled a newspaper cutting from his pocket. He passed it to Beth. It was an advertisement.

Wanted. Estate manager, Llanfair ym Muallt, Wales. There were brief details of the duties but whoever had written the advert had sent a message in the last line. It read: *House on small plot of land (but overlooking endless view) available for rent or purchase by the successful applicant.*

Overlooking endless view. Beth met Selous's eyes and was going to ask him if he'd applied but he said simply, 'Beth, I've got the job. I'm moving there next month.' He held her gaze and she dared to believe that her long solitude was coming to an end. She found her face turning up towards his as he turned his down to hers.

'And?' she said softly.

He smiled back and, before their lips touched, he said, 'Beth, it would be as if I possessed the world if you'd care to come with me.'

It's November, three years from that evening when Beth took a call from Twicare and crossed the threshold to a new world. There's a view of the world from Beth's living room window. She can see for miles down the valley over fields lightly brushed by early snow. Their ploughed furrows are inked along their white crests by streaks of black soil like lines of text on a page whilst dry-stone walls – silver bookmarks – divide the fields. The trees along the river in the valley are etched in ice against the hills beyond, whose forests are a library of myth and lore. In the other direction she can see the town and in certain lights the town's silhouettes resemble the battlement-like kopjes of the Matobo Hills. It is all too beautiful, as Fortunate would say, but she sees that it's more than a pretty view, a charming landscape; it holds memories and stories, struggles and symbols. For now, other people's stories but, in time, it'll hold their own. She and Selous will take possession of the land.

She's just said goodbye to Alena and Preeti, and to Christina and her gorgeous little girl. They had a ball and will be back again before long.

I was staying in the area (interviewing Beth as part of my research for this book) when Beth's friends were visiting. Before leaving, Christina took me aside and said, 'I can't blame you if I come across as an impulsive whore in your book but I want you to know one thing. When I first met Selous in Zimbabwe and Beth disappeared into Lindi's house to fetch Bismarck's keys, I said in Selous's ear, "I've had the clap, I'm incubating a baby and I've got issues, but you'll find Beth's the most gutsy, kind, surprising, jewel of a woman any man could ever have the luck to find".'

Beth (not her real name, of course) is a partner at a practice in the town, trying again to help her patients with their stories, her surgeries still running late. She knows now how easy it is to be blind to other possibilities, to discover alternative narratives for one's own script.

She's learning Welsh at evening classes. One day she hopes to be able to sing *Land of my Fathers* in Welsh, whoever her fathers – and her mothers – were. It's of little consequence to her, that not-knowing (at least for now) as her children will know theirs.

There are two mementoes pinned to Beth's kitchen message board: Cavafy's poem of course, but also an unopened envelope addressed to the Prince of Wales. It's a permanent keepsake because Beth's done with delivering letters. If the Prince would like it, she'd be happy for him to collect it, but she and Selous are miles off the beaten track, out here in the land.

ACKNOWLEDGEMENTS

I owe particular thanks to the many Zimbabweans who have generously shared their lives, homes and experiences with me over the last three decades. They have extraordinary stories to tell and almost all are more valiant and noble than the characters I depict in my novel.

I'm grateful for the help given to me by Elspeth Parry in my background research on the rock art of the Matobo Hills, although any errors in the text in that regard are my own. For one of the scenes in the novel, I drew on the late Yvonne Vera's description (in her moving novel, *The Stone Virgins*) of combatants returning to normal life after Zimbabwe's war of Independence. The books *Voices from the Rocks* by Terence Ranger and *Prehistoric Rock Art — Polemics and Progress* by Paul G. Bahn, were especially helpful.

I am also grateful to Mollie Baxter, Dinah Ceely, Sheila Cross, Michael Drucquer, Rod Duncan, Elizabeth Harris, John Makin, Suzanne Sharp, Corinne Souza, Alison Timmins, Jan Tozer and several Zimbabwean friends – whose anonymity is probably advisable at the time of writing – for commenting on the draft or for editorial help.

CAVAFY: THE COLLECTED POEMS translated by Hirst (2007) 8 lines from "Che Feche... Il Gran Rifiuto" p.11. By permission of Oxford University Press.

ABOUT THE AUTHOR

Andrew JH Sharp's first novel, *The Ghosts of Eden*, won the 2010 Waverton Good Read Award and was shortlisted for the 2011 International Rubery Book Award. He spent his childhood in East Africa and has worked in southern Africa as a medical doctor. He is based in the East Midlands in the UK.

www.andrewjhsharp.co.uk